Genesis

The Children of Thoth

Eugene E. Whitworth

Previous publications by the same author

Nine Faces of Christ

Eternal Truth: A Metaphysical Trilogy

Diary into the Unknown
The Song of God
The First Christmas Tree
Tomorrow Dawns Today
Bay Bridge Murder Mystery
Wild Love Affairs with Life
Eternal Easter
Christmas Enduring

Four Musicals:

Grandma Gets Her Man
Boots to Match
The Jaguar Prince
Tale of the Terrible Dragon

258 Radio Dramas, 1933–38

Forthcoming books by the same author

Quest for the Lost Gods

The Jaguar Priest

Casa Na Balam (House of the Jaguar)

Genesis

The Children of Thoth

Eugene E. Whitworth

Lion's Wing Press
Hygiene, Colorado
USA

ISBN 0-9642778-0-8
Lion's Wing Press First Edition

Last Digit in Print Number: 9 8 7 6 5 4 3 2 1

Lion's Wing Press
PO Box 257
Hygiene, CO 80533
(303) 678-0864

Cover by Tony Stubbs

Printed in the United States of America

About the Author

Dr. Eugene E. Whitworth is founder, Chairman of the Board, and President of Great Western University. He has enjoyed a distinguished career as a businessman and entrepreneur, specializing in executive training. Over the years, he has taught business management psychology to corporations, as well as in colleges and universities.

As the founder and master teacher of the Great Western Brotherhood, Dr. Whitworth also trains his students in the development of their highest mental and spiritual potential. His knowledge of comparative religion is encyclopedic. He and his wife, Ruth, have traveled extensively to the far reaches of the Earth to record religious rituals, dances, and songs.

In the East, they have been accepted as equals by Indian Saints, Tibetan Lamas, Zen masters, and Buddhist priests. In the West, they are recognized as teachers, authors, scientists, and lecturers. In the Southern hemisphere, a cancer research center has been founded in their name, and in the Northern hemisphere, temples have been dedicated to their work.

Dr. Whitworth has received many honors for his creative works. He continues to lecture worldwide, spreading the significance of the universality of religious thought to help bring about world peace.

Dedication

This book is lovingly dedicated to Ruth E. Whitworth, my wife, to the inspiration of all the students of Great Western University, and with deep appreciation to the inspiration of Thoth, the First God and the First Man, and to all his children.

Contents

Foreword and Warning

Reader, believe you hold in your hands a treasure from antiquity, one of the books of Thoth, First God and First Man. It is intended for his Sacred Children who are responsible for the preservation of planet earth.

You who read absorb some of the pure, ancient energy, which goes from one particle to another as both are transformed. It is a primitive, natural force which forms our universe and embraces the cosmos. It is a fundamental flow that shapes and improves all.

With that divine energy, you also absorb a responsibility and a problem. For when you read of the training and techniques that turn men into Gods and women into Goddesses, you may grow impatient with the limits of your fleshly self. You may want to slip the bindings of earth. As you read you will learn the process and much of the technique by which this may be done.

However, you may lack one key ingredient, which is the presence of Thoth, God One, or of your spiritual teacher. That, and one other special, indispensable thing: the exact methodology of the Sacred Breath.

THAT is the key to your problem.

For *no one who knows* dares teach anyone the sacred skills needed for Initiation into Wisdom, without first putting them under a strict obligation to secrecy, face to face.

And, too, an energy passes from teacher to aspirant, a power most needful for life and happiness. For Wisdom has cosmic power. Within it is the same energy as that of the speeding proton; or that of the forty-eight forces which formed the universe—and you.

You are part of that cosmos envisioned by the Mayans (that race of mental giants) to end when creation returned to its beginning. They said:

> *Where there was neither heaven nor earth sounded the first word of God. And He unloosed Himself from His stone and declared His divinity. And all the vastness of eternity shuddered. And His word was a measure of grace, and He broke and pierced the backbone of the mountains.*
>
> *Who was born there? Who? Father, you know. He who was tender in Heaven came into being.*

You who "was tender in heaven" do not think you can read this book as a story only. Oh, it is a glorious love story, an adventure story, a horror story, a war story. A story of your life. A mystical story of love for family, home, country, and life; but also a story of duty, determination, and struggle against threat, hatred, and anger. It is a story of consistency of behavior in the face of the threat of a fiery death. It is the story of Genesis of the Children of God One, Thoth.

This book is a guide to the gate of your own Temple of Divinity. Once you lift the latch and open that gate, you can never again be as you are now. For you will be endowed with a power of Creative Wisdom that will demand expression. It will drive you, plague you. It will make you become worthily divine through uncontainable and unexpected creativity.

Ancients taught that those with creative drive were touched by an inner sacred fire of a god. Antiquity, according to the great Tertullian, thought that authors were Gods, and not merely inspired by them. Thoth, the Great Creator, for the guidance of His Children, authored forty-two other books which were considered sacred, and that have given to mankind all of the Universal Knowledge it will ever need, from material science to ethereal spirituality, with equal respect for each.

As you read this work you will, yourself, (by absorbing His power) become the Scribe of God, the amanuensis of Divinity. With your reading you take on the burden and the joy of service to Divinity, which you can never put down. Some of the dedication of its creator is absorbed into every "smallest particle" of your being, into every cell Indelibly, the lessons of your mind will record on the seed-atom of your heart, and you will become sacred and the fecund matrix of all the glorious future of the human race.

A swift glance inside this volume is enough! Even if you glean only a small grain of Cosmic Wisdom, you are wrapped into an awesome responsibility. For it is known of old that you will never be able to rest in peace until you have passed on to another, duly prepared and ready, the Cosmic Wisdom you have gained. Your soul takes on a burden that must be given through to others, or your spirit will strain forever against the storm wind, your energy will combat the lightning, and your voice will strive with the thunder. And if this volume goes with you to your final rest, you will cause peace to dwell with you and yours forever.

Be aware. As you read, Wisdom of Divinity will be impressed from the author to you. Once it is yours, you are made divine, you are become one of the Children of Thoth, Child of the First God. You must then create other Children of God, as did Thoth, Hermes, A-Sar-U, Ast-i, Mut, Horus, Bes, Vishnu, Rama, Ramtha, Jesus, Krishna, Mohammed, Teotihuatl, Buddha, Brahma, and Ra, and pass on to these children that which is good for the future of the race of mankind.

Such is your problem. Such is your glorious burden. Such is your promise of love that will last forever.

And you must pass onto them **the energy for GENE-SIS,** the power to raise themselves to become the Sacred Race, the Dearly Beloved, the Children of Thoth.

Before The Beginning:
The Creation

The beginning subtle energy of the universe was soul.
Nothing else existed, no force attractive,
Until the Supreme, Thoth, felt all should be active.
Thinking the world into being became His goal.
    In the beginning all was without form,
    All was void, and nothing moved. Forever the rude
    Intertwining mass called chaos had stood
    In the endless darkness neither cold nor warm.
        All was inert weight and held no creative charms
        For growth in physical things in disarray.
        No sky, world, or moon or shining sun held sway.
        No earth gave form to embrace of ocean's arms.
All was without form and void and all was stark
As death, floating in the unending dark.

But in the eternal stillness, need and mood
Was set by the endless blackness. In that hour
Thoth's Self-Existing, Undiscoverable Power
Pierced the endless night with Thought therein to brood:
    He, Who only mind alone can perceive,
    Whose Essence eludes through time eternal,
    Poured forth more thought than darkness could receive.
        Then even He, the Soul of All Things, shone forth
        In a form not seen or dreamed since time began,
        And the Pristine Will with endless force then ran
        To form the Universe, and to give it birth.
And matter without form, or power or pole
Was shot through by Thoth's own shining, Golden Soul.

In that Force-field of the Ages, before Time
Was marked by the earth-sun's ceaseless round,
Or the light of the four directions could be found,
Or the living seed was ready and was prime
    The Gentle Heart of Heaven relentlessly willed
    Out of His very substance, his Golden Mead,
    The Creative Thought, the form-creating seed,
    With which the vast universe was quickly filled.
        Then by Thought and by force of Pristine Will,
        The Golden Egg in time was burst asunder
        And there was formed a voice like thunder
        Which spoke forth earth and heaven and was still.
The seeds were bright as Golden Sun, or near it,
And were the Golden Eggs of All Creative Spirit.

From deep within the Self Supreme there came
The rising source of all-creative mind,
Which nothing physical could ever bind;
It came to bear a sacred, holy Name!
    The Voice spoke again in Creative Thunder
    And brought forth mountains vast, and dale and ocean
    And living things of beauty, kind, and motion—
    But lacking inner worship or great wonder;
        Each living thing Thoth gave creative mind,
        With mastery of its own power of birth,
        And sent it forth to the farther ends of earth
        To have dominion and reproduce its kind.
And then, Supreme Crown to His Perfected Plan,
In swift ascending glory, Thoth created Man.

The Will of Thoth

(For The Children Of Thoth)

I am Thoth, God One, the endless force which created Itself. I am the Creator. I gave birth to myself and to all things. I was before time. In the Beginning I am, and no other thing. I am eternity. I am Father-Mother, Son-Daughter, Scribe-Servant of Divinity and mankind.

I am Thoth, source of Divine Mind, Lord of the Cosmos. I am *Meket*, the energy that gives life to mankind and Gods. I am scribe of the Gods, Lord of Sacred Speech. I speak *Hekau*, Words of Power. What comes from my mouth springs into being.

I am Thoth, God of All, the physical, mental, and spiritual. I am Life, Death, and Birth. I am the God of healing, the inventor of all sciences and healing arts. I gave mankind all learning and all culture. I give Words of Power as the gift of speech; as power for bringing and restoring life; power by which the spirit may raise itself to eternal life; Power of Speech to pronounce for the infant the Name which turns Gods into men and men into Gods.

I am Thoth, the outward expression of mankind's most divine inward self. Those who become Masters and Avatars, as well as those who are born so, are My Children.

I am Thoth. My heavenly wisdom existed before, and is hidden in the land which became Celestial Egypt. My forty-two previous volumes of Cosmic Wisdom are inscribed forever on Pillars of Light. By My will some of it has been hidden until now in pure elements that work unseen except by the eyes of True Initiates, My Children.

I am Thoth. This is My will:

> Mankind may now know that Wisdom which was with Me before time; may know of Cosmic Lore and Techniques that lead toward Eternal Life, Everlasting Love and the Mystery of Being.

I am Thoth. This is My will:

> This fragment of the vast Pillars of Wisdom shall be carved in ink on wood that all who seek may see and be satisfied.

I am Thoth. I have spoken. It therefore is.

Authority Structure

Supreme Spiritual God-e.
Supreme God-e, Lor'd One of the Pleasant Planet (Flesh made spiritual)...held by ATL, then RA, then Thoth, then A-Sar-U.
Lor'd One of Wisdom...held by THOTH.
Lor'd One of War...held by JE-SU.
Lor'd One of Religion...vacant (Thoth)
Lor'd One of Knowledge...held by BRAHM.
Lor'd One of Information...held by MA-NU
Lor'd One of Science...held by SOM.
Lor'd One of Population...held by RAM.

Names and Meaning

Major Characters—Male

A-Ra: The Supreme Divine God-e, Eternal Spirit never in flesh.

Atl: The Supreme God-e (Before Ra and Thoth), the Highest representative of the Supreme Divine God-e in the flesh. Owner of all things on the planet, Supreme Lor'd One.

Thoth: Lor'd One of War, then Wisdom, and, finally, Lor'd One of the Planet, and then the Supreme God-e. Master Teacher, great benefactor of all mankind. Seer of the future. Uncle to A-Sar-U.

A-Sar-U: Son of God-e Ra—by unregistered Virgin Birth—Lor'd One of War, then Wisdom, Lor'd One of the Planet and by appointment, Supreme God-e.

Je-Su: Cousin of Thoth, Lor'd One of War, swarthy, black-eyed, powerful, devious, and treacherous, reborn in terms of his faith in his ability to control all mankind and its thought, for their own good.

Horus:	Son of A-Sar-U and Ast-i. (aka Heru)
Set:	Almost-twin brother of A-Sar-U, devotee of Je-Su, Commander of the Armies of Je-Su. Treacherous and jealous of A-Sar-U, secretly in love with Ast-i.
Po-Si-Don:	Legendary figure from antiquity who supposedly had led the peoples of That Other Planet to this new Pleasant Planet. He founded the temple-state based on the worship of the divine and eternal, on an individual basis, by trying to become like the ideal Supreme.
Brahm:	Lor'd One of Knowledge, younger brother of Je-Su, who believes he can control the destiny of all men through the force of his mind.
Ma-Nu:	Lor'd One of Information, who believes he can control all mankind by laying down specific laws as codes of behavior, with severe punishments for the slightest infraction.
Bes:	"Lor'd One of Nothing," great, short-legged warrior, secretly the representative of Ra, father of Ast-i, by unregistered Virgin Birth. Commander of the Temple Guard. God of Children. True protector of the ancient faith and confidant of Thoth.
Som:	Lor'd One of Science, small, brilliant, with all the material science of his race stored in his almost unfailing memory.
Ram:	Lor'd One of Population, small, emotional.
Africanus:	Seemingly materialistic-minded, powerful, brilliant, and charismatic leader of a clever tribe. Admirer of the leadership strength of Je-Su.

Lady Goddesses of The Pleasant Planet

God-ette: Chosen Woman of Ra, Mother of A-Sar-U, First
                Virgin of the World, Companion of God-e,
                Mother of the Virgins.
Siri: Lady of the One Great Star.
Ast-i: Lady of Eternal Truth, Chosen Woman of
                A-Sar-U, Mother of God-e Horus, Goddess of
                Love.
Er-Ru: Lady of Beauty.
Ir-Ma: Chosen Woman of Set.
Isi: Lady of Space.
Isi-Ankh: Lady of Eternal Life.
E-ma: Lady of the Radiant Dawn.
An-ki: Lady of Life.
Ma-ri: Chosen Woman of Je-Su.
As-Tar: Chosen Woman of Bes, Mother of Ast-i,
                Goddess of Power, Force, Knowledge, and
                Wisdom.
Lak-Shi-Mi: Chosen Woman of Brahm.

Explanation of Names

*Some names are hyphenated as are names from ancient
Egypt brought into English*

1. The letters -e, -i or -U as a suffix to a name means:
   - The individual has mastered the spiritual discipline
     needed for eternal existence; or
   - The individual had become part of the Great and
     Learned Priesthood of the Planet.

2. The -Ankh added after a name shows:
   - That individual is thought to have attained to eternal
     ·life in the spirit; or
   - That the individual may be able to pass on to others
     the eternal subtle energy or spirit needed for eternal
     life.

3. Internal hyphens within proper names, (for instance,
   A-Sar-U, and Ma-at) were used by the Ancient Egyp-
   tians.

1

The Childhood Ends

It was Westsun 2999, Eastsun 28, in mid-second watch, since his ancestors came to E-Den. In three generations since they fled disaster on That Other Planet they had developed a Warrior society to control the rebellious and more primitive tribes. They called this the Pleasant Planet. It was A-Sar-U's 200th birthdate, or would be when the Westsun blazed its path over the planet at High Light of the Eastsun. It was a joyous time of celebration, for he was coming of age!

So he was not as alert as a young Warrior should have been. What he said about his dream caused unusual tensions among the assembled Lor'd Ones and their Lor'd Ladies. He did not know why.

Tensions always rose as the Westsun swept across the Pleasant Planet and made all things suffer. This was the time when cattle and animals of all kinds dropped their foals.

Women gave birth to children or paid the dues of their femininity. Tensions were always greater, because of interruption in the gentle pleasures of life in an ideal society on a fertile planet.

A-Sar-U, first-born son of Ra, Lor'd One of all the Empire of E-Den, had gone through 199 celebrations of the return of the Westsun. Always, exactly on time. Precisely when the Golden Pillar fully fifteen arms high on the Sundial of the High Porch of the Temple of Po-Si-Don cast no shadow to north, east, or west, and only a fingerwidth to the south—the Westsun blazed its meteoric, glaring path across the land.

Always! On the twenty-eighth day of the rising of the Eastsun!

Always there were human tensions which matched the rising wind and the following downpouring rain.

1

This 200th celebration of his birth, up to this breath, had been the happiest of all.

Now, as Som, Lor'd One of Science, watched the shadow of the Golden Pillar, the Sundial of the planet, close to a palm-width, the tensions had suddenly risen. The first hint of the garish, hard, glaring light in the north-northwest overrode the light of the Eastsun and made the lines on the faces of his uncles seem more deep-cut and, somehow, ominous.

Je-Su, Lor'd One of War, stood rigid, his swarthy face deeply scowling, his black eyes fixed like twin lances upon A-Sar-U. His expression was between that of hatred and joy.

Bes, who liked to proclaim himself "Lor'd One of Nothing," and was adored by all children, rested his ample, powerful body evenly on legs that were only half as long as they should have been. His face was benign. His ever-present smile was slightly askew. A-Sar-U thought it was more warning than pleasant, as it usually was.

His favorite uncle, Thoth, Lor'd One of Wisdom, seemed to be telling A-Sar-U by his glance to be wary of Uncle Je-Su. A-Sar-U knew that Thoth was the greatest Warrior in the Race of God-e. The race had been rulers on That Other Planet. The Empire of E-Den, on the Pleasant Planet, required Warriors to hold in obedient peace the wild tribes the God-e found when their space cruiser crashed. Everyone adored Thoth, even tribesmen waiting to rebel at the moment of choice. He was the perfect example of Warrior strength and fighting skill. Also, Thoth had that sacred wisdom that turned man into Man-God; and all persons who had the power and the will to become God-like, into Divine God-e.

A-Sar-U's twin, Set, large, broad-shouldered, hardened by training in the Young Warriors' School, glowered his usual brotherly disapproval of A-Sar-U's actions. There was no way ever to please his twin brother, born fifty breaths later and always trying to catch up to and outdo him. Toward Set, A-Sar-U held no animosity, did not consider him a rival. Set always was angry about anything that had to do with A-Sar-U. A-Sar-U gave Set's black, in-turned looks no further thought.

The dream was, he thought, fascinating. A-Sar-U rushed on telling it until he was stopped. Thoth's laugh died. He bellowed, "What did you say, A-Sar-U, Son of Ra?"

A-Sar-U saw the tensions growing on the faces of his uncles even as his mind groped for the exact words he had said only moments before. Lor'd Je-Su was deeply angry. His anger showed, stark and mean, as his swarthy face and black eyes fixed into a hostile mold.

Uncle Bes was now clearly shaking his head "no." His short legs brought him down so that his eyes were slightly below A-Sar-U's. Clearly his darting eyes were signalling caution and to be wary of Lor'd Je-Su.

Brahm, Lor'd One of Knowledge, younger brother of Je-Su, stood with an implacable look of non-attention on his face. He prided himself on being all-knowing without knowledge, of being divinely detached in fierce attachment. He said that all men might as well worship him and thus save the bother of striving to understand the Supreme Spiritual God-e, for he was the Great Teacher of faith and moral precepts, the God-e on the planet in flesh. His face was inscrutable, but not scowling.

Ma-Nu, Lor'd One of Information, scowled deeply. He was always angry. He made rules and laws so fast no one could obey them all, and was furious when they did not. He laid down codes of obedience and behavior with exact, swift, and severe punishment for the slightest infraction. When Thoth became Lor'd One of the Pleasant Planet, he forbade Ma-Nu to enforce all his laws. Ma-Nu had been in a pet ever since!

Som, Lor'd One of Science, and his twin, Ram, Lor'd One of Population, stood near each other, impassive and diffident. Their tall bodies were too slender and weak for prolonged combat. They were not in competition for further advancement through the Tournament of Combats. They said they held their offices by brilliance. They were likeable but a little disdained by Warrior-trained men who knew that only Warriors could hold the rebellious tribes together. They were never positive in their public reactions. A-Sar-U liked them, but he could not admire them...at least not enough to really care what opinion they held of his dream.

The dream seemed to be as important as it had been unusual. A-Sar-U felt that as the First Born of Lor'd Ra he could not stop. Yet he wondered why all the men of his family were so tense—even beyond the usual tension caused by the onrushing Westsun. His eyes flicked to his mother, God-ette, Lady Companion of the God-e, Mother to the Virgins of all the Temples of the Pleasant Planet. Her attitude was most important. She was wise and learned. She might have been Lor'd Lady of Religion, for Thoth thought she should be and was qualified to be. But she turned the office down saying, "One will come back to fill that job whose coton I am not even worthy to mend." Thoth, therefore, temporarily took that office himself but depended upon God-ette for advice and direction. She was smiling at him with her usual fondness.

Er-Ru, Lady of Beauty, sister of his father, was laughing gaily.

Far over under the shelter of the overhang, he saw Ast-i, daughter of Lor'd Bes and Lor'd Lady As-Tar. She was one Westsun younger than he, his life-long playmate and secret love. His memory of her was acute in his head. Oh, young Warrior, too, too acute! Ast-i was two arms tall, less half a span. Not as tall as he was at two arms plus half a span. But he thought she was a perfect height.

Her skin was the translucent, golden hue of alabaster. It molded a figure that in repose was excitingly perfect in dimensions. In action it was a fierce fore-wind. Unpredictable and unstoppable! In their childhood, before he was sent into the Young Warriors' School, he had taught her the way Warriors fought with hands, elbows, knees, and butting head. When she went into action her lithe beauty became as fierce as a pouncing jaguar...and at times, he thought, nearly as deadly.

She had hit him many a blow that hurt. Yet he always enjoyed the lost bouts with her. About her always was a kind fragrance that seemed to be a combination of orange blossoms, lemon rind, wild-wild ginger and...posanga fruit. Yes, for when he was near her he was like a posanga zombie, with no will to see anything or think of anything other than her charms.

Ast-i was not frowning. Quick to criticize and correct his awkward ways and manners, she was swift fury on those who chided him unjustly. She was, he thought, even more protective than his own dear mother.

Ast-i was looking at him, and there was laughter on her pretty face. She saw his glance, reacted to it with a self-conscious toss of her reddish-golden curls that made the gossamer bodice of her Virgin's dress ripple over her beautiful, womanly body. Soon, he knew, he would have to ask her if she would be his Chosen Woman.

She probably would reject him. But he would try... soon. Very soon. Oh, Yes, very, very soon. She sensed it, he was sure. She was now a woman, not the feisty girl he had played with and adored all his life. Now she was in the School of the Virgins. Since childhood, she had been alternately sweet and severe with him. She was not now scowling or tense. So, he reasoned, she must have found nothing wrong with his relating his strange dream.

He decided that the black humor of his powerful uncles was due to the fact that they stood out from under the protecting overhang of the High Priest's raised platform. The light where they stood near the Golden Sun Pillar was already beginning to turn garish.

Even if they were scowling because of what he had said, he would say it again. It had been his dream. To his family dreams were important. His father encouraged him to remember and to talk about his dreams.

Myth held that Atl, ancient adventurer, formerly the adored Lor'd One of the Empire, had said:

"Dreams are the way tomorrows talk to today, and yesterdays correct their mistakes."

All dreams were very important!

A-Sar-U continued quietly. "I said, 'Last night I dreamed that I had grown big and strong. I could leave my body in a radiant form. I could reach up and bring the Westsun and the Eastsun together so that with only one sun we could be...' "

His eyes were on the pretty face of Ast-i. He saw her lips open, saw the moist, pink beauty of her tongue and the roof of her mouth. Then she was reeling sideways it seemed. Her scream startled him.

He realized that it was he who was twisting backward through the air.

5

He had not felt the blow. Now, in mid-air he did. He knew that his favorite uncle, Thoth, Lor'd One of Wisdom, had sent him tumbling.

Why?

Well before his body slammed down upon the marble floor that covered the upper porch near the Sundial of the Temple of Po-Si-Don, the question was firmly in his mind.

Why?

The blow was strong but not cruel. It was more a push. The crash to the marble was no greater than those he had twenty times each day in his exercises, drills, and mock-fights with the class at the Young Warriors' School. But the blow seared the question into his brain.

Why?

The long slide across the foot-smoothed marble did not shake it away. With that agility which comes of many practice tumbles, he was instantly on his feet, on guard and wary.

Both his mind and body were alert now. He saw the puzzled expression on the face of his mother, God-ette, First Virgin of the World. He saw the blank amazement on the face of Er-Ru, Lady of Beauty. Too, too clearly he saw the beautiful pink-tongued mouth of Ast-i close to reveal again the prettiness of her oval face. But it also brought something more into his mind to wonder about. He saw the concern filled with a slight contempt upon her sensitive and expressive face. Her sky-blue eyes were aflame with either fear or derision or both.

Thoth, Lor'd One of Wisdom, was reaching for A-Sar-U. Beyond his large body, the angry bulk of Je-Su, Lor'd One of War, seemed threatening and implacable. The body of Lor'd Bes, big and burly, seemed strangely unthreatening on the too-short legs. Brahm's eyes stayed serpent-dead in his impassive face. Ma-Nu chewed his thin lips. Som and Ram stood delicately indecisive, like birds about to fly.

"Enough! No more! You speak of the sacred suns. Say no more. Someone might think you malign the God-e and his power."

A-Sar-U stared up into the loving, large, blue-green eyes of his beloved uncle, Thoth. His anger at the affront to his dignity was evaporated by his uncle's actions, as the Westsun evaporated the water in the shallow birdbaths. As

Thoth reached large, war-trained hands toward him, his eyes were filled with love. One lid closed in a slow half-wink. There was even a hint of pleasure in his large, sword-scarred, sensitive face. It was gone too swiftly. It was reassuring against the anger of Je-Su's grim face.

Thoth's voice held no special tenderness when he spoke again. It was a softened version of the voice he had used in commanding the Warriors in the fighting when he was Lor'd One of War. It was resonant, firm, commanding—and undisputable.

"God-ette, Mother of the Virgins of the Planet, this son of yours will report to my care tomorrow before the setting of the Eastsun in the west. He will be trained in the cadre of the Warriors of Wisdom."

He fixed A-Sar-U with blue-green eyes that seemed to search the depth of mind and thought. "In case you wonder why, you will be trained in the beliefs of our planet, in the way of the life of the God-e. You will be taught the ways of divinity so that you can never again even unintentionally question the great power. Do you understand?"

A-Sar-U thought he saw the hatred in Je-Su's black eyes soften somewhat, at least to indecision. He clearly saw the love in the eyes of his favorite uncle.

Thoth moved him firmly yet gently toward the shadow of the overhang. As he did so, A-Sar-U thought he saw a nod of approval, secret between the two of them.

The fore-winds were due. The people of the plains of E-Den braced against it, as did the Lor'd Ones and their families on the Porch of the High Priest at the south end of the Temple of Po-Si-Don.

The Temple—one of fourteen built by the great Atl, last commander on the space cruiser—center of all life on the planet, was set in the middle of E-Den plain. It sloped gently from the sheer, impassable Atl Mountains to the north over one hundred thousand paces to the ocean called the Sea of Ra. Water from the sea surrounded the Temple. So did water from the Atls. Therein lay danger from the raging Westsun.

Water from the wild rivers of the Atls was caught in huge reservoirs and then fed into wide canals that brought it to the Temple Complex. On the way across the plain, those waters were diverted and filled three of the five canals that circled the Temple Complex and fed the fertile fields of E-Den.

The Temple sat on a man-made island. The Temple Complex was surrounded by five great moats. Water from the Sea of Ra was led into the outermost circular canal and, by cross channels, into the third from the outermost. On these great ships could sail.

The raging Westsun lifted the waters of the ocean and the canals. It lifted the water in the sea-fed canals much higher than the water in the mountain-filled canals. The levees were constantly in danger of being overflowed. Each Westsun seemed to raise the water higher.

Part of the duty of the Young Warriors was to build the levees ever higher and stronger. If the sea-water overflowed, salt would be left upon the verdant lands.

Water from the mountain-filled canals was siphoned under the sea-water canals and sent to many convenient reservoirs dug into the land. These were lined with smooth stone, close-fitted by workers under Som, Lor'd One of Science. The waters in these tanks sometimes burst out in fury, and there were many tanks around the inner Temple Complex that always acted strangely during the Westsun.

Only once A-Sar-U had seen it all. When he and Ast-i sneaked up to the raised platform of Ra on the top of the Temple. From there they could see all the plains of E-Den, the Temple Complex, the tanks, the circling canals with their levees also made into protecting breastworks. Most exciting had been the tan-colored sails of the mighty sea-ships and the broad pathways across the plains on which the commerce, manufacture, and foodstuffs were moved to and from the thirteen other Temple Complexes of the Empire.

He felt that standing for even one brief moment on the Window of Ra was worth the punishment he received for that childhood breach of decorum. For he had stood in "the Place Where the Supreme God-e Is Seen."

As the Westsun fore-winds began to howl around the statues along the pathway to the Temple below, A-Sar-U wondered if they would ever stand there again.

The fore-wind increased until it was difficult to stand. The Lor'd Ones and their families stood near each other, but each individual was pulled together in one's own way.

Yet they were closely grouped, as men always became when the forces of nature were beyond their ability to understand or change. The glare of the Westsun as it streaked overhead made the Eastsun seem to fade from the sky. The light changed from a golden white to a blackish red. It bounced back from the white marble in shafts of brilliance.

"Bounces like pebbles of visible energy."

Thoth spoke into his ear above the screech of the wind. The description fitted perfectly. It was as if energy was connected to light and flung in bunches of spears upon the surface of the planet.

The very air began to crackle with excess energy. Light leaped upward from high places, from trees, from the top of the Golden Pillar rising so high above them. Lightning began to form. It was like shining, jagged lances thrown upward into the sky toward the Westsun. It was a battle between earth and sky!

Tension grew between the Westsun and the land. Water was raised in all the tanks about the Temple Compound but did not overflow. Water in the birdbaths bubbled and evaporated swiftly. It seemed that even the top part of the water in the tanks changed to the form of a gas. Flashes of lightning exploded this gas above the surface of the water of the tanks.

Each explosion caused a flash of blue light that died swiftly to a pale yellow and then vanished as if it had never been. Unlike fire from wood and burning soil, it did not smoke. The sound of each explosion was that of a thousand swords upon a thousand shields...strange ripples of sound. Each ripple was not loud, but the thousands coming close upon each other caused a violence in the head like practice-sticks upon a helmet.

Then the lightning began to come from the sky toward the earth. It was as if the Westsun was tired of retreating and came forward now with brazen lances that zigzagged into the ranked archers of the land. Thunder came. Rolling, thought-stopping, fear-creating crashes of thunder.

Even as he cringed a little in himself, A-Sar-U saw that Ast-i stood tall, her blue eyes wide open, filled with an excitement that had nothing to do with cringing or fear. The fore-wind pressed her Virgin's dress tight against her body, and he saw such beauty that he forgot to cringe. The blood in his ears was matching the thunder. His heart was beating for a cause all its own, and fast, oh, far too fast!

As the Westsun reached the spot in the sky almost directly above the Golden Pillar it seemed to pause in its flight, to hover and linger to have extra time to punish the land with more heat, more lances of fire, more lightning, and more terrible thunder.

The heat became oppressive. Sweat formed upon all foreheads—except the cool bronzed-marble of Ast-i's lovely face. Breathing became a chore. Breath that had flown inward and outward with ease and without concentration of thought, now could be had only by thinking hard and breathing deliberately. Each breath in had to be concentrated upon. Each breath out was an equally mind-consuming task. It seemed that the lungs wanted to collapse, that they did not have enough power to work smoothly. Time stood still. Each mind was concentrated upon the simple task of breathing deeply enough to stay conscious and alive.

When it seemed that the Westsun had stood still almost above the Golden Pillar forever, that breath would never again fill aching lungs, that time had ceased to be and would never be again, the rains came. Not the fragrant, gentle droplets of the rainy season of the Eastsun! This was a violent dumping of the oceans of tears of an anguished heaven hatefully upon a despised land. It was torrents. Millions of baskets of water deluged out of the angry sky upon the captive land.

Then, it was over. For twenty-eight glorious days, fragrant with delights of life and abundance of soil, it was over.

In the time of one hundred breaths, the raging Westsun curved its way from the northwest to a point overhead and slightly to the north of the Pillar of the Sundial. There it seemed to pause—at least to A-Sar-U, who knew it could not pause, it only seemed to—before it swept onward. Relentless, it curved from the northwest, southeastward to the Sundial, then northeastward again.

It was said that the Temple of Po-Si-Don had been built at this exact spot in order to mark the furthermost south the Westsun traveled in its meteoric arc. The Temple—and another far to the west and still another far to the east—was on a line exactly between the paths of the two suns. It was the fix-point of all land, the beginning point of all history.

It was here, so the story was told, that the ancestors of the planet had landed three thousand Westsuns ago.

Ancestors were to be worshipped. On That Other Planet they had learned to become God-like, to become God-e. But, now, many did not really believe that they had come from another planet. Many said that the story was only a tale told by priests when they could not think of other things to say or wanted to scare children.

Even after the Westsun disappeared beyond the horizon curving to the northeast, there was little attempt to talk. It was as if the experience was too great for words. Laughter would come easily later.

A-Sar-U saw that people below were moving about very slowly and acting as if they were coming out of some strange benumbing lethargy.

Many of those present had moved moments before to relieve one part of their bodies from the buffeting wind. A-Sar-U had moved, skillfully and unnoticed, he hoped, to be near Ast-i. Her soft hand crept into his and tugged gently until the two of them seemed to drift naturally downwind and out of earshot. His thoughts were upon the perfection of the grace with which she moved. Her thoughts were, it seemed to him, practical. Nothing more! Even knowing this, his heart continued to beat far more swiftly than he thought it should.

Ast-i was to him the most beautiful person in the world. Fun to be with. Fun to tease. Fun to play with, as they had played through the years. She had some of the easy, powerful grace of Lor'd Bes, the great, if modest, Warrior. They said she had the regular features, blue eyes, reddish-golden hair, and deep-skinned beauty of her mother, As-Tar.

A-Sar-U tried to remember the sad story of As-Tar. She had strangely disappeared while attending the duties of the High Priestess of the Temple of Po-Si-Don. Even the Ama-Sones could not find her or Ra, his own Divine Father, who disappeared near the same time. Ama-Sones sel-

11

dom failed. They never gave up trying to find anyone and especially those who broke the Law of the Pleasant Planet

His thoughts were sharply broken.

"You're dumb!" Ast-i's whisper sounded more loudly to his startled ears than had the recent thunder.

"Why? How dare...?"

"Quiet! Listen! You don't even know why Thoth shoved you to shut you up, do you?"

A-Sar-U stiffened. He was proud, for he knew he had great physical strength and a bright mind. She was, after all...

"No. You don't either. How could you know what I don't?"

"Listen! How I know—pure accident! You think I'm wrong...oh, oh..."

A-Sar-U felt the baleful, angry eyes of Je-Su upon them.

"No time now. You'll step on the reason if you walk around the Golden Pillar of the Sundial."

As suddenly as the fore-wind had begun, the aft-wind stopped. Voices could be heard behind him now.

"That's craz..." The look of loathing and fear on Ast-i's lovely face made him stop with the words half-formed. But the thought completed itself forcefully in his head. *It was crazy to think that the reason he had been hit could be stepped on by walking around the Golden Pillar. It had to be crazy!*

He looked at her in amazement. Surely she was joking. She had a strange, sometimes over-imaginative sense of humor. There was no way he could have formed an answer to her without hurting her feelings. Before he could think of anything to say, Je-Su spoke.

Je-Su's face was covered by a mask that must have been meant to be a smile. It was a muscular rearrangement of features. His tight lips did not press so hard upon his slightly protruding teeth. His cheeks were reshaped so that the hollows were less pronounced. The corners of his mouth were pulled back, but not up, for they seemed to be defeating muscles unaccustomed to lifting. An arching of his black, full, overhanging eyebrows into what he must have fancied was a light and friendly look did not lighten the angry look in his black eyes.

"Your dream. Most interesting, my boy! Did you talk with anyone, oh, say, like your mother, about it?"

Ast-i pulled herself inward as if she wanted to escape, and her animated face went dull.

"No, Lor'd Uncle. I only dreamed it last night."

"Ah, yes? But I meant, before. Have they talked to you about anything that would make you dream so...about their dreams...their beliefs."

Ast-i moved quickly, as if disturbed by a sudden dread. But her face was wreathed in a beautiful smile as she asked, "But Lor'd One of War, does not the Creed of the Planet tell us all what we may—must—believe?"

Je-Su's body did not display his annoyance. He said, perhaps too sharply, "I thought they might have discussed other possibilities. For instance, do we all believe the same? Sometimes I think I do not believe exactly what I'm supposed to believe. What do you believe, lad?"

There was something in the way Je-Su moved his tall, powerful body that made A-Sar-U remember the serpent he had seen pounce upon a bird. His mind was fully alert now, and had taken the warning in Ast-i's apparently harmless comment.

"I believe the Creed, Lor'd One. Only what I am told."

"What were you told?"

"About what, Lor'd Uncle?"

"Why, lad, about the two suns. About Radiant Bodies rising out of the physical body. About anything that would have caused you to dream such a strange dream."

"Oh, Lor'd One of War, I think I dreamed about me more than about the Radiant Body or the two suns. I dreamed I had the power to handle the two suns. It was very interesting, captivating. I fear it was a rather conceited dream."

"Yes, it could be said to be the dream of a big ego, couldn't it?"

A-Sar-U blushed. "Perhaps, Lor'd Uncle, I was dreaming that someday I would be as big and powerful as you are. You control all the Warriors of the planet."

A tiny flash of approval came into the black eyes.

"Ah, but not the Temple Guards and the Ama-Sones. Therefore, I am so little in importance compared..." His eyes flashed with anger as they rested on Thoth. His voice trailed off. "Ah, compared to anyone. It is only the Supreme God-e, Lor'd of the Pleasant Planet, who is great."

"To be as great as you should be enough, Lor'd One. How many times you have risked your life and won!"

The flash of approval came into the bright, black eyes. This time it stayed longer. But it was replaced by a gleam of fanaticism that grew more intense with each word of the many that came tumbling out of his ever tighter lips.

"Remember, lad—both of you—how you think of Divinity determines your welfare in life and your salvation after death. Dead you must someday be, for that is the punishment of the Supreme Spiritual God-e upon disobedient flesh called man.

"Accept with grace your burden of eternal sin. Repent the sins of your forefathers. Make amends. Atone! Cast yourself on the mercies of the Eternal. Work to make up for the willful sins of the flesh."

Je-Su was beginning to pulse to the rhythm of his eagerness. He was whipping himself into a frenzy, intoxicating himself on his own words. Words repeated over and over until they were drills in unconscious acceptance of half-truths, A-Sar-U thought.

"Be obedient to God-e. Submit your will. Support with your life his divinely selected priests. Escape the talons of lust. Find that inner peace. Serve God-e. Serve his priests. Do not sin in body, mind, morality, soul, or spirit."

Je-Su's voice became more unctuous. He was vibrating with his words. They were coming in short bursts. He was becoming more rhythmic, more sing-song.

"Sin not in look, word, gesture, or action. Sin not in pride, falsehood, heresy, deception, or deviation. Sin not—as you almost did—in dream, thought, concept, or mood. You almost committed the unpardonable sin. You almost imagined yourself equal to the Supreme. Unforgivable. Punishable. Even if unintentional, still despicable, unforgivable, and punishable. If you had talked of these things previous to dreaming them, it would have been treason to the planet. Blasphemy to the God-e. It would have been the deadly sin of a mind uncontrolled, which should be punishable by death."

14

Bes, the Magnificent Warrior, moved up beside them. Ast-i smiled with pleasure. "Lor'd Father, we are enjoying the religious thoughts of Lor'd One of War."

Je-Su's strange, self-fascinating rhythm of speech broke. He seemed to A-Sar-U to come down from some great emotional height.

Bes smiled, his head on one side, his blue eyes filled with his usual confidence and good humor.

"I heard. Je-Su may someday be Lor'd of Wisdom. I hope he will not then find too much on the planet that is punishable by death."

Je-Su stopped in mid-stride. "Do you challenge the laws of the God-e?"

"I, Je-Su? Of course not. Look, I'm only two-thirds of a man. Is that big enough to challenge the guardian of the Eternal Laws? Relax. This is a party, not a War Council inquiring about morals." Bes moved on, walking in a waddle because of his short legs.

Je-Su called sharply. "We should always be in a War Council on morals. Sin is ever present. Even slight deviations, slight insults to the God-e grow toward revolt against the ancient laws as they are carved by fire upon the Columns."

"Hey, friend! Surely you don't think that you will find rebels to the laws of this planet here. Not among the families who shed their blood, gave their lives, to keep the people from overthrowing the God-e and his laws?"

"Everywhere there may be spies, tricksters, blasphemers who undermine the God-e."

"Not here, Je-Su. If the God-e is ever undermined, it is we here who will turn our swords to placing him back in power."

"Will you fight for the God-e?"

"I have all my life. Why change?"

"Will you be subservient to his priests?"

"If they are clean and pure, not tricksters or charlatans."

"Ah, ha! Even you reserve the right to judge the priests for yourself rather than by his appointment."

"Je-Su, would you fight and die for a false priest?"

"If appointed over me...unquestioningly!"

"Good. Oh, I'd fight. But I'd ask a lot of questions."

15

"Are you saying you might be treasonous to the God-e?"

"Oh, no. It a Warrior's duty to die if need be! But the God-e has never said I had to die without asking questions. Certainly asking why is not as bad for our planet as are those who try to impose beliefs and shackles upon the minds of men so that they may never think for themselves in any matter, even the smallest."

"Who does that?"

Bes swung about so that his blue eyes held fast on the fanatically bright eyes of Je-Su. "Je-Su, I've heard it said that there are groups who claim special privilege as the chosen people of the God-e. Individuals who want it whispered that they are the first and only Son of the God-e. People who want high place and privilege they do not yet have strength to take or wisdom to earn. Have you heard of such people who malign the God-e by making him partial to a special people?"

Je-Su seemed to swell. His swarthy face became a deep ruby color. His eyes almost closed. He panted, as if choking on choler. At last his voice came in a strangled, unintelligible burst that ended with "...and I know of no group that claims privilege they do not deserve. Otherwise my Warriors would..."

Thoth came easily into the group and took Ast-i and A-Sar-U by the hand. "It has been a wonderful day. A great anniversary for each of you. Come, let's go."

He led them away and the group followed. Ast-i said, "I'd like to walk around the Golden Pillar of the Sundial. You want to come with me, A-Sar-U? It might bring us special luck."

A-Sar-U felt his heart leap, and also the urge to walk around the whole planet with her. He was interested in holding her slender, fair-skinned hand, not in seeing what she thought was the reason he had been forcefully stopped in relating his dream. They would have pulled away, but Thoth held them firmly.

"Please! Do nothing more that might be taken to be superstition. There is unrest and suspicion everywhere. You must be careful what you believe. Even more careful what you say. More careful still of what people think or say you believe. Walking around the Golden Pillar for luck

16

may bring you the bad kind. You can die for what certain persons think you think."

His grasp upon their hands was willfully strong and compelling. Together they walked down the upper promenade for the High Priests of the Temple, down the ramp toward the inner courtyard. The temple had never looked so large and beautiful as it did now, glistening in the gentle Eastsun. The vast walls, seven thousand arms in length on each end and nine thousand on each side, seemed polished with pure silver.

They turned back on the lower floor of the galleries, passed underneath the golden-pillared Sundial, and out into the front promenade. A-Sar-U was always impressed by the vastness, the beauty, the awesome grandeur of the works the hands of man could create for his worship of the Divine. They crossed over the wide avenues leading past the imposing statues, over into the front fields.

Thoth stopped. His voice was gentle. "You are obviously in love."

Ast-i blushed. A-Sar-U merely said, "Of course, Lor'd Uncle. She is the mate I have chosen as soon as we reach the permitted age for priestesses to marry."

"You never told me," she said.

"I've been telling you with every act of my life all my life. You are my chosen. Am I yours?"

"Ease off," Thoth said with a gentle laugh. "If you are to choose to be a priestess rather than a Virgin of God-e, you must decide soon, Ast-i."

"I want to be a priestess. I want to have only one man, not many. I want children and a home, not the Temple of the Virgins.

"Then listen well!" Thoth's voice took on a commanding tone. "Decide soon. If you wish to be a Bride of God and wish A-Sar-U to be your consort, you will have my support. But you cannot delay. Hear well. Wild forces threaten us all. Things you cannot dream of are about to happen. You no longer have the luxury to enjoy the innocence of your youth. All too soon disaster, your beliefs, your faith, or old age must overcome you. You are in equal danger from each."

He paused, reflected. "You decide now. I will talk with Lor'd Bes about it."

17

A-Sar-U felt suddenly older. The chill of the dreadful warning was upon him. The heat of his adoration for Ast-i was also upon him. "What was he warning us about?"

"I don't know. But it has something to do with those black streaks on the white marble to the south side of the Golden Pillar of the Sundial."

"That sounds so... so..."

"Unbelievable! Yes. But it is true, A-Sar-U. Believe me it is true."

"How do you know?" He intended to argue. But he saw stark terror in her eyes. "Holy God-e, Ast-i. I believe you."

"Oh, A-Sar-U, I am so glad. I was afraid you might not. I get so frightened by what I know. I know when I know. I know what I *think* I know. But don't know why I know. You must not tell. We might be killed."

"I will not tell." In his thoughts he added that no one would believe him if he did. Great persons, Priests of the Temple of Po-Si-Don doing murder over black streaks in white marble beside a Sundial! No, he could not tell, for it would send him to the headsman for the insane.

Ast-i was looking at him in a way she never had before. It made his knees weak. "Do you want to...I mean... the Ordeal of Virgin Birth, the Bride of God? Would you— could you—keep yourself for me only until we conceived a child by Thought-Force. Oh, A-Sar-U...I yearn so...can we...?"

"Yes. I want no woman but you, ever."

"Oh, A-Sar-U."

"Will you take me as your Chosen Man so we may work on the desire together? So that I may father your child by Thought-Force alone?"

"Yes. Oh, yes!"

"But only the first child, Ast-i. After that I want you as my Chosen Woman. I yearn for your physical body in my arms."

"I madly for yours. Understand, if you are too strongly attracted to any other woman...remember, I am yours any time you wish, any way you wish. May we try...not physically...for a while?"

"Oh, we'll make it work. You will conceive and bear my son while yet untouched by man."

"How I'd like that, A-Sar-U."

"You know the dangers of the Ordeal of the Virgin Birth, the Bride of God?"

"If I am found wanting, I die. Yes, I know."

"Is your mind made up? Shall we ask our families' permission to risk it? If we fail, they will be dishonored."

"Yes. I know. But, Oh, A-Sar-U! If we succeed, I shall be honored above all Virgins, and you above all Warriors."

"I know. I can wait for the honors. I'm just not sure I can wait for you."

Hand in hand, glowing with radiance, they turned back toward their family group. Both knew they had, in the last thousand breaths, passed beyond childhood and youthfulness.

Together they faced a stormy future, made more doubtful by the meaning of marks on white marble at the Golden Sundial.

2

Ordeal of Virgin Birth

Ast-i knew that few chose to risk death in the Ordeal of Virgin Birth. It was honored as a divine power usable only by divine mankind—at least so priests said. It had been commonly used on That Other Planet. Great Atl had been of Virgin Birth, and he was a cosmic personality. But few, it was said, lived past the preliminary tests, and none in three thousand Westsuns had registered in advance and achieved the Holy Miracle. She had known from her earliest childhood that she wanted to strive for it, was born to achieve it—and with A-Sar-U.

Never once had she ever faltered in her desire, and only at times in her faith in him. At those times, when he seemed to slip in his behavior, to be less than perfect, she had been swift and severe to pull him back to the perfect path. He had always been strong, sure, quiet. When other girls looked at him they melted away in delight. Ast-i knew what she wanted, and she intended to get it.

She had expected A-Sar-U to declare her to be his Chosen Woman...many times. Or she had dreamed he might, or hoped he might, or whispered the mantra for the Supreme God-e. A-Sar-U had never said he wanted her. Yet he was always near her, towering over her in protective strength, with humble laughter and such studied reserve and indifference.

Sometimes she delighted in punishing him with unnecessarily hard blows when they played at hand-fighting. Then she was secretly sorry.

"Oh, A-Sar-U. You've always been my Chosen Man and we were always destined for this Ordeal," she thought.

Ast-i held proudly to A-Sar-U. Since her earliest memories he had been her idol. As children they had played in the back reaches of the Temple grounds. Often they had quarrelled over childish things. But always he had been so firm, dependable, and supportive. His face, so open and filled with intelligence, often filled her dreams. As the daughter of a man with a visible deformity she was often teased, but not when A-Sar-U was near. He teased her, but always gently. No one cowed him or her when she was in his presence.

Never had he told her that she was his Chosen Woman. How proud that made her. To be Chosen Woman of the Son of Ra, the God-e of the Empire of E-Den, was honor enough. To be Chosen Woman of A-Sar-U, bravest and swiftest of the Young Warriors, and the only Young Warrior her own father ever had complimented in her presence...oh, that was too, too wonderful.

As they approached the family group, she saw them all looking quizzically at her. Was her gossamer Virgin's dress awry? Had the Westsun, wind, and rain...?

"Lor'd Ones. Beloved priestesses, if we may, we have something to say that all the Empire will want to hear."

A-Sar-U's voice was firm and strong. She could not have spoken, for she was trembling inside.

The group converged upon them in curiosity. A-Sar-U continued. "If it please the Lor'd Bes, Father of the Virgin Ast-i, if it please the Beloved Mother, God-ette, know that I wish to take Ast-i as my Chosen Woman."

Ast-i saw the look of pleasure on all faces except those of Je-Su and Set. They looked angrily at each other. She put that fact into her mind, then turned to the expressions of joy from the members of the family.

Now, in the custom of the Pleasant Planet, she must make her statement of desire. She moved slightly forward and noticed the glowing face, smile, and clear sky-blue eyes of her chosen.

"Beloved Lady Goddess, Lor'd Father, Lor'd Ones, and especially Lor'd Thoth, Master of Wisdom: If it please you all, I, lacking one Westsun of being of the age required, ask permission that I be allowed to become the Chosen Woman of A-Sar-U, my Chosen Man."

There was excitement, laughter. Er-Ru cried out with surprise and joy. All seemed greatly pleased except Je-Su and Set. Why? What caused their black looks?

She did not have time to find out. She had to speak the words that would set an Empire into motion. She and

A-Sar-U had chosen the path on which so many failed, and which could lead to death as punishment for breaking a vow...or if either could be proved to lack the virtuous and virginal qualities needed for the highest honor of the planet.

"If it please you further, and is approved by the Lor'd One of all the Empire, we wish to apply to enter the Ordeal of Virgin Birth. With the power of Thought-Force in the mind of my Chosen Man, I wish to become the Bride of God. I wish to become a Virgin Mother."

There was a stir indeed, and many joyous exclamations. She saw Je-Su nudge Set, whisper to him, and both almost smiled while shaking their head knowingly.

Bes came to her swiftly and held her protectively in his arms. "Are you sure you want this Ordeal of Virgin Birth, the Bride of God? So many fail."

"I'm sure, Lor'd Father."

"If I refuse my permission because you are not of the age?"

"In one Westsun I shall be. Then..."

"Say no more, you determined little wench. I did not raise you to be a sweetling only, but a helpmate to your Chosen Man. I am proud of you."

Bes turned to the gathering and said quietly but firmly, "I give my permission."

The noise of comments rose. A-Sar-U stood and looked at them and did not seem tense at all. She so admired his coolness. Inside, she was turning to quivering terror. What if she...?

Thoth held up his hand. Silence was immediate, so great was their respect and love for the Great Lor'd One.

"A-Sar-U, are you willing to undergo the Ordeal?"

A-Sar-U actually smiled! She could not smile, her face was frozen with terror.

"Lor'd Uncle, I welcome the Ordeal. I hope we two may at last prove the training of our race and bring the line of Divinity back to the Pleasant Planet."

Thoth raised his arms above his head and clapped his hands together nine times in a strange rhythm Ast-i had never heard before. It's effect was that in three breaths a band of Warriors with drawn swords came swiftly from the compound of the Temple Guard. As they approached, a line of priestesses, all in Virgin's dress, hurried from the compound of the Virgins of the World and marched hurried beside them. To Ast-i they seemed an army as they stopped in formation nearby.

"Let it be done! These two, Ast-i and A-Sar-U, wish to risk the Ordeal of Virgin Birth, that she may become the Bride of God. In a few Eastsuns they shall, before all the Realm, on the Window of Ra, be examined separately and together. Prepare the front of the Temple of Po-Si-Don. Take them now separately. Keep them pure for examination.

"Lor'd Bes, may we let the Drum speak!"

Her father raised his arms and signalled the Guard. In less than three breaths, the deep throats of the drums of the Empire began to tell the citizens of the Pleasant Planet all the story.

So swiftly it went! Hardly was her decision made when she was encircled in the coils of the Empire, Ast-i thought. It was frighteningly swift. The unknown added tensions and terrors she had little dreamed of as a child.

The Virgins moved in precision. In honor of the five canals, and also the Serpent of Eternal Wisdom, they made serpentine coils around her. They wound themselves around Ast-i as if they were the canals and she the Divine Temple. The first two lines moved into place by circling right. The next line circled left. A fourth line circled right. Then the outermost line, like the outermost canal connecting to the sea, formed itself by circling left.

The Virgins moved with precision. They drilled much to be lithe and beautiful in public displays. They were wards of the Empire, privileged to live as well as the Priestesses of the Temples. They might choose to become priestesses and undergo the long training needed. They might choose to be the Virgins who served the needs of all men. Or one might choose to be a Chosen Woman, serving and loving only one man through all her life. Once she was a Chosen Woman she could never belong to any other man on penalty of death.

Ast-i saw that the Temple Guards, practiced Warriors, formed a fighting square around A-Sar-U, isolating him from all others as the Virgins had isolated her. The Guard then moved away, almost running, as if in a hurry to pull him away from her.

Her feelings were torn between her concern for her actions and behavior amid the stress of all these new things happening to her so swiftly, and the fact that A-Sar-U was being hurried away from her. She longed to caress him with her fingers as she did with her eyes, as for one-half breath of time she saw him across space and the bobbing heads of moving escorts. He stood half a span taller than most.

She looked back toward her family and Thoth. But she saw only Je-Su and Set. One brief glimpse sent near panic through her. Je-Su was speaking close to the ear of the overly attentive Set. As he spoke, both curved their middle fingers into the form of a hook. Other fingers were folded away from it. The last thing that registered on her was the sudden, vicious thrusting, pulling, and tearing motion Je-Su made with his finger. Set's burst of glee and the delight on his swarthy face was sickening to her, and she wondered how the twin, the darker twin, of the man she loved could be so cruel and hateful.

Ast-i was moved swiftly along the south face and then turned to the left down the east side of the Great Temple. They went beyond the Temple to the north for another three thousand paces, then entered the west gate of the complex of buildings that made up the Temple of the Virgin of the World. It was set far east, almost upon the bank of the innermost canal. It was the center of training for the Virgin Priestesses of the Realm and under the guidance of the High Priestess of God-e, God-ette, Mother of the Virgins.

It was not half as large as the main Temple of Po-Si-Don. Yet it had a grandeur and beauty that was particularly its own. The buildings were perfectly formed in rectangles of seven to nine proportions. Each room was designed to meet perfection in the eyes of those who observed it. It sat like a proud lady in the midst of verdant fields. It was made of white marble with a slightly golden hue. It was resplendent and beautiful with a haunting, almost ethereal beauty in the lowering light of the setting Eastsun.

As she was hurried through the high postern and past the Ama-Sones, six giant women in full war gear, she felt a sense of safety and relaxation. She knew that six of these warlike women were on duty at each gateway at all times, light or dark. Many were stationed at the doorway of each house within the walls of the compound, and some even stationed in hallways to the inner rooms. Each had shield, breastplate, armor, lance, sword, and knife.

The Ama-Sones were fierce fighters, larger by half a span than most men. They guarded the Virgins. They were charged by ancient laws, inflexible and unchangeable, with one very special duty to the Empire. Any man who touched a woman without her permission was by law to be slain immediately by the nearest citizen, male or female. If he was not, it was the duty of the Ama-Sones to hunt, find, and kill that citizen pleasantly, with a single sword-swipe that took off the head. Then they were to find the attacker, cut off his private parts, cram them into his mouth, slit his belly open, and let him die in horrible agony. Women had to be safe anywhere in the Realm. Any time. Under any circumstances.

This ancient law of the Empire made it possible for women to move about between the fourteen Temple Centers, nestled like jewels on a string of jade along the verdant rivers underneath the benign Eastsun.

The hallway of the outer Temple was filled with Virgins. Each wished to see Ast-i, praise her, and wish her well in the Ordeal. The spontaneous outpouring of affection was pleasing to her, though she blushed under the teasing about how much nicer a man must be than a ghost.

The Mothers of the Virgins soon quieted the babble and shooed the Virgins through the many entrances into the great council chamber of the inner temple. It was near the sanctuary and the statue of Mut, Goddess Mother of the World. Many thought—and Thoth did not deny—that God-ette was Mut, reborn in order to serve the Empire. The statue was seven arms high, in grey-blue granite, and the figure of Ra as a child in her arms was a full arm in length. The statued face of Mut was so beautiful as she looked with pride and love upon the infant god in her arms that it often made Ast-i weep. Mut was Goddess Mother of

All Men, yet in her expression was a sign for all women. It poured out love upon her child. It spoke to women of their duty to handle all the trials of life and still love fondly their own children beyond the capacity of man to love anything. Ast-i knew that she could and would love her child no less than Mut obviously loved hers.

Soon the Virgins were seated, elbow to elbow, line after line, and row after row, upon the marble floor. Only when all the Virgins were assembled did she realize that there must have been more than a thousand who were sent to the Temple for education and training. How fortunate she was, for she was literally the foster daughter of the Mother of All Virgins, the greatest woman in the Realm, God-ette, Chosen Woman of Ra.

God-ette entered the room with the lithe flow of a tigress, purposeful, poised, and relaxed. Her hair was long and fell in large waves to her waist, its blond beauty fresh as that of a girl of a mere fifty Westsuns. Her eyes were a blue-grey, her nose straight with a flare at the end that gave her a light and pleasant look even when the burdens of her duties demanded severity from her. Her lips were full, curved more delicately than were A-Sar-U's lips and perhaps a little more red. Her chin was strong, and she carried herself with such strength that no one, not even Thoth, ever rose against her.

Every Virgin knew that she accepted no maiden into her temple who was not assigned to her totally, her will, her mind, her very life. When she spoke, as she was now going to do, every Virgin was alert, for she spoke for the Empire.

"A-Thena, Re-Gina, Balina—are all your Ama-Sones here who are not on duty?"

"Yes, Mother of the Virgins."

"Good. Though you worship the Goddess Athena, Queen of War and Chase, and we worship Mut, Mother of All Mankind, we have much in common. We all think women are more wonderful than men."

The Virgins laughed gaily, but Ast-i thought perhaps they did not know her beloved A-Sar-U.

God-ette continued, her light but firm voice carrying throughout the huge room.

26

"We are singularly honored. One among us has decided to risk her life for our greater glory. Ast-i has chosen A-Sar-U, my first-born son, and with him desires to enter the Ordeal of Virgin Birth. As soon as all is in readiness, in front of the Window of Ra, we may watch her official examination for purity. If she fails, we may catch her head as it falls from the Window and spit in her face.

"She will attest on honor her purity. It will be tested. I believe in her. To my knowledge she is pure. But you Virgins have your little ways and deep secrets."

The tapers of burning-flax in tallow flickered from some stronger wind outside. The Virgins drew their secret guilts and little lies closer into their consciousness and sat in hushed expectation.

"Women! How private we all are. How surely we take everything as personal. We need to be more universal in our outlook, in our dreams, in our aspirations. We need to let go of our private loves, fears, hopes and ambitions, and private lies—and live in a larger world. If we were not so pulled in upon our private selves, we could outdo any man anywhere anytime.

"One among us had decided to risk her life to bring our sex back to the respect which it has not enjoyed for three thousand Westsuns. We need to know our power— not as a group of beautiful and desirable creatures, but as individuals wielding the power of the Eternal Spiritual Supreme.

"Rulers may make laws concerning physical things, in terms of men and their ideas. When women refuse to obey them, those laws are void, moot.

"They may not be repealed, for the word of the King is forever—but they have no force.

"Why? Because men are kinder as a group than are women.

"Some women think that men delight in fighting and killing. Perhaps they do. But they do it by rules and with honor in upholding those rules and yet conquering a worthy foe.

"Woman is far more implacable as a foe. She hesitates to fight until she thinks all hope is lost—then fights with no rules. She is sensitive and knows terror and horror and

27

how to inflict them upon mankind...and she does it with a fearful, self-satisfied, loving smile.

"Death to woman is abhorrent. That's why she so enjoys the Holy Combats. Men have made the rules for these ancient Combats and follow them with honor. But unless women enjoyed the Combats and the defeat and death of men, men would never submit themselves to the Combats. It seems to women, sometimes, that death is not abhorrent to men, but is just a sad end for some.

"Woman wants these Combats. She wants the strongest and the bravest to be selected by the sword. She wants one of those so selected to be father of her children and give each child the bloodline of bravery and courage. This is well, for it gives our race hope of a future against all foes and all predators.

"Ast-i has chosen a Holy Combat for her Chosen Man and for herself. It will be dreadful. But I believe she, my foster daughter, my charge as a Virgin and my beloved friend, will win. That means, of course, that my son, A-Sar-U will win. Of each I am personally proud. To each I extend the thanks of the Virgins of the Realm. We may again be respected as we should be and once were.

"Women were goddesses. Women now are slightly lower than goddesses, only slightly, and higher than men. Women can love as hard as men fight. As I said, they can hate and destroy more viciously unless they are aware of their kinship with the God-e Supreme.

"Woman is humanity's footbridge to eternal life. In flesh and in spirit, woman is the easiest and most convenient way to continue life on the planet or in the heavens above it. Lest you tend to conceit, know she is not the only way. She is the easiest, if she remains natural, true to her physical nature.

"Sex has instant gratification and long-time rewards. However, if woman wants to delay gratification and have *eternal* rewards she may make herself a spiritual footbridge. It is quite possible for any woman.

"The requirements are quite simple. Simple, Virgins, not easy. These are:

"For a lifetime be absolutely pure in body, mind, morality, and spirit.

28

"Contamination of spirit is easier than you think. The soul of woman runs too often to tears, excitements, and self-pity; she makes her spiritual self impure by bringing it under the sway of her wide-ranging emotions. She is born to curiosity and to resisting authority.

"To hope for this absolute purity she must:

"First, discipline her mind until it is instantly obedient to her will.

"Second, curb her incredible ability to take everything that happens as personal.

"Third, curb the wide swing of her curiosity and emotions.

"Fourth, develop a wisdom greater than the natural wisdom of her physical body which says that by flesh alone may new life be born.

"Fifth, develop a pure emotion so universal and powerful that when turned inward to herself it will become the love of a single man.

"Sixth, be born with the ability to make one man love her more than he loves life itself for all her life from her earliest days. This is so he, too, will be pure and prepared.

"Seventh, be willing to risk her life, and possibly sacrifice his, for the good of all mankind.

"Eighth, be born with, or develop, a pristine will that can master every emotion, control every thought, and at last raise her flesh-self to the level of Divinity."

Ast-i was silently weeping, and saw the tears flowing on the cheeks of all Virgins near her.

"Children, I told you the way to become a Virgin of God-e was simple. I warned you it was not easy.

"Now, all to your quarters. When nature will permit we shall be greatly honored or greatly condemned by the Realm. Good sleep, pretty princesses. Light be your dreams."

The Virgins crept silently away, tears gleaming unashamed upon their cheeks. Ast-i sat still and wept until she was relieved of her stress. She was then brought food, and a small ordeal began.

When the petty ordeal was over, Ast-i sighed with a private relief. She had allowed herself to be fed a sparse meal of ground grains, nuts, boiled roots, ripe fruits.

She was fed. She could not by rule feed herself. By the same rule she could not be touched by anyone except God-ette. Little did she know how much pleasure she took from doing for herself until, by rule, she was forbidden to do so. Little had she known how reassuring the touch of a warm hand or sweet embrace could be!

When the meal was finished, she was shown to quarters at the far end of an open-air passageway which was lighted by smoking tapers of the wood of the fire tree. Inside her apartment was a giant bath, usually used for all Virgins, but for this Ordeal reserved for her alone. It was a deep pool of clear water, dropped from a stone reservoir which had been heated by the Eastsun.

When time would permit her to enter it, she found that the water was just at her body temperature.

Her guardian Ama-Sone, to whom she had become accustomed looking in on her, watched her float in the water with a total indifference.

Ama-Sones despised comforts. They slept on stone floors, seldom ate hot foods, and wore rough leather clothing or simply plates of metal as an armor. They worshipped war. Their greatest desire was to die in the midst of combat after killing ten of the enemy.

Ast-i held no such desire for discomfort or death. As she floated in the water as if borne up by her own body heat, she decided that the only death she would ever want would be to be squeezed to death in A-Sar-U's enraptured arms.

"I bring clean," the Ama-Sone said, waving her Virgin's uniform. She then moved out of the room with an energy that was akin to that of the Westsun.

Ast-i relaxed and dreamed. The warmth of the water was like a caress. It was soothing, lulling, and to her it was also exciting. She leaned her head against the stone edge of the bathing pool, closed her eyes, and let her imagination go. Her fantasies were so wild that she sat up breathing quickly, slightly flushed at the things her mind could do to her body.

Deciding she could stand no more of that longing for A-Sar-U, she stepped from the pool. Droplets of water made jewels upon the symmetrical beauty of her firm, up-pointed breasts, her strong wide-hipped body, and her long, slender legs. Her reddish-golden hair, now wet, clung in wavelets to her head and fell in curls upon her breasts and shoulders.

She busily dried the water from her body with the palms of her hands, expecting the Ama-Sone to return at any moment with cloth and clothes. When, after too long a time, she did not return, Ast-i called.

Her voice rang hollow in the room, and echoed strangely to her ears. It was the voice of a girl suddenly bewildered and afraid. She went toward the entrance but there found her passage blocked by three large persons in the uniforms of Mothers of Virgins. She stepped back, almost fell, and screamed in fright.

"Oh, my child! Such a noise." The one in the center spoke in a low, throaty, not very feminine voice. "You should thank us rather than scream at us. You do not know it yet, but at the next rising of the Eastsun you will be called for examination. The Drum has spoken. We have come to save your life."

Ast-i stood straight in the innocence of her naked beauty. She noted how slowly the six eyes searched and examined every part of her body. She did not like it. She resented it greatly. She must, she thought, be overwrought, for she was intuitively revolted by the very presence of the three. She had been given no reason to expect them. They might be her benefactors, but she was terrified by them.

"How may you save my life?"

"As Mothers of the Virgins, we are charged to determine if you are as you say. If your head is to be cut off tomorrow the committee wants to be forewarned. So we have been sent to examine you. If you are as you say, we will rejoice. If you are not, and if you wish us to do so, we will spirit you away and keep you alive in some far, safe place."

They were, she reasoned, possibly right. The House of Virgins would be deeply embarrassed if one of their own turned out to be false. But her intuitive self screamed warnings.

"I am as I say, Mother."

"We do not doubt it. But the committee does not want to take any chances. You understand."

31

"How would you determine...?" She did not need to finish the question. She saw the extended middle fingers fashioned into the form of a hook.

She recoiled with a slight scream. "No. No, thank you, Mothers. I will risk death rather than be touched."

"My child, control yourself. The Temple of the Virgins must insist. You carry our reputation to that Window of Ra tomorrow."

"No. I will not submit. Do not touch me!"

She screamed again as the three lunged toward her. As they parted on leaving the entrance way she saw the head of her Ama-Sone guard rolling in its own blood as if it had been severed from her body by a sharp sword. She screamed more loudly than before.

"Silence, my child. Do not be hysterical. We have orders to examine you from the highest authority. We will do so. If you relax it will all be over in a moment. We trust you know we must be sure. Our reputations, child."

The three slowly advanced, as if they wanted her not to panic. They spread out as if to take her in a net so that she could not slip away.

"If you touch me, you die by the law."

"If we do not touch you we die. The Temples of the Virgins may also die at the hands of angry people who can no longer trust our Order to keep their daughters safe and teach them. You understand, Child. You must understand."

Ast-i eased back a step, very slowly. "It is my life only I risk with the coming Eastsun."

"Your life. Our reputation. Our future."

The sight of the three curved fingers made her skin shiver. She then shivered inside her being. In her memory's eye she saw again the fiendish joy on the face of Je-Su and Set, and the ripping, tearing motion of that hooked finger.

One lunged at her, touched her shoulder with hands too calloused to be those of a woman. She slipped sideways as A-Sar-U had taught her to do and broke the grip. Another caught at her arm. She twisted free and retreated a step further.

Space was limited. She could not back much further or she would be pinned in the corner. She kicked at the third and felt the hard outline of a scabbard under the flowing gown. She screamed, "Help me. Help me."

Escape was no longer possible, she felt. She was of the blood of the Lor'd Ones, and she must fight. She had been taught to attack when in danger with no escape. Attack she did. She attacked to hurt and maim. Her fist slammed into the neck of the center one, who coughed and staggered back, gasping. She slashed at the second with her elbow, and heard the grunt that covered a cracked rib, she hoped. The third caught her from the side in a vice-like grip, pinning her arms, and squeezing the air from her lungs. Darkness began to settle over her mind.

"Stop!" The grip lessened and light flowed back into her brain.

"Let her go!" It was the voice of God-ette. Yet, Ast-i thought, it was asking, not demanding. If it was a command, it was a most reasoned command. Her attacker stepped back.

"Priestess, we but do our duty to the Temple. It must and will be done."

Ast-i saw the hand that slipped inside the flowing robe of the attacker nearest her. She knew it sought and gripped the handle of a sword.

"They have swords!" she cried.

"Nonsense, child." God-ette looked at her with a frown of disapproval and a slight shake of the head.

"They have swords!"

"You are a foolish girl, Ast-i. Mothers of the Virgins are never armed. The law protects them. Now be silent so we can get on with our business." Her voice was cutting and cold, and her head signalled her severe disapproval.

"Again, just why are you here?" God-ette asked of the intruders.

"Honored Lady, we are from the Joint Council of Mothers of Virgins in the Main Temple."

"You are?"

"Yes."

"And your duty is...?"

"To protect all Mothers of Virgins we must be certain that with the coming Eastsun she will prove to be as she has claimed."

Ast-i saw the signal that sent two of her attackers into position to attack God-ette. Was she blind, could she not see that she was putting herself in danger?

"Oh, that would be wise. Are you carrying swords as she says?"

"Yes, Mother of the Virgins. Of course! We are commanded to do so by our superiors when we are assigned swift and delicate jobs such as this one. The Ama-Sones can be most unreasonable and cause great delay."

"Yes. Yes. They certainly can. Did you cut off the head of the Ama-Sone guard at the door?"

Ast-i wanted to scream. God-ette was nonchalantly proceeding with her questions as if she had all the time in the world. Did she not see that the three were more intent on evil and more destructive than the wild Westsun?

"It was most lamentable—and necessary. She was unreasonable—even argued our authority."

Ast-i recognized the implied threat to God-ette...and the lie. There had been no words outside that entrance. The Ama-Sone must have been taken by surprise and murdered. It could not have been any other way. Surely God-ette could see that.

"I understand. You are under the need to hurry on official business. Very understandable." God-ette turned aside slightly and walked slowly, apparently in deep contemplation, five paces over, then two paces back. She stopped as the attackers seemed about to spring on her. "Ast-i, why do you not submit to authority?"

"They are false. They mean to...to deflower me."

"Nonsense. Why?"

"So I fail my testing and my head..."

"Oh, Child. How dramatic you are." God-ette turned to the attackers. "You see...so excited...so upset. Shall we leave her alone for a short while and let her recover her senses?"

"No, Mother. We must do it now. Our duty must be done and now!"

"Yes. I know how pressing these things can be." God-ette turned away, five steps over, two steps back. "Ah, I have a duty, too, you know. I must ask this. You know she is protected by the Law of A-Ra. She has not given you

34

permission to touch her. One of you has touched her. Have the other two?"

"No, no. We were merely trying to get her to stop to reason. If she would just lie down...a second..."

"I see what you want." She whirled on Ast-i, her finger pointing with absolute authority, her voice a sharp command. "Lie down. This instant. There. You know I am authority. I have life and death power over you. If you disobey me another instant you die. Lie down!"

All the years of training in obedience to the Mother of the Virgins struck at her confidence. She felt she must obey, yet she knew physically and intuitively that those hooded ones were false, and dangerous.

"Lie down, now!"

The command was like a whip that struck the strength from her legs. She sank to the floor, her eyes large with dread and wonder.

God-ette suddenly threw herself down upon the stones upon which she stood.

Three gleaming spears came through the entrance. Ast-i heard the impact of the spear in the body of her nearest attacker then the grunt of anguish. But the attacker struggled to bring out a sword. Before the sword was half drawn, the Ama-Sones were through the door and slashing at the attacker's groins.

Quivering in terror, Ast-i crawled into the corner. She did not want to watch, but could not keep her eyes away from the scene. The Ama-Sones were like posanga zombies who went about their grisly task with precision and indifference. She saw the bleeding flesh ready to be shoved into the mouths of her attackers. She saw in fascinated horror the swords of the Ama-Sones seeking and poising at the bellies of her attackers.

"Who sent you?" The peremptory command was heightened by a slight puncture of the belly.

"The Council "

A deeper thrust of the swords cut short the lie.

"Who sent you? Tell us and you die by one merciful stroke and lose your head. Refuse, and you die in increasing pain. Who sent you?"

"We don't know..." The moaning voice seemed to be telling the truth. The Ama-Sones ground their swords

35

deeper. "Swear by the Supreme Spiritual God-e. Met by hooded Mother paid...mercy on us. Mercy!"

"I think you know who. Tell."

The swords bit deeper and deeper and the pain seemed to echo in Ast-i's own flesh. At last she could stand it no more.

She groaned and turned away in sheer horror. She was so busy being sick in the corner she did not hear the dying moans of her attackers. During the long time of anguish she sobbed quietly into her hands in the corner. She roused only when the Ama-Sone spoke in a flat, matter-of-fact voice.

"Mother of the Virgins, we have done as you and the law required. We will take these three swords, three knives, and one teste of each as proof." The Ama-Sone almost chuckled. "We have some small proof they were not Mothers of the Virgins."

God-ette was equally matter of fact. "Take all the proof you need. You don't have to prove to me they were false. I knew that the moment I stepped through the entrance there. I knew, too, they were men and armed. That's why I sent for you."

"Good thing you did. They were determined. We got nothing from them."

"Did you really expect to?"

"Oh, perhaps not. No matter. It is nice to see men suffer."

"Not a feminine thought, Ama-Sone!"

"No, Mother of the Virgins. A true one."

"Our dramatic Virgin there almost forced them into killing us before you could get here."

"Oh, don't blame her," the Ama-Sone chuckled. "They were men. She enflamed them. If she weren't so small she'd be beautiful enough to be an Ama-Sone."

The Ama-Sones threw the mutilated bodies over their shoulders. "We'll take these to be displayed by the Cryer in the pathway to the Temple for the coming activities. Thank you, Mother of the Virgins. It has been a pleasure to serve you."

At the entrance the Ama-Sone turned and looked long at Ast-i. Her eyes ran like extended fingers over her form. "All that beauty...to be wasted on a man."

She turned and was gone. Ast-i looked down upon her body and wished she had thrown it into the lustful arms of her Chosen Man. By now she could have been a happy, well-loved Chosen Woman.

While God-ette was busy giving orders about how to clean the place and purify it with torches, Ast-i slipped back into the water. It seemed to wash away some of the filth and horror of the past fifty breaths. Once again she began to feel like a woman in love, not a ploy in a power-play of the Empire.

God-ette stopped at the side of the bath with a cloth and a clean gown. Something of a sad smile was on her face.

"You must not be sad. You've just been through a little trouble. Your problems have just begun. The pathway to Virgin Birth is over corpses."

"But why? It should be such a divine path. It promises so very much for the Empire."

God-ette sighed. "Ah, yes. Perhaps it is so valuable because so many powerful people want to prevent it. You and A-Sar-U must become two people against many in the Empire who are powerful and will do anything to defeat your spiritual success. Equally, you must be willing to do anything to assure it. Anything!

"Courage, Daughter, a new Eastsun comes soon to test your will."

3

Je-Su, Son of God-e

The Temple of the Warriors was directly west of the
Temple of the Virgins. While it was much larger in dimensions, it was not as beautiful to Je-Su. The marble
selected for its structure had slightly bluish veins and took
on the feeling of emotional indifference rather than inti-
macy. Its compounds were far more open. The courtyards
were paved with blue-grained granite to stand the pounding of martial feet in training and in preparation for wars,
or the Combats when they were permitted.

All rooms were sparse, even hard, except one. It was
the quarters of the Lor'd One of Warriors. It was fitted with
all things he desired for his comfort. The women kept the
balsa mats clean and tidy and made patterns of the giant
tiger skins which he strewed around to remind all visitors
of his prowess as a hunter.

The cured hide of a one-horned creature of enormous
size hung on poles in one corner. He had killed it with his
sword as it charged him. He did his visitors the favor of
letting them know that he had done so. For their own self-
protection they needed to know how powerful he was, how
courageous.

Now, he, Je-Su, Lor'd One of Warriors, was impatient.
Though he did not dare admit it to himself, he was also a
little frightened. What if the plans went awry? What if the
bumbling fools bumbled again in spite of the detailed instructions and warnings he had ordered Set to give them?

Why didn't Set come to his quarters to report? It was
well past half the dark time! Je-Su plucked impatiently at
specks on the tiger skin on which he sat, threw the imagined particles at the entrance near which hung the many
shields of those he had beaten in combat. All those shields
proved his ability as a Warrior. In all the Realm only one
man had a right to his shield. One man!

38

One man stood between him and his rightful place!

With head sunk on his chest, his breath coming fast through flaring nostrils and compressed lips, he recalled the moment of his defeat. He had out-thought and out-fought, had the sword beaten high so he could go in low under the shield with a crippling cut to the leg! It was good strategy. It had worked many times. Then he could slowly move in for the kill on his helpless opponent, letting him understand in his last moments the foolishness of challenging Je-Su, Only Begotten Son of the Supreme Spiritual God-e.

One man had luckily escaped his power. Sheer luck. A flashing sword came down upon his shield, parried his own sword high, ducked under and drove past the parry up through his own sword hand. He was impaled and weaponless. He stood defenseless.

Sweat poured from his forehead even remembering that moment.

One man!

One man had stopped him. It must not be! He was First-Born Son of Divinity. He was divine. He deserved the honors. He was the chosen one. He was the Son, the Heir to the Realm. All this was rightfully his. By birthright. He should not have had to fight for it. He was the heir physically and spiritually. His commands were the ones that should be obeyed. His voice commanding all the people. Now it was permitted to command only the Warriors in training and at war. Someday he would loose his legions, his hidden legions. He would change all the laws so that his blood would inherit the kingdom forever. Someday! The waiting was such a waste of his great skills, his great mind. All wasted. Because of one man!

The effrontery! Defenseless he had stood before that man, ready to die the glorious Death of the Warrior. It was denied him. Denied! He was not given death with honor. He was given life with false praise, false honor.

That voice as it pronounced his doom! Unctuous. Flattering the crowd at the Combats! Appealing to their sense of fair play to deprive him of honor.

"Je-Su is a Lor'd One of our Realm. He is a Warrior of great skill and endurance—as you have seen since we two have fought now for two Eastsuns and more than half of another. He is powerful. He has courage. He is brilliant in defense and fierce in attack.

"I want him to live. Not only because he is my kinsman, but because he is good for the Empire. I ask you all to realize that he lives because he is the soul of honor of the Empire. I want him to live as my right hand in defense of the Empire we all love. Do I have your permission to let him live?"

Oh, the shouts of the crowd as he was reduced to the second place in the structure of the Empire—and in the affections of all the people. Worse. His divine ideas, divine rights were rejected! He was not allowed to openly insist that the people realize how great his religious ideas were.

He alone could show them how to get universal salvation for all souls. Salvation. Eternal life. Merely by accepting the facts as they were, as he proposed to state them:

"Believe in God-e. Believe in me, First-Born Son of God-e, heir and participant in his powers on earth. Bow down before the priests I appoint to serve you. Give obedience. Be subservient. Delay your pleasures. Cease to sin, sin, sin!

"Cease to sin and peace can be yours. You could know my divine love for you. It will fill you. Love can then flow out from you to all mankind.

"Believe, have faith, and I will bestow divine blessings upon you. Peace in life. Life in this very body after death. Salvation unto life everlasting. Bow down before me."

One man! The needless delay. Peace would come. Love would flow out from man to man or every head would roll. They would believe! They would not sin, sin, sin. He could make them obedient to his power. He would have that power. He was building his hidden armies, readying his priests. His ideas would prevail. He would rule the Empire. It would bow down before him. It would reach its salvation and life everlasting. It would know how great, how truly great, he was. It was coming. It could come soon. Soon. Soon!

Delayed by one man. Who insulted him in the moment of defeat. Degraded him! Gave him life with spurious honor, not glorious death. Death was better than living in second place. Beneath the one who had defeated you. Then, most insulting and degrading—When Thoth was appointed by Ra to be the Lor'd One of Wisdom, to announce to the gathering of all the Warriors in the Empire that he had chosen—Holy God-e! Chosen! Like a Chosen Woman! Chosen! The mighty Je-Su chosen to be Lor'd One of War, in charge of all the fighters of the Empire. Except the Temple Guard and the Ama-Sones. An insult! Just to build up an ego!

Ego! How little attention anyone had paid to his ego, his feeling of worth. Even his parents...Oh, it was a long conspiracy starting with his name. Why did people never understand him? Why? Because he was not what his name declared him to be.

His old anger and hurt flooded over him swiftly, causing the sword-wound over his left temple to throb.

"From the beginning everyone was against me. Even my parents. That's why they let me be called by that weakling name, not the great name they intended to give me. JeeZUU. Should be strong name. It was meant to be like the name of Ptah, *PuhTaah, the first great artificer.*

My name should be pronounced KuhJaahZUU, meaning the great Builder of Civilization.

"Why do people always defy me? Or ignore me? Why?"

Those wrongs would be righted. People would call him by his true name. And that insult!

That insult should be avenged. He would avenge it. Soon. He would take by brilliance what had been stolen from him by a lucky sword thrust. He would crush...oh, yes, he would crush!

How like a fawning God-e that damned Thoth liked to behave. Open smiles. Friends with everybody. No rules of self-righteousness. Friendly even to those who sinned. Careless. Casual. Ah, ha!

Perhaps because he had sinned himself!

True, everybody fawned upon Thoth.

But they really loved Je-Su. Deep in the core of their beings, they loved Je-Su. He would soon destroy that fawning, sinning, lucky, casual Thoth. Soon.

4

Thoth, Lor'd One of Wisdom

He thought, "Thoth, Lor'd One of Wisdom, Supreme Lor'd One of the Planet! How far I have come! How grateful I am."

Thoth glanced from the sheepskin on which he sat to the many shields in the corner. They blended with the marble of the room beside the apse of the Temple of Po-Si-Don. He liked that. He wanted to forget that he had been forced to win much of his progress, his place of authority, by Combat. That was the law.

The same law demanded that he take and keep the war-shield of each Warrior he defeated.

Defeated, ha! His thoughts gouged his memory with the admonition of his Master Teacher, Ra, when he was appointed temporarily to this, the highest office in the Empire.

"You have won your way to near the top. But you have never defeated anyone. It was the power of God-e working through your huge, well-trained body, supported by your lightning-fast mind. You never defeated a Warrior. You didn't really defeat Je-Su in the contest for the Lor'd One of War. He defeated himself."

His first Combat was for command of a Line of Twenty, his first command of a body of the Warriors. Then the Combat for the command of the Twenty Lines of Twenty. Then the company of Twenty Twenty Lines of Twenty, followed by Combat for Lor'd One of War, Commander of the Warriors of the Realm. From there, Ra had appointed him to be Lor'd One of Wisdom. If Ra did not return, he was assured of his position for life. But by honor he was severely restricted in some things because of his public promise to Ra.

He had hoped for a greater destiny than commanding the Warriors. When Ra was forced by...well, events and decided to leave, Thoth was ready.

Ra had done much. Always he turned to Thoth for help and guidance with the citizens of the Empire. He sent Thoth out among the peoples. All tribes, without fail, all tribes! Ra had the welfare of the people at heart. The endless battles with the desert people, the Shumen under Africanus, had consumed his energies and his mind. Often he said to Thoth, "I teach you that you may teach all men. I will conquer the rebellious Shumen and Africanus. You must conquer the hearts of all the peoples of the Realm."

How he, Thoth, had tried. Sometimes too hard, he thought. With some success. Many people of the different tribes loved him, accepted him and the training he took to them, with open hearts and grateful lips. Much he had tried to do. More, by far, was yet to be done.

So much to do. So little time! Oh, so little time if the marks upon the marble at the foot of the Golden Pillars of the Sundials of the Empire were telling true.

Thoth stirred restlessly. It was as if he warded from his mind a silent sword-stroke of destruction. His face was placid, but beads of sweat on his upper lip showed the stress of even thinking of the horror that might befall. Just the thought!

He had sent scientists as observers to fourteen points, the giant Sundials of the Empire, to triangulate the Westsun, its path and its behavior. Thirty-six Westsuns had come and gone, and they could not be positive. Or didn't want to be.

"Scientists!" he grumbled half-aloud, "Always *tomorrow, need more data, or maybe. I can not live on maybe. I need to know, and to know now.*"

He smiled. He heard in memory the calm voice of Ra, "Thoth, you are yesterday, today, and tomorrow. You know everything. Yet you always have to know more. You were not born. You were unbegotten by knowledge."

Unbegotten! Yes, but in knowledge only. He had been begotten in the flesh by a mental-spiritual force using a special technique coming down from A-Ra, the God-e.

Thoth had been assured that he had been born by Thought-Force, by Virgin Birth. As had Bes, Ra, As-Tar,

God-ette, A-Sar-U and Ast-i. Like his birth, their births had not been recorded or heralded by the Empire. But they should have been. They would have been but for the almost overwhelming onslaught of the Shumen under Africanus.

Officially, no Virgin Birth had been recorded in the Empire for three thousand Westsuns. Three whole generations. He knew better.

He stirred slightly, but it was enough to redirect the thrust of his meditation and revere.

Thoth knew he was allowing himself to be too concerned about the possibility of disaster to the Empire. That was why he had suggested to A-Sar-U and Ast-i that he would support their choice at such an early age. He knew they were in love, had been all their lives. He believed them pure. He needed someone with the strength, the brilliance, and the ability of A-Sar-U to help him save the lives of the citizens.

Je-Su, second in the Empire, should be his right-hand man, his trusted confidant. But he could not trust Je-Su. Je-Su was a good fighter, a good Field Commander, with endless energy and a flashing mind. Yet, he could not trust him. Not with a secret that was so important to the Empire.

Brahm, Som, Ram. Each was too narrowly set in his opinion to see the total good of the Empire. Each was too inturned upon himself to see the problems of the whole planet. No! He would have to wait. The time for training A-Sar-U would be a time of dreadful doubt and hazard. But that was the only hope he saw for the Empire.

A-Sar-U was a man grown already. He had been born wise. He was truly one who could say "I am yesterday, I am today, I am tomorrow."

Soon, all too soon, Thoth knew, A-Sar-U had to have the techniques, the abilities, the knowledge, and the will to be able to truthfully say, "I have the power to be born a second time." In a way, to be saved from destruction, every person in the Empire had to learn how to be born a second time. They had to be taught. A-Sar-U, the only hope of the Empire, had to be able to uncover the hidden soul, create gods, and feed Divinity. Otherwise the Empire might...

Thoth tossed his hands in the air, sighed. He must not borrow from time. You could not win Combats by pre-supposing where the sword stroke would land! He did not win all those shields, so needlessly stored face-down in the corner, by borrowing from time or from trouble. He had to keep his mind clear and confidently meet any challenge.

Thoth scolded his racing mind with a whispered, "You are planning for the long future when you should be thinking of tomorrow."

He had not intended for the two young ones to risk their lives so soon. It came in a rush, as if they secretly had been planning it for all their lives. No doubt they had. Thoth knew the hazards they were to encounter. He must do all he could to help and protect them.

First, he had to get them through the Trial tomorrow. The ritual, the pomp, the pageantry was all arranged. It was standard. A show for the people.

He was Lor'd One of Wisdom. What wisdom could he give Ast-i, that sweet child-woman, tomorrow? Too soon she was flung to the ravages of the powerful ones of the land.

He looked at the room to confirm his readiness. His sword, his spear, helmet, armor, and robes with mantles were ranged on the walls. The golden armor and headdress to be worn tomorrow was polished and resplendent in the light of the grease-tub tapers in the holders on the walls. All seemed to be ready. All...but he, Thoth.

He concentrated upon the meaning of the ritual coming tomorrow. It had deep physical meaning, deep moral meaning, and deep spiritual meaning. His thoughts seemed to take over and speak in clear voices inside his head.

"A woman is wiser even than nature in selecting her mate. Nature puts men and women together by birth without selection. Women select. They select wisely, too. In the areas of life where men with great mental ability and learning are required, women select the mental giants for their mates.

"Women would prefer one Eastsun with brilliance than a dozen Westsuns with dullness. They chose the brilliant father for their children. Women select better than nature to upgrade the race.

45

"In the spiritual area only, woman is not wise. She leads man toward spirituality. She desires spirituality for herself and for man. But she does not interconnect her spirituality with her sexuality. The spiritual she does not consider sexual; the sexual she does not consider spiritual. Yet it truly is. The priest who performs a beautiful ritual is as stimulating as a Warrior who wins in the Combats.

"This is obvious to men; but it is not obvious to women. In this case, women need help. How great is the one who can lead people to realize that the end result of spiritual life is the creation of physical life.

"If the ancient Wisdoms were true, all life began as the attraction between stray particles of matter. These particles can be moved by some of subtle energy. Thought is a subtle energy. Thought can move these particles solely because it, too, is energy.

"No woman can be made fecund physically unless she is in health and ready by age and mental leaning. No woman can be made fecund spiritually by Thought-Force unless she is spiritually in health and ready by training and mental leaning. Her Chosen Man must also be in spiritual health, ready, and most desirous in his mental leanings. They must be wedded in emotion, in body, in spirit.

"Both must be ready at the same instant. They must have an emotion great enough to support the transfer of fecundation through the subtle energy of thought."

Yes. Yes! He could say that. He could add a thought from his heart.

"We, Peoples of the Empire on the Perfect Planet, are privileged to live in this time when two come, strong in body, firm in mind, true and perfect in spirit. They may teach us again of our greatness, of our heritage of the spiritual universe of the Goddess Mut and her offspring, the God, the gods, goddesses, and the peoples of the land. Two come to lead us back to our own, our true spiritual beginnings."

If only the people of the Perfect Planet could be led back to their spiritual beginnings! Those divine beginnings before the great dispersion, before the shaking planet drove their Divine Race to this Pleasant Planet. To the time of Thoth-Khnum, First Male God, the All-Creator, and the time of the First Female God, God-ette or Mut, Goddess of All Life, Mother of All Things, Source of All Gods, Queen of Heaven.

They had sent down their powers through the chains of births. There had been developed the three classes of celestial beings in bodies that could never diminish or melt away. The All-wise Avatars that were the true Gods, reborn afresh to every age, to meet the needs and aid mankind. Surely these had filled the spaces of heaven, all the land. Surely they had pre-known all the joys and terrors of E-Den, the fertile Empire. Surely they filled all the times, past, present, and future.

Since they did, Thoth, Ra, Atl, Bes, As-Tar and God-ette, inheritors of that Godly race, were then, now, and forever! *(And so were their offspring, physical or spiritual!)* They moved and had their beings in a continuum of time. They were flesh to occupy the spaces of the planet. They were also spirit to occupy all the spaces of heaven. This he *knew* he was. For he had been taught the technique by which he could raise his spiritual self out of his physical body. He had been given the disciplines that produced everlasting life. He had raised himself in the spirit and found that he could function in all times and in all spaces.

The skills had been taught to him. Could he now teach those skills to A-Sar-U and the two of them teach those exacting disciplines to the seven million persons of the Pleasant Planet, and do it before another disaster drove his race from a planet?

If those skills needed to be taught! If the disaster he suspected was indeed...

No! He must not let his mind speculate on the horror. He must live in the present. Live for the *now*, and forget the specters of the possibilities of the world of the *What Ifs* of tomorrow.

In a way, tomorrow was on him now. If the two he had selected could develop swiftly enough to produce a registered Virgin Birth it would help, greatly help. The people of the planet, who mimicked anything the God-e did, would turn again to spiritual things and spiritual practices. They would be willing to work and try, to study and learn, to experiment and report. So much depended upon those two near-children, and upon the accuracy of his estimate of their abilities, wills, and determination.

Had he been wrong in hurrying them? His only excuse was that they were so desperately needed to change the drift of the Empire away from the teachings of A-Ra the God-e.

So much to do. So little time.

He was both helped and hampered by the laws of the Empire, the customs, the ways of doing that sometimes had no reason, were beyond rationality. He was Supreme Lor'd One of the Realm. He owned all things. He owned all men, all women, all children. He owned all lives. Yet in an equal way, they owned him. For his actions were studied and followed. His thoughts were echoed, sometimes when they made no sense to anyone but himself. Every expression was picked up, every thought. He must not dwell upon that unthinkable thing. The people would detect his tensions and become tense when they needed to be most relaxed. He had to go back to the techniques of relaxation he had been taught.

He had to be able to relax every muscle in his body. He had to be able to control his thoughts so that he could stay relaxed even when the swords were swinging at his head. Not just relaxed, but so relaxed that nothing could bother him. Not life, not pity, not love, not pain, not joy, not death. He had to once again gain complete control over his body and his mind so that his spiritual self could be freed from his flesh to move through space and time, and return safely.

Oh, much more. He had to be able to teach A-Sar-U those disciplines, those techniques, those skills in a time so incredibly short that it would seem only a hundred breaths.

So much to do. So little time.

Eternity stood at his elbow plucking at his sword arm. Time was not his friend. Time was the deadly enemy of him, his plans, and the planet of people he loved.

Thoth called his server. He was made ready for sleep. Perhaps the wisdom of dreams could help him understand whether or not what he suspected was true. The great Atl had said that it was well known that dreams spoke to the

ears of the *Now* words of the *Then*. He badly nee
wisdom from the future.

Tomorrow he must show the face of joy to all the thousands who would come to the Ordeal. He must not allow
his mind to dwell upon a single worry or the people of the
Empire would detect it. This he knew. So many times he
had been with them. They knew him well. His worry became their worry. They must be relaxed. They must be
trained. They must have no worry.

Like the good Father he must give them the divine
tchefaut food as if they ate ordinary corn.

He must render to them *maat*, perfect justice. If he
did, their lives would be saved, somehow, he knew not
how.

But if he was not a kindly father, leading his family to
safety, they must surely die.

He put all thought from his mind. All thought. Even
the thought that there was so much to do in so little time.
Then he went seeking wisdom from his dreams.

He wanted three understandings:

The first was an understanding of women that he
might aid them, for they were the true hope of the future.

The second was an understanding of all the myths of
the race, especially the myth of the unknown fashioner
and builder who formed the first egg, hatched it, and
brought forth the suns of the Pleasant Planet.

The third was an understanding of why a planet paradise under the sway of the benign Eastsun should be
plagued by the vicious and possibly dangerous Westsun.

Was this a symbol of human life which seemed to have
its pleasures and its pains in a reoccurring cycle, a rhythm
that taught that there was purpose in each? Was there
some great energy exchange between the *now* and the
then, between the certain and the possible? Ah, he was
drifting into one of his mystic phases. Enjoyable as it
might be, he must set it aside. For tomorrow was the time
for absolute mental discipline and physical control.

As he drifted toward sleep he wondered why the ancient myths did not mention that there was a Westsun.
Did God-ette, ah, Mut, know?

Someday he must inquire. So much to do. So little
time.

5

Bes, Temple Guard

The noise was like a happy battlefield, Bes thought. Tens of thousands had assembled in the dawn-light for this Testing for the Ordeal of Virgin Birth. Runners had not been sent to every part of the Realm to deliver their messages, as was the custom. The past few times there had been intense resistance to their passage by Je-Su's Warriors. Je-Su was getting to be too confident of himself. But the time to handle that was in the future. If Thoth would only order the Combats opened again, Lor'd One of War was open still to challenge in the Combats by anyone who had not been defeated by Je-Su. Bes had never been. He knew he would never be. He could out-sword and out-last Je-Su. Not by much. It would be close. If it became important enough, he would challenge and defeat the in-turned Lor'd One of War.

Instead of the runners he had decided to use the Empire Drum. The Drum was on the fourth level, above the south courtyard of the Temple of Po-Si-Don, protected by the Temple Guard under his command. The Drum was the pride of the Empire. It was twenty-two arms long, and two tall men could not touch fingers around it. The slit in the center of the mahogany log was a full hand across. When struck with the drumsticks those lips spoke across a distance of thirty thousand arms.

People in far places could hear the message of the Po-Si-Don Drum. Each temple had a drum almost as large and mellow, and relayed the messages. Drum-talk went from temple to temple. The people then knew about it within fifty breaths for it was relayed through the loud voices of the Cryers of the Empire.

Almost all who learned of it would come to such an important religious activity. Sturdy and willing, they would travel at a near run through most of the cool of the dark time of the Eastsun. Excitement built at every step. As group joined group along the curving, stone-paved footways of the many districts, babble and rumor increased. Whole families had come. Whole tribes had come. As he looked out from the height of the Temple's fourth level, he thought perhaps the whole Empire had come to Po-Si-Don Temple.

Bes stood on the top of the fourth pyramid level of the Temple of Po-Si-Don. From there he could see all the members of his Temple Guard and they could see him. The archers placed around the edge of the third level of the Temple could place shafts in any body on the vast grounds below. Along the outside of the Temple grounds, and on the levee of the inner canal, archers were stationed. In the crowds his specialists in short-swords mingled, betraying their presence only by sometimes glancing up to him to see if he had directions or signals for them.

Sometimes there were scuffles among the citizens. Tempers. Tribal prides. Fatigue came from the long time of travel. When combined with pride of tribe or self it made tempers flare. Egos, or the desire to show-off, to prove courage, brought such temper-flares to blows sometimes. Few were hurt. A few teeth were lost, noses broken or bloodied. Rarely anything important. Friendly fights were laughed about. The first hand that touched a sword was disgraced among his own people.

Within the Temple Compound all beings had Sanctuary of the God-e. To injure badly was the privilege of the God-e or his second. Whoever transgressed the law of Sanctuary was disgraced and then beheaded. Before the sword fell, however, the family, kin, tribe, and even district of the culprit was shamed by the Cryer, in a loud voice from the Window of Ra. Thus family and society together were responsible for curbing the natural rebellion of the individual. His transgress was their disgrace. Therefore, the unit disciplined the individual or the Empire disciplined the unit.

His was a small force. Each man was carefully selected. Each man had a family in the Temple Compound. Each man would fight to the death any outbreak of violence in the crowd. They would be protecting their own kin by being obedient to his orders. Only thus could he trust his men against the blandishments of Je-Su and his cult of fanatic admirers. No. Worshippers. Je-Su had begun to demand that he be worshipped. Publicly demanding repetition of that ridiculous religious formula...

Yes, someday, perhaps soon, he would have to challenge Je-Su to the Combat.

A few bad ones keep the system from being perfect. But what in human beings was ever quite perfect? Thoth? Thoth was almost a perfect statesman, Warrior and swordsman. Scars on Thoth's face proved that even he was not perfect. A-Sar-U promised to be even better.

Bes interrupted his thinking to rub the scars on his own face. Yes, the swords would get through!

Perhaps the only perfection, even in the justice of the Empire, was the inflexible Law of *Ma-at, Eternal Truth Unchangeable.*

Bes shifted himself around on his short legs so he could look down the east side of the Temple Complex. The red tabards of the Temple Guards made dots the length of the levee and through the grounds. Exactly spaced, reserved and motionless, they were almost unnoticed by the people near them, some of whom were still sleeping where they had fallen to rest. His guards were treated like friendly walking statues, with great respect, for they alone might touch hand to sword in the Temple Complex, and then only on signal from Bes.

There were the Ama-Sones! They, too, were carefully selected for combat skills, but, oh, what bodies to waste on minds like theirs!

They were part of the Temple Guard—and as deadly as they were dedicated. They moved like tall goddesses. Their knee-length leather skirts, their skin-covered breastplate that sheltered only the left breast, their full-helmeted armor, sword, knife, bow and arrows, and spear made them stand out to the eyes of the people. He could see that a triple guard was stationed around the golden Temple of the Virgins. Ama-Sones from other temples moved with stately grace in full armor among the people. They were admired, respected, even revered.

Yes, Bes thought, but not loved. No, not loved. They were proud, efficient, haughty, and disdainful sexists. They decried men. Yet, in what they said was a bitter and much damned defeat of nature, they had to choose men by whom to have children. This, by command of their community, they did at each thirty-sixth Westsun until they mothered a girl child. They went into the temples, laid down their weapons, and took men.

From the children produced they kept only the girls. Boys they put in oil-soaked baskets of balsam and rattan and tossed into the sea. Those who were found and rescued lived. Those who were not drifted out to sea to the fate the Ama-Sones thought they deserved.

Strange women! Proud of their Warrior skills. Unwilling to fight with or for men in a general war. Yet they served as part of the Temple Guard faithfully, well, and courteously.

A-Thena, Chief of All Ama-Sones, respected him, Bes, as her superior. He smiled wryly. Perhaps that was because he was only two-thirds of a man! He felt the grin on his face. How many shields he had got because Warriors could look down upon him. He had learned the hard way that a sword even in the hands of a practiced child, who could last the three days of the Combat, could be deadly.

His attention was jerked from his reverie. Thoth, that God-e-in-the-making, appeared at the giant gate in the front wall of the Temple Compound. The crowd shouted wildly and surged toward the pathway he would follow in approaching the ramp to the Temple.

"Thoth. Thoth. Thoth."

Bes signalled the Cryer who began his commanding chant:

"Bow down, bow down, bow down. He comes now. He comes now. Thoth! The miracle of eternity in which man and God-e meet. The son of God-e. He who speaks the words of *Ma-at, Eternal Truth*. His words are truth. His will is resistless.

"Thoth gives hope to the hopeless, faith to those without faith. To the hungry he gives food. He demands little of those who love him. Only that they:

"Do justice to all peoples they can.

"Provide for the homeless.

"Fight for the downtrodden.

"Keep the widow and the orphan.

"Honor their family.

53

"Keep Eternal Truth in their hearts.

"Treat all mankind as equal to the God-e.

"Not allow skin, tribe, nor history to make one lower than another.

"Love peace and eschew war to have the blessings of the God-e.

"Reap no field you have not sown or otherwise transgress against the general good.

"If you do, Thoth directs that all such shall be punished. Those who err because of anger shall be informed and led aright.

"The good of all shall come before the privilege of one.

"Every person shall be willing to die in honor for the rights of his tribe. He who will not, disgraces himself and his tribe.

"Bow down. Bow down. Bow down."

Bes checked himself with a half-laugh. Was it the many times he had heard that spiel or his admiration for Thoth, his comrade in arms? He almost bowed down! It was not his duty to bow down, it was his duty to protect. Once he had faced Thoth across the sword. They were a match. It would have been luck that won the Combat had they ever joined. Then, Ra came to them with his heavy burden, his great need. His urgent need for the good of the Empire. Bes had taken the lower way, but to him the more important one for the future of the people of the planet.

The crowd below was chanting again. It was more a howl. Thousands of voices, each trying to out-shout the other. Fervor. Energy. Love.

Thoth deserved it. Yes, he deserved it well. He had earned his place through brilliance and ability.

Thoth was coming into the Temple Compound from far outside the levee. He would wind among those persons far out, then cross the levee, and come down the pathway leading to the front ramp of the first pyramid level of the Temple.

Bes was uneasy at this time—always. But Thoth would have it no other way. Thoth was well outside the Sanctuary of the Temple. He was relatively unguarded. He might fall prey to an attack. Yet he would not have guards move with him. He would wear those two short-swords in the sockets on each side of his helmet. They were loose. Only the tips were within the carriers. Thoth had announced to the people why two swords were there.

"I shall try to make you all love me. Sometimes I cannot. If any of you has the idea he cannot stand me any further, let him take one of the short-swords and try to take my life. He will have the advantage of surprise. I will have the advantage of skill. I want you to know that though I own you, you own me. I am you even as you are the Realm."

Damned foolish ploy. It worked! No surprise, everything worked with Thoth.

Thoth moved slowly among the throngs. He stopped to chat, to ask about crops, about fruits, illness. His gold breastplate and helmet, and especially the sundials between the two short-swords on his helmet, caught the light of the early Eastsun with the glow of a thousand hearth-fires. His shepherd's crook and flail in his left hand contrasted oddly with the spear and shield in his right.

Thoth came across the inner canal at the Lion-bridge. He paused before stepping from the bridge onto the Sanctuary land of the Temple.

"People, guardians of the Empire, by your pleasure I rule. By your pleasure I am empowered to send officers among you to keep justice. They are, and I know I am, your servants. Servants who have time to help you learn how to plow, sow, grow, reap, and store more food with less efforts. Do they serve you well?"

The Cryers relayed the words almost as they were spoken, so that everyone in the vast throng knew exactly what was said. The answering shout was loud, swift, and long. The people loved the exchange. So did Thoth. Bes decided that Thoth was, after all, a born bard with a flair for the fanciful and exciting.

"Do you have enough food, water? Is there sickness among you?"

Again the answers were positive, vigorous, and long. Bes thought he saw Thoth looking directly at him on the fourth pyramid level. Was that a wave to him? Was that wide smile meant for him?

"Laws we make to keep justice among you. Ministers we send to administer those laws fairly. Thus you may live in peace with your neighbor and rest secure from your enemy. Do those laws and those ministers distress rather than serve you?"

Almost before the Cryers had relayed the message a giant old Warrior who Bes recognized from the recent Shumen fighting shouted: "The laws distress us when we lose!"

His bellow was so loud it must have been heard by half the thousands before the Cryers started, for the laughter was long and honest.

Thoth laughed with the crowd. "Taxes. The produce of your lands we take from you that we may live and have leisure to guard you and improve your lot. Are the taxes fair?"

"No!" The voice was penetrating and mournful. "But it's not fair that my Chosen Woman nags me, either." The laughter was long and loud, and the women put on a mock-show of disgust. Before the Cryers could begin over the hubbub, the voice came again. "But, Lor'd Thoth, I get more from your taxes than I do from her nagging."

The men teased their Chosen Women, who responded with resounding whacks on the shoulders of their men, and much finger-shaking.

"If you feel the laws are fair and fairly administered, still there may be those among you with private matters. I would like to walk slowly along the pathway leading to the Great Temple of Po-Si-Don. All who have complaints against the ministers of justice or the laws, or against me or any other man, come and speak it with loving lips close to attentive ear. Law is only as good as the fairness with which it is administered."

The shouts of approval made a noise that echoed along the nine pyramid levels of the Great Temple.

When it had died down again, Thoth asked: "Have I your permission to enter Sanctuary to perform a ritual in the Temple?"

The answer was deafening and long. It was positive and many people added loving words meant for Thoth's ears but which were lost amid the noises. Thoth reached up and removed the two short-swords from his helmet and handed them to a guard. He then gave over his shield and his spear. Only then did he move forward into Sanctuary. Bes breathed a sigh of relief and sent the pre-arranged hand signal to all the Temple Guard. They were obviously relieved and pleased.

The laughter and good-natured ribbing went on as Thoth moved through the crowd. He touched hands with all. He embraced old fighting comrades. When asked, he spoke the magic Words of Power over the newborn children to bestow upon them their full rights as citizens of the Pleasant Planet, and to welcome them into the religion of Mut-God-ette and Thoth-Khnum, the Mother/Father God.

6

The Ordeal

Thoth made his way amid the adoring people until he reached the ramp leading to the second level and the Window of Ra. The guards stopped all others and he mounted the long plane alone. Once he was up to the front edge of the Window he turned serious, although the crowd was not yet ready to give up its holiday spirit. He advanced as far as he could and took off his helmet.

"Is this not true: we believe that once the gods were born of women?"

The question took the crowd by surprise. They slowly quieted down as the Cryers repeated his question to all the masses. As was the custom, the Drum sent it to all the other temples.

"No longer do we believe it. Why? If it was true in the days of our great ancestors, why is it not true today?

"We believe it has always been true that men were born of flesh. Flesh bears flesh to borning. Why is it not true still that man is born of spirit? That spirit is born of flesh? That spirit bears spirit to borning in flesh?

"Is there any reason why this Empire should not undertake to re-establish this belief firmly in the minds of all citizens?

"All who hear me, all who hear me and believe the true words, all those who hear me now may speak to others not here concerning what I have said. Let all the Realm know that if two can do it, all of you can do it. What they can do, you can do. Divinity may return to flesh at long last.

"What does divine borning require of you? It requires that you willingly discipline yourself; that you protect the fleshly temple of the Eternal Supreme which is your human body; that you spiritualize your mind; and at last, that you have the will and courage to raise your Radiant

Spiritual Self from your human physical body and then send it forth to do the work of both nature and divinity.

"We speak of birth in a Virgin untouched by man. Of Virgin Birth! We have worked on reviving an ancient technique. If Virgin Birth is possible and the techniques we have revived are helpful, will each of you pledge yourself to learn these disciplines in the very near future? Will you pledge to teach others concerning your Radiant Divine Spiritual Self? Will you strive for life everlasting in the spirit?"

"Divine Thoth, Lor'd One of Wisdom: Do you mean that we may learn to live forever in the spirit?"

"Yes. I do."

The crowd swayed and murmured, then settled down again. And the voice spoke as if for all. "Divine Lor'd One. We've fought for you. We'll die for you. Why not live forever for you?"

The cheering was tumultuous, but short lived. They seemed to want to know more, and to know it swiftly.

Thoth smiled. "Hey! Not for me, Sab-e of the Temple of Ptah, with me. With me!"

The tension was broken with laughter.

"We're with you, Divine Thoth. We are with you!"

"Good. We'll storm the heavens of the gods as we stormed the haven of the Shumen in their desert."

"We'll win, too," came simultaneously from thousands. Many slapped their chests to indicate the sealing of a contract that could not be broken.

Thoth slapped his chest and the crowd applauded.

Thoth waited for the crowd to settle into seriousness again before he nodded to the trumpeters. Three silver trumpets blasted three notes three times, and finished with a gliding up-note that demanded close attention.

Bes, from high above, signalled the Drum to begin its resonant beat. Its throat seemed to cry dread. The beat was slow, very, very slow.

A procession left the compound of the Temple of the Virgins led by three Ama-Sones. At the same instant, a procession left the compound of the Warriors led by three Warriors. These processions turned outward from the Temple of Po-Si-Don to form a long line of marchers to the east of the Temple and also to the west. This moved them solemnly and slowly among the people.

The Ama-Sones came first in their line. They were such large, beautiful women. They came in full battle dress. Their animal-skin skirts and left-breast guard, shield, helmet, sword, knife, and spear were in evidence as usual. For the festivities of this occasion they had added leg, shin, and heel guards and breastplates of silver, and attached two red plumes to each helmet. Each plume was not less than an arm in height and moved gracefully as the Ama-Sones advanced. They had formed a rectangle of Ama-Sones, two abreast on each side, and four abreast at front and rear. Within this formidable rectangle they had formed a triangle, moving with its tip forward as an arrow in flight.

A-Thena, famed for beauty, speed, and courage in the hunt and kill, was the tip of the triangle. Three Ama-Sones formed each side and the back. At the right side of the arrow-point Re-Gina moved with regal stride that showed her right to the title "Queen of Strength." At the left side of the arrow was one who moved with the lithe grace of the jaguar after whom she was named, Balina, "Little Jaguar." She was not little. Her beauty was incredible.

Inside the arrowhead, just behind A-Thena was Ast-i. Her beauty was so great that all eyes sought her and sighs of delight came up to Bes's ears. She seemed to glide. Her reddish-golden hair floated at each step and glowed with the colors of honey, gold, and hints of fire-opal. He was so proud of her. So proud.

Behind her walked God-ette to the right, and Er-Ru representing As-Tar, Mother of Ast-i, Chosen Woman to Bes. Behind them came four Virgins, carrying between them a headsman's bench. As if to emphasize the somber threat of the occasion, behind them came two Virgins carrying the heavy, curved headsman's blade and the blood-cup.

Close behind the point of the arrow, almost like the shaft, six Ama-Sones carried between them with careless indifference the bodies of Ast-i's attackers, the false Temple Priestesses. A spear shaft had been run through each throat. With the spears resting on the shoulders of the tall

Ama-Sones, the legs and hands of the corpses waved in frozen dismay.

Behind them came the Virgins, four columns abreast. They were in their celebration uniform. The wide belts of silver spangled cloth snugged them from hips to rib line, with a slight rise in front to a peak between their breasts. It emphasized their narrow waistlines and delightful hips. The loose, pleated skirts were of a diagonal weave and so thin they floated around the legs at each step. Silver sandals with toes arched up and backward made the off-white skirts seem to sparkle. Each Virgin wore a thin mantle. It was arranged as if it had been thrown carelessly over the shoulders. But the arrangement was so artful that it floated in the air as they moved, fluttering over the firm young breasts.

The hair of each Virgin was pulled back from a center part. Each side was caught in a silver clip over the ear. The luxurious hair then cascaded down the back and over the breasts of the beautiful girls. Their hair was a mix of glowing colors, from silvery white through blonds, browns, and blacks to the glory of the red-haired ones.

The soft, glowing folds of the Virgin's robes seemed strangely in contrast to the martial splendor of the Ama-Sones. Each seemed to emphasize the other, as if in the bodies of living women a great Eternal Truth was being stated—woman is capable of all things from tender love to harsh war.

To the west of the Temple the spectacle was no less moving. The Warriors came in full armor. They had formed a rectangle also. For this occasion the Warriors had thrown over their armor long banners of cloth that almost reached the ground both front and back. The cloth had been dyed in achiote until it was a deep scarlet. Bes knew this must be for special honor and promise to A-Sar-U. Such variations from uniform were only on occasions that signalled great combat to come or a singular victory.

Within the leading rectangle was the arrow head. Inside it marched A-Sar-U, in full dress uniform, covered by a flowing silver-colored robe with two embroidered suns on both front and back. The upper sun, representing the Eastsun, was large, of pure gold thread, with coruscating

61

rays intershot with white. The lower sun was reddish and its rays were crimson with thin traces of black.

The two processions moved in perfect cadence. The booming voice of the Drum was like a whip upon the back of emotions. It forced them to follow its resonant voice in its slow but ever increasing rhythm. Six men, three on each side, held two drumsticks in each hand. They moved in rhythm along the lip of the Drum's mouth. Thus they made it speak in rhythmic tones constantly shaded. There was no monotony. There was a cadence that beat itself into the very marrow of the bone, hid itself in all the crevices of the head. It made the heart beat to its rhythm. It commanded the movement of the processionals. It enchanted the crowd.

Bes, looking down from his fourth-level advantage, saw how colorful and effective it was. A momentary burning of tears let him know that even a grizzled old Warrior could be touched by such a parade. True, his beloved daughter-of-the-spirit was approaching possible death. True, his beloved foster-son was also in hazard. But... But... He had taken many bodies on the point of his sword. It had not bothered his emotions.

Yet, looking down upon the glory of this spectacle, the precision and order that bespoke a great civilization, enjoying it in the warm glow of a benign sun upon a verdant and fertile planet—he was struck with how soon it all might be destroyed utterly, without hope of survivors.

He glanced askance to see if anyone saw his descent, even for a nostalgic moment, into emotion. Then his eyes, blinked clear of tears, again took in the two spectacles.

7

Brahm's Conspiracy

The sound of the Drum startled Brahm. Not because it was loud. It was on the fourth level of the Temple of Po-Si-Don, on the far side from his rooms. Though it could be heard for thousands of arms, it did not seem loud to him. No. He was startled because he was not yet in full armor. He hurried to get into his breastplate harness, throw on the tabard with his own crest and motto tatted and then sewn upon it in thread dyed purple by the small sea mollusk.

It was his own tabard. For too, too long he had worn the tabard of Je-Su. Now he was free of that. Any man who wore the tabard of another man was a fool, a coward. Death was not as cruel as is the weight of another's blessing and protection upon the shoulders of the True God-e.

Man controlled his own destiny, worked out his own fate. By force of mind...trained mind, disciplined in the faith of Brahm...any man could work out his own destiny. Any *man*!

Brahm struggled with the lanyards of his breastplate and snugged it into place with an impatient jerk. He knew it was too tight. Small and flat as his belly was from the exercises of the eighty-three positions of the asanas he put his body through each morning and evening, it cut at his hips. Fat hips! Terrible. Impatiently he untied the knots and set the harness to a better fitting.

His small, dark face was bland, his black eyes intense. Only his hands and the cords in his neck showed his anger, frustration, and anxiety.

The procession was moving. He would have to join his guard, and then merge with Lak-Shi-Mi who would be marching with her women. All would be waiting at their assigned stations. His chosen would be angry with him, as usual. If not about being late, then something—anything.

She seemed to think she knew everything better than he ever could. She was as stupid as she was beautiful!

She did not realize that he had the way to Divinity. He was Brahm, Lor'd One of Knowledge. His secret followers knew that the whole world belonged to those who accepted Brahm as the intermediary between men and God-e. To them, Brahm was God-e. They did not need to strain to reach a higher plane, for he had the ability to fill them with his blessings.

Soon he would be strong enough to take his rightful place and order his own creed to be the one memorized by the people and repeated before each meal. Ma-Nu would prepare the laws the way Brahm told him to prepare them! Brahm would then see that they were carried out to the letter. His creed would be short, simple, and commanding:

"God-e is the spiritual, unapproachable, unseeable deity. Brahm is a seeable deity. Brahm's priests sustain the world. It is by their favor that God-e reigns in eternity. What priests, who are followers of Brahm, speak never fails to come true. Their wisdom orders all lives and all tribes into obedience to the inescapable Law. All Lor'd Ones and rulers, all teachers and trainers, all Temple Priests and chieftains are subject..."

The scabbard clanked loudly as he belted on his sword. With red-plumed helmet in hand he hurried toward the entrance. As he hurried through he almost collided with Je-Su.

Je-Su! How fawning he was as he pretended it just happened. That it was not planned that they walk the length of the Temple of Warriors together.

"Brahm, Lor'd One of Knowledge. How is it with my younger and much-loved companion and friend?"

"Je-Su, Lor'd One of War. Praise be to my older and much-admired friend. How are you?"

"Well. But not as well and content as when you were my right arm which I could trust."

"The sword has proved my right to wear my own livery and colors. I am distressed you are not totally well. You look as if your night had been sleepless."

"Oh? Yes. Yes. It is this Virgin Birth. It must not succeed. Do you think it might?"

"Might. But not if nature is obeyed. Nature has the way. Let's say it is Brahm's way."

"Oh, nature's way is Je-Su's way. Yes. Yes. Nature's way. Nature has been known to be fickle."

As if drawn into conspiracy, they walked closer together and lowered their voices to intense meaningfulness, biting meaning into each word spoken. "You think it might happen?"

"It has not for all the time our race has been on this planet. Some three thousand Westsuns so they say. But many things go on in the main temple that I do not understand or trust!"

"Ah, your people have picked it up, too?"

"Yes. Why is Bes, Lor'd One of Nothing, made great with command of the Temple Guard, and yet plays constantly with the children?"

"He is a great Warrior. Fools say perhaps greater than my own great friend and former mentor."

"Then why is he not Lor'd One of War? Why is he in charge of carefully selected, picked troops who have more authority within the Temple Compound than even my own war-scarred Warriors?"

"Because it was the will of Ra before he went away. The law was proclaimed abroad."

"Oh, yes. Yes, indeed. Ma-Nu clearly proclaimed the law and it is inescapable. But where did Ra go? And where is As-Tar, wife of Bes, mother of Ast-i? What could possibly keep a mother from seeing the Ordeal of her first-born? What kind of mother is she?"

"Not a good mother—if she could help herself!"

"Ah? You think she is a prisoner in the Great Temple?"

"I do not know she is even in the Great Temple."

"But you suspect?"

"Beloved friend, I suspect even you as you suspect even me. Like you I suspect that much will be done to make this Ordeal fail."

"Have you plans to make it fail?"

"Why, dear friend, such a question. Of course not. But you have. What are your plans to make it fail?"

"How can we harass them so much they will be too disturbed to succeed?"

"Why, Lor'd Friend, wouldn't that be against the law of Ma-Nu?"

"Why, my, my! Yes, it would be, wouldn't it?"

They laughed with mutual understanding of the irony and moved on to the beat of the Drum in a closer, almost companionable attitude.

"If nature can be set aside and borning come of spirit only, we may never be able to command minds and loyalties of the Lor'd Ones. Som and Ram would never join us. Ma-Nu might not. We would be alone. The true will of the people of the Empire might be turned awry. The True God-e might never take his rightful place."

Brahm's lips barely moved as he spoke. He slipped his helmet into place. He missed the look of delight that came into Je-Su's face.

"Thank you, beloved friend, for so clearly stating that fact. Be certain I will someday be Lor'd One of Wisdom. I will rule the Empire. Then the True God-e shall be made known. You will then be the Lor'd One of Religion, no longer forced to risk the annual Combat if challenged. You will be the great Priest of all the Empire of the Pleasant Planet."

"I'll become one half of Thoth, you the other half?"

"Ah? So to speak. But that is possible only if we can prevent this thing...this pretense...this turning nature upside down. It is well known that nature will not bend her laws any more than Ma-Nu will bend his. To create a child by Thought-Force alone in the womb of an untouched woman is impossible!"

"You said that before. But you remember that the myths say it was common on That Other Planet three thousand Westsuns ago. And you have great doubts?"

"Oh, not about nature."

"Then why disturb the young ones? Why risk the law?"

"Because nature might be fickle. Nature might also be lied about. Understand? Those mysterious movements in the Great Temple might be used to delude and hoodwink the people. To make them believe that divinity may come through a common Virgin's untouched womb.

"Divinity can come only from the womb of such as your or my mother. Out of the loins of such men as our fathers. The Only Begotten First-Born Son of such a holy couple must be the Divine God-e returned to the planet to serve mankind. The Only Begotten First-Born Son of God-e must rise to his rightful place. Must be freed of all restrictions. Must have the power as well the right to rule all the Empire. No man shall have the power to gainsay him, for he speaks truth and must be instantly obeyed on pain of death. He will bring back again the ancient days when all men worshipped the Living God-e and dwelled in paradise, in the real E-Den, the garden of perfect peace. That perfect time of peace and beauty, when all men had plenty, no man knew want, worry, doubt, or strain; when all men worshipped humbly the One Divine. That holy time must come again.

"It must come again by strength or stealth, by blows or deceit, by truth, half-truths, or lies. I will make it come again to our beloved Empire. My Empire of peace and prosperity, of graciousness and joy, of purity and love for the True God-e in flesh shall last ten thousand Westsuns."

Brahm noted that Je-Su's rhythm of speech and intensity had increased as the tempo of the Drum increased. He was into a frenzy, speaking softly, but as if he was envisioning before his inner eye a planet full of adoring worshippers. The force and energy of his speech carried into his face. His eyes were intense balls that seemed to have flames dancing in them. Secretly Brahm wondered if these were flames of desire or flames of insanity. So strange, his older, more powerful, more aggressive companion. So strange! But not so smart. Not so wise. Brahm could and would outsmart...what was Je-Su saying? His own creed? The Creed of Je-Su?

Je-Su paid no attention to Lak-Shi-Mi who waited with her women near the corner of the Temple of the Warriors.

Lak-Shi-Mi! Brahm remembered how once those deep violet eyes had raced his heart. Her long lashes fluttered to a cheek smooth and brown to captivate his being. Her tiny figure made even his small stature seem adequate—in the beginning. Her face was mobile and controlled. Only when he was defeated at the annual Combats and seemed not to be able to rise higher, her eyes had turned hard-purple. Her lashes ceased to flutter. Her once ready smile turned to a near sneer. She began to try to force her own ideas upon him. At times he thought she should enter the Combats, win, and force her plans upon the Realm. Oh, she was a beautiful picture of deceit; a heart full of anger, a head full of chicanery, a body full of flaming passion, and a face full of beauty. She seemed to forget her criticism of him only when...

Brahm forced his mind back to the moment. Memory was the terrible trap of weak wills and wandering minds! Discipline must overcome all.

Her hard-violet eyes were blazingly and critically on Brahm. When they swung to Je-Su they softened to adoration. From hate to love in one look! Brahm made note of that fact.

Je-Su hurried on in his rhythmic deep-study. "We shall establish the new, universal creed so that all the Empire may learn it and know exactly what one must believe to be given his rightful place in this paradise we will build. The creed will be simple, true, universal. The very act of saying it will shower blessings of the God-e upon the individual:

"I believe in One Supreme Spiritual God-e, maker, owner, and master of all things.

"I believe in and adore his First-Born, Only Begotten Son, who is God-e in spirit, mind, and flesh, the very likeness and essence, identical in will, power, and love!

"I believe in and I submit humbly to the Son all my hope, mind, will, fortune, and bodily strength. I will receive his grace and my spirit's salvation.

"I believe in the Divinity of the priests he appoints over me, for his words have made them divine also. They are the earthly heirs of the power of God-e through his First-Born, Only Begotten Son.

"I believe the priests are rulers of the spiritual and temporal domain. I will accept their wishes as the command of God-e, and fulfill them with my life for therein lies my only hope of salvation and everlasting life.

"I believe that all who are disobedient to the First-Born, Only Begotten Son or his priests are guilty of the unredeemable sin of apostasy and are spawns of outer darkness.

"I believe these heinous sinners are to be shunned utterly, despised utterly, and destroyed utterly."

Brahm was listening to the cadenced words as spoken by Je-Su, but hearing the voice of Lak-Shi-Mi repeating them softly, almost under her breath. Not quite! So intense was her ardor she said the words of the creed loud enough for him to hear. It was clear she had repeated them many times. It was clear that those once-dear and fond eyes of his Chosen Woman were now fixed on his indifferent older friend with blazing passion.

Her eyes shifted to Brahm's own eyes. Her face hardened. Her eyes seemed to turn into flints. They turned to blazing hatred as she repeated, "I believe these heinous sinners are to be shunned utterly, despised utterly, and destroyed utterly."

Yes! It was hatred! Foolish woman. She did not realize that her station was being lowered by Je-Su who was usurping Brahm's rightful place; breaking the law by repeating any creed but the one required by the Lor'd One of Wisdom; and planning to lead the minds of all the Empire into a blind flurry of hatred and suspicion or outright entrapment into helplessness.

Incredibly gullible and stupid woman. Like so many others, adoring the man who led toward her own downfall!

Brahm was glad it was not clear to him where her criticism came from. He had thought it was his smaller stature, his less overwhelming strength. That would have been bad enough. But to have been seduced by the megalomania of his half-mad former friend, to be blind to Brahm's own true worth and obvious divinity. Intolerably vile woman. She must die! He had to be able to replace her with a Chosen Woman who helped him. One who did not hinder and belittle him with endless criticisms over the smallest things. He could do nothing to suit her. Even his most divine acts she criticized and made small. Yes, yes, she must die. He must be free of her.

He must be free of Je-Su, too. Not yet. When the time was right and his death would lead Brahm to his rightful place. Or...if Je-Su was caught trying to harass the children in the Ordeal of Virgin Birth. Caught trying to turn aside something that would be good for the Realm. Then his execution would be certain. How could that be worked out? With Lak-Shi-Mi included!

The three, followed by their retinues, joined the curving marchers as they turned back toward the Great Temple ramp on the west side. Each took the place reserved and moved on at the head of his own guard.

Marching to the slowly increasing cadence of the Drum, they moved upward and northward toward the extension of the north face of the first level of the pyramid, thirty arms in height. They were to stand near the Window of Ra for the ceremony. In Brahm's mind the accelerating beat of the Drum repeatedly whipped one word of anticipation through his being:

"How? How? How?"

The clamor of his mind almost drowned out the now racing beat of the Drum.

8

The Headsman's Couch

Slowly, yet with increasing cadence, the two marching columns came to the front of the Temple of Po-Si-Don. They mounted the inclines on each side of the Temple, climbed to the second pyramid level, then on up to the overhang on which was built the vast area known as the Window of Ra.

Ast-i moved on legs that seemed caked in hardened mud. She knew her legs moved. She saw them move. But her heart was a ball so tight in her chest it squeezed almost all sensation from her body.

She knew a smile was on her face. It was so broad and immobile it might have been plastered on by earth and pine-tar. Her mind seemed squeezed to a thorn's point in her head. She was cold. Cold inside her body and cold outside.

Yet droplets of sweat formed between her breasts. She felt them begin to run down in cold rivulets as if to make a lake of her navel.

The weight of her feet seemed more than she could lift. Her legs ached. Her hips hurt. Her back pained. Between her shoulder blade was a spear, thrust deep and twisting.

Light came in ever-narrowing beams into her eyes as if through waves of water. Nothing was clear and distinct. Everything in the procession moved at a speed so slow that she seemed to hardly move at all. Her breath came in. But it did not satisfy her craving for air because of the bands around her ribs. Bands as invisible as the spear in her back that seemed to tighten more with each step she took toward her unknown future.

Her mind was too tired to understand all the things that happened in her body. She was squeezed from head to foot as if by the arms of a thousand fierce Ama-Sones. Her body was too full to hold all its contents. She fought

71

her desire to evacuate, to urinate, to vomit. She was, she realized, in the grips of a horrible dread of the unknown, a fear that ran cold through her body. Her heart throbbed in her temples and in her ears more loudly and far more often than the Drum.

All this she knew in some distant way. It was as if she worked on two levels. In her body with all its stresses and strains. Also, somewhere up higher. She saw, heard, and felt things as if they were happening to some other person.

For one fleeting moment she saw her father high above on the fourth level of the pyramids. He beamed a smile down on her and she felt herself respond with a nod. She meant to wave, but her hand seemed too heavy to lift.

At the turn of the ramp, bodies parted so that she saw her beloved A-Sar-U. He was in full Warrior armor over which was thrown a shimmering band of silver. Beside him three Warriors carried his shield, spear, and sword. The sword was held high to signal to the multitude the events that might come. It was a signal she knew everyone in the Empire recognized. By custom and practice, it said that if anyone dared impugn her virtue or his, he challenged them to an immediate combat to the death. No quarter. Death only could prove innocence.

A-Sar-U could be fierce. Now his face was blissful. So serene, so self-assured! Oh, how she wished for some of that self-assurance!

How proud she was of him, how ashamed of her own feelings of fright, of panic. Such a man had become her Chosen! Surely he would not expect her to be a weakling and collapse with fright. Or disgrace herself in public view.

He glanced her way and smiled. Some of the dark dread let go its hold upon her mind. Some of the cold within her warmed.

Across the Window of Ra she saw Thoth, his giant form resplendent in golden armor, his big face smiling at her with the affection of a true father. The greatest man in all history looked with such pleasure upon her! She felt forced to respond. She squared her sagging shoulders and bobbed her head in recognition of his approval. He did not seem to doubt she would pass the Test. Why should she fear?

She shouldn't, but she did fear! All her life she had been active. She could climb, jump, romp, roll, fight, and tussle with anyone. Also, A-Sar-U had taught her to fight with sword, bow, spear, and shield. She had gone through the strenuous leaps and falls of Warrior training. Perhaps a blow during a fall had destroyed what the touch of man never had. If so, she could not prove her purity and her head would fall to the mob below!

She stood straighter, a little defiant of her fear.

"If my head falls, good life to the first who spits in my face. I will not die a coward's death," she thought almost aloud.

She squared her shoulders a little more, and forced her legs to be more attentive to their job. She raised her hand and waved at Bes. He waved back.

"Death is nothing," she thought. "Dying is only an inconvenience. I refuse to die by drowning in the sweat of my terror over and over. Why should I? The three greatest men of the Empire look upon me with approval and confidence. At least, I can refuse to borrow death from the future, to wallow in incapacitating thoughts of what might happen."

"Might happen is not will happen," she muttered aloud.

A-Thena looked quizzically at her. She returned the glance. Such a model of feminine beauty and masculine mental precision! A-Thena would be true and swift if the sword must fall. The blow would be merciful and accurate if it had to come. A-Thena was her friend...well, as much as the emotionless, Warrior-like Ama-Sone could be. Her sparse, spare, harsh way of treating her body had not dimmed the luster of her beauty or impaired her mind. A-Thena was brilliant, informed. She could speak eloquently when stirred beyond the monosyllables normally practiced by the warlike.

Ast-i saw Brahm across the platform of the Window of A-Ra. His face was an angry shadow. Lak-Shi-Mi's face was aglow as she looked up admiringly at Je-Su. Je-Su was also aglow and animated as he always became when he was talking of sinning or of his own importance as spokesman for the True God-e. He was talking. As usual he had worked himself up to remarkable heights. The

73

three fell into the line of march. Their retinues split, some going on up the ramp to the second pyramid level, some out upon the first level, and some further out to the Window of Ra.

Much of the whole procession moved out upon the Window of Ra. Though she had played there in times past with A-Sar-U, she revelled then in being in a forbidden place. She was now astonished at the many hundred persons it could hold.

The Drum was speaking more rapidly now. Faster and faster it moved her toward her testing. The last of the lines were moving into place. Time was running now, as if to catch up with how slowly it had moved before.

As Je-Su moved into place, she saw the look he flashed upward at the mighty Warrior, Bes, on the fourth level of the pyramid. Either she read the look, or Je-Su's thoughts, or remembered her own curious wondering:

"Why is no one allowed to go above the fourth level of the pyramid except Bes and his Temple Guard? What is the secret there? What are they hiding? Why?

"I'm reading Je-Su's thoughts. I never wondered if there was a hidden secret up there," she whispered fiercely to herself.

Her mind was pulled back from that intrusion into Je-Su's angry mind by the sudden change in movements around her. The moving column stopped. A-Thena moved to the front edge of the Window of Ra. The execution couch was placed at the very edge of the platform by two Virgins who smiled at Ast-i a fleeting apology. The two Virgins who struggled with the beheading sword lugged it to A-Thena. She hefted it easily in her fight-trained hand, and raised it to her shoulder. She placed herself facing the headman's couch. From there, Ast-i knew, A-Thena's discipline would not allow her to move until she struck the sword down at Thoth's silent signal, or at his command, handed the glistening, sharp weapon back to the Virgins.

How very much she admired the Ama-Sone. How very terrified Ast-i knew herself to be as all the sensations of fear returned to grip her. The sweat rolled in rivulets downward to overflow her navel.

74

9

On the Window of Ra

Thoth stood at the front edge of the center of the Window of Ra. The two columns stopped on the platform behind him. The rectangles and arrowheads continued to advance. When they were near the front edge of the Window they spread apart. Ast-i was placed at Thoth's right, A-Sar-U at his left. Six Ama-Sones moved to the front edge of the platform with three corpses dangling upon spears between them. A-Thena, Re-Gina, and Balina placed themselves, swords drawn, near Ast-i. The signal was clear to all below that even now she was under guard.

When they were in place, six long blasts on the three silver trumpets caused a murmur of expectation.

Thoth pointed at the three corpses. "Listen to the Cryers."

The loud voices proclaimed and the Drum relayed to the Empire: "Behold! These are the ones that violated the laws of the Realm. They touched a Virgin without her permission. That which the Ama-Sones have done to them is that which is commanded by law. Their private parts were cut away and crammed into their mouths. Their bowels were split. They were impaled upon spears. They will be thrown from here down so that their bones will be crushed. Then they will be later taken to the land to the south and left for the bone-eating jaws of the wild jackal. Behold! Obey the law."

The people standing below the dangling bodies forced the people behind them to step back so there would be room for the corpses to fall.

Thoth raised his arms for silence. His voice was loud enough, when reflected from the face of the pyramid-level, to reach even those outside the walls of the Temple Compound. "Hear me, again. Once we believed that gods were born among men. Such gods as Khnum, Atom, Atl, the divine Ra and..."

"... Lor'd Thoth!" a voice interrupted.

The crowd cheered in full assent.

"Thank you. Not I, beloved people of this pleasant Empire. I am but the forerunner, teacher, and servant of one who is to come. One who may bring you life more peaceful and lasting than even this Pleasant Planet may afford you. He is the one who is yet to come to bring you life.

"Today, here, now, we hark back to the old laws of God-e. There was an old theory. By certain techniques demanding a discipline so long and intense that it is unendurable to most persons, the spirit-form of man can fecund the pure Virgin. Never touched by hand of man she may then bring forth a spirit-child through Virgin Birth.

"Such an action renews our faith that we are the children of the Eternal Supreme. We are the blessed ones. We are the favored race. But no one has dared to publicly try for Virgin Birth for three thousand Westsuns.

"Why?

"The demands are great. The punishment for failure is death. Some exceptions...but death. If there is known to be a blemish upon the character of the male, his accusers are commanded to come forward. Their accusation he may disprove, if he can, either by witness or by immediate combat to death. It is a dangerous thing to claim purity that does not exist. It is also dangerous to claim it does not exist when it does.

"The Virgin may be tested in a simpler, more visual way. Three women citizens of the people are selected to examine her. They examine her here, before you, on this sacred porch on the Window of Ra. They then show their findings to you by the usual sign. Thumbs up for truth, thumbs down for falsehood. For she claims on her honor, punishable by death if she be false.

"Death will be quick. For she will be upon the headsman's couch, the axe will be poised in the hands of A-Thena. Her duty will be to sever that neck with one stroke and the head will fall straight down to you.

"But if she is found to be as she claims, then what?

"We will train the male in special ways to send forth his Radiant Body, his spiritual self from his body self. The

76

ways require disciplines that are unbelievably difficult and time-consuming. They cannot be given to anyone who is not of pure mind and pure body. They cannot be used successfully by anyone who is not of firm confidence, strong will, and relentless determination.

"The Virgin will be guarded night and day. No person, not even her guards, will be permitted to touch her person on pain of death. No man will be allowed into her presence, not even her father. She will remain pure for ten Westsuns. If she is then found to be with child, she will be admitted into the presence of her Chosen Man alone and no other man until after the child is born.

"By this means we will determine that the spirit of pure flesh may beget in pure flesh. That spiritual birth is possible to every person. That gods can be and are born of human desires and out of human flesh.

"That you may know for certain that there are no tricks, we will choose three women from among you to be the examiners. I will choose one. Bes will choose one. A-Thena will choose one.

"If these arrangements please you, let us know, and we will go on with the ceremony."

The crowd below began to moil and turn. Murmurs ran from one group to another. At last an ancient Warrior spoke for the crowd.

"Your selections, Lor'd One of Wisdom, are pleasing to us. But we ask you to explain more to us about the idea, the theory, the techniques of Virgin Birth."

"Very well. The ancients held a theory that by disciplined Thought-Force a pure man could create a child in the womb of a pure woman. It was a theory that he could raise a spiritual self from his flesh self and send it forth with fecund seed. Thus spirit was born in flesh. Thereby, gods were born of spirit in woman.

"The theory is important. By pure living and preparation mankind may attain to Virgin Birth by means of Thought-Force alone. In theory it is simple, but it must be done in pure and perfect Virgins. This purity we test for here and now. The penalty for failure is death. This discourages those who might come forward for the sake of the attention they would get from their peers, not caring if they failed the test. Law was made very strict around this sacred act. To express the desire to start the Ordeal of Virgin Birth sets instantly into action all the powers of the Empire. We rush toward the hope that we shall again have gods born among men as we are assured and, I believe, they were in ancient days.

"It is said that once all the priestesses were trained to bear children by this means. The offspring from those early births led That Other Planet to the highest civilization ever known for the good of human kind. They also led this Pleasant Planet from a wilderness of warring tribes to the present state of glorious beauty, gracious friendships, productiveness, and good living. This was done in only three full generations. The priestesses were then indeed goddesses who led mankind upward to unparalleled greatness.

"Then came those who wanted the honor without preparation. They caused much waste and dashed many great expectations. Strict controls were put into the laws of the God-e. The maiden who claims to be a Virgin but is not is a horror before the Supreme. One who enters the Ordeal lightly, with so little determination they soon want to forgo it, is a blot upon womanhood. It became the law of the God-e that in either case she forfeit her life to the singing sword in the hands of the Chief Ama-Sone. Thus the Empire protects its ancient rituals. Thus the honor of all women is preserved. Thus the divine ritual is kept pure.

"If the woman stays six Westsuns in the Isolation of the Ordeal, not touching anyone, and not being touched by anyone except the Mother of the Virgins of the World, and does not become pregnant with spiritual child she still may live. No one blames her if she has done all things correctly.

"But if she does not conceive in the spirit through Thought-Force, or if she deserts her place or leaves her pledge in less than six Westsuns, she is a criminal by the Laws of Ra. She then must be beheaded.

"Concerning the technique. It is private instruction between teacher and man, and between Divine Mother and the Virgin mother-to-be. Soft-spoken words from loving lips to attentive ear. If the man cannot perform his part, no one is blamed after six Westsuns. But if he deserts his post, he is a criminal.

"When he is successful in sending the Radiant Spiritual Self through Thought-Force, the Virgin begins to show the signs of pregnancy. Three Westsuns thereafter, all the land is informed and the three examiners are brought back to the Temple of Po-Si-Don to reexamine her. If again she pass the examiners, all the Realm rejoices. For a young god promises to come forth among us.

"These are the old laws. Have I explained them to your satisfaction?"

"Yes!"

"Let it be known. Here is A-Sar-U. He is the first-born son of Ra out of the body of God-ette. Both are known to you as the benefactors of our Realm. Both are of the Lor'd Ones, and each is of great Lore. A-Sar-U swears on his honor that he is pure. If anyone has knowledge otherwise, or wishes to accuse him, let that one now speak or forever be silent before the God-e and his fellowmen."

Thoth waited for several dozen breaths until he thought it was clear that no one wanted to bring an accusation. He had expected trouble. It came. Belatedly, as if one had needed time to steel himself to do that which he was under command to do. A young Warrior moved forward on the ramp of the Window. He was lank of body and face, with the yellowish skin of the Fen People. When he spoke, his voice had a haunting overtone of the whistle of the sand-bird of the marshes .

"Hav' I permiss'n t' speak, Lor'd One 'f Wisdom?"

The vowels were broadened, the consonants slurred, and the words so rushed and jumbled together it did not sound like the speech of an inhabitant of the Pleasant Planet.

"Come forward," Thoth invited. "Let all the people see you as you speak."

Thoth did not miss the look of pleasure that came over Je-Su's dark face as the young Warrior moved forward to the front edge of the Window of Ra.

The young Fenman was blue with the cold of dread, and sweating. He seemed driven by some power beyond mind. He was agitated and concerned. Yet he moved wooden-like. It affected his gait in that strange way which Thoth had seen only on a posanga zombie. The posanga zombies were almost mindless except for the will of their master. These addicts of the extract of the juice of the posanga fruit moved through the land as intruders into a well-ordered society. They were unable to function without their daily ration of the white powder that came from the juice cooked down. They sniffed the powder and moved to a realm of no-mind. They were fully dependent on the one who supplied the posanga fruit and became helpless in a wild sickness when they could not have it. This lad, not much older than A-Sar-U, seemed badly in need of his daily portion. For that daily portion, Thoth knew, the addict would do anything. Even, as this lad was about to do, risk death itself.

"You may speak only on the Ordeal. Before you do, know! If you accuse and cannot prove your accusation you may die. For you will be challenged to immediate combat to death. If you accuse and it is proved you lie by witnesses, you must die by the sword of the nearest Temple Guard. Do you understand?"

"Yes, Lor'd One." The bravado of the young voice cracked.

"You are trembling in a strange way. You are sweating in the way of the posanga taker. Are you here for the truth or for posanga?"

The youngster looked wildly about as if searching for someone to help him. When he spoke his voice rose, broke, and ended almost at a whisper. "I com' f'r th' Empire, f'r truth."

"Then speak."

"I 'm E-Don, Son of Da-Na the Fenman. I 'm in th' Young Warriors' School. My berth 's in th' alcove nex' t' that 'f A-Sar-U. Please check tha' fact." The speech had been hurried as if the youngster would forget his memorized lines.

"Thoth turned to A-Sar-U. Is the berth of E-Don, Son of Da-Na the Fenman, in the alcove next to yours, A-Sar-U?"

"It is, Lor'd One of Wisdom."

E-Don seemed to take courage. "In th' dark ten East-suns agone, when th' new watch was changin', A-Sar-U cam' inna my alcov', 'ntered my berth an'...did that t' me...which... He 's no Virgin an' can't prove he is! I confess this 'n all shame f'r th' great sin I committed by 'llowing his greater stren'th..."

80

The outburst seemed so sincere that the crowd reacted with sympathy. For many breaths no sound was made on the platform other than the lad's weeping.

Thoth turned to A-Sar-U. "You heard the accusation? What is your answer?"

A-Sar-U's voice was steady and undisturbed. "His statement is false in every detail. It is not true."

"Can you prove it is not true?"

"No. No more than he can prove it is."

The crowd stirred as if in their minds he was guilty as accused. Thoth realized how clever the plan was. If the lad, obviously weak and no true Warrior, was challenged and died on A-Sar-U's sword, the accusation would linger in the minds of the people. If a true Virgin Birth was then achieved, it would forever have a shadow upon its full acceptance. Somehow Thoth had to prove the lie and not permit the deadly combat.

"Was that the only time, the dark of ten Eastsuns ago?" Thoth watched Je-Su's face as he spoke and saw the instinctive, subtle shaking of the head that was meant to signal the lad to answer no.

"Yes, Lor'd One. The on'y tim'."

Je-Su's face turned to a mask of disgust and anger. He glanced at Thoth, saw his scrutiny, and forced his face into a pattern of relaxed interest.

Thoth felt a surge of hope, and a secret delight in twisting the thrust further home against Je-Su.

"No other time? No other time at all?"

"No. On' tim' on'y, Lor'd One."

"You are absolutely certain?"

"Yes. Yes. Yes. I'm not a want'n. I do n't do such things. Nev'r! 'Cept this one tim'. He...he forc'd me. I w's weak, once! I w's he'pless. I would n't confess this an' bring dishonor 'pon myself, my family, my tribe 'cept f'r th' great'r good 'f th' Empire. It 's f'r th' Empire that I 'spose this false 'an' lying..."

E-Don grasped for words. This part had not been rehearsed, Thoth thought. It was spontaneous.

The lad's words rang with such passionate patriotism and love for the Empire that it influenced the crowd. When he broke into tears again, real tears, the crowd leaned forward, scarcely breathing. Thoth sensed an agitation among

81

the crowd, but did not take his eyes from the lad. Surely there was a clue, a way...

The agitation became apparent among the tribe of Fenmen. They were arguing. At first they argued quietly. Then explosively. At last they came to some agreement. A big Warrior stood forth. He was big and gaunt as the swamp-dwellers usually were.

"Lor'd Thoth! I speak f'r my tribe. We'll no' accep' this dishonor t' our tribesmen. I'm Da-Na, father 'f E-Don. Beside me's my Chosen Woman. Her remembrance, an' th' remembrance 'f our tribe's this:

"From fifteen darks 'f th' Eastsun agone, t' six darks agone, th' division 'f Young Warriors t' which my son b'longs was on trainin' runs throughout Fenland. They ran all dark six darks agone, eight darks agone, ten darks agone, and twelve darks agone.

"E-Don, my son, was 'n his home resting between each 'f the runs. He could n't have been 'n th' Warriors' Compound and seduced by A-Sar-U. A-Sar-U's honor 'n' th' honor of the Fentribe's *maat*, it's true and pure."

The reaction from the crowd was instantaneous and would have continued, but Da-Na bellowed, "Quiet!"

"Lor'd One, ther' 's more. We beg th' 'ndulgence of the Empire 'pon my son. E-Don was able t' stay 'n his home f'r th' first time 'n twenny four Westsuns. He 's changed. He 's a posanga zombie. He's addicted. He does n't know truth fr'm lie. I beseech you, allow us t' tak' him t' his home 'n' try to save him from this spawn 'f th' Westsun. Please, let this be y'ur will.

"But 'f 't 's not y'ur will, our hearts shall ache wi' his fallin' head. The Fentribe asks me t' say, E-Don's lying. We swear he w's runnin' all dark through the dark of ten Eastsuns agone. We swear, too, to chall'nge to immediate combat t' death 'ny person, tribe 'r Empire that throws the gage 'nto our throats. The tribe 'f Fenmen has spoken."

The denunciation by his tribe caused the crowd to turn in fury upon E-Don. Quickly their anger was expressed even before the Cryers could repeat the challenge of Da-Na. Aghast at the angry waves of energy from the crowd, E-Don collapsed almost to his knees. With great effort he was able to straighten up again.

82

Thoth spoke quietly. He felt like gloating so much that he did not even look toward Je-Su lest he give in to that all too human emotion. "E-Don, Son of Da-Na the Fenman. You have heard your tribe witness against you. You may challenge them to combat or you may prove you are not lying.

"Do you wish to challenge a tribe to combat?"

"No, no, no!"

"Can you prove you were not lying, that they are wrong?"

"I nev'r meant 't t' come t' this..."

"Are you lying, E-Don?"

"Yes." The voice was so weak and strangled it hardly reached Thoth's ears. He thought it best that the crowd should know what was said.

"Louder, E-Don. Were you lying?"

"Yes. Yes. Yes!" The voice rose to a hysterical shout.

Then a subtle change came over E-Don. He stood straight, with all the dignity his addicted mind had left him, and said in a loud, clear voice:

"Yes, I lied. A-Sar-U was m' frien' 'til posanga powder stol' my will, made me captive t' its desires. That my tribe may know, I was tol' that all that 'd happ'n here t'day was that I 'd cast doubt on th' valid'ty 'f Virgin Birth 'n' that this was f'r th' good 'f th' Empire. I warn all who 're takin' posanga fruit, you 'll die from it. So die early. Do n't disgrace yo'se'f, yo'r people, yo'r tribe 'n' th' Empire.

"I as' f'rgiven'ss 'f my frien' A-Sar-U, my fam'ly, my tribe 'n' th' Empire. Posanga gripped me. I lied!"

E-Don's voice rose to a screech as he hurled himself from the edge of the Window. There was a gasp and then a hush as his body hurtled twenty arms downward.

The sound of his body breaking against the stones so far below held the crowd in check for a second. As the crowd began to surge forward, Thoth's voice cut commandingly into their ears.

"Stop. Stop. Stop. Hold, friends, hold! I know each of you wishes to be the first to spit in his face to express your contempt for a liar and one who defames the honor or his tribe and the Empire. But I beg you to reconsider.

"Was E-Don a weak liar? No. He could never be if he came from the loins of the Fenmen. They hold truth and honor and courage above all things dear. You all know how the Fenmen fought to keep safe the Empire. Will you spit upon one of such a tribe?

"At his last breath, E-Don became again the loyal, loving, and honorable Warrior he had once been. In his last act he became a true conqueror. He was captive and helpless in the horrible grip of the habit of posanga. But for honor to his tribe and the Empire, with his last ounce of courage and will, he broke from it. He conquered posanga, the deadly enemy of us all.

"Shall we be forgiving of his momentary weakness? Shall we? Shall we thank him for so warning our young who want to experiment with posanga fruit but have not believed in its horrible powers? Did he not serve the Empire and every family in it?

"Yes, he did. I ask you, for your love of courage and the Empire, bear up his body and tend it lovingly. Tend it with admiration and with honor for his family and his tribe. In my mind he proved with his last breath and his last act that he was the honorable son of an honorable family in a tribe of honorable people.

"What say you, my friends? Will you bear him up, weeping for his last moment of greatness?"

In a few breaths action proved their mood. The people made a platform of raised hands as if they bore him up on so many shields of honor. They then passed his crumpled body along in solemn silence until it was delivered to the Fenmen.

When his body was placed on the ground again, the tribe of Fenmen wept quietly with its happiness. E-Don was not a disgrace to his tribe, and their honor was saved. They wept partly for joy, partly for the departure of one of their friends.

Again Thoth's voice rang out. "Is there another accuser. Let him speak now or forever be silent before the God-e. If he has a secret, tell it now, or forever be silent for the honor of his fellowmen and the Empire."

After a long, expectant silence, Thoth turned to Ast-i.

"Let it be known. Here is Ast-i. She is the first-born daughter of the Great Warrior, Bes, Lor'd One of the Realm, out of the body of As-Tar, Mother of the Virgins, Priestess of Power, Force, Knowledge, and Wisdom. There above, at his usual duties, stands Bes. As-Tar is away on duties for the God-e and will be proud when she returns. If anyone has knowledge that is not favorable to our continuing with this Ordeal, let them now speak or forever be silent before the God-e and his fellowmen."

Thoth waited expectantly.

10

The Testing

As Thoth turned to her, Ast-i felt her body again turning cold. Her knees were suddenly so weak she had to force them to hold her body up. Her kneecaps were shaking so hard she was sure they made her look ridiculous. Thoth spoke directly to her.

"Ast-i, daughter of Bes out of the body of Mother As-Tar: The hopes of the Empire are placed on you. We trust in you. We give you our love and our appreciation for the great risk you take for our good. You shall not fail. But even if you should seem to fail in these severe tests, you will have done much for the future of mankind. You shall have moved us all some small step closer to our own ultimate salvation. You will also have caused many young people to concentrate upon the goodness of flesh and of the spirit that is the foundation of our orderly Empire.

"Your tests shall be these:

"First, three selected women shall visually examine you to make certain you are as you claim you are and we all believe you are.

"Second, you will be placed under strict guard and constant watch. Only one person may touch you. You may not give yourself any foodstuffs or water for ten Westsuns. It must be administered to you. This is to prove to you beyond doubt that you are the treasure of the Empire and entirely dependent upon it for all things.

"If, at the end of ten Westsuns you are not with child, you may leave the trial with honor. If you are with child you will in time once again be examined by three select woman to make certain even the constant scrutiny has not been violated; that you are some Westsuns with child and still virtuous.

"If so, the whole Realm will rejoice. Undoubtedly you will, too. Are you ready for the Testing?"

The fear in her rose like the bouncing rays of the Westsun. She tried to speak. Her throat was dry. She sucked her tongue, swallowed, and tried to smile at Thoth. How pitifully small her smile must have been, but he smiled back. This gave her courage.

"Yes, Lor'd One of Wisdom. I am ready for the Testing."

The silver trumpets blared. The people cheered so loudly that it echoed through her head. God-ette moved up and helped place the headsman's couch at the very front edge of the Window of Ra. Ast-i's head was to fall clear if it must fall! So close were the legs to the edge that two Ama-Sones were told to kneel and hold the couch so that it could not slip and toss her over the edge.

Directed by God-ette, Ast-i lay on her back. Her head and neck were stretched out over space. As she lay back the Virgins advanced with their many banners. At God-ette's command they dropped the banners down all around her, hanging from the staffs. A banner even fell across her neck. They made a room of banners. Only her head was outside the room. She could not even see her own body! She would not be able to see those who examined her.

Thoth's voice came from beyond the house of banners. "Three women have been selected. Let them run swiftly up the ramp to do their duty for the Empire.

"First, the Chosen Woman of the Chief Warrior of the Altmen.

"Second, the Chosen Woman of the Chief Priest of the Temple of Fen.

"Third, the High Priestess of the Temple of Shumen.

"Are all those three here?"

The shouts were positive. Long, loud, and sometimes bawdy comments brought guffaws of laughter.

"Then run to your duties. You alone are honored to be able to touch her with permission of the Empire."

Ast-i knew he must have signalled to Bes. For Bes alone in all the Realm might cause the Drum to speak. The pulse began, low in volume and about one beat each two heartbeats. The volume increased, so did the tempo. Slowly, exactingly, the beat increased until it seemed to throb inside her head. She wanted to cry but dared not. She wanted to jump up and run away. Possibly she would have done so, but her knees were suddenly thrust apart. Three times she was touched by knowing women.

"Turn face down," God-ette commanded.

Ast-i felt the jar in the pit of her stomach. She must have failed. Oh, surely she had failed!

Obedient to the command, she turned on the headsman's couch. Her head was so far beyond the edge she could look straight down to the stones below...and into the upturned eyes of the people standing on the very stones upon which her head might soon fall.

Why, she wondered, did peoples' mouths fall open when they looked straight up? The thought filled her mind as if it was dreadfully important to know. She bit her lip and concentrated on the question. Then suddenly she knew why. She was simply beside her normal self with fear. With this realization came the realization of how silly she was being. She felt so silly she giggled a little. With one hand free, she waved at the staring eyes and open mouths below.

The straining, upturned faces that had seemed so impersonal a moment before broke into delighted smiles. The people waved back.

So this is the way it is to end? Her head at least would be spat upon by persons who once had been friendly! She arched her neck so she could look out upon the thousands of faces in the Temple Compound. They made her giddy. She giggled again.

"Oh, God-e," she thought, "I'm losing all control."

She was being foolish. Was it becoming? Was it appropriate? Was it according to the best thinking?

Suddenly she didn't care. Perhaps she should care about her behavior in situations that were standard, tested, and tried. Her behavior should then conform to the tested, accepted ways of her people. For then she had the advantage of thousands of life experiences to help her in moments of tension when clear thinking was not likely, when instinctual reaction was not acceptable and trained reaction had to serve. Given time enough she would, perhaps, come to the same behavior so many before had tested and approved. Now she was in unknown space! No woman in three thousand Westsuns had gone through all this. Who could tell her how to behave?

Tickled to the point of laughter by her own mental twisting, she waved at the entire crowd. The response was instantaneous. Every arm was raised as by the fountain of energy that rushed up to her from happy throats calling to her such things as:

"Good luck, Ast-i."

"Plucky girl."

"Tomboys sometimes win!"

"No spirit for me. Make mine a man!"

The Drum had risen to a great volume of vibrant sound. The beats were now so fast it was impossible to count the strokes. She heard the trumpets sounding.

She glanced at A-Thena who stood impassive, the huge sword ready, her eyes fixed on Thoth.

The Drum stopped. The trumpets sobbed their way to silence. The crowd below stood still, as if impaled on the last, lonely note of sound. The hush was so great even the birds did not sing.

Thoth spoke. "Select women. Stand forward to the very edge of the Window of Ra. Now ball your fist and stretch forth your arm. Now signal to the people of the Empire what you have found. Thumbs down for disgrace and death. Thumbs up for honor and life."

To Ast-i, time stood as still as her heart. Her breath caught in her throat. It formed a large, aching block. Her brain swam like piranhas among her senses, gobbled them until she was near fainting. So long it took. So long!

Did no one move anymore? Why was everyone so very still? Why was each upturned face filled with an open mouth?

Such silly thoughts. Would A-Sar-U be thinking such random, undisciplined, unimportant thoughts? Would he remember her after—many Westsuns from now it seemed—the sword fell and those friends below caught her head? Would...?

Her own thoughts were making loud clamor in her head. Her eyes saw the surging mass of people below. She saw women melt into tears against their men, as if the strain had been more than woman could bear. She saw men dash tears from their eyes. She saw faces bulge and become red from the force of their shouting.

Finally her eyes caused her thoughts to hesitate in their own unheeding rush. Then she heard the wild clamor of the Drum, the shrill singing of the trumpets, the clapping of hands, and the deafening disharmony of thousands of voices shouting.

Bodies below her began to whirl strangely. Feet stomped. Hands beat out a rhythm. There was a wild energy released, seemingly inspired by the trumpets, the Drum, and the stomping feet.

At last she realized that she had not even breathed out the breath she had breathed in. When? So long ago it seemed. Was it possible that all this had occurred in the space of one long-held breath? No, not so much, only one long-held half-breath.

"Three thumbs up. All thumbs up," Thoth called joyously.

Ast-i collapsed in tears. Weeping, she saw the people below laughing up at her. They threw her kisses, then hugged and kissed each other. They were riotous with joy.

She could only weep. Sobs raked her body and hurt her throat.

"Stand up, Ast-i, Virgin of God," Thoth commanded.

Ast-i tried to ease back on the headsman's couch. Her arms were so weak she could not lift herself. She collapsed weeping. The people below went even wilder.

"Stand the couch up with her on it," Thoth called.

The two Ama-Sones holding the couch merely straightened their legs. Ast-i and the couch were up-ended. When her feet touched the marble, Ast-i felt weakness run up her legs. She could hardly stand. She clung to the upright of the headsman's couch, weeping helplessly.

The people below went wilder still. Either they despised her or they understood her emotions. As she was wondering which, a loud voice came with a jolly roll:

"Hey, Ast-i, now you know what its like to win in the Combats."

"Combats! By God-e, she won a whole war single handed."

"Good girl. Weep it out."

After a long while Ast-i found she could move. The retinue, led by the Ama-Sones, started down the ramp. At the edge of the Window of Ra she turned and waved both hands at the crowd. They cheered so much that she was no longer ashamed that tears streaked her cheek and soaked her breasts. She loved those people below who felt with her some of her great release from intolerable strain.

"Oh, woman," she thought, "a moment ago it was sweat, now it is tears that make a lake of your navel!"

As she moved down the ramp the people began to bow low before her. In waves they bowed, all the while calling to her terms of encouragement, bawdy advice, and sheer love. As the group moved across the lower level, they came to the weeping group of Fenmen and Fenwomen. In their midst was the crushed, crumpled, and bleeding body of E-Don.

As Ast-i came near they rose and bowed. How she longed to reach out comforting arms to that weeping mother. She dared not. She bowed low to the Fenwoman.

"I sorrow for you, mother. My arms are forbidden to do so, but I embrace you in my heart. I sorrow for all his kinsmen. But be proud of him. He did not disgrace you."

"Goddess Ast-i," the mother said in the singing tones of the marshland, "We 'r' proud 'f E-Don. We 'r' proud of the way he died. We 'r' proud 'f Thoth, 'n' our Empire." She smiled and looked at Ast-i with love in her large hazel eyes. "We r' proud f' you, Virgin of God. We love you 'n' what you risk 'n' do f'r us. Sur'ly you 'r' blessed 'bove all women."

A-Thena spoke to the Fenwoman directly. "What is your name, Fenwoman?"

"Ama-Sone, I am the Chosen Woman of Da-Na the Fenman."

"Yes. But have you not a name of which to be proud?"

"Yes, Ama-Sone, a name 'f which t' be ver' proud. I give 't you ag'in. Chosen Woman of Da-Na the Fenman."

"You are proud of only that?"

"Ah, Ama-Sone! 'T is such a proud thing t' be Chosen Woman 'f a great man 'n a great tribe 'n a great Empire. What more cou'd anyone want?"

A-Thena smiled wryly but broadly. "Fenwoman, you have made your bitter point. Yours are the teachings of Mut. Mine are the teachings of A-Thena. In your way, be happy always."

"I promise' Ama-Sone, 'n' thank you f'r th' wish. I sh'll be 's happy 's my Chosen Man 'llows me t' be."

"Ouch!" A-Thena turned away with a friendly shrug. After several paces she said softly, "She seems so loving and tender, that worshipper of Mut. Yet she is as hard as I and as unbending as a shield. I like her. What a Warrior she could be if she would only learn to fight."

As the group moved along the side of the Main Temple toward the Temple of the Virgins, God-ette said almost under her breath. "The way to Virgin Birth is over corpses!"

"How many, Mother?" Ast-i wondered aloud. "There are five already! How many?"

"As many as it takes," A-Thena said and her usually flat voice was filled with a lift of emotion.

"As many as it takes," God-ette echoed.

A-Thena's voice ran on, thrilled and filled with notes of music. "If hundreds die that Virgin Birth may be proved again, it is a good exchange. Women are goddesses in the making and thus may prove it."

"If they prove it," God-ette said, "divinity will walk again publicly on the land even as it does now secretly."

"Secretly, Mother?"

God-ette lowered her voice to a soft whisper. "Yes. Secretly. In you and in A-Sar-U. You both were Virgin Born but not registered. We were too frightened to let what we were doing be known. Now you will make it public. Much depends on you two. The future of the people of this Empire now rests with you.

11

Words of Mystery, I

A-Sar-U stood with his guard of Warriors and watched Ast-i with her guard of Ama-Sones, priestesses, and Virgins disappear down the east ramp. He was so proud of her! His pride somehow increased his desire for her. As he saw her beautiful form moving with such grace among the others, his yearning made thunder in his ears.

When she disappeared, waving both hands in her joy and exhuberance, he allowed his gaze to wander up the levels of the pyramids of the Main Temple. From where he stood he could see the lines of the Temple converging in steps until the apex seemed to float contentedly in the blue sky.

Above the first level there was a second pyramid. Like the first it was truncated. The third pyramid sat in the top surface of the second pyramid, and around it on each side was a flat surface much like the courtyard below. The fourth, fifth, sixth, seventh, and eighth pyramids were smaller and smaller replicas of the ones below them. At the very top of the eighth pyramid was a building that continued the slope of the sides of the pyramid but was fitted with entrances to a floor that contained nothing at all visible from below. It looked empty. A vast building, pyramidal in shape and empty.

The entire Temple reached probably one hundred fifty arms above where he stood on the Window of Ra. Ramps led upward to the top of the third pyramid. Many times the Warriors were permitted to assemble there when participating in rituals.

Insofar as he knew, only priests and priestesses were allowed on the second and third levels at other times. They had rooms inside the walls. Rooms that could be reached only by those who knew how to open the large slabs of marble that closed the entrances.

No one other than Thoth, Bes, and the High Priests and their servants, was allowed to go above the fourth level. At all times Temple Guards stood at the top of the ever-narrowing stairway that led from the fourth level by steps up to the building that formed the apex, or the ninth pyramid. Bes stood on the fourth level now, as was his duty in times of ceremony. His select Temple Guards stood there at all other times—even, it was said, during the fierce fore-wind, bombardment, rain, and aft-wind of the Westsun. No one was allowed beyond that point without permission of the guards.

He interrupted his musings as a body of Temple Guards came in formation down from the fourth level. They approached him and his Warrior Guards rapidly and with purpose. Thoth came forward and placed himself beside A-Sar-U.

"Warrior Guard. Give your charge into the keeping of the Temple Guard and return to your quarters."

The Commander of the Warrior Guard reacted quickly. "Lor'd One, we are commanded to keep A-Sar-U safe at all costs. We must return him to his room under our protection. He is a Warrior."

"Whose orders are these?"

"Lor'd Je-Su's. They are standing orders. Warriors take care of Warriors. It is our sworn duty."

"Commendable duty, usually. You are relieved of that duty now!"

"Only Lor'd Je-Su can..." the Commander placed his hand on the hilt of his sword and began to draw.

Thoth's reaction was so swift even A-Sar-U standing almost chest to chest with the Commander did not see it clearly. The Commander was flat on the floor and his sword was in Thoth's hand, point at his throat.

"Only Bes can give an order I cannot countermand, and that only concerning the Drum. Commander, is that clear?"

"Yes, Lor'd One of Wisdom. I meant no offense. Only to do my duty as a good Warrior."

"Most commendable in other times and other cases. But this is most unusual. It requires unusual procedures and instant decisions. I commend you and your Warriors. If my action is swift and uncompromising, these are the times that try man's trust. You will now take your Line of Twenty to your quarters. You and they are released from all responsibility for A-Sar-U. He is now the property of the Temple of Po-Si-Don."

Thoth changed from a fierce Warrior to a smiling priest in a quarter breath. He extended his hand to help the Commander to his feet, and carefully brushed him while clucking in good humor.

"Commander. One day I will show you that trick. You will be surprised at how simple it is and how little strength is needed."

The Commander smiled rather ruefully. "Lor'd Thoth, your reputation as a clever fighter has just been proved. If I offended..."

"No more, friend! I should have been offended if you had given up your charge too easily. You guard the property of the Empire. I guard the property of the Empire and the Temple."

"Are they not the same?"

"At times I wish I could be absolutely sure," Thoth said with a laugh.

The Warrior Guard marched away and disappeared down the ramp. Thoth motioned the Temple Guard and they formed a square around A-Sar-U and Thoth. Thoth then signalled Bes who cried: "Servants, bring food and drink for a long march for twenty Warriors. Do it now!"

Almost instantly ten servants appeared on the fourth level carrying earthen pots. They wore the long loose-flowing talpa-skin robes of the servers of the Temple, the green vestcoats with short sleeves, a red stripe on the right side and a yellow stripe on the left. They wore green and gold caps of soft squirrel-skin pulled low over their foreheads.

"Release your armor quickly," Thoth whispered. "Do exactly as you are told. Do it swiftly. Your life may depend on the next few minutes. You will exchange dress with the first server, helmet and all."

The ten servers moved through the Temple Guards around him, and they all converged as if to take their share from the pots. Quicker than A-Sar-U could believe, his armor was lifted from him and put upon one of the servers. His helmet was moved from his head to that of a server. In two breaths he had been covered with the server's cap, the varicolored vestcoat, and the loose robe had been draped over him. A huge pot was set on his shoulder. It was done so deftly, and they were so close together that it must have seemed, even to Bes looking from above, as if he had bowed low and then straightened up again

"Serve the Guard," Thoth commanded. "Bow so your face is not clear. Then go with the servers. Walk like one, too. You stand too proud!"

A-Sar-U bent to his task. In twenty breaths he seemed to have changed from Warrior to server, the Guard formed up again, and his armor and helmet marched away in the center of the Guard. They marched down the ramp, under the overhang of the Window of Ra and out toward the Lion's Gate, with Thoth leading them.

Slowly the servers moved around A-Sar-U and they carried the pots up the ramp to the third level, then up the narrowing stairs to the fourth level. Bes stood aside and allowed them to turn around to the east side, away from the Temple of Warriors. The servants slid through a narrow opening, climbed a circling inner stair and entered the bottom of the seventh pyramid. A narrow stair wound upward about twenty arms, then ended in an interior corridor. Down that corridor they entered into a large room that was apparently servers' quarters. A-Sar-U was silently guided to a corner and motioned to sit upon a pile of cow hides. The servers went about their business as if he were not there at all. After several hundred breaths he dozed.

Perhaps five thousand breaths later Thoth appeared in the room with two servers bearing large jars as if they were filled with water. They advanced and poured out of the jars his armor, helmet, sword and knife.

"These are duplicates of your armor. Put them on. As you do, listen to me. You will soon be led toward the inner secret chamber of the pyramid. It is the sacred sanctuary. Even to enter it you must be initiated and pass a test. You must tell the guards that you seek eternal life.

"Before you may enter upon the seeking of eternal life you must understand these ancient *Hekau*, these words of power, these words of mystery:

"I am the hidden soul. I create gods.

"I have the power to cause gods to be born in flesh.

96

"I have the power to be born a second time through spirit.

"I am yesterday. I am today. I am tomorrow.

"I partake of the tree of life. I feed on the flesh of divinity.

"I drink the blood that gives eternal life, I quaff the elixir of divinity.

"I am all three of the classes of celestial beings with bodies that never change, diminish, or fade away.

"I am now. I was forever. I will be eternally."

A-Sar-U repeated the words over and over until he was certain he had them memorized. They rang like the sound of trumpets in his mind. Each time he spoke them he felt a new energy rising within himself. He did not understand why, but they created an enormous energy within him. Every word was clear. Yet the total meaning of each sentence and of all the words together escaped him. The sentences bore a weight of wisdom too great for his mind to bear.

"Who could be yesterday, today, and tomorrow?" he asked.

"Only one who could pass through the barriers between times. Or, maybe, one who could stand outside time. To suspend time would be to stay in the now eternally. To command time would be to be able to be in any time at will."

"Am I to re-enter my mother's womb and take a second life? How can I do that?"

"Why do you ask that question?"

"I have the power to be born a second time in spirit?"

"Wonder about it!"

"All men think that humankind was created by the Supreme God-e. Yet I learn I am the hidden soul. I create gods."

"Dwell on it!"

"What is the meaning of this strange saying, 'I partake of the tree of life? I feed on the flesh of divinity'?"

"Ponder it!"

"Explain so I can understand this: 'I am all three of the classes of celestial beings with bodies that never change, diminish, or fade away.' Surely that is a joke meant more to puzzle the mind than spur on the spirit."

"Think about it! But know, you will never understand it by mind only."

Thoth waited patiently until A-Sar-U finished trying to think out the meanings. When he gave up with a smile and a shrug, Thoth moved with a burst of energy. They went to the inner wall, Thoth tapped three times, waited, tapped three more times. The wall swung open and they passed into a complex of rooms and stairways inside the pyramid. A-Sar-U thought they must be in the topmost pyramid, near its very center. Each room opened into another except one, which was a barracks room for Temple Guards. Six were there. Two stationed at the door, swords drawn. Two were sleeping in corners far separated from each other. Two others were cooking food at a small stufa. All guards rose to attention as Thoth strode in.

"A-Tem, Commander of the Guards of the Body of God-e, this is A-Sar-U. He is a candidate in the Ordeal of Virgin Birth. He will not leave these quarters until I give permission. If he tries, kill him."

The simple nods of the Guard spoke loudly of their intention and ability to obey.

"A-Sar-U is not to be seen by anyone but me. His body is in holy trust to the Empire. Many may try to find him, to disturb him, or even kill him. Defend him well, he is worth your very own life. To the degree he is harmed you are harmed one thousand times more. Feed him through the slot. Taste his food and drink to be certain it has not been poisoned. If he dies, you die. If he is poisoned, a poisoned spear will be run through the bowels of each of you. Understood, A-Tem? And does your Temple Guard understand?"

A-Tem looked at his Guard and received nods of understanding.

"Understood, Lor'd One of Wisdom. We accept the honor with its burden."

Thoth stepped beyond the next entrance into the inner room. It was fully thirty arms long and twenty arms wide. Its ceiling was mounted on five tapering, square, fluted columns. Between each column and the next, or one of the walls, the weight was supported on crossbeams of one single hewn stone.

In the far corner was a raised platform with a small wooden cover. Thoth strode to it, unlocked a wooden crossbar and lifted the cover. The sound of water running in the cloaca could be heard.

"Lock even this when it is not in use. Our enemies will swim through filth to kill you. Take no chances at all."

"But I have no enemy, Lor'd One."

"Everyone is your enemy until your task is accomplished. Quite a few would be willing to kill you to deny the Empire even a chance that you will succeed.

"If you do succeed, every religion but one will lose adherents. Je-Su, Brahm, Ma-Nu, even Som and Ram, have religions they wish to foster or force upon the minds of all the people."

"Why, Lor'd Uncle? Why?"

"Ego. Pride. They think it makes one more honored to be head of a religious movement. They cannot out-sword or out-last me. So they try to win converts by any means.

"If...ah, when...you succeed they will fall further out of favor with the people. You will prove again the validity of the old beliefs. New beliefs will be crowded out.

"You are a threat. Je-Su will do anything. He is obsessed with the importance of his own birth."

Thoth turned toward a raised platform of marble in the center of the room, paused and said reflectively, "Perhaps I should have given him the Honorable Death. But why should so many of our needed, good Warriors die with one hand tied with a vine to a pole. I know it is ancient custom. But it is such a waste!"

He stopped at the platform, pointed. It was about hip high, and covered with soft rabbit-fur spreads.

"This is your Mound of Desire. You will not lie on it until you feel you are ready to contend with nature to force your creative will upon spirit. At all other times you will rest where you can, if you can.

"Right now you will remove all your armor except your sword. Your sword must be near at hand at all times. If anyone enters this room except me, it is against the orders of the Empire. He means to harm or kill you.

"While you are in this room you will remove all your clothes except one sandal. You may cover yourself with a rabbit fur if you wish. When you work, you must be neither barefoot nor shod, naked nor clothed, fed nor hungry. You will work, physically, every Eastsun."

Thoth walked to the far end of the room and pointed to a pile of huge, square-hewn, oblong stones stacked neatly there.

"You must keep your strength. When you come out of this confinement you may need to join combat. At the rising of each Eastsun you will take those stones from the entrance and carry them here. At the setting of the Eastsun you will carry them back to make a barrier at the entrance. Each stone is the weight of a big man. There are thirty three of them. By moving them twice each Eastsun you will surely stay in strength.

"Food! Food will be given you three times each Eastsun. Water, too. It will have been tasted at the entrance. Wait fifty breaths. If no one calls to you, eat one bite, drink one swallow. Wait yet another fifty breaths. If you feel distress...well? Otherwise eat and drink in peace and good health!"

"Now to your training..."

Thoth was interrupted by a heavy pounding on the door of the chamber. A momentary surprise came over Thoth's face as he answered the knocking with a rhythmic code. The aperture was opened and A-Sar-U saw the face of A-Tem.

A whispered conversation took less than ten breaths. Thoth said: "Tell Lord Bes I come. Triple all guards. Do it now."

Thoth turned. "Do you know a Commander of a Line of Twenty by the name of Luflin?"

"Yes. He was the Commander from whom you took the sword."

"Ah? Your opinion of him?"

"He is of the Altmen, the High Mountain tribe. He is strong. He does not enjoy Je-Su or Set but serves them well."

"Thank you. I must be gone a while. Please rest. It is the beginning of the third watch of the dark. We will work as soon as I can return."

Thoth was soon gone, and the giant room seemed to echo with memory of his energy.

12

The Grace of Je-Su

Luflin, the Mountain Man, was the Commander of the Warrior Guard whom Thoth threw and disarmed. In his own spinning mind he was sure that the unwilling fall he took was the beginning of an unwilling fall, perhaps even to death, in his standing with Lor'd Je-Su. Je-Su in a fit of anger, had commanded his name be changed from *Luflin,* to Lu-Flin, an insult to his tribe and his dignity.

Je-Su had sent him to the Trials with specific whispered instructions, among which was: "On pain of death, never mention to anyone the content of these instructions. Ever!"

Luflin's instructions, made more onerous by the Lor'd One's unblinking eyes, were simple:

"Take A-Sar-U to the Trials and Testing with a Line of Twenty to back you up. He most probably will be discredited and ordered to die by the sword of the Empire. If so, you will then kill him quickly. Personally! Quickly! Understand? Quickly!"

Je-Su strode back and forth over the tiger skins on the floor of his quarters, his black eyes feverish with intensity, his swarthy face working against the weight of a frown. He brightened and came close to whisper to Luflin, "What will you do if he is not discredited and ordered killed? Just this. You will bring him back here swiftly. Warriors take care of Warriors. We will take care of him. You will especially and personally take care of him."

Luflin did not personally like Je-Su but enjoyed the many special trusts placed upon him by the Empire's second greatest Warrior. He did not understand why he, a simple Warrior from the Altmen, a High Mountain tribe, was chosen for such special assignments. But he accepted the benefits that came with the responsibilities, and tried to serve well and faithfully. He wanted to serve better than the marshland Fenmen, or the desert Shumen of Africanus, or the Plainsmen. He wanted to prove that his tribe, although it had been conquered by the coalition of tribes, was better than the other tribes of the Empire. His place and knowledge of the techniques of war and the might of the Empire War Machine, might someday help his tribe triumph when next they revolted. Someday they would, and he thought it would be soon.

After Thoth overthrew him and took possession of the person of A-Sar-U, he marched his Line of Twenty down the west ramp of the Temple of Po-Si-Don. He saw the lack of discipline shown by the Temple Guard, a Line of Twenty. They jostled the servers as they rushed to surround the cooking-pot to grab for food. Je-Su would never have allowed such lack of discipline to go unpunished.

On the level ground, he angered his men by making them drill near the South Gate although they were still in festive dress with heavy armor, as they had been since before the rising of the Eastsun.

He delayed for a purpose. He saw A-Sar-U's splendid armor and colorful helmet-feathers as the Temple Guard hurried through the Lion's Gate, along the embankment, and then turned northward along the trail that led over Loba Ridge toward the frowning Atal Mountains. Only when he was sure in his mind he knew where they were headed did he march his men into the Warriors' Compound.

He was met by Lor'd Je-Su and Lor'd Set, both with conniving curves to their upper lips that passed as kindly smiles.

Scowls came black and terrible as they saw that A-Sar-U was not among the Line of Twenty.

"Commander Lu-Flin, where is our most treasured Warrior?"

Luflin heard the black threat in the words and trembled. "Lor'd Je-Su, he was taken from us by Lor'd Thoth, by trickery and force."

"Trickery? Were you not ready for trickery? By force? By force, when you had a Line of Twenty of the greatest young fighters of the Empire? Why did you give him up?"

Luflin saw the rising fury like the onsweep of the Westsun. "Lor'd Thoth had a sword at my throat, and many

102

Lines of Twenty of the Temple Guard close to his command."

"You *gave* him up?"

So much venom in so few words!

"Lor'd One of War, he was taken. We were outnumbered."

"I personally gave you orders. I, Je-Su, Only Son of God-e, carefully gave you orders. You know the Supreme God-e was whispering his orders through me."

"Lor'd Thoth had a sword at my throat, ten lines of Temple Warriors, and the Temple Guard Archers on the walls. He had all the power and the authority of the Empire to call upon. I had one Line of Twenty."

"Silence! You disobeyed the Son of God-e. It is a sin against the Empire. It is treason. It is heinous. It will not be, it shall not go unpunished. You must be punished. All of you! By your inaction you sinned against the God-e."

Ra-Lu, Leader of the Line of Twenty spoke quickly. "Lor'd One, why should I or my line of men be punished? They obeyed all orders spoken to them. They did not, could not, know of your secret orders."

"Silence!" Set's anger sounded in his throat like the yowl of a spear-thrust bear, and he was rewarded by a light nod of approval from Je-Su. "Your punishment must be greater because you fail to understand that you all have sinned. Sinned against the Living God-e."

"How have these men sinned?" Luflin managed to croak from a dry throat.

"Silence! You sin still more by doubting the will of the Son of God-e. Do you study to sin?" Je-Su stalked the length of the Line of Twenty and back again. "You all know that the Warrior's Code demands that you be alert, aware, and obedient, and give your life in defense of the Empire.

"You fools were not alert.

"You were not aware.

"You were not obedient.

"You did not even try to defend the Empire. You all know that conspiracy runs amuk in the Empire to deprive the Only True Son of God-e of his birthright." Je-Su slammed a balled fist upon his own breastplate for emphasis and said in a strangled scream, "You all know that A-Sar-U and Thoth are part of that conspiracy. Indeed, they are the very poisonous heads. They mean to destroy you, your tribes, your families...all."

Je-Su was panting with rage. "Are you standing before me now?"

His black eyes seemed to spew venom upon every member of the Line of Twenty.

"You know you are standing before me now.

"Therefore you did not do your duty. You did not die in defense of the Empire. You broke your Warrior's Code. You sinned against God-e.

"You were cowardly deserters. You sinned against me, your loving protector, your Lor'd Supreme Commander of War, your benefactor, your patron."

Je-Su turned to Set. "Do you agree, Lor'd Commander of the Warriors of Je-Su, that they have not given their lives in combat for the welfare of the Empire?"

"I agree. Indeed I agree!"

"Do you agree that all should be punished?"

"Of course! Lor'd One, you are Supreme Commander and beloved champion of all the Warriors of the Empire. If you decree that they must be punished, I will see that the punishment is inflicted—as will every other Warrior of the Empire."

"Thank you, Lor'd Set. Punishment they must have. They have most grievously sinned against the Son of God-e."

Je-Su stood very still, his eyes closed tightly, for many breaths while the Line of Twenty sagged under the threat of his awful rage. When he opened his eyes he was almost smiling.

"Those who sin should be punished in such a way that they will have time to repent of their sin. To confess their error. To do all they can to make amends and proclaim to others that which is just and right.

"This then shall be their punishment:

"Each one shall be hung by his fighting arm so high that only his toes can touch the ground. He shall be given a wooden sword with which to defend himself against any young Warrior who may wish to practice upon him the art of killing.

"He shall be given neither food nor water until he is killed by a student Warrior, or dies...

"Except, in our mercy and pity, we order that he shall be given one mouthful of water after each eighty breaths he has spent shouting at the top of his voice 'I repent that I sinned against Je-Su, Only Son of God-e.' "

Set smiled broadly and said, "If one was hung in each Warrior Training Compound, it would spread the message."

"Very good idea. Thank you, Lor'd Set. But the message will also be spread when their bodies are sent to their families to dishonor their tribes." Je-Su turned to face Luflin. "What have you to say, Sinner? Is it fair punishment, in case Thoth should ask?"

"No punishment that takes a life is fair." Luflin's voice quavered so much he could not continue. After several gasping breaths he managed, "You have the power...but I know the direction they have taken A-Sar-U."

"Oh? Good. Tell me and I'll send Seven Lines of Twenty to rescue him from his kidnapers."

"Into the Atals. But...I am a Mountain Man. Would Lor'd Je-Su want us to...?"

"Are you trying to escape just punishment for your sins? That is another sin in itself!"

"Is it a sin to wish to live?"

"It is a sin to try to escape the will of the Only Son of God-e" Je-Su was instantly in another giant rage. His swarthy face bulged with his passions, and turned a muddy purple.

"Lor'd Je-Su," Set said. "I have a thought. You do not want these Warriors to sin further by trying to escape punishment. They would like to do something for the Empire to delay or remove the punishment.

"Would it be just to allow them to go in pursuit of A-Sar-U? You might let them know that if they found him, rescued him from his kidnappers, even if he was killed in the encounter, they would be granted a reward..."

"Are you deserting me, too?"

"...A reward in this way. They would not escape full punishment. No! After they have succeeded, your decree would be carried out, exactly as you direct.

"Their reward would be this: Warriors who die for cowardice, which is a sin against the Empire and also against Je-Su, Only Son of God-e, bring dishonor upon their family and their tribe.

"In your Graciousness, you might grant that their bodies will be cut down, carried to some fighting front, and then reported to have died gloriously in battle.

"You would gain the allegiance of their families. These Warriors would have much to work for. Their punishment would be just. Their families would not suffer from their cowardly sinning."

"By the God-e!"

At Je-Su's expletive, Set startled. "If I have displeased with my rambling thoughts I withdraw..."

"You have pleased me greatly. Ah, Set, you are growing wise under my teaching. I like it. Fair. Equitable. Sin will be punished.

"You, Commander Lu-Flin of the Warrior Line of Twenty, and you, Ra-Lu, leader of the Line—to you I grant a special boon.

"When you are hanging we shall give you more time to understand why and how you have sinned. Time to repent your sinning. We will allow no bumbling young Warrior to fight you and kill you abruptly.

"No. Each day we will give you three bites of food and three additional gulps of water. Your life will be prolonged and you will have more time to plead for forgiveness.

"Turn now. Turn now! Do it! Go to that place where Thoth is holding A-Sar-U against his will. Rescue him.

"Then bear his body back to me in great honor, with thousands weeping beside the track you follow.

"Go. Do your best for the Empire. Do it!"

Set looked at Je-Su with admiration. "Lor'd Je-Su, how very gracious you are. You have the divine forgiveness that befits the Only Son of God-e."

Luflin hung for a moment between fear of the wrath of Je-Su and knowledge of the foolishness of wearing colorful dress into combat. "Lor'd One, do you mean for us to leave without changing into our combat gear?"

"And why not?"

"Dress gear is stiff and heavy. We will spoil these bright clothes given us by the Empire."

"Spoil them. You will wear them to the hanging anyway."

Je-Su and Set laughed. The sound of that raucous, mocking laughter was in Luflin's ears as he took his Line of Twenty out of the Warriors' Compound at double-quick step.

13

Rebellion In Mind

Luflin, Commander of a Line of Twenty thought bitterly, "Pines smell of space, strength, and freedom," as he topped the ridge and looked down into the upland valley.

Bitterly. Because behind him, up the hillside trail, struggled twenty angry Warriors. Good Warriors, trained to kill, who held him responsible for the death sentence imposed upon them by Je-Su. He could not have prevented what happened, even if he had been given all the facts. But he knew that any of the twenty would gladly run him through if they had a chance. Yes! And they'd make that chance if he was not wary. He must now run his race as if on the edge of a precipice. He must keep them busy, and too exhausted to hope to overcome him or temporarily care if they could or couldn't.

Luflin shut his mind on the danger from his own men. For the fragrance of pines ran the remembrance of freedom into his brain. Remembrance of the days of childhood and youth of a Mountain Man, born to the highest reaches of the Atal Mountains. The recollection brought a half-smile of pleasure to his face and a bitter sigh from his heart. He recalled the early days when he roamed free—free even of clothing. When he lived in complete and joyful freedom, bound only by the need for food and the inescapable love of his mother and father. Even as a youth, when he was taught by his father the ways of the tribe of Altmen and the skills of Warriors, he was free. Free to challenge any one. Free to speak his mind, his likes, his wonderings. Free to be himself with confidence in his acceptance by his family and his belongingness to his tribe. Free to be important, if only in his own mind.

When he had done that which duty to his family, friends, companions, and tribe required, he came and went, thought and spoke in complete freedom.

A mask of fury settled over his face as he recalled the coming of the Shumen, under Africanus and the Plainsmen, in ranks of shields and spears. The years of oppression, and then the coming of the Men of God-e, and the Empire of the Pleasant Planet in greater ranks of shields and spears, and flights of metal-tipped arrows and the glittering, hard-cutting swords. They overran the Shumen overlords and also the men of the Atals, and freed them a little by making his mountain-fasts into a part of the Empire of God-e.

Again Luflin felt the searing fear he had seen in the tear-dimmed blue eyes of his mother as he was chosen to go as a Hostage-against-Rebellion. And the blazing anger on the face of his father penned in by a ring of blades.

As High-Chief and Priestess Mother, his father and mother were the final force, authority, and conscience of his race. He, as their son, was heir-apparent to their domain and authority. Yet, though young Warriors of the Atals followed him, his parents had made him earn and earn again each position in his life.

When he had been hustled by Warriors from his highland joys to the deadly routine, discipline, and restriction of the Temple Center of Po-Si-Don, he had wished to die. Then he saw that he could learn much that would serve his own tribe in some future time. He applied himself to learning.

For a long while now he had kept buried the remembrance of his boyhood pleasures, of still-hunting in the oak and pine forests, of arrow-fishing in the cold mountain streams, and of bathing his weary body in the flowing water only a few arms from the melting snow. His days had been filled with work and joy, and even now he dreamed often of lush forests of sweet-smelling pines, sturdy oaks, and brooks gurgling to him of happy things.

The fury of his strides lessened as he came to the crest of the Loba Ridge and could see the trail descending into the Loba River Valley. Twenty Warriors behind him, still in heavy dress uniforms and bearing the heavier weight of being condemned to death for something they truly had no part in, sagged in near exhaustion as soon as he stopped.

He had run them for too long and too fast without rest in the attempt to overtake A-Sar-U's guards from the Temple of Po-Si-Don. Also, because he could feel the danger that came at him from a Line of Twenty ready to rebel against all authority.

So hardened had he become under Je-Su's training that his conscience had not pricked him at all until his anger and frustration were softened by the bright, clean smell of his beloved mountains.

"Stop, Commander! I'm on to your game. You may be in charge of us, but I am the Leader of this Line of Twenty. They will follow me if I say *Stop*. You have run them for half an Eastsun. I will not..."

Luflin swung angrily to face the Leader. "Leader, you will do as you are commanded to carry out the will of Je-Su. I am Je-Su here. My word is his command. Clear, Leader?"

"What can you do to punish us? We're already condemned to die."

"Yes. It is not a question of what, but how soon. I am your only chance to delay. Do you want to give up that chance?"

"No. I want my men to live as long as possible with honor."

The Leader's voice was now less harsh, but Luflin knew that here was a hard-minded but fair man.

"What now, Commander?" The Leader's voice had lost its edge and now held the lilt of the Fenmen.

"Your name, Leader?"

"Ra-Lu, Commander."

"Leader Ra-Lu, you are panting. We all pant in our hurry to catch those..." his hands indicated the empty tracks across the meadows of the Valley of the Loba... "those Temple Guards."

"Why hurry so?" Leader Ra-Lu squinted up at him. "The sooner you find them the sooner we all die for sinning against Lor'd Je-Su." There was a long silence except for the labored breathing of the Line of Twenty before he added, "I wonder why we should die at all."

Luflin turned away quickly to hide his face. He felt a small chill of delight, but held his countenance as impassive as he could. "Because Je-Su wills it."

"But why? The death of anyone decreases the power of the Empire."

"So?"

"By the God-e, you sound resigned to death."

"Looking forward, Leader Ra-Lu." He meant it to be light but could not keep the bitterness from his voice.

"Yea-ah, to our special treatment. We get fed enough to prolong our lives so we can have the benefit of understanding the enormity of our sin." The Fenman was taller than most of his tribe, his brow big inside his helmet, his yellowish skin glistening with beads of sweat. His eyes were angry, but not mean.

"Leader Ra-Lu, you know I am not really to blame for..."

"They think you are." Ra-Lu's eyes jerked toward the twenty men glowering up at Luflin. "They'd like to see you suffer."

Luflin held his eyes steady. But his face lifted in a tense smile. With a self-deprecating laugh he said, "Sweet thought. Thank you for reminding..." Luflin's voice dropped to a whisper. "Look, a buck."

"Where?" Ra-Lu followed the silent pointing finger. "I see...a three-prong grazing beyond the..."

"Feed twenty-two hungry men?"

"Just barely. But he's too far. Sixty arms if a span."

"Downhill. I can get him."

"Oh, sure. And I can kiss the Westsun."

"Watch." Luflin eased his shield to the ground and slid out of his breastplate so slowly it did not spook the buck to flight. With the slowness of a dream, he took a wide-spaced stance and brought his spear above his right shoulder. His arm glided backward to its fullest throwing strength. He felt as if he floated in a special, super-natural space. He knew, with a sure, surreal knowing, just how to arc the spear into its flight. His arm shot forward. The spear sailed upward, the heavy metal tip high.

Luflin was not concentrating on the spear but on the spot on the buck he wanted the spear to hit. Dimly he saw how it sailed effortlessly, like a hawk in flight, until the point began to drop below the level of the butt. Then, like a hawk swooping to the kill, the spear seemed to increase its speed.

Apparently the buck sensed danger rather than saw it. It sprang high into the air an instant after the sharp point

111

crashed through it's heart and came out the far side. The buck collapsed.

What had been a thing of beauty and grace in motion hung awkwardly on the spear hasp. The grace was gone from its muscles, the power from its life before it crashed to earth.

"Oh, Good God-e," Ra-Lu murmured in admiration. "But, it knew it was in danger. Why didn't it bolt?"

"My will for food requiring death was stronger than its will for life requiring flight."

"You willed the spear...?"

"Of course. I willed the spear to bring it instant, painless death." For a moment he stood silent. When he spoke again it was to the dead animal. "Little Brother, your flesh will give food I need. I did not wish you pain. I did not wish you dead except that I might live a little while fed by you. Little Friend, let your shadow self go peacefully into the tomorrows beyond life and take with you our gratitude."

Ra-Lu looked hard into Luflin's face and grated angrily, "Damn you. My men and I want to hate you enough to kill you. But you feel, too, that all life is precious. You'd make a good Fenman. We know," he indicated the Line of Twenty, "at least *I* know, that all life is precious. Far too precious to be wasted on the whims of man."

"Any man, Leader!"

"Is Je-Su a God-e, Commander?"

"He is as you believe him to be, Leader Ra-Lu."

"Commander, I believe him to be a man. Only."

"A man he is, then." The two stood looking hard and deep into each other's eyes, searching for assurance that the words they spoke would not lead to dishonor for their tribe...for to them death was already promised.

"I do not think Set is a God-e."

"You know you sin. You know you speak rebellion in mind. You know you speak treason...all by Set's order?"

"Oh, I know. But so do you, if you agree with what I have said."

"If I don't agree?"

Ra-Lu shrugged indifferently. "Well, if you are lucky enough to live until you get these Warriors back to their unjust punishment, you can turn me in...for any good that will do. You might save your own life by defaming my tribe with my dishonor before my death."

"Yeah? You know I'd never live long enough to enjoy it. You Fenmen are a touchy race, and you never forgive anyone who harms one of your own people. Besides, I'd dishonor my own mother and father and make a lie of their training in duty. For my duty is to speak truth. In truth I agree with you."

"What'll we do about it?"

"Think on it and trust each other." Aloud he commanded, "Leader Ra-Lu, make camp by the River Loba. Roast the venison and eat in relays. Keep four outpost guards alert at all times. By newlight we must go find the Temple Guard and A-Sar-U. Move!"

At Ra-Lu's command the sagging guards broke into a run, seeming anxious to obey and accept the first positive thing that had happened to them in a full Eastsun of degradation of spirit.

Luflin stayed at the crest, for even before the Warriors moved, he was studying the land carefully, his inner senses resonant with echoes of sounds of danger. After a hundred breaths he became aware of the fear in Ra-Lu. Some shadow or chill of danger seeped into his mind, although his eyes did not find its cause in the valley ahead of them.

He studied the activity in the campsite, the wafting smoke of the fire, the blue slither of the Loba River. The lines of trees behind the camp, the rising land beyond the river, the scattered trees, and the scattered clumps of grass and brush gave no indication to his practiced eyes of the cause of the unease in his mind. But he felt a strange force, like hostile eyes staring.

Suddenly Ra-Lu shivered and grunted hollowly, "Eyes!"

"You feel them, too, Leader?"

"Eyes. Yes, Commander. Eyes. The terrible force of eyes that scream silently. You feel them?"

"Yes. Like the eyes of bears once around my night camp high in the Atals."

"More like madmen's eyes around my scared tail!"

"Well put. I can't see them—anything."

"Nor I. But they are there. Fenmen know."

"So do Mountain Men."

113

Luflin pulled himself erect and felt a cold hand sweep up his spine. He shivered slightly. "They hurt, like the memory of a bad dream. Could it be that we are feeling guilty for thinking aloud our sin against the glorious leaders of our kind Empire?"

"You jest, Commander. But Thoth is our true leader of the Empire and he is glorious, kind, helpful, and understanding. Only Je-Su and Set make death-giving decisions under those stupid, punishing laws."

"Again, agreed. But now we are sinning against the maker of those laws, Lor'd Ma-Nu. Under him to breathe is a sin, to even think protest is to die. Where can we go to hide from the laws of Ma-Nu and the stupidity of Je-Su? His orders rule the Empire."

"Not quite. Only the Warriors of the Empire."

"Great! We'd be safe if we hid among the Ama-Sones. They report only to Bes."

"Ummm. Doubt we'd be safe. The Ama-Sones would work us to death." He waited to see if the Fenman would catch his attempt at humor.

Ra-Lu answered:

"Better far a death while grinning

"Than a slower death for sinning.

"So give me, I say with lowered breath,

"Freedom, or the sweeter, faster death.

"Ah, yes! But in that case, I'd prefer to hide among the Virgins."

"Hey, good thought, Commander. Then you could have swift death for touching without permission or sweet death from touching with permission."

"Ra-Lu, at the slope of that rill beyond the river...watch the bushes. Do they creep?"

In the long silence that followed, Luflin felt a surge like a chilled hand gripping the inside of his stomach.

"Bushes creep? Yes, slowly, those bushes are moving to create a tightening circle around our men. But Commander, they show no partiality. They are also closing around the two of us."

"Pure joy joy!"

"And you without breastplate, shield in hand, or spear." Ra-Lu whistled shrilly and long. The twenty men down the slope were instantly in fighting stance, swords in hand, looking carefully about themselves.

Luflin saw a slight speed-up in the movement of the bushes on the hillside near them. He was aware that behind him clumps of tall grass scurried across the ground, ever tightening the circle around them.

"Blazing Westsun! What is it?" Luflin's voice felt like half-chewed grass blades in his throat, and he was a little ashamed at the fear he felt. "Wolves sit in a circle while they wait for the big male to lead the kill. But they don't hide in creeping bushes and clumps of grass."

"Crocks circle in our waters, luckily also, not in bushes." Ra-Lu glanced at Luflin with a strange light in his eyes. His lips were drawn thin, but he managed something intended to be a smile. "Commander Luflin, do you believe in ghosts?"

"Shadows of Energy. Yes. But not in moving bushes in bright Eastsun."

"Then, shall we run for it and rejoin our men?"

"No!" Luflin leaned down slowly and picked up his breastplate and shield. He tightened the straps on his buckler and hung the shield on the marching-hooks on his shoulder harness. "No, we shall walk slowly, talk loudly, and stand tall. There must be a thousand, so chin up. No sword in hand, right arm at ease. Now, with me, forward at Parade Pomp."

They moved together down the slope. Luflin steered them directly toward a clump of grass which he knew he had seen move. They walked across a soft, slightly spongy mound some two arms long and four spans across. It sloped gradually from the ground to the height of some two spans, then was almost flat for its length and breadth. Grass was apparently growing from each outer edge.

Apparently!

His mountain-trained eyes told him the grass was newly transplanted into a thin layer of dirt on the mound, dirt not quite the same as the land around it. He paused on the mound, walked its length, about three heavy strides, and then continued toward the river. He felt better for having taken some action, but knew he had not solved the unknown.

"I saw! You cool son of a..."

115

"Cool! That's why I'm trembling and sweating?"

"Oh?"

"That one at least was long enough, wide enough, and high enough to hide a Warrior in full armor, a buckler, a bow and arrows, and just maybe a short spear. And it sounded hollow to my steps."

"O.K. So how do we handle it?"

"Parade Pomp, Warriors in camp under drill conditions. O.K. with you Leader Ra-Lu? Got a better idea?"

"No. O.K., Commander Luflin, I'll back your play, smart or dumb." He called to the Warriors, "You Line of Twenty, you're not in Je-Su's compound. Hustle that grub. Make camp. Before the dark make ready for the arrival of Seven Lines of Twenty."

"Seven Lines of...?"

"Just a little thought I tossed in for luck."

"Good. Luck we may need if those mounds cover fighters and they attack in the night."

As they neared the camp, the two leaders marched along as Parade Pomp Commanders should. "If they charge in the night, shall we fight, flee, or spit in their faces?"

"Leader Ra-Lu, you may spit. I can't."

"Why?"

"Too scared. No spit!"

Both men laughed aloud and strode into the camp with more natural confidence. A sense of trust and comradeship showed in the very energy that radiated from them. It was not lost on the Warriors, who seemed to take some assurance from their leaders.

The late Eastsun seemed to draw out the aroma of the roasting venison. To Luflin it was stomach-warming and memory-inspiring. When, as Commander, he was handed a spit of warm meat, he thanked the Warriors and sat down near the fire to eat with them. He was pleased to see that, hungry through they were, all Warriors did not sit down at once. Nor were all sword hands greasy at one time from handling the cuts of meat. He was pleased, too, to see their eyes studying the terrain with careful casualness. They, too, felt the power of frightful eyes upon them.

Luflin studied the campsite for defense. He was not pleased. The river bank on both sides sloped gradually down to the gently purling water. The river was not deep.

116

And there was no drop in the river bank to delay a charge of man, beast, or thing. There was no rampart behind which a defense could be mustered. The space of the campsite was bare of trees, but was ringed by trees from which anyone, anything, could sally in sudden charge. There was no best spot where such a charge might be met and delayed, if not defeated.

It was not a strong place. It was a worrisome place. Most worrisome were the few tufts of grass and mounds of brush that were within the tree-line. Like regularly spaced stepping stones they led down to the river. The intervals were almost exact. Too regularly spaced!

He counted them and felt his face become suddenly gaunt and empty as his mind. Twenty-one. Twenty-one!

As casually as he could he walked to where Leader Ra-Lu sat, his knees drawn up, his head resting upon arms folded across his knees. Softly he said, "Leader Ra-Lu, the brush covered mounds within the tree-line of this camp...?

Without raising his head Ra-Lu said in a voice that showed he was both tired and puzzled. "Twenty-one, the Warriors say. No, these mounds did not move like those did that are across the river."

Luflin fought to keep his own voice from showing anxiety. Danger for himself, or in action, he could face. Unknown danger for twenty-one men under his command spun whirlpools of thought in his head.

He walked slowly through the camp, speaking to some of the Warriors casually. Their expressions told of the tensions in their minds. Their eyes overbrimmed with questions that glistened like tears of fear.

His mind ached with inactivity. Yet he knew he should not break camp and march exhausted men into a strange territory in the night. No, here they should make their stand. But either decision could be wrong.

He walked back to Ra-lu. "Leader, in a hundred breaths the Eastsun will turn the planet black. Do we stay or march?"

"Either way we may fight. Wisdom alone will tell us which is best."

"Wisdom comes from applying knowledge to a changing situation, does it not?"

117

"So we have been taught, Commander. But where do we get knowledge, the exact knowledge we need here, now?"

"We dig for it."

"Dig for it?" Ra-Lu's face came up and confusion was on the Fen-yellow of his taut cheeks. "You suspect that under twenty-one mounds..." He shivered. "It is an awful thought and a slim chance. But we should dig!"

"Right. We stay. Prepare the camp for night defense. Gather firewood for four huge fires. One on each of three sides of the camp and one at the river's edge. Fell trees and put them around the camp as barricades. Pile the brush high as arrow stops. Then dig."

"Dig, Commander?"

"Dig. Body holes. Redoubts. Put dirt and brush around each for protection. Dig exactly where I say. Two body holes here at the center. Then one in each of the twenty-one clumps. Do it!

Understanding replaced confusion on the Fenman's face. He called, "Warriors, we stay here. Bring wood for four big fires. One on each end and side of this space. Fell trees for ramparts. Then dig body holes and surround them with dirt and brush for arrow stops. Two here. One in each of those mounds where the turf is softer and easier to dig. Get set to sleep if possible and fight if must be. Do it. Now!"

Well before complete dark Luflin was beginning to let himself relax until Ra-Lu came toward him. In the half-light his yellow skin seemed brown and his eyes were big as if in surprise.

"Commander, come! Please!" He led the way briskly to a clump of Warriors who stepped aside as he approached and held a taper so he could see more clearly that which had put puzzlement on their faces and fear in their stance.

It was a Warrior in full Temple Guard dress. His helmet was on his head. His shield was on the carry hook. All his weapons including bow, arrows, sword, and spear were beside him. Beyond his dead body was a split shell that, had it been turned upside down, could have been a body-fitting grave dug into a half of a tree trunk. It appeared to have covered his body like a movable wooden room. Luflin reached for the wooden shell and easily lifted it with one hand.

"One half of a split log of a cotton-puff tree," Ra-Lu said. "A child can carry an entire tree ten spans around. Yet it is strong enough for spear shafts."

The shell was cut so that the wood extended flat for a full span all around the opening for the body. The body hole had room for weapons to be carried in loops carved in the wood. When the shell was turned over and laid flat, Luflin saw the grasses and brush tips imbedded in the soft wood. Many stalks of hollow cane were shoved through the shell so that air could circulate inside the shell even when it was close over a man's body. At the front, peepholes had been set with hollow-grass stems, and a breathing hole arranged for emergency air. Yet from the outside it looked like a low mound of grass with bushes growing in it.

"What is it?" The Warrior who spoke was trembling and the fear he showed was beginning to affect them all.

Luflin snapped, "Warrior! When you cannot grip your sword for protection you grit your teeth against fear and the unknown. Stand to, stand tall, all of you. Your mind is an instrument of war more cutting than your sword. But you must never let it cut yourself. Tell me, what is it, Warrior?"

The Warrior raised dark brown eyes filled with consternation and terror. Slowly, as their eyes locked in a struggle for the processes of mind, the terror lessened.

"It is..." He swallowed hard. "...It is a dug out half-trunk of a cotton-puff tree, Commander. You should know that!"

Luflin recognized the flippancy of a boy trying to show courage. But he felt the tension in the Warriors, for he could take it as impertinence to an officer and mete out punishment. Luflin saw the tension in the eyes of his men and in the way they stood. The realization came that they did not know him, his reactions or his abilities, yet he had authority over them, even to death if need be, for the smallest infraction. They were afraid. They were feeling guilty for feeling fear.

"I know!" He softened his voice. "I now know. Thank you, Warrior!" Some of the tension went out of the Warriors and he laughed aloud. "I've just been told by a Warrior almost as scared as I am."

They all laughed and relaxed still more.

Luflin sat back on his heels, keeping himself below the Warriors. His father had often told him that it was hard to fear that which is lower than you and smaller, unless it was a snake. "But, I'm damned if I know why this chunk of cotton-puff was carved in the first place. Anybody got an idea?"

He saw the looks that went from man to man. They were puzzled. One Warrior ventured, "Commander, could it be an emergency shelter from the Westsun?"

"Good thought. It would make a good one, wouldn't it? Then why have we never heard of it from the Cryer? Let's turn over every mound in this campsite. All twenty-one. But dig your spears under the edge of the mound and tip it over. Don't split it with a spear thrust?

"Do it. Now!" Ra-Lu commanded.

Within fifty breaths, the last of the twenty-one clumps had been upturned to expose twenty bodies of the Temple Guard in full dress with all weapons. Closer examination showed that each had been garroted with long-strand hemp. The blue faces, the swollen and protruding tongues, and the looks of horror and surprise did little to settle the fears of the Warriors.

"Why? Who?" The questions beat in Luflin's mind as he walked from one death-tortured, grotesque body to another. Slowly, anger rose in his being so hot that it overcame the chill of fear.

The Warriors huddled near each other, as if the heat of body contact could replace the cold horror in their minds.

"Now, Commander, what do you suggest?" Ra-Lu stood with the frightened Warriors close behind him.

"About what?" Luflin was stalling for time to let his benumbed mind bring reason into his thoughts.

"About these twenty dead Temple Warriors!"

Luflin faced the angry men. He knew that discipline was clawed thin by fear. If his answer was wrong it could turn them into a mob, senseless with fear, and bent on destroying him. He didn't blame them. But destroying him would not solve their real problem.

"Are you fearful about these twenty dead bodies?"

120

He took the chorus of disgusted grunts to mean yes.

"I'm not."

The wall of anger and suspicion hit him like an avalanche of high-mountain snow, and surrounded him with cold, unspoken questions that hung on droplets of confusion.

"Why not?" The question was flung with the force of a well-fletched arrow.

"These bodies are not yet stiff. They have not been dead half an Eastsun. Whoever killed them must have done it less than a thousand breaths before we came over the crest of Loba Pass, and must still be in Loba River Valley."

Luflin had been letting his mouth do his thinking and was roused within himself by the sudden intake of twenty incredulous breaths. He had not thought out a plan of action, but let his mind go free and search for words to express its running.

"Have you Warriors let yourselves be so filled with anger over things of the past that you have not paid adequate attention to things of the present that might possibly save your lives?"

"By God-e! We're sentenced because of you. We are surrounded because of you. The dark is on us because of you. Why should we trust you?"

Luflin felt his Warrior's mind urging him to answer in threatening anger, to declare his innocence, to justify himself. He set his will against it and felt his face turn into a self-satisfied smile.

"Two reasons. You know I'm not really to blame. But more important, I'm the only sensible chance you have and only I have the plan to save you."

"What plan?" The question sounded so loud in his own head that he failed to hear it from twenty voices.

What plan indeed? His conscious mind boggled at the circumstance and he knew he must soon have a plan in his head or a spear in his belly.

"You may not have guts enough to make it work." After several breaths he continued. "It may, but it may not work to save you from the Warrior's hanging of Je-Su." He let them mull the ideas for a while and then added. "And some would say it will lead to sin and treason."

"Try us," was the challenge.

"In a breath or two. But first, the most specific thing against it is..." He paused and looked hard at each of the Warriors. "...is the twenty-first body."

"The twenty-first body?"

"The twenty-first body. The body of a leader or a commander, one body that must have been planned for and is not here. That is the one body that could upset our plan and bring us to the death we are trying to miss."

"How?" He heard the question this time, for a plan, thank the God-e, was beginning to form in his mind. It was indefinite, incomplete, sketchy, had holes in it, was foolish, but it might be better than a spear thrust. At least, he thought, for a little while.

"First, is anyone here willing to commit treason against the Empire? Wait, treason as Je-Su, Lor'd One of War defines it. Which is not believing in him as the Only Son of the Great God-e?"

"Do you take us for posanga zombies? None of us believe in Je-Su," Ra-Lu snapped, and twenty heads nodded agreement.

"Good. My plan is this. You change clothes and arms with the Temple Guards. Change everything. Keep nothing. Nothing, not even personal things by which you could ever be known at later times. Then we go on into the hills toward the High Atal Mountains. But you go as the beloved Temple Guards of Bes, not the hated Warriors of Je-Su. As Temple Guards we can stop at any small Temple Compound for shelter. And take supplies from them for our onward marches."

The Cryer would tell the Empire!" Ra-Lu grunted, "And the second temple's guard would kill us right then."

"Maybe. But do you think they'd not tell the Cryer if we made the Commander of the Temple Guard believe we were hurrying after rebels and must move in secrecy?"

"Maybe not for a while, at least. But, I'm against it, almost as much as I'm against going straight back and dying at Je-Su's orders."

"It is a chancy and tough choice Warriors. All must make it or none of us can safely do so. We must swear secrecy forever, or until I give permission to speak. My thought is this, we will get to the High Atals and hide among my tribe for about three Westsuns. We will then come back down to the plains of E-Den and make a long search, circling from temple to temple around the Empire. Finally we will go back to the Temple of Po-Si-Don."

"Crazy," a Warrior cried.

"Yes, Warrior. Crazy...or bold. Or both."

"The Temple Guard at Po-Si-Don will know their own.

"I hope so. For we will tell Lor'd Bes *in person* what we have done and throw ourselves on his understanding and mercy. We will pray the God-e that Bes is more understanding and merciful than Je-Su."

"It is a lousy plan," Ra-Lu said. "One lousy plan."

"Got a bett'r 'n', Ra-Lu?" a big Warrior asked.

"No, damn it!" Ra-Lu was silent for twenty breaths. "No. So do you want to go for this one lousy plan?"

There was a long, strained silence. At last the big Warrior stood up from his squatting position. "Don' wanna go for th' lousy plan, but gotta. There's a big Guard over there, 'bout my size."

The Warriors, men of action, stood, showing they were ready and planned to change uniforms and equipment.

"Wait. Sit down again," Luflin commanded. "I have a feeling, an intuition, call it a hunch. The ones who strangled these Temple Guards must have been very many and very strong, and struck with complete surprise. The Temple Guards are the very best in the Empire. Their murderers must yet be in this valley. They may even be in those mounds that creep. If so, they must not see what we do."

Once again anger, confusion, and fear settled over the Warriors and threatened him like arrows drawn to the reach of the bowstring.

Ra-Lu voiced it. "How can we change into those uniforms without someone seeing us? How can we make sure that no one sees the change?"

"Blind those who can see into our camp."

"Sure." Ra-lu's hand swept toward the mounds as if they were all around. His voice showed his anger and disgust. "Sure. While I play catch with the Westsun."

"No, Leader. While we play catch with firebrands."

"With firebrands?" The question rasped from twenty throats.

"If men are in those mounds—which we do not know, but strongly believe—how many could see us changing clothes, personal things and arms with...?" His hands indicated the dead, and the shiver though his body made clear what he felt.

"Beyond these trees, probably no one could see us. Beyond the river on the slope close enough to see what we're doing...I count twenty-eight."

"About three for each of ten volunteers."

"To do what?"

"Cross the river with firebrands...naked and without weapons...and set fire to the end of the grass clumps facing us and see that they burn. We must go to the furthermost one first and..."

"That puts a possible enemy between the volunteers and the river, and the river between them and help."

"Right, Leader. That's why I am asking for nine volunteers...and our weapons right on the river's edge."

"You said ten volunteers just now, then nine."

"Right, Leader. Nine and me."

"You? Why should a Commander go? You give the orders and we..."

"O.K. I give this order. Only nine may volunteer and I will go with them." He half rose and looked down into the solemn eyes of the Warriors. Some small change had occurred. The arrows of their eyes seemed no longer drawn to the fletching. "Thoth, they say, never gives an order, and never asks anyone to do what he cannot and will not do. I'd like to be like Thoth. Besides, I've never crossed a river, climbed a slope for fifty arms, ran down again while setting fire to at least three mounds, made sure they were burning and then got back across the Loba River."

"Don't you trust me to lead my own men?"

"I'm not going to lead your men. Nobody can lead them. I'm going to help them. If you want to volunteer, you may. Before we go we'll select the mounds each of us is to burn, and each will get back as soon as his job is done. And Fenman, your set jaw and the cast of your skin tells me that anyone can trust you for anything."

"So?" Ra-Lu rose to a half crouch, an instinctive position of attack.

Luflin studied him gravely and read in his stance an inward anger. Yet, he, Luflin, had to go and make certain that every mound was burned. "Trust you, Fenman? I'm trusting you with more than my life. I'm trusting you with my naked ass. I love my..." He stopped mid-sentence.

For ten counts no one breathed or moved. Then with a great explosion of breath, Ra-Lu and the Warriors all laughed. With that breaking of tensions, Luflin felt he had become the Commander in fact, not in name only. Cautiously he thought, "Now if I can just keep it, I may live out this adventure."

Aloud he said, "Volunteers only, let's go and choose our targets." As he stood up so did all the Warriors. He stepped away, all followed.. "Are you nuts? It may get real dirty over there."

"Au, 'a soKay. We need a bath anyway," a Warrior said in a mock grumble.

"SoKay," Luflin mimicked with a smile. "You nine pick yourself." He busied himself with cutting ten long oak limbs that could be set strongly aflame at one end to serve as torches.

The Warriors, with the hassle and strong words usual in such things decided which nine were to accompany him. It took much more time than it would have if he had appointed them. But he knew they'd done a job more satisfactory to them than any leader could have done. They could not now escape the extra surge of elation that always came to him when he felt he had used self-determination.

Luflin dropped his clothes behind the line of brush on the river bank. Then he picked his way through the protecting brush, and deposited his sword, spear, shield, bow, and arrows near the water's edge. He then went back to catch the firebrand tossed across the brush to him. When the others were ready, he moved cautiously into the river. He felt the cold water as it rose swiftly up to his armpits. Then the bottom leveled, and he walked on tricky, rolling, small stones and intermittent bands of sand.

The current was strong, but not strong enough to sweep him from his feet. The bottom was not filled with suddenly deeper holes that would slow them down in case they needed to make a swift retreat. For this he thanked the God-e.

On the far bank they fanned out along the river, and climbed a gradual rise until they were at the last mound at the top of the slope. At Luflin's signal the Warriors applied their firebrands to the grass and brush of the end of each mound. As soon as the flame took, they hurried to the next mound and set it afire. They set fire to each clump of grass or bushes until they reached the shoreline. Luflin came last, rechecking every blaze, and rekindling those that were not burning brightly enough.

When they were all at the water's edge, on impulse rather than by pre-planning, he thrust the butt of his fire-brand into the mud. The other Warriors did so until there was a line of torches at the water. They plunged into the cold river and hurried to the shore.

As he stooped to take up his shield, a scream tore at his ears. It was loud. It was long. Yet, it was not a scream of pain as he might have expected. He searched his mind for a word to describe it. Though his mind rebelled at the thought, it was a scream of *joy*!

Yes, joy. Joy mixed with pain. But not defiled by anger.

He snatched up his shield and spear and whirled. A figure in white! No, the entire figure was white. The face was the color of paste made of ground wheat. The hair was long and white as river sand. The mouth was open wide but couldn't hide a nose that was gracefully formed.

The eyebrows seemed made of sand. The eyes. Oh, God-e. The eyes were wide open, fixed and staring and were a brown faded almost to white.

The tattered cloth that floated around the hurtling figure had once been white. It was not a cloak. It was nothing but a strip of cloth some four arms long and six spans wide with a head-slit at the center. It flew aside with each long step, to reveal a thin, more, an emaciated, figure. Not as tall as Luflin, but tall. The shins were wrinkled and flabby, like one just up from a long sick-bed, and dull as the white of a long-dead fish's belly.

In its left, claw-like hand it brandished a club two arms long and three times the heft of a spear shaft. It brandished the club expertly, like the deadly weapon it could be in practiced hands, and charged on as if to kill.

As it came into the line of firebrands, it shattered two of them with a single vicious swing of the club.

As the white figure raced past the line of firebrands its eyes were blank, fixed, and staring. But the face was smiling. Smiling! It raced smiling into the water, did not flinch at the cold water, and strode, almost as if the bottom were dry land, through the river.

As it neared the shore, the screaming dropped to a low chant, a monotonous repetition of words that seemed to have no connection with the body or the blazed eyes and the fixed smile.

"Halt!" Luflin commanded.

The wraith came steadily onward. It raised the club to attack height. As it weaved for advantage in attack, Luflin could clearly hear the words of the chant.

"You have joy in serving Je-Su, your Lor'd One,

"You will strangle these soldiers and nothing can stop you.

"Not even death.

"For you will have the joy of dying for Lor'd Je-Su.

"Only Begotten Son of the Supreme God-e.

"For Je-Su, do or die in joy, joy, joy, joy."

On shore it paused at seeing a line of spears blocking its path. With the club it shattered the spear-shaft of the Big Warrior then lunged toward the Warrior, arms outstretched, gnarled hands grasping.

The Warriors on each side thrust it through with spears. But it did not flinch or cease chanting or charging. It seized the Big Warrior, shield and all, and tossed him over its head. The huge frame soared five arms through the air and splashed down into the river.

Luflin stood in the path of the charging apparition in white. He thrust his own spear through the chest and held against it with all his weight. But the figure continued to churn forward, three spears and a Commander hanging from its chest. The eyes were vacant, fixed staring.

The smiling lips repeated over and over again: "You have joy in serving." It coughed, but continued, "You will strangle...nothing will stop you, not even death...dying for Je-Su...only Begotten Son...do...die in joy, joy..."

The white cloth was now crimson across the chest. The voice began to weaken. But the body moved relentlessly forward, though mortally wounded, seemingly held up by the power of mind supported on the magic of words repeated over and over.

The Big Warrior charged out of the river. His anger was obvious in the viciousness of the swing of his shield against the back of its head. It stumbled slightly, righted itself, and without changing expression or missing the rhythm of its chant, continued more weakly, "You have joy...nothing will stop...dying for Je-Su...only Son...do...or die...joy, joy, joy."

Again the Big Warrior struck with his shield against the unprotected head. It stumbled and sagged to its knees. Its voice was weaker, yet the smile grew bigger and its eyes focused slowly from Warrior to Warrior.

"Thank you," it said clearly. "Thank you. You help me to die for Je-Su in joy, joy, joy...j..."

It twisted on its side, then slowly turned on its back, and stared directly at Luflin with eyes alive with joy and a smile—a ghastly smile on its face

Its body crumpled as if all strength went out of all its muscles at the same time, as if life went out of the body in a spurt. But the finger of its right hand flicked to point at Luflin, and though the lips did not move he distinctly heard, "Die for...joy...thank...you."

The light went from its eyes, and it sank lifeless, three spears thrust through its body, and a giant Warrior's shield held ready for a third blow strong enough to kill any normal man.

The nine Warriors and Luflin stood looking upon it with expressions mixed between hatred and pity. Incredulous eyes seemed almost to fill with tears. Luflin felt the moisture forming in his eyes and his fear gave way to an inner anguish, a silent cry of spirit that any human being could be so estranged from nature and self-preservation as to behave as it had. The face, now relaxed in death, returned the eyes to a normal size, and the mouth settled into a gentle curve of well-formed lips.

The lips were full, although now bloodless. The face took on a tenderness, a gentleness, a strange sort of beauty. In death it found a peace it had coveted and not found in life.

The Warriors looking down upon the crumpled figure, sucked in air as if it was hard to swallow physically what their minds tried to digest. As to a hero, their swords came up and then down, smartly, in a salute of respect to one who had died bravely. Luflin felt a pressure catch in his throat, as if he had eaten sour meat.

The Big Warrior spoke the thought that had been forming in all minds. "Good God-e! He can't be older than a hun'red fifty Westsuns. A chil'. We have killed a chil'!"

"If a child, a wild and dangerous child," Luflin said quickly. "A child who tried to kill us and may have killed the Temple Guards."

"Not alone, he didn't. Two hundred like him, maybe."

"Maybe. Maybe we'll never know."

"So, what you gonna do?" The Big Warrior lowered his shield with a look of distaste.

Luflin did not hurry to answer. With the black of the Eastsun settling around them like arms filled with hurt, mystery mounted upon mystery. Deaths piled up like on a battlefield. He felt sick and sweating even with the wind-of-the-dark on his wet and naked skin. Confusion flooded over him like rays of the Westsun, hot and uncomfortable.

"First,..." He tried again. "First, I'm gonna puke."

The words tumbled out of him from some energy source beyond his control. He was inwardly startled when he heard them, afraid the Warriors would take it for weakness. For several breaths they looked at him in a strange fascination, as if they saw someone they had never seen before. The subtle sneers he expected did not show on their faces. He waited. He saw the looks that passed between the Warriors, then almost as one they said:

"We'll help you."

They turned aside, each to hide his own weakness, and retched. Each wept gently. Luflin was a Warrior, trained to fight and kill. But not to fight children not yet in training as a Warrior. Not to kill one who could not have known what he was doing, or why. What great things had gone wrong, he wondered, to change the Pleasant Planet to a place of conflict and doubt?

Luflin forced himself to go back and look carefully at the strangely handsome youth who lay dead upon the river bank, and his heart lay heavy inside.

"Why"? he kept shouting at himself in his mind. "Why"?

He was roused from his thoughts by the wondering tones of the words of the Big Warrior. "Ha'f my heft. Ha'f my heft, yet with stren'th 'nough t' throw me over his head an' five body len'ths 'nto th' river. Where'd he get such stren'th?"

"I don't know. But if there is one like he was under each mound in this valley we are deep in danger. More important, the Empire may be in deep trouble."

"So much stren'th, so hard to kill," the Big Warrior mused. "Throw over 's head the son of 'n Ama-Sone 'n' not even pause."

Gingerly, with some kind of strange awe and respect, they examined the body carefully but found no clues of any kind to help their understanding. They then took the body inside the defense perimeter and placed it under an empty mound. Then in the darkness when the fires had died out, all but Luflin changed into the uniforms of the Temple Guards and put their own clothes on the dead Guards. They exchanged all personal items, and all weapons.

"Wonder which'un was A-Sar-U," Luflin said as they assembled again and began to build up the fires.

"He ain't here," the Big Warrior said.

"What?" Luflin jerked erect. "I saw him marched away with the Temple Guard inside a box formed by a Line of Twenty."

"So did we," the Warriors said.

"But one mound was empty until we put the raging child into it," Ra-Lu began.

"Is A-Sar-U...?

"He ain't here," the Big Warrior was positive. "He's th' only Warrior Cadet as big an' strong as me. He jus' ain't here."

"Then we have a big, big decision to make, and fast. Our decision may influence the Empire."

"The likes of us influence the 'mpire? Ha!"

"Yes. Let's assume A-Sar-U escaped with his life and may return to the Temple of Po-Si-Don to carry on with the Ordeal of Virgin Birth. If he is dead...out there somewhere, something very important for us has been changed. We can lose ourselves in the Temple Compounds, as we planned, for many Westsuns. No one will know or care. But, if A-Sar-U is alive out there somewhere, we may change the destiny of the Empire if we help to find him."

They were all silent for a long time. Ra-Lu cleared his throat and the sound made Luflin jump.

"You are saying, we might go free, get away, save our lives. Or what?"

"Or, we might return to the Temple of Po-Si-Don with our important information and greatly serve the Empire."

"Yeah? How?"

"If we can get to Lor'd Bes and tell our story..."

"Big *if*, Commander."

"Big *if*, Leader."

"Damn," the Big Warrior exploded. "Why'd th' God-e make decidin' so hard?"

"What decisions, Big Warrior?"

"Whether t' start our dark run back t' Po-Si-Don now, 'r res' a hun'r'd breaths b'for' we start."

"You want to go back, knowing we all..."

"I wanna go back f'r I b'lieve that provin' th' Virgin Birth may bring A-Sar-U 'nto power 'an' change th' government 'f our Empire. It may giv' all 'f us greater freed'm. Au, Whirling Westsun, ain't it jest th' bes' thing t' do f'r ever'body?"

In the long silence each Warrior squirmed his feet on the ground to match the ideas whirling in his head. The Big Warrior spoke again, softly, "'Cides, A-Sar-U 's a big guy lik' me. He don't seem smart, but he is. An' people just love him. Not b'cause he's bright, but b'cause he loves back. Loves ever'body back, ev'n a nobody lik' a nameless son of a' Ama-Sone. 'Most nobody loves a hulk lik' me. He does 'n' I love him back. For him I go now to Po-Si-Don. I go back now."

He moved a pace before Ra-Lu snapped in a harsh, military tone. "Without permission from your Leader? That's desertion punishable by hanging."

"So hang me right aft'r Je-Su gits through."

131

"What about your honor? And dishonor to your tribe, your people?"

"Leader, a son 'f a Ama-Sone has no honor. He has no tribe to dishonor. No fam'ly t' love 'r t' love him. On'y the Empire. And...and sometimes someone like A-Sar-U."

"What about Thoth? He is the Great God-e. He does much for the Empire. People love him."

"Thoth 's great. He'll teach A-Sar-U t' be greater. Greater f'r some special...uh...cause."

"How do you know?"

"Inside me som'wher' somethin' knows."

"Are you an untrained seer?"

"Seer? I don' know what 'seer' means. But I know somethin' 'nside me knows what I know."

Ra-Lu turned a face toward Luflin which had on it the look of amused compassion. "Commander, what do you think?"

"Leader, I think you want to help the Big Warrior. So do all the others." He looked from Warrior to Warrior and all heads nodded yes. "So I think it would not be wise to do so..." he paused and saw the looks of disappointment on the faces of the Warriors, "...until the fires are out and our eyes have become adjusted to the needs of a dark run."

After the first few hundred breaths, while they crept single file to the top of Loba Ridge—with guards out for protection from surprise attack—it was downhill. Luflin set a pace he thought they could hold for the distance, with a hundred-breath rest once in a while. But he knew he must get the detachment inside the Temple Compound and out of sight before first light, or risk being recognized by Je-Su's Warriors.

Luflin was astonished, and pleased, very pleased, that a tired Line of Twenty could run so fast and so in harmony. He felt that he had acquired wings upon his feet. Then he realized that the wings were upon his mind. That heavy and angry thoughts, useless and energy-draining, no longer weighed upon his legs. That hope was needful to make men work for a purpose.

Well before fourth watch they raced into the compound of the Temple Guard. They were received on the threat of spear tips.

132

"Halt!" The command came from the quavering voice of a youngster. "Who comes? What do you want?"

Panting, Luflin's voice did not sound strong as he said. "To see Lor'd Bes on urgent business of the Empire."

He heard whispers and ". . . can't disturb the Lor'd One."

"Who does he think he is?"

"Tell him to wait until after first light and come back."

Luflin felt the anger run through his body and his voice boomed out with authority. "You, Guards, take us to Lor'd Bes. Do it now."

"Why?"

"Because business of the Empire is not for you to question. Do it!"

There were more whispers and then, "Yield up your arms."

"Line of Twenty, make ready to yield up your arms into their gizzards if they do not take us to Bes within twenty breaths."

"Wait..."

"Business of the Empire cannot wait. Take us. Do it. Now!"

"Lor'd Bes sleeps."

"But not dangers to the Empire. Wake him and take us to him. Do it now."

"Commander, I have taken ten breaths. Shall we draw."

"Leader, give five breaths more."

"We'll take you into the assembly hall. Come."

"Good. Now rouse your full guard on watch and surround the assembly hall. Then allow only Lor'd Bes to approach unless he commands otherwise."

"Why?"

"Because you do not know us and Lor'd Bes would expect you to take every precaution."

Luflin followed the moving shadow in the dark, and the Line of Twenty followed him. Within ten breaths they were in the dark assembly hall and groped their way to line up defensively against the walls. Luflin stayed nearest the doorway. His ears were sensitive enough to hear the tense breathing of the Warriors but not sharp enough to

133

hear Bes as he entered. He felt him, like a sudden shaft of Eastsun, warm and moving in the blackness.

"Lor'd Bes?"

"I am."

"Shall we first surrender to you our weapons?"

"How many are there of you?"

"A Leader with a Line of Twenty, under a Commander."

"So few may keep their weapons. You are no threat to me."

Luflin almost smiled. It was no boast, just a simple statement of confidence in combat skill.

"We know, Lor'd One. We are tired, hungry, and confused. We are under sentence of death from Je-Su, and in uniforms of your Temple Guard, and we come because we bear strange knowledge. But we are no threat to you. It is our hope to bring you important information, but not to be seen or reported to Je-Su."

"Do you negotiate to save your lives?"

"Lor'd One. We come with confused knowledge that may serve the Empire. It is in regard to A-Sar-U."

After a long silence Bes spoke softly. "I shall call in lights. Turn your faces to the walls where you stand until the servers have gone."

When the lights were in and Luflin turned again, he saw that Bes stood unarmed by the door, a relaxed, almost pleasant smile on his big face.

"Lor'd Bes, I am Luflin, Commander. This is Ra-Lu, Leader of this Line of Twenty from the Warriors' Compound."

Bes nodded. Encouraged, although each breath seemed to lodge high in his chest, Luflin recounted his secret orders to follow after, find, and kill A-Sar-U, or take him back to what he believed would have been certain murder. How the entire line had been condemned to ignoble death because Thoth had taken away his prisoner. The run over Loba Ridge in pursuit of the Temple Guard and A-Sar-U. The mounds, and the encounter with the bodies under the mounds. The incredible charge and mantra of the sweet youth of great strength and his willingness, nay, eagerness to die for Je-Su. Their confusion and their decision to return to and throw themselves upon the mercy of Lor'd Bes because A-Sar-U might need help. That to them,

A-Sar-U and the Virgin Birth Test seemed more important to the Empire than their lives prolonged a few Westsuns.

Bes listened impassively, nodding at times when Luflin hesitated over-long in the telling because of nervousness. When the story was done, he looked at the Big Warrior with compassion.

"Big Warrior, I think you and I are blessed in our individuality. Being different means we must be better, and..." His tone was serious-bantering when he continued.

"An' what, Lor'd One?"

"...and we must pity all those people who are not normal like us."

"Sir?"

"They only *think* they are perfect. We know we are."

Luflin laughed as did the others. But he saw the Big Warrior begin to stand tall. Pride in himself started to work its magic and remove doubts from his mind. Luflin mused that conforming to the norm of any society could be self-destroying to some individuals. This, he resolved, he would remember and use.

His preoccupation was broken by the voice of Bes issuing requests from the entrance-way to someone in the dark outside.

"Please. Swiftly bring food, sleeping mats, bath water for twenty-one. Go and ask Som, Lor'd One of Science, and also the Commander of the Temple Guard of Twenty Lines of Twenty—whoever may be on duty—to please attend us here immediately.

"Yes, Lor'd One." The military voice came from the dark outside.

"Oh, Commander Tao. Three things more. How grows your Chosen Woman?"

"Big, Lor'd One."

"Will she be ready by the next Westsun?"

"Let's hope so. Her belly is big enough already for a lion to come out."

"My regards. And attend her well. Shift duty if need be."

"Thank you, Lor'd Bes." Luflin heard the pride and... yes, love...in the unseen Commander's voice. He could see that the Commander was bound to Lor'd Bes as an indi-

135

vidual as well as part of a command. He resolved to re-member that and use it.

"Commander. Please. Also go personally to the apart-ment of Supreme Commander Lor'd Thoth. Inquire quietly. Find him, wherever he is or send to him. If he is awake, ask to see him personally on my spoken pass. There, ask him if he would come quietly here, unattended except by you. Would you do that for me, please?"

Luflin heard the short answer and knew from the tone of the voice that the commander would have charged a Line of Twenty bare-handed for Bes. Such respect and honor...

His mind floundered in mid-thought. Was it respect and honor that caused the charging youth to fling himself with incredible strength at the ten of them on the river-bank? Was that what caused him to seem to seek to die for a cause...some cause...and to die with joy and thank-fulness to those who, tragically unwitting of the limits of the danger, had met him with maximum, killing force?

Luflin found that his thought ran tiredly. He was glad when they were told to go into the attached room and bathe. When they came out, clothed in soft linen sleeping clothes, great bowls of foods, fruits, and cakes waited for them.

Before they could settle down, Lor'd Som and the Com-mander of Twenty Lines of Twenty came in with speed and flourish. Shortly there came silently through the entrance-way a tall, hooded figure in a common brown robe. But Luflin felt the room begin to vibrate with energy as if the Eastsun sent its heat through the thick stone walls. Before he heard the resonant voice, he knew it was Thoth. Thoth, who moved like a silent God-e. He sat beside Luflin.

"Commander, may I join in your food?"

"We are honored by your presence, Lor'd Thoth. We thank you for the food since the Empire is yours."

"Ours, Commander. Ours. I am chief custodian, that is all."

As they ate, Bes repeated their story word for word, stopping only occasionally to check on an obscure fact or make clear a feeling. When he had finished Thoth spoke softly. "Warriors, I'm sorry that my trick of disarming your Commander caused you all to be sentenced to death. I, like you, think it is unjust. You may think that Bes and I can right now change or remove that threat. By rule and custom in our Empire—and you will admit that it usually runs quite well—we cannot change the Rule of a Commander except by open trial.

"This above all else you do not want. Ever. This above all Lor'd Bes and I do not want *at this time*. There are things afoot in our Glorious Empire that strain belief, and demand our immediate and complete attention. These things can only be solved if all the peoples are at peace with each other. Your trial would put tribe against tribe. You understand?"

Thoth thought for a while and then said. "I must, for the good of the Empire, delay your trial. Would you be willing to go back in secrecy to the camp on the Loba River and carry out your plan to find and help A-Sar-U, or to get lost in the far country? And stay lost for many Westsuns?"

The feeling among the Warriors was heavy, Luflin knew. They had not been assured of immediate release from their sentence of death.

"If Je-Su's Warriors see and recognize us...?"

"Were his orders to you to follow, find, and capture or kill A-Sar-U?"

"Yes."

"Then, follow his orders. He did not say how long or where or in what uniform you should look for him, did he?"

"No."

"Then, Commander Luflin," Thoth's voice was firm and sure, though a slight smile played impishly around the corners of his mouth, "by law you may follow his orders all your life until you capture or kill A-Sar-U. I quote: 'The Empire supports any Commander who follows the order of a higher Commander in his assignment, and no other Commander shall have authority to change his orders except that same higher Commander, in person.' "

"You mean, no Commander can make us..."

"He means," the Big Warrior said and laughed, "you c'n order us t' go on looking until Je-Su gives you orders 'n person t' stop. Not even Set can make you stop."

Luflin turned to the Line of Twenty. "Leader Ra-Lu, Warriors. You may stay or go. It will be rugged."

"You can order us. You have the power."

"I have the power to have you killed if you do not follow my orders in defense of the Empire. Leader Ra-Lu has the power to refuse me the right to order you to risk your life without option. Only you have the power to commit your life for the Empire."

One by one the Warriors nodded assent. "We'll go," Luflin said to Thoth.

Thoth nodded. He seemed lost in the depths of his thoughts as his eyes measured Big Warrior. "Big Warrior, are you as big as A-Sar-U?"

"Why, yessir, mos' nigh."

"Would you be willing to wear his uniform?"

"It'd be a' hon'r."

"If Lor'd Bes likes the idea, he will arrange all details?"

Bes nodded agreement.

Thoth rose. "Good! Go find A-Sar-U. Search for him quietly throughout the land. Once in a while, appear at different temples, for moments only, in his uniform. Come again only when the Cryer and the Drum announce the final Trial. Or the success or failure of it. We hope it will proclaim that there is to be a Virgin Birth. Then return here, directly and secretly, and report to Lor'd Bes."

Thoth nodded to Bes and understanding seemed to pass between them, Luflin thought.

Then Thoth was gone as silently as he had come.

14

Words of Mystery, II

Thoth returned and the training began.

A-Sar-U found himself caught up in a delight almost too great to bear. Thoth turned his full attention upon him. The love and magnetism which held crowds attentive was almost overwhelming when focused single-mindedly upon one person. It was also stimulating. Every nerve and muscle in his body was alert to the drive of his mind and will. A-Sar-U did not need this admonition:

"A-Sar-U, you must strive to master all I can teach you in a very few Eastsuns. There will be little rest, little food, no real sleep. We will work until we pass out from fatigue. Then we will work on in lethargy.

"Here are some basic principles by which you turn your flesh-self into a Radiant Being almost identical with Divinity.

"First, the Radiant Being must be created in your body. Then it must be loosed from the bindings of your flesh. It must be freed from your body's last grasping hold. Then you must have the will and knowledge necessary to send it into space and time as your other body, as your obedient but Divine Self.

"It must perform tasks you set for it with full memory. Memory of what it is to do. Then memory of what it has done.

"It will then be returned to your body. There only, as yet, it may gain that energy which gives it life. Your great task in the future will be to free it permanently from your flesh, to give it independent, everlasting life. But more of that when you fully understand the words you have just memorized.

"For now, your Radiant Body will always return to your body. At all times you will be able to see it. It will be attached to you through an energy cord, glistening, grey-

139

blue-white. It is much like a baby's belly-cord that attaches it to its mother at birth. We cut that cord to give the child independent life. If we cut the cord to the Radiant Body, both it and the physical body die. At least as yet. Of this more later. Much more.

"This cord attaches through the back of your head. It can be felt inside your head in a special area of your brain. It is a source of constant energy needed for life: for physical life and also for spiritual life.

"Energy! All depends on energy. You have enough energy of a special kind in your body for the present."

Thoth thought deeply, seemed to change his mind. "Something else waits. Something else that I assure you will demand more energy, more of you.

"It will be important to all people of the Empire upon the Pleasant Planet. You are their only hope.

"Enough of that now. I will not make it clear as yet. You must not wonder about it. Your mind, will, concentration, and energy must be on this one task first.

"In order to become part of the infinitely small, you must yourself become infinite and also small. This is another puzzlement to you?

"Let me explain it this way. Think of yourself at this moment as being God. You are God-e! You have grown through space. Now, you must go backward. You must go backward in size through all the material levels until you become the clod.

"Then you must go further back until you are the grain of sand. Then until you are the smallest particle, the unit within the grain. For there is endless energy or power in that attachment of each unit with the grain. You must be able to release that power. You cannot do so unless you can become small enough to enter the grain of sand.

"You must be able to travel through time. Therefore you must be able to travel through time by becoming time.

"Sound strange? Yes, it is strange. But this you must do. You must reach that stage where you command time to your will.

"Badly said! Time must not ever be your enemy. Time must always be your friend. When you make time your friend you will be able to eject your Spiritual, Radiant Body from the grains of your flesh.

140

"You wonder at the words. Spiritual, Radiant Body. It is a being like you. It must be grown within your flesh body, within the grains of your flesh, by the use of the Divine Breath.

"Divine Breath! Yes. And of course your Divine Mind and Divine Will. By a technique I will teach you, you grow your Divine Radiant Body within your flesh.

"By breath, will, energy, and luck you become the kin of the clod and then project yourself to begin the borning of God-e.

"Hear me well. You must become the simplest, lowest, most primal energy before you can start the birth of the most complex, highest, and most divine.

"Strange! Yes. A paradox? Yes. Impossible you think. Almost. Almost impossible. Impossible to most people and to all who do not have the confidence of faith in themselves and their teachers. But you can do it. Yes. Will you do it? Yes. Yes or die or be disgraced.

"How will you do it? First, you must learn how to relax every muscle in your body and still every thought.

"It is not easy. You must memorize the feeling of muscles when they are doing only what nature and land-pull compel them to do to hold you in whatever position you find yourself. When you know how, you can relax in motion to some degree. You can relax while standing by getting balance in your stance.

"Stance. You can hold the weight of your body on a platform made of your feet, legs, hips. Your body is then held without unnecessary tension in the muscles. This is possible if you have the right stance and the right posture. Stance is your platform. Posture is how you hold your relaxed body upon that platform.

"Posture! Chest lifted and arched. Shoulders back and down. Spine erect, neck extended, gently extended. All done on muscles meant by nature to hold the weight of your body against land-pull.

"Breathing. You do not breath into or move your chest. It is raised as high as it can be. It does not rise and sink when you breathe. Never. Never. Never.

"Now we will practice stance, posture, and breathing. We will practice them standing, sitting, lying on face, on back. You will stay in posture even when you are asleep.

You will breathe correctly even when you are not conscious of breathing at all. You will breathe correctly at all times.

"Come! Enough talk. To work."

A-Sar-U approached the exercises with a near smile. He was, he thought, a trained Warrior. He was used to running, jumping, fighting. What could the exercises do to fatigue him?

Swiftly he found out. He was sent time and time again to the wall to get stance and posture. His shoulders ached from being brought back and down at the same time. His ribs hurt from holding his chest up and out of the way of his breathing. In five hundred breaths he was exhausted.

Thoth kept after him. He did everything he asked A-Sar-U to do. Did it three or four times. When A-Sar-U felt he would drop, Thoth was fresh and smiling, and still doing three exercises to his one.

"With practice it gets easier. Never really easy, but easier," Thoth assured him.

When at last he had learned to move quickly into stance, and to hold himself in a relaxed posture the breathing exercises began. Despite Thoth's warning, A-Sar-U was confident his Warrior's skills had taught him how to breathe. In six breaths, although Thoth had warned him to stop at three, he was dizzy and his head was swimming wildly.

"Stop!" Thoth commanded. "Your eyes are glazed. Rest a few breaths."

Rest! It sounded wonderful to A-Sar-U. Thoth's idea of rest was to guide him to the wall by a mighty hand. He rested from breathing while struggling again to get relaxation in a posture that was satisfactory to Thoth only when it seemed impossibly hard to A-Sar-U.

To rest from that fatigue, he went back again to breathing. This time he made six breaths before his eyes glazed and his head spun.

This time he rested by lying on his back on the floor near the wall, trying to get his body into posture against the floor as he had been doing against the wall. He struggled into a seemingly stiff and awkward position. He had almost mastered it when Thoth commanded, "Now, breathe!"

Thoth sat beside him with one hand on his belly, the other on his chest. A-Sar-U started to breathe. Sharp tones stopped him.

"Breathe only in your belly. You chest must not move! Ever. Ever. Ever!"

A-Sar-U struggled to master the posture and the breathing. He had welcomed the thought of lying on the stones of the floor. Soon they were hard against his aching shoulders which were pulled back and down. His spine was forced flat upon the floor until Thoth was not able to shove his fingers into the space between the small of the back and the stones of the floor.

Still he worked. Posture. Breathe. Posture. Breathe again correctly. He did the exercises until he wanted to drop. Then he worked more and harder.

Thoth drove him on by example. Every exercise Thoth asked him to do, Thoth first demonstrated, then practiced along with A-Sar-U, then did again to show him how to correct or improve it. Thoth was doing at least three times as much as he, but gaining strength and freshness as A-Sar-U folded into fatigue. The skin of Thoth's face took on a pink, youthful glow. He seemed to grow younger as he gained strength and relaxation. A-Sar-U asked Thoth, "Why?"

Thoth laughed, seemingly well pleased. "Thought you'd never ask. Been waiting for you to see on me the effects it is having on you. Now you will learn! Now you have an immediate goal to work toward.

"I use the Pathway of Gold. I will teach it to you if you wish. If you really wish!"

"I really wish!" A-Sar-U said.

"It is a trick of mind. You must approach it with extreme care and caution for used wrongly it can delay your progress, or worse.

"You use this trick of mind to make your mind, your will, your *concentration* work upon the air you breathe.

"By this special trick you take out of the air a special energy. This energy turns to strength in you. It is a mystery. A deep mystery, I suppose, because neither Ra, Bes, God-ette, As-Tar, nor I understand why it works. In our early youth Po-Si-Don's Priests, the last living guardians of the ancient ways of That Other Planet, taught us how to do these exercises. Even those wise priests of Westsuns gone did not understand or would not say exactly how the magic happened.

"Many times we asked. They would not tell us why the magic happened. 'It is an Initiate Secret,' is all they would tell us.

"But the magic does happen if you do the exercise perfectly. Then, you must use the magic correctly."

Thoth studied A-Sar-U's face intensely, as if looking for any doubt or hesitation. A-Sar-U did not doubt his divine uncle's truthfulness. He did not doubt it would work. He only doubted that he could hold his body up long enough to learn the exercise. Seemingly satisfied with his long searching, Thoth continued. He was now excited, joy-filled, crammed full with energy like a Warrior who has won his first Combat!

"You breathe in and cause your mind to take from the air the strength you seek. The energy is in all air at all time. It is in caves in the land, it is at the highest point of the Atl Mountains. The ancient priests said to us many times:

'The energy for eternal life comes from dying light.'

A-Sar-u looked puzzled and Thoth laughed uproariously. "That's the look Ra had on his face and Bes on his when we first heard that saying. In your mind is a question. How could energy for eternal life come from dying light?

"I do not know. I have asked Som, Lor'd One of Science, to find what the saying means and explain it to me. When you study with him you must remember to ask him."

Thoth turned away, his big face clouded slightly, his Warrior's hands clenched in a small fury. "Ask him! But don't expect your answer soon. He and all his scientists have been working three dozen Westsuns to explain simple black streaks..."

Thoth swung back. His face cleared and he began work as if his mind had not caused an interruption.

"Your mind can take out of the air a special strength. This strength, or energy, turns to gold in your head. Therefore it is called the Pathway of Gold. When you have your head all aglow, you let the golden strength settle down

144

through your body. It is like warm, golden honey throughout every grain, nerve, fiber, muscle of your being. It is
warm. It is relaxing. It pours energy, strength, health, and
happiness into your body. It fills your body with a love too
great to hold, a joy too sweet to be yours alone. Here is the
way you do it."

Thoth showed him how to bring in the starting puff of
breath, use his mind's force to extract the special energy
by force of will, qualify that energy to warm, golden, relaxing light, and let it settle like warm, golden honey down
into his body.

A-Sar-U had never been forced to concentrate so intensely, to visualize so exactly. For a long time he felt
nothing. Then he began to feel the power. It lit up certain
regions of his head. He felt the energy flowing in. He saw it
turning into golden light. He felt the thrill of it run through
his body. He felt his heart racing in his excitement of new
discovery of the marvelous, no, unbelievable abilities of his
body and mind! The glory of the golden energy enchanted
him. The power of the energy caused him to glow all over.
Thoth danced around him, almost shouting words of encouragement.

"Good stance! Good posture. Breathe a little deeper—
belly only! Good. Good. Now, create the gold in your head
by the force of your thought and your will.

"Ah, ha! It is working on you. I see the pink blush of
renewed youth in the skin of your face. Now, on your back.
Try for deep relaxation. Fill yourself with the golden light!"

A-Sar-U lay on his back and found he could ease into
the formerly difficult posture. He concentrated on the technique of breath. In seven breaths he began to feel the
warm, golden, honey-sweet light flowing through his body.
He felt the blush of youth in his face and in his body. He
opened his eyes and looked at his body and his hands.
Underneath the skin the flesh had taken on a baby-pink
glow, as if returning itself to its earliest youth. He closed
his eyes, lay back and continued the breathing exercise.

He began to feel younger, healthier. He was no longer
bone-tired, certainly no longer exhausted. He felt the pull
and ache of his muscles and bones, but it was if they
belonged to another. As he worked he realized that dark of

145

Eastsun had given way to light and then to dark again many, many times.

Sometimes Thoth was called away on Empire problems. Many times they worked Eastsuns without food or rest. Still, he and Thoth worked on, stopping only when A-Sar-U had to shift the stones. This he did quickly, always anxious to get back to the glorious exercise.

"Stop!" Thoth commanded. "We must have food. We must rest some."

"But I don't feel tired!" A-Sar-U said.

Stop they did. Food was all handed in through the feeding slot, tested. A-Sar-U began to realize how hungry he was as they waited the required fifty breaths after tasting the food. Sitting on the floor they ate goat-milk curds, nuts, cut-meat from the fish of the sea wrapped in patted bread of corn, papaya fruits, and legs of rabbit.

As they ate, A-Sar-U was excited over his new learning and asked to learn more, and learn more swiftly.

Thoth smiled broadly. "A-Sar-U, you are an apt student. Also you are an eager student. I am well pleased."

They ate in silence. A-Sar-U was glowing from the compliment and slightly shy because of it. His mind drifted to Ast-i, and his body glowed even more. He missed the first words Thoth said.

"Using these techniques you will change your body. You will build within that physical body of yours a golden, Spiritual Body which is the exact duplicate of every part of the physical. It is this Spiritual Body that will do your bidding and do your work."

A-Sar-U asked questions to assure himself he understood all that Thoth had told him of the theory—a theory which secretly, at first, he had doubted. He did not know why, or how, but the exercises had set his body aglow with youth, strength, health, and a strange sense of joy. They had robbed his body of accumulated fatigue. Whatever the energy was, it was powerful!

"Now we must rest," Thoth said as he rolled over on his back.

A-Sar-U felt he would rather begin again in the studies. But Thoth told him to lie down in posture on the floor. Then breathe correctly, each breath turning his body more and more golden.

146

"Now! Go to sleep breathing correctly."

Thoth lay back and in seven breaths was fast asleep.

A-Sar-U was so excited he expected to be wakeful. In three more breaths he was fast asleep.

15

Woman's Duty

Ast-i saw A-Thena's lithe form standing at guard in the entrance to the apartment. A-Thena's shield, always at the ready, tilted slightly in a near salute, an honor paid only to the Mother of the Virgins. God-ette swept into the room on an energy storm.

"Her presence is a force," Ast-i thought, "a radiance seen with the skin."

The general effect was like a small sun in a whirlwind of love and efficiency, with a hint of laughter and a sense, a subtle and almost imperceptible sense, of urgency. In her presence things had to happen, thoughts brighten, wills rise to the higher occasion, and minds concentrate upon things most important and timely.

Ast-i felt the power of her eyes fixed upon her.

"Ast-i, Beloved of God-e, we start now to teach you all I was taught and learned in preparing the body to receive and become fecund by the seed of spirit."

"Oh, I am ready, Mother of God-e. I yearn for companionship." Ast-i felt that she blushed for such bold confession, but God-ette merely smiled a somewhat knowing smile.

"Good. Yearning will make you work harder. Hard work makes time pass quickly. Would you like news of A-Sar-U?"

"Oh, yes, yes."

"Your brother and Chosen Man does well in his trials."

"Oh, good news. But I have done little more than mental exercises in these ten Eastsuns."

"Perhaps much more than you think, Divine Child. You have learned the first lesson of womanhood—to be at ease and quiet in yourself. For you it has not been an easy lesson to learn. But you have stilled your yearning for activity, you have learned to turn inward to the Divine Self,

148

and to rest easy with yourself and with events you cannot control. It took me four Westsuns. You have learned it in ten Eastsuns."

"Oh, Mother of God-e! Thank you for reassuring my doubts."

"Hold no doubts, Young Goddess. You will have problems enough without doubting yourself. You are adequate. You are chosen. Now, I will train you the best I can."

"Please. And swiftly, Mother, please."

"As swiftly as your sweet friend, Time, will allow you to learn."

God-ette began now to speak in a slow, measured cadence that etched each concept into Ast-i's brain as if by brands of fire. Each concept was made of ideas, as if jewels were enlarged and fastened onto a statue of pure gold.

"Woman's first duty is to recognize that her divine creativity requires quiescence. Physical activity must give place to spiritual peace. Man creates by activity. Woman creates by energized passivity.

"Woman is the matrix of eternal life. Acceptance of her divine role is contrary to her normal nature. But it is essential to her spiritual fecundity. Until woman can be still, at utter and divine peace, and see her body as the pure temple of the active Divine Spirit, she cannot conceive by Radiant Spirit.

"Therefore, most women can never become mothers of spiritual progeny. They enjoy living in their normal, emotional nature. Their minds are filled with the smoke of half-burned thoughts, their cells are filled with the smoke of half-burned passions. Such unholy smoke brings tears to the eyes of approaching spirit.

"To ready yourself for divine motherhood, you must master your emotions fully. You must be supremely indifferent to all things around you, yet fill all things with your benign love and with your appreciation of their individual worth, value, and beauty. You must let go completely your natural, feminine capacity for finding and dwelling upon little faults, for fussing over minutia, for being overly concerned with details. Instead, you must change your mode of thought until you as readily see the whole pattern as you see any small portion of it. You must be able to visualize in yourself the creative act completed and yet in no way care how or why or even that it was completed.

"You must have absolute confidence and no doubts.

"You must be able to praise the Divine for the birth you desire even before you accept the spiritual seed. You must realize that spirit works wholly, perfectly, and instantly when it works. It works only on its own terms and in its own time, a most annoying thing to the mind of a woman. She wants all things to work on her terms and in her time.

"You must give yourself up wholly to the spirit. You must not question time. You must prepare your body, mind, and life to become the lowest of the low, and yet at the same time to be the most refined and highest spirit.

"You must know the lust of mass for energy, the thrust of energy toward life, the lift of life toward spirit, and the kinship of spirit with Divinity."

God-ette stopped with a shrug of helplessness and indecision. "I used ten word-formulas, ten rhythmical statements to help me. They were mine. I do not want you to take them, but listen and then make your own. I will repeat them to you, but you must put them into your own words, your own ideas. They may help you. Do you want them?"

"Oh, yes, yes, Divine Mother."

"You will say them only when your mind and will are at ease, when you can concentrate on them with all your being?"

"I will say them only then."

"Then enter your private temple of thought, as I have taught you, and I will say them for you."

Ast-i took an easy position, breathed the seven Divine Breaths, and created within herself a golden radiance and power. She felt her body glowing with the gentle and urgent warmth the exercises always created in her. After a moment God-ette began to speak, her voice coming from some far place, but with a sweet and personal insistence.

"I am the child of God-e, the heir of Divinity.

"I am the hope of the Empire, the salvation of mankind.

"I am *now,* the past, and all eternity.

150

"I am the strength of God-e in special form, and all things are possible to me.

"I am the darling of time; it is my special friend.

"I am the joy of creativity.

"I am the laughter of the All-Good.

"I am the wisdom of fecundity.

"I am the knowledge of eternity.

"I am Chosen Mother of God-e."

The melody of God-ette's voice ceased, but the song of wisdom continued in Ast-i's mind. When she decided to move she found a will stronger than her own holding her to her place in perfect comfort and joy.

Later, much, much later, she seemed to come from some far distant place back into the room of her apartment and to all the familiar things about her. She formulated the concepts into her own words. As the time wound on, she found a new delight in each passing Eastsun. Seven times each Eastsun she said the formulas aloud, and she thought upon them constantly. One Eastsun ran into another. She lost count.

Each time she felt her emotional, feminine nature begin to assert itself, she repeated the concepts with fierce concentration. She slowly—oh, far too slowly, she thought —became able to go from lowliest clod to highest God-e in the space of seven breaths.

When this happened she sensed that a pull was exerted by her body upon all nature and that spirit sat atremble over an abyss of love and joy.

Indeed, she was joyful beyond words. Her emotions swept her up in clouds of delight until she wept with her joy. She called upon the ground below and the sky above to witness her joy and accept her boundless love.

"I am blessed above all women for Divinity is my lover. I know such joy as fleshly woman may not know, for I am an instrument of eternal destiny. I laugh aloud for my love of Divinity, for in me It moves and has Its being. I am rich with the blessedness of womanhood made fecund by spirit. I am the Chosen Woman of God-e. I am the heir of Divinity. I am the mother of the Divine. So greatly am I blessed."

151

16

Words of Mystery, III

One dawning, A-Sar-U awoke to a full Eastsun. Thoth was bathing, standing in the trough above the cloaca. He poured water over himself from earthen pots.

"Come, lazy bones. Up! The stones. The stones! Before you can move them from the entrance and bathe, it will be time for food again."

A-Sar-U moved the stones to their place against the wall, then bathed. He was pleased to see that the ruddy, youthful color was still in his flesh. He felt strangely detached and contented. He experienced a sense of inner peace that was foreign to him. He felt warm, relaxed, strengthened, and ready.

They ate a porridge of Ra's-eye and dates, and bread of patted corn. Soon they were back at work again.

Thoth said: "I am the student. You are the teacher. I know nothing. Teach me all I need to know and do to become the Radiant Spirit. Make me do it right."

All that Eastsun they worked, and through the dark, pausing only for A-Sar-U to move the stones. Thoth tested his knowledge, his observation, and his skill. Sometimes his patience, too. When, as sometimes he was able, A-Sar-U caught Thoth in some almost invisible action that produced tension or detracted from the effect of the exercise, Thoth seemed to be especially pleased.

He had to teach exactingly, and insist upon the most perfect performance. At last A-Sar-U was able to teach to Thoth's satisfaction.

A-Sar-U began to realize that he was being trained in the sacred skills exactly as one had to train for the Combats. He went long, almost unendurable times with no food, no rest, under intense tensions. Then he was allowed food and rest.

Always his physical strength was most important and basic. The body was built as strongly and as swiftly as the mind. The body, mind, and spiritual self were being strengthened in the same exercises. He realized, too, that these exercises were both ancient and sacred, dedicated to the God-e Supreme.

"You can teach me," Thoth said, "Therefore, you can teach others when the time comes, which it will, and far too soon. When I am away, you must teach yourself. Don't think you cannot. You must. Fortunately, if you make mistakes, these Sacred Exercises have built-in protections. You cannot harm yourself even if you do them badly or wrongly. But you can delay your development! That you must not do, for we have so little time."

Thoth called for the Temple Guards to bring Bes. He and Bes talked in low whispers through the food slot for several breaths. Thoth returned to A-Sar-U smiling.

"Tensions are rising. Bes thinks we still have time. We will continue."

Thoth took on the role of the teacher again. His presence was like a flow of energy. Around his body a light seemed to dance almost like an energy too great to be confined to the body alone.

"You have worked hard and long to develop the golden energy in a body that is relaxed and ready. Now we must go to another exercise. It will help you get the good from all your work and practice. You will now qualify that golden energy and use it to create the golden, Radiant Spiritual Body inside your flesh body.

"You now turn that Golden Body to spirit! You create a radiant, golden, Spiritual Body inside your physical body. Exact duplicate. Perfect!

"You will feel the pull of this Spiritual Body upon your physical body. It will wish for release, urge itself toward a life all its own. When this urge has grown great enough, you will be taught how to release it from your body. You will release it from the pull of your flesh.

"Your flesh will be the temple and also the trap of your Spiritual, Radiant Self. The last trap is like an invisible hand at the back of your head. It is inside, in your brain. You will want to release your Spiritual Body from this last trap of the physical body, and it will want to be released.

153

The pull will become great. It will tug toward release. You will want it to go free. You may even will it to go free. At first it will not."

"Why?"

"Because you will try to free it with the wrong will."

"Wrong will, Lor'd One?"

"Yes. To release your Radiant Self from the last trap, the lock in the back of your brain requires a very special will. It is a very ingenious, selfless will that gives the special energy you need to thrust the Spirit Self free of your physical self. It is a deliberate, special set of mind that is needed to give life to the spirit and send it forth with all the powers of the physical self—and more. It will have mobility. It can travel at speeds much faster than sight. It travels at the speed of thought which, the divine Atl said the ancients taught, is the speed of sight times its own self.

"You will make visible the Divine Spirit you have caused to be born in your body through a special technique and with the blessings of the Supreme God-e.

"You will feed to that spirit the divine food, the *chefaut*, which is dying light. You will fashion it into a separate being with energies and a life of its own as long as it is fed with energy from the glistening cord attached at the back of your brain.

"When you can do all this, you can free your Radiant Spirit and it can go to your beloved and make her fecund."

Eagerly A-Sar-U began the work. For three Eastsuns they worked, with little rest and little food. That which he began with such great hope seemed to elude him. Time after time A-Sar-U built the Golden Body inside the flesh and tried to externalize it.

He could not externalize the golden Spiritual Body which he felt he had so perfectly formed inside his flesh body! Each time he tried, something pulled him back. Each time he felt he was going free, his Spiritual Body slammed back home to flesh. Slammed hard! It stung. His flesh prickled as if swiped with stinging nettle. He fought down his frustration. He choked back his anger. He struggled to keep down the silent tears of his disappointment.

Thoth was ever attentive, ever helpful. "Start all over at the very beginning each time you fail," he advised. "Each

154

try is a new time for success. Always start afresh. You may have tensed yourself with your very first breath. Start new."

Again and again A-Sar-U took the posture against the wall or on the floor. Again and again he went through the breathing cycle. He could light the Golden Pathway that turned his flesh young and made visible the Radiant Spirit within his body. He loosed it from his body. He felt it floating out of his flesh. He felt a sweet assurance and joy. Then came the jar at the back of his head! The Radiant Body immediately slammed back with nettles in his flesh. Over and over he tried.

"I'll never get it, Lor'd Uncle," he said. "I just can't make it work."

"Never say *can't* in divine work.

"First, because you are not the final decider. The Supreme Spiritual God-e must bestow His grace or you can do nothing. Second, never is a long time.

"You've only been working now ten Eastsuns. Not even one Westsun! So you have eighteen Eastsuns to go before the first Westsun will have passed of the ten the ancient law allows you for the Ordeal. So relax and be at peace. Even after the Westsun next coming, you will have nine more. Don't rush. Time is not your enemy. Time is your friend."

Thoth laughed long and loud. "You feel frustrated? You should have seen us. We did not know anyone who had done it. Now we can assure you that it can be done. That should give you courage. Does it?"

"I'm disgusted with myself. I get so near. Then I fail. Oh, I know it is possible. But is it possible for me?"

"The impatience of youth! In youth, we want everything one Eastsun ago. Better, make it two. We don't want to wait for the Supreme Spiritual God-e to work his will upon us or upon events.

"You can be as impatient as you wish. The God-e will give you complete release when He decides you are fully ready. Not one tittle of breath before. When it comes it will come like a spear in the night, and you will wonder from where.

"Think for a while on your beloved Ast-i. Visualize her in your mind. Then, keep working.

155

"You know how. You seem to be doing everything right. You taught me the right way, you found my errors. Now teach yourself afresh each time and find any possible errors. But just..."

Bes called Thoth to the food slot. Thoth went with a smile on his face. When he returned the smile was gone.

"Affairs of Empire press upon me," he explained. "Now, where...ah, yes. Just keep trying. Keep trying and keep thinking that time is your friend. Don't try too eagerly.

"Remember, you must be so relaxed that even the thought of tensing a muscle is too much tension.

"Your discipline, your will, your training, your control must be so perfect that even those stones there, if dropped on you, will not disturb you!

"Your concentration must be so great that no thought, except the thought you have trained into your pristine, pure, and willing mind, can reach even your back-mind and certainly not your front-mind.

"Your feeling of knowledge-of-success must be so complete that you are filled with joy each time you fail for you are one trial closer to success.

"Your determination must be so great that pain, fatigue, hunger, walls, alarms, and dangers will not deter you.

"Your detachment must be so great that you are serenely indifferent to either success or failure."

"Oh, Lor'd Uncle. To be detached from success in this case, my insanity would have to be so great that I believe all these things are possible to me."

Thoth laughed gaily, and the laughter lifted the heavy look of care that had come to his face. "Yes, a little insanity helps, a lot helps faster."

Thoth looked toward the entrance. "I've taught you all that you need to know for the Virgin Birth. There is much more that you must be taught and asked to do for the Empire. But it must await your first success. I must leave you now for cares of the Empire. The rest is up to you and Ast-i."

"I will to do it. How shall I know when it is done?"

"The Drum will tell you. But you will know, positively know, long before the Drum speaks. When you are in her presence in the radiant form your mind will be able to

156

count every honey-golden hair on her head and remember the count. You will know.

"The Drum might also tell you if we are being attacked again. It is better to depend on your own certain knowing. Either way, you will be released soon after you hear the Drum, either to fight or to go to the rituals and then, maybe, to celebrate the coming of a new God unto mankind."

"I have told you how to do this divine thing. But I have not showed you. I have a few breaths of time. Come! Watch me!"

Thoth strode to the Mound of Desire, pushed the coverings aside, lay down upon his back. He breathed slowly with measured rhythm seven times.

His body seemed to sag into the stones so relaxed had he become. After several breaths he stirred as if from a deep rest, but did not sit up.

"Ra, your Divine Father, lay here to engender you."

"I am Virgin Born? Truly?"

"Truly. Yes. Unfortunately not registered. We were merely testing the old sacred training techniques. They work. You are one proof. Ast-i is another. Both Virgin Born of the techniques I have taught you. Watch me carefully, Son of God-e."

Thoth breathed slowly. His face began to glow. The bluff, hard look of the Realm's greatest Warrior faded. The suave look of the Empire's ruling head dissolved away. Around Thoth appeared a glowing halo of golden white which expanded until it engulfed A-Sar-U in a warm flame.

Then from Thoth's head leaped an intertwining caduceus of white and blue light. It rose high in the air. Then, as if it were in truth serpents interwound with each other, it turned slowly toward the pile of stones. It fixed itself upon a stone, and lifted it to twice the height of a man. Slowly it moved the stone across the wide room.

It passed above the Mound of Desire, above Thoth's physical body. At the entrance to the room the stone was fitted into place. It was then lifted and returned over Thoth's body to the pile of stones at the wall.

Thoth lay very still a while. To A-Sar-U's incredulous eyes he looked the epitome of all godly power and beauty.

He glowed with a power and energy that charged the room. Suddenly he was sitting up. His eyes twinkled.

"Easy, you see. Now you do it."

A-Sar-U grinned. "Lor'd One, passing a stone of a full man's weight over my head may require some more learning."

Thoth laughed. "Wise! Very wise. I just wanted to show you that it can be done. You have the techniques. These things I hope you learned from this:

"First, that a busy man, hurried with the details of problems of the Realm, harried by enemies—a battle-scarred Warrior of physical action—in seven breaths can change into the likeness of the godliest. Lesson one! Strong men, busy men, harassed and harried men can become as effective as recluses in things divine.

"Just as swiftly, too! You need not be soft to seek to become divine. Do I make that lesson clear to you, Young Warrior?

"Manfulness and fighting ability are enhanced by Divine Grace."

A-Sar-U walked, disconsolate, to the far end of the room and back again. "All I must learn to do is to relax so much that a stone dropped on me will not disturb me. To breathe the magic breath that builds divinity in the tiniest grains, or cells, of my body even in the midst of strife. To create a Radiant Body out of the divinity within my cells. To send it forth with confidence that it can and will do what I desire at the time I desire. And then return it to my body with clear memory. That's all I have to do?"

"That's succinctly stated. But, yes."

"Good. If that's all it will only take me about a thousand Westsuns!"

"You don't have a thousand. Only about nine. It will not take more than three. Possibly two. Less if you desire greatly and work swiftly. You might be able to do it in three Eastsuns not three Westsuns. You, Virgin Born Son of God-e, you might take only two Eastsuns."

"If I had your faith,"

"Ah, but faith you do not need. You will accomplish all this, *if* you use the techniques, whether you have faith in them or not. The exercises do the work.

"Your need is for will and determination. And for a vast desiring. If you have these and do the work, the exercises will change your body and give it the chemicals of divinity. The work. The exercises. That and will and desire are all you need. Clear?"

A-Sar-U nodded. He was dumb with the enormity of the task before him.

Thoth moved toward the entrance as lightly as if he had not worked the most part of ten Eastsuns, both light and dark. At the entrance he stopped and turned.

"A-Sar-U, Know! The future and salvation of the people of our Pleasant Planet are up to you." After a pause he added, "You will need some further training. The task is great and the time may be short. You are our only hope for their salvation."

Thoth was gone in a whirl of energy. The room seemed to gradually lose its crackle. His presence was a charge that wore down slowly.

When Thoth had gone, A-Sar-U wandered aimlessly around the large room. He finally sat on one of the large stones and dropped his head into his hands. He felt the weariness of the work and a heaviness of defeat.

He knew he must not allow himself to be depressed. He had no time for rest, for self-pity. He had work to do.

He got into position on the floor. He checked his position carefully. When satisfied with it, he went slowly, carefully through the exercises.

They worked.

He saw the glorious Pathway of Gold in his head. He felt the warmth seeping down through his body. The sense of relaxation flooded over him. He felt the creation of the golden man, the duplicate of every cell of his body in resplendent light. He felt the Radiant Self release itself from his flesh and start to rise upward. He was filled with joy.

It slammed back into his body. He burned as if rolled in nettles.

Angrily he sprang to his feet. He stumbled over one of the thirty-three stones. He carried one to the entrance and put it into the place designed for it. He ran back for another. Carrying it, he ran around the room. He enjoyed punishing himself with the weight that was on his shoulder. He enjoyed the punishing pain and the ache of his

159

lungs gasping for air. He put the stone into its place and ran back for another. Each stone he carried twice around the room before he put it into place. He kept at it until his muscles trembled from fatigue and all the stones were in place.

Then with equal self-deprecating fury he began to carry them back to their place at the wall. Each time he ran around the room, trying to increase his speed, carrying a stone of his own weight. When the stones were all against the wall he began again to take them to their place at the entrance. He was carrying them around the room for a fourth time when his heart and head began to thump from fatigue.

He knew he was tired. Too tired. He was also angry with himself. Punishment was not enough. He must...

He was passing the Mound of Desire. It struck him that Thoth had never allowed him even to sit on it. Now, in his frustration he wondered why.

Fatigue, curiosity, anger, and frustration all exploded within him. He sat on the side of the Mound. The rabbit fur lay half across it. His hand touched the soft fur and a swift surge of emotion came over him. He was filled with a great longing to see and to touch Ast-i. To hear her laughter. To see her beauty and the radiance of her smile.

Disconsolate he threw himself at the Mound. Something caused his body to slide from the edge to the floor, pulling the rabbit fur under him.

He was so tired he was trembling, and too exhausted to care.

He fell face down beside the mound, pulled the rabbit fur over his body. He wept.

After a long while he realized that he had rolled over on his back. The tears in his eyes slowly dried away, as did his hope. He had done his best. It had not worked. He was not even able to be angry any more.

Utterly hopeless, he lay in complete exhaustion.

A weeping Warrior! He stormed at himself inside his mind. Yet he did not really care. The great driving energy was gone, expended in useless effort.

The only thing that had not gone was his desire for Ast-i.

160

His senseless, all-consuming desire for Ast-i. All else was gone.

All was emptiness. All was the echo of despair in his mind.

17

A-Sar-U and Mindforce

A-Sar-U rose from a short, exhausted nap and again attacked the stones with an inburning fury. He raced to move them from the doorway side of the stone crypt to the outside wall. He grabbed each stone, though it weighed as much as he, as he ran by the piles in his race across the room. He ran and slammed it down into its place.

In his mind was a burning. A red, painful burning that seemed to be a sliver of stone driven up from his spine into the center of his head. There a picture wavered and flared like flames in a storm wind. Each stone was to him an enemy. An enemy of a thousand faces. Faces sardonic, jeering. Faces smug, judgmental. Faces of derision. Faces of hatred. Weary faces. Burning faces. Anxious faces.

And a thousand hands. Hands reaching for him like falcon claws, swiping at him like blunt swords, striking at him like dueling sticks, hammering at him like hard-swung maces. Bleeding, grasping, clawing, hurting, dangerous hands. Life-threatening, grasping hands.

Faces, hands—all striving to harm him, hurt him, cripple him. Each a threat to him, his future life. Each sucking a little breath from his lungs, a little light from his mind, a little life from his body.

His only weapon in all that danger was his ability to move the stones from place to place in the almost empty vault. His brute strength against an array of futilities, jeering, mocking futilities.

He could not make his body obedient to his will, and his will obedient to his desire. He knew the jeering faces were right. He was a failure, a tiger without teeth or claws, a useless hulk of flesh without force of mind. He was a muscle without brain. He was eyes without sight. He must have seen whatever it was near the Sundial on the porch of the Temple of Po-Si-Don that Ast-i had observed and understood. He did not know if it was ominous. He did not know how to see or understand or do anything except heave rocks from place to place. Why?

He stopped in mid-stride. The heavy stone in his arms was stained with the sweat and tears that frustration dripped from his nose and chin. Where they landed they showed as a dark cloud spreading on the grey-white granite, spreading, spreading. His breath was racing through his nose with a sound of stirring unswallowed tears, a gurgling as if through symbols of weakness.

Why?

Standing as if a statue of stone himself, he felt the word thunder in his head. And heard echoes from a thousand jeering throats.

"Because Thoth said to do it! Who is Thoth? A Lor'd One who could not do officially what he expects you to do. An aging Warrior whose sword hand will soon grow weak and slow. Why should you listen to Thoth?"

Why?

A-Sar-U placed the stone in the center of the room and sat on it facing the mound of stones against the outside wall. It was a careful and deliberate act, and his muscles trembled so much that his body shook.

Why?

He could simply declare that he wanted out of the contract to attempt Virgin Birth. He could admit defeat, inability to perform such high duty for his people, for the Empire. Surely, they could expect only that he do that which was within his ability. Could they ask more?

He swiped tears from his cheeks with the back of his curved right wrist, the wrist that was trained to hold the sword of defense for his people. He was a good fighter! Not a...a miracle worker. Could his people expect him to be a miracle worker? No. They could not.

The plateau of peace his logic had built on his mountain of angry frustration and despair of self-perceived weakness crumbled into an avalanche of certainty. People would not expect much of him. For they did not know what was beside that Golden Sundial on the white marble floor. They might not have understood it if they had seen it. Even more, they might not have seen it. Even he might not have seen it.

No! No. No. No.

He must have seen it. He just had not understood it.

He lay back on the stone, liking the punishment of the rough surface on his skin.

Yes, he had seen and not understood. But Ast-i had seen, observed, and understood. Thoth had seen, and Bes. They understood and knew that something was indicated there that was important to the Pleasant Planet and the future of all persons on it. They had selected him to participate in a scheme that was clearly important to the future. They had chosen him. They had faith in him. They risked much on him.

He was failing them.

He wanted to quit, to admit defeat. But he knew what he was doing, that which he was attempting. It was simple.

Thoth was his spiritual mentor, his Master Teacher. Thoth was the Great God-e. But more important he was A-Sar-U's guide!

His Master willed it.

His Master wished it!

He might fail himself, and the Empire. But he could never fail his Spiritual Master.

He lay backward and squirmed further up on the rough stone and let the tears of anger and frustration flow through the aching in his chest. The sounds he made were those of a baby ashamed to cry.

He must have dozed. Suddenly Thoth was sitting on a stone beside him.

As he awoke, he blurted out his frustration to Thoth. "I feel anger at myself. It feels like a bloat in my belly, like a fist of ice squeezing outward. Always in my life before now I have been able to do something, to take an action to relieve such pressure. Now I feel helpless, in the grip between the needs of my body, mind, and soul, and the requirements of my position with my people.

"I feel swept along on a river of expectations that grows with each person I know, and the millions I have not yet met. Each is an added duty, which causes my expectation of myself to increase and the thongs of time to become more knotty upon my mind. A man grown, I am more helpless than a baby in swaddles."

Thoth let his bulk seem to inhabit the giant stone on which he sat as if it were a throne. His very *isness* was a special feeling as solid as the stone. After a long wait he spoke slowly.

"I hear you say that you are feeling frustrated, helpless, and controlled. And you should. Because you are all three. Anyone who selflessly serves his fellowman is helpless in the given circumstance, frustrated of ever reaching his full desire, and controlled by the requirements of one's duty."

"Why?"

"Within the law of duty and morality one puts oneself into gyves. But it is a self-accepting restriction. You are free to leave your pledge."

"I know. And I may."

"At times, many would like to escape the oppressions of duty. You can break the moral or social law, the law of the land, or even the Law of Je-Su, if you are willing to take the consequences."

"What consequences?"

"For breaking the moral law, a lifetime of guilt. For breaking the social code, a period of rejection by one's peers. For breaking the laws of the land, a sliding punishment depending on someone's judgment of its severity. For breaking the Law of Je-Su, death."

"I did not help to make any of these laws."

"Yes you did."

"How?"

"That which was done for you reaches back through time to the first of your ancestors. You, as an event and a personality in time, brought to bear your future potential in the thinking, behavior, and life of your ancestor. You, *even as the hoped-for offspring that was eventually to come,* were the cause of formation of laws and customs, of agreements between persons, groups, and tribes for mutual protection. Out of this grew the laws that allow the Empire to regulate those who are not amenable to accepted patterns of behavior."

"Then I can change them."

"Yes, you can change them. But until you do, you cannot escape them. For they are founded on ideas that have

165

come out of the living experience of mankind. Ideas are hard to develop, impossible to destroy.

"A-Sar-U, you are now and will forever be responsible to future generations for what you do. Even what you think. You are this very moment fashioning thoughts that will mold your actions in the immediate future. This will influence your impact on generations far into the future. What you fashion now by your thoughts and actions, and by the powers, energies, and wisdoms I soon will be able to pass into you, will echo in the births and deaths in your lineage until the end of time. You are to be the first in my line of avatars. All who follow in the future will be Children of Thoth. But each will be a special individual partaking of your very energy."

"I am not capable. Must I die to escape my failure?"

"You cannot escape. Not your failure, but the sacred duty I have been assigned to assign on to you. Your assigned destiny.

"You are not ordinary. You are priceless in the gifts poured into you with the connivance of history since the first God-e, Khnum, and of course the grace of Ra, the One God-e Supreme. You are being fashioned as an ever-living spirit that may become the common property of every person who wills to partake of it until the end of time and beyond. You will receive, and eventually pass along, the divine energy that will birth the god-men of races in the future.

"You are the way-shower, the pastor, the guide. You will make it clear that Children of Thoth, those born in the line of Avatars of God, by whatever name in whatever time, are worthy of worship by all individuals. For they benefit all mankind by their very birth as examples.

"Also, you will make it clear that Divinity may be developed *in everyone*, out of human flesh by discipline and will. Everyone, not just the few, you avatars, the Lor'd Ones. The common man—all humankind for all ages will be better because of you."

"Lor'd One, I have failed..."

"A-Sar-U, you have tried. You have not succeeded yet, but you have not failed. Finally you will come to know that you can try too hard, and then you will thrust less. You will know that when your will and your desire are as one,

166

and you have foreseen the outcome clearly, you will allow the Divine in you to make your effort good. In so doing you will show everyone that Divinity may reside in man."

"Who will care?"

"All humankind through all future ages. Oh, they will be too busy with personal things to pay much attention. But you will make laws for them they cannot escape. Laws of love, life, and self that reside in their thoughts as the taste of sweet fruits reside in memory"?

"They will forget."

"Yes. Oh, yes, they will forget. That is why your avataric energy will return in a new form with the same wisdoms in a different personality each seventy generations. Again and again your same old message of Divinity in man, and worship of the God-e, will be received anew. Many will strive, most will fail. But in each appearance you will convince a few more to try, and the world will be better for this.

"They may never be quite as good as you. But you are now making the laws that they will obey. You will time and time again be the Sacred One in human form, proof that man and God-e are always *almost* one. You will be the reason for Communion Feast, the ritualistic consuming of the flesh and blood of the ever-renewing avatar. You will show time and time again that by special training in the use of *Meket* and *Hekau*, by selfless love, by endless effort, by bending the will and desire of common man to a selfless task for the good of all mankind, remarkable good may come. That uncommon gods walk upon the planet among common men."

"Can't I just walk out?"

"You can quit. But you cannot just leave. You cannot escape the contract you have made with Ast-i, the Empire, and Divinity and live. I speak with the accumulated and administrative wisdom of that Divinity. I pass to you the Powers of Destiny, Universal Knowledge, and the Cosmic Power, the Sacred *Hekau*. You are to be one of the many Divine Ones who, for the good of all humankind, shall speak in all sacred aspects for all time down through the times.

"But you heard my orders to A-Tem, who mounts your guard each day and night. They guard to keep harm out.

They also guard with their lives to keep good in. If you try to leave without my presence and permission they will drive swords through your body until it is dead, and I shall be first to spit in your face!"

Thoth rose and walked toward the door to the guard room. He stopped at the half-door, his hand raised to send the signal to let him out of the chamber.

"Before I go, let me show you that control of mind and will are possible."

Thoth lay down upon the rough stone floor. He folded his hands in a ritualistic way. He breathed slowly three full breaths. Breathed again fully three breaths. Then as if prepared, he took one long, slow, infilling breath and held it.

A radiance began to appear as if coming from within his heart. It pulsed with a jade-green light, so beautiful and intense it seemed to shine through the bones of his chest. Then a golden radiance began to appear around his face, as if it was a light too bright to be hidden. The radiance increased, grew in brightness, and began surging from head to foot. It pulsed, gaining intensity, in some joyous rhythm with the breathing he resumed.

Then, beginning at the top of Thoth's head a Golden Body seemed to stand up out of his physical body, This translucent body appeared as a vapor rising from a boiling pot. Suddenly this Radiant Body was standing five paces above his physical body in a body-form so radiant that it hurt A-Sar-U's staring eyes. A glowing jade sun was his heart.

Slowly at first, but with gathering speed, the light-body moved toward the stack of stones at the outward wall. The Radiant Body lifted and carried a stone and placed it beside Thoth's supine body, long-ways, on the right side. Another stone was placed end-to-end with it. Two more stones were placed on the left side.

Thoth's physical body now lay as if in a trench.

The Golden Body brought six stones and laid them crosswise over Thoth's physical body.

Thoth now lay in a closed tomb.

The Golden Body moved stones until they formed a circle-like octagon at the foot of the tomb. Then at the head the Radiant Body extended the tomb and added stones like arms reaching out from about the level of Thoth's physical shoulders. A-Sar-U saw in it a rough Cross of God-e, the Symbol of Thoth-Khnum or Ra, the promise of life after death. Oh, much more, it was the Symbol of Eternal Life from the flesh of Man made God.

Thoth's Golden Body paused, as if enjoying the look of wonder on A-Sar-U's face and the admiration in his astonished eyes. Then, in a swift moment of intense activity, placed one stone crosswise on the tomb, and stood another on end behind it. In two breaths that light-body had created a rough approximation of the Seat of Ra on the Window of Ra on the porch of the Temple of Po-Si-Don.

Then the Golden Body floated up and seated himself in apparent comfort in the Seat of Ra, and seemed to inhabit the stone in utter peace.

A-Sar-U felt the wonder on his face. But curiosity was stronger in his mind. He tried several times to think out an intelligent question but finally blurted out, "Who...what ...are you?"

"I am who I am. I am that. I am."

"You...You are Thoth, God-e, Lor'd One of the Pleasant Planet?"

"I am the Radiant Body, spiritual, non-material except as light. The Eternal Radiant Body of an entity that has taken physical body as Khnum, Ra, and Thoth and will take other physical bodies as required."

A-Sar-U was so excited he almost danced. "By the Holy Word of Khnum, creator of All, how did you do...do all this?"

"By the divine energy and pristine will of my physical self, disciplined and made potent in my Radiant Body."

"But, if you are non-material except as light, how did you learn to do this?"

"By discipline, discipline, moral and selfless living, and still more discipline. And also, being obedient to the desires and directions of Divine Masters. By accepting Divine Mastery from my birth."

"Then you could...you could cause Virgin Birth?"

"Oh, yes. Even as I, in the form of the First God, through Atl's form, caused mine, Ra's, and Bes's. Ra caused yours and Set's. Bes caused Ast-i's."

169

"Then you have the Power? You could cause Virgin Birth in Ast-i?"

"Ah? I have the Power. Yes. But, do not let your concern show so. I have the Power and could cause Virgin Birth. But not in Ast-i. Only you can plant the New God in Ast-i."

As A-Sar-U was about to protest his inability, the Golden Voice said, "...and will. You will because you want to, you wish to, and you must. Not only for her sweet sake, but for all the people of this planet and the future of their lives."

In the long silence, A-Sar-U stirred. As if taking the body action as a signal of readiness in mind, the voice continued. "Only you, A-Sar-U, an Unregistered Virgin Born Son to Ra (son and also father to Thoth-Khnum), and God-ette, (daughter and mother to Mut) can cause Virgin Birth through Ast-i."

"Why?"

"Because she loves you and you love her. As arranged by the gods, love is the grace the Great God-e gives through spiritual means to achieve physical things that lie beyond the beliefs of man.

"Love locks in all desired things and locks out all undesired things, even the power of the gods in personal things. Love is part of that energy that gives eternity to life and grows gods out of clay. Therefore, unless that special god-given love runs between man and maid, Virgin Birth cannot occur. It lacks one prime ingredient, the energy of the two Radiant Selves focused as twin suns of love."

A-Sar-U felt his own confusion and doubts. He had endless questions that would have come from his lips had he not forced himself to be silent.

Why was Virgin Birth so important?

Why did all the gods seem to be parent and offspring of each other and of themselves?

Why did all the gods seem to be identical in...well...in a way?

He forced himself to be practical and almost shouted, "How did you learn it, and where?"

The Golden Body seemed to smile, but the radiance was so great A-Sar-U could not be certain. "I will answer your spoken questions. Also, I will answer some of those you wish to ask, but decided not to ask."

"How did I learn this? In my present physical body, exactly as you are learning it, as everyone must learn it, but without the pressures and dangers that beset you. I was prepared through a youth of love and service. My moral character was as strictly overseen as yours has been. My desire to serve mankind was increased as yours has been by careful example. My masculine ego was enhanced by contact with a glorious 'girl' called Ma-at. Ma-at means 'eternal truth and justice.' She glowed in my presence and my heart. All avatars and also all god-men, trained or self-taught, are the inheritors of our energy.

"My training was that of all young Warriors. Young Warriors must learn and desire to protect the tribe, their people. We were caught on a planet where war is needless but is constant. Constant only because men of grandiose mind-set inhabit, even illegally, without consent of the tribe, seats of power. We had and you have inherited a society that has far too many who want to control with power and confusion, not through service and love.

"The point is that to be a potential God-e you must first become stalwart and acceptable to the ways of a community. For the good opinion of one's fellowman, even the acceptance of non-speaking life forms, is almost as important as love in achieving success in Virgin Birth.

"Then comes desire. Desire, not to be important or achieve great personal things, but to help one's race achieve all it should. Desire is a force of will that heats the sword-blade of success.

"Then comes discipline. Discipline that focuses the will, the relentless hammer that time and time again assaults with force the rude form of chaos until the flashing sword of success is fashioned and ready.

"Yet two things are needed. The first is the will and blessings of a trained Master. A Master is one who has been trained through time, purified and tested through turmoil, strengthened by opposition, disciplined by will, and empowered by grace. A Master alone may pass along that other absolute necessity one needs.

"A vital necessity beyond the Master, yet but an extension of him—as Gods are but an extension of one another—is the grace of the Supreme God-e. He is the Master of all things, the director and controller of life. That grace, like love, is given specifically to the individual. Unlike love, it is usually given only to those who, through preparation and control and purification of self, have earned it. But like love, it is sometimes given to those who do not truly deserve it, at least not yet in that moment of time.

"Both true love and grace from the Supreme God-e cause men to rise to Godhood.

"Where did I learn this technique?"

"And why?" A-Sar-U shot in hopefully.

"Where? In an initiation chamber. As if here in this vaulted room of hope and despair. As if here amid stress, great like you have, and tears of anger, frustration, self-doubt, and possibly greater self-criticism. Amid protestations of inadequacy, of inevitable failure, of defeat, or desire to abandon the plans of the Great Cabal of the God-men of Thoth."

"What is that?"

"A Secret of Initiation you will come to share when you succeed in your present assignment. One you will need to know and to share with all living things on this or any planet. And that is the answer to 'why' I did this and why you are doing it. It is to save us all.

"To answer your unspoken question, 'Why is Virgin Birth so important?' As breath is fundamental to life, Virgin Birth is fundamental to belief. And belief is fundamental to the success of the Great Cabal of Thoth, Khnum, Atl, Ra, As-Tar, God-ette, Bes, and Myself. It is one way Goddess Maat and God Khnum as Thoth can be reborn and bestow their eternal energy.

"Why do all gods seem to be parents and offspring of each other and of themselves? Because they all come from one divine energy, eternal, life-sustaining. As such you are my father, my son, and myself.

"Why do all gods seem to be identical in a way? Because they all come from the same source in a channel of time, like snow-melt in a river. What drop did not come from the snow?"

The Radiant Body rose from the stone and in thirty breaths had returned the stones to the outside wall. It then went to Thoth's body, floated in the air above it for a few breaths while aligning head to head and foot to foot, and then began slowly to descend. The nearer the Golden Body came to the flesh body the faster it seemed to close. It rammed into the body with an audible sound, and seemed to be absorbed into the flesh as the Eastsun into darkness. For a moment, the Jade Heart continued to glow, but in six breaths it had faded.

Thoth rose with a single bound. "Ah, that was a nice rest. I showed you something few persons have ever seen, and fewer still can do. Atl and Khnum used these skills on That Other Planet, and taught them to only a few."

"Will you teach them to me?"

"I will see that you have mastered the secret. You will need it in your present task. Especially after the planet accepts you and Ast-i as God-e and Goddess, as two of the Nine Holy Faces of the invisible Thoth. Accepts you two as the rightful inheritors of and able to bequeath the unerring rightness and justice of Goddess Maat, and the creative power of God Thoth as you bestow their energy upon man."

Thoth was gone in a breath, and A-Sar-U felt the loneliness of the room like wisps of morning mist are felt on the skin.

18

Ast-i-Ankh:
Lady of Eternal Truth

Ast-i tossed on her bed. Her mind raced with her concerns so much she could not sleep. It had raced all during the light-time so much she could not eat. But she could weave.

She sprang from her bed and began to weave. She did nothing else but weave. All the time, until the Ama-Sones told A-Thena, who told God-ette, Mother of the Temple of the Virgins, "Ast-i is killing herself with anxiety. She has not slept, will not eat, cannot rest."

"I'll come. Thank you."

Ast-i sat on the side of the raised stone that served as her bed. It was covered with a reed mat. Long, pith-filled reeds were cross-woven with shafts of willow bark, then tied into a second layer. It made a long, pliable, soft padding as thick as her finger was long. This was covered with skins of the meadow-land doe, and over this had been spread skins of the mountain sheep of the high Atals. She was constantly under the watch of the Ama-Sones. Occasionally, oh, far too seldom, she thought, she was visited by the Mother Goddess, director of the Temple of Virgins.

Ast-i asked for and got armloads of the long, fragrant water-reeds, dried and ready for splitting. These she split. Feverishly, she drove herself to weave the split reeds into baskets. She forced her mind to keep busy, and her body to be tired, by working intensely on the basketry she thought she would need in the space in the Temple Complex that would be assigned to her as the Chosen Woman of a famous Warrior.

If she was tired enough there would be no energy for her mind to hold the slightest doubt that she and A-Sar-U would succeed in an open and announced Virgin Birth.

No matter that the Mother Superior said that Ast-i and A-Sar-U were born through Virgin Birth, but unregistered. That the method was known. It could be taught. It worked. They could not fail. They must not.

To stop the thoughts that jammed into her mind, she made her fingers race faster and faster at her basket weaving.

She had to be certain, calm, cool, *certain.*

But she was, wasn't she? Didn't she know that the tears that welled up in her eyes were because of the slow pace of her fingers? That the anger was because the reeds had not split evenly? That the frustration was that she was not as swift as...

"Weeping and working, Daughter?"

Ast-i's head jerked up so swiftly that the tears in her eyes flowed over onto her cheeks. She looked in the direction of the Mother Superior, who was a blur beyond the tears. She brushed the tears from her cheeks and eyes with the back of her hand and saw that her finger was red.

"Weaving, weeping, bleeding." The voice was low. It would have been gladsome but for the sub-tone of maternal wisdom. "You are doing woman's work, alright."

Ast-i turned to her a tear-streaked face. She wanted to be so strong, to have no doubts. But her resolve broke. She rose and flung herself into the fragrant warmth of loving arms.

"Oh, Mother, I am so happy. So proud. So confident. I really am. Really, really am. But I am so unimportant! Who am I that the Supreme God-e should choose me to mother a new Savior of Mankind? Blessed I am, above all women. Proud...but I am so *unsure.*" She sobbed against the loving shoulder. "Does being certain, proud, and unsure make sense?"

"No. Except to a woman in love."

When her weeping had spent itself, she allowed herself to be guided to sit again on the reed mat.

"I'm being foolish," she managed.

"Well, yes. Foolish! Foolish and eternally feminine. We women live on suffrage. We must have approval. Approval is in the judgment of the beholder. Therefore we are always insecure, always doubting our own selves until others have approved of us."

"But not you, Blessed Mother. You are always so calm, so sure, so poised."

"Thank you for your approval. Poise may be pose, you know. With experience comes the ability to hide our feminine insecurity. But it is like being able to dodge a sword cut. You must always be ready to dodge the next one. It will come again.

"But," she drew a deep breath, "some things make us glow inside so brightly that we overcome the secret mental shadows and darkness our sex has inherited from our race. My brightnesses are that I have been a Chosen Woman of a Great Warrior and bore him two sons by Virgin Birth.

"My shining brightness is that I am able to be the Highest Priestess of the Temple of Po-Si-Don. Because in that office I can serve you, the Chosen Woman of my Godly son, and help to begin a registered dynasty of God-men that will serve all mankind forever and, if need be, in other worlds."

Ast-i studied the calm face of her Priestess Mother. "You don't look as if you had ever had a care."

A gay smile brightened the face. "Oh, never! *Positively ne*-ver. No more than other women. But the workings of our bodies are so very strange that it influences our minds to sensitivities, to passions. If we have passions strong enough, we take courage enough to overcome our doubts for a time. In the intensity of causes, we overcome our inward insecurities."

She picked up Ast-i's hand and looked at the bleeding fingers gouged by the sharp reeds. "Ah, though sometimes we hurt ourselves, this makes us adamant followers of causes we choose, unstoppable when we have passions strong enough to force us to lead."

As God-ette began a movement to leave, Ast-i clung to her. "Oh, Mother of God, don't leave me just yet. The lights are long, the darks are..." Her unspoken movements and expression told of the loneliness, the oppressive loneliness. "You mentioned other worlds. What do you mean?"

"Well, I may stay, just for a little...here, let me wash those cuts. There! Now, if you will, lie back, become cozy and secure and expectant of fecundity. You must see yourself made pregnant with the God of Tomorrow's Planet.

You must *know* you are. Imagine the joy. Visualize it. Allow no doubts. Feel, *know* yourself fruitful, made so by Thought-Force, through space and time. For what you hold strongly enough in your consciousness, in time will come to be. By concentration and time, the chaos of 'might be' becomes the beauty of 'is'. The reality of thought becomes the fact of life."

God-ette talked slowly, but her experienced hands soon had Ast-i lying back on her bed, partly covered.

"Ah, yes. Other worlds or planets. To begin: I quote: 'In the beginning all was void and all was dark and time was not. To become a Goddess you must go beyond time. In the darkness you must see the true light. In the nothingness you must see all that may ever be. You must go in on one of your nine bodies, where knowledge is not. And in a divine consciousness, you must go where the mortal conscious cannot go. You must go where worlds cannot be and all worlds are there. Then your Radiant Body can rise out of your flesh body, and in that place where life cannot be, it will have eternal life.' "

She laughed softly. "Men! Men could never understand that. They would reason and *think,* and it would become nonsense to them. But we women *know* it is the true story of creation as told by our ancestors and remembered by every little particle of our bodies. We *know*, don't we?"

Each time Ast-i breathed or moved, God-ette breathed or moved. Each time Ast-i blinked, God-ette blinked. After a dozen breaths, God-ette began to slow her breathing and to blink less often and move less often. Ast-i found she was lulled, lulled and made sleepy by the gently, musical voice and the rhythm of the words that gradually came slower and slower. Without waiting for Ast-i to answer, she continued.

"Other worlds. Ah, yes. I must tell you the story of our people and That Other Planet. This is what was told to me by the former High Priest and confirmed by the former High Priestess. You can close your eyes and rest while I tell you the story.

"We are from a planet far away. That Other Planet we call it, because the name is too sacred to be known at large. The memory of its godliness is too sweet, too sweet to share. We, our family, were of the race, or tribe, that ruled. We were the Favored of the Supreme God, the Children of God, God in Human Form called God-e. Well, to be absolutely honest, we were born to wisdoms, powers, and knowledges that worked mental, physical, and spiritual magic among all humans—no, more, among all things!

"We were the learned ones, given the lore, or wisdom, of our race, a race that had descended from the days of creation. We were Lor'd Ones of special wisdoms. We had some skills in common, some very singular and special. But we were the rulers, not the doers. We thought and planned, others built and operated. You look sleepy, dear.

"One day a shaking began on the planet. The Lor'd One of Planets warned us all that we had to leave that planet by the space ships we had invented and constructed. We had enough ships for all the people of the planet. We tried to bring them to safety. But only a few thousand came.

"At the last breaths, many others accepted the dogma of false prophets, grew doubtful, mean, unruly and tried to destroy the ships. They stormed the ships which contained the great scientists, artisans, builders, and mechanics, and in senseless fury tore them apart.

"Then they turned their fury on the ships of those who were lored in the sciences and in healing, and destroyed them. But our ship escaped as the mob approached. We were shot from the shaking planet by a force—we cannot explain it, for the Lor'd One was injured and died before the lore could be passed on to others. It is alright for you to be sleepy, dear.

"Oh, we escaped, but so much was lost that we have never recovered the grandeur of our former life.

"We lost, partly at least, instant healing of any ailment by force of mind. The ability of everyone to read thoughts, and time and distance. Also, how to raise our Radiant Bodies and have life everlasting. How to change our bodies from material to Radiant Thought-Force and back again at will. How to build vehicles that fly over the surface of the water and the land on a cushion of...oh, something that made them float or fly at great speed, but stop quickly.

"And vastly more important now is the fact that we lost the knowledge with which to build ships that are little worlds and can fly from planet to planet through the Universe, as the Great Atl did. Som may know, he is Lor'd One of Science. You may drift into sleep if you wish.

"Anyway, we—well, really I mean *they,* for that was three generations agone—had troubles with the space ship, and fell by accident to this planet... This destroyed our ship, for it sank in the sea on the south side of this planet. Actually, less than two thousand of our race reached safety on this Pleasant Planet. But we are fond and fecund and many times bring forth twins. Slowly, because we are lored in special ways and know how to rule, we gained control of the warring tribes of this planet...

"I see you are really sleepy. That's a dear girl. I love you...very much for you are so wonderful."

Silently, she left the room, a pleased smile on her face. She winked at the Ama-Sones on guard at each side of the entrance way.

"She fell asleep right while I was talking."

One Ama-Sone said archly, "Now I wonder why!"

The other laughed. "You! Oh, you!"

19

A-Sar-U's Mindrace

A-Sar-U began again to redo, repeat, and again and again redo and repeat all the basic exercises Thoth had taught him. He checked himself to be certain he used the three relaxing breaths, followed by the three energizing breaths, and then the empowering breath. He held his mind in sharp concentration on the process. He saw, thank Atl! he saw the radiant light filling every part of his body. He felt it, saw it, running like sun-warmed, clear honey into every particle of his body. He felt the warmth that played along his skin like shafts of the Eastsun on a morning-cold body. And he began to relax. He felt the warmth seeping through each muscle and let himself drift into pools of silence. He saw himself gliding into fields of peace, heard himself drifting into worlds of light. He was so at peace, so joy-filled, so filled with energy, health, and happiness.

He was so sure in his mind that he had conquered his mind that he thought, "This is it!"

Incredibly, he was suddenly fully aware of the pressure of the stones on his back, the feel of the cool stone in the vaulted room. The sound of his own breath thundering wildly into his chest then could barely make room for the beating of his disturbed and angry heart.

The thought alone was enough to flip him from awareness of his desired inner universe to the harsh dimensions of his outer world.

Suddenly he was wildly alert. There was no divine peace in his being, no joy in his body, no warm relaxation in his mind. He felt the flow of disappointment, frustration, and anger like a wrestler's grip on his heart and his mind.

With a jerk of exasperation, he flung himself to his feet, his body at combat stance, his anger, frustration, and despair like sword-tips inside his body. He beat his fist

180

into his palm. Then he beat his head with the heels of both hands. Then, in the extremes of despair he fell sideways, brought his knees up to his chin, wrapped his arms tightly around his bent legs, and wept in despair.

"Oh, Atl, why do I fail? Why do I betray myself, my beloved Ast-i, my family, my tribe? Why do I fail? Why do I fail? Why do I betray my teachings, my training, and my Master Teacher?"

He heard his voice, like the cry of a dying loon, echoing through the room. He buried his face against both knees and wept. The sobs wrenched his body about on the stone and punished his ribs with exquisite excess.

Did he enjoy his failures? Did he enjoy his inadequacies? The thought jerked from his throat a gasp that echoed in the room.

"No!" His mind screamed the words inside his head. But it was a cry of protest, not of conviction. "No," his pride cried again, but his conscience whispered its own correction. "No, no, no. I am not a weakling. I am a champion." The spoken words echoed long in the vault of the room, but there was no echo of conviction in his heart.

Slowly his inner voice began to speak. It seemed that Thoth's voice filled the room and rumbled in his ears.

"Humankind, in general, likes to fail. For then, like hurt children who return to motherly comfort, they can have at least momentary attention and assurance of worth. For a moment, they can return to the community-blessed safety of non-aloneness. They can forget the terrors that being alone accentuates. They can be reassured of belonging.

"To many persons, assurance of belonging is more important than success. Being one of the crowd is more important than leadership. Belonging to the gang is more important than belonging totally to one's higher self. It is easier, too, for it takes less effort.

"There is an instant reward and gratification for failure. The gratification and reward for success is sometimes long delayed, or never given, or even denied by authority—or worse, simply ignored after much effort."

A-Sar-U let go his legs in astonishment. It was as if he had read the thoughts of his Master and turned them into words of truth. Slowly he forced himself into the sitting position and faced the neatly stacked stones against the outer wall. They were the inert things of life, the innocent and un-meaning things of life that most persons used as a sword-dummy. Things that were made important so that truly important things could not enter. Empty things, habits, thoughts! Baseless daydreams and uncontrolled night dreams that took time, thought and energy away from self-improvement and progress toward a goal.

A goal. His goal! What was his goal? Was it some ill-defined thought of self-aggrandizement through a rare and ego-satisfying action. Was it no more sharply defined than the daydreams of those who fail? What was his goal? Was it truly more than to have all the adorable and exciting womanly charms of Ast-i as his singular possession? Was it at base nothing but selfishness?

What was his goal?

What was his plan, the steps to reach that goal?

He lay back on the rough stone and allowed his greater mind to speak to his lesser mind as Thoth might speak to him.

His goal, no, no, my goal is to fecund Ast-i through the use of divine Thought-Force. With her help and acquiescence, to use love as the carrier of Life-Force through space to impregnate her in preparation for human birth from a Virgin untouched by man. Then, it is my goal to help, as Thoth or circumstance may direct, my fellowman to ready and protect itself from all hazards of the future, expected or not.

But you don't even know what hazards to expect, his lesser mind screeched.

True, his great mind acquiesced, It is not yet clear. But it is important to the planet. I shall be ready to do my part.

My plan?

First, I will discipline my self to absolute control and benign indifference. I will practice the Sacred Exercises intensely. But gently! As a mother caring for a child, not fiercely as a Warrior conquering a foe.

Second, I will practice the Divine Breath, sending it to all the sacred particles of my body, carefully and repeatedly, but without force or command, to produce a result in a short time.

Third, I will find the meaning of the relaxing breaths, not force them to my will. For they are old in the annals of time and were designed and tested by crafty, lored, and wise men.

Fourth, I will allow the energizing breaths to give me more energy, not try to wrest the energy from time by force of will.

Fifth, I will fashion my concentration and use my will to control my mind in order to ready myself for success. I will not force my opinion of success upon circumstances or persons. I will remember that the Sacred Exercises are as old as time and have worked for so many, changing their lives and making them better, stronger, healthier, and wiser. I do not need to force them.

Sixth, I will let the Sacred Exercises work by doing them exactly as taught and not try to force them to work on me.

Seventh, I will prepare myself painstakingly, as a sacred trust, as a priceless wisdom, as a rare knowledge, as a Lor'd One filled with disciplined skill.

Eighth, I will then send my life-forming energy to Ast-i, my Chosen Woman, the woman I love, the woman who loves me. And then? For a moment he felt doubt welling up in his body like a dreadful chill. And then? Oh, Holy Atl, what then? Thoth, what then?

He shivered and threshed about on the stone. But his greater mind shot streamers of warmth through his tense muscles. As if from far away and above, beyond the orbit of the burning Westsun he heard the words spoken in his ear.

Ninth, I will do that which I must do and do it the very best I can, without attachment to the results. The best I can now. For if I do, through this, my present life, and my lives through all future ages, the God of man will fashion it to the immediate service of my fellowman, and make it good for all ages and all men to come.

Tenth, I will project my Radiant Body, the exact duplicate of my physical body, anywhere in the universe to serve my fellowman...

A-Sar-U allowed his mind to stop talking to itself. He again took in the three relaxing breaths, three energizing breaths, and the seventh breath dedicating him to the

183

service of others and obedience to God. Again, he felt that quieting, euphoric feeling that seemed to say to his body that it was totally at peace with itself and all things around. And to say to his mind that he could accept that peace and stop the racing of ideas. He could bring his body totally under control and his mind almost under control. Why, then, could he not bring it totally under control?

A-Sar-U let his mind wander. Just wander. He decided to let that which would happen, happen. But he guided the happening. In his head he held a picture, an ideal, of his Radiant Body in all its shining, golden power rising slowly out of his flesh body. This vision he held without attachment. If it happened, that was enough. If it did not happen, that was beyond his will, his skill.

Again he felt himself gliding swiftly into euphoria, that wonderful floating delight. The stones did not press upon his skin. The air was not filled with the dew of first-light chill. The wall was not supporting the pile of stones he was yet to move to the other side of the room without reason to do so. Drifting, drifting into satisfaction, ease, forgetfulness, and peace. Drifting, drifting into a non-caring joy. A non-caring joy.

At a place beyond the measure of breaths or the tyranny of feeling or the tantalizings of thought. At that place he seemed to poise. To poise and drift. To drift and float in peace and in joy. In incredible joy, in rising, floating joy.

In some way, beyond the five senses he felt himself begin to vibrate. To vibrate like a struck sword blade through every particle of his body.

It was strange, but it was not totally unpleasant. His mind did not react to the feeling. Then, from some ancient well of racial experience, he felt his Radiant Body gather itself into a True Self and begin to lift out of his physical flesh. It seemed to float upward and then stand on the floor. But he felt an enormous pull and demand from his physical body upon that radiant form.

Then he was aware that in some wonder, some joyous wonder, he was walking away from his body against that strong pull, and that it grew less with each step his Radiant Body took.

His senses were in him, but in some strange limbo, between his two bodies, seeming to be created in his physical body but felt in his Radiant Body.

Somehow, without consciously willing it, he moved further away. Near the far corner of the chamber he felt free of the pull. But he was aware of a silvery cord that ran from the back of his physical head to the back of his radiant head. There it seemed to attach to the head and the heart in such a way that it did not restrict or bother him.

The joy of his new success buoyed him, emboldened him. Thoth had moved the stones by his Radiant Body. So would he. With a strange twist of his will he directed the Radiant Body to lift and carry a stone. In his extended senses and sight he saw the stone float through the air to the inward side of the room. The sound of its being fitted to the wall and floor was slight, but he knew in the waters of his deep river of unconsciousness that it was done.

Again and again he desired a stone to be moved, and it floated over him and was fitted into place. The mood of infinite joy was in him and all went swiftly. Then, as a stone was sailing above his physical body, the sense of wonder and joy turned to questions, to what what-ifs.

What if? What if I could not get back into my body?

What if the silvery cord were to foul on some stone and be cut?

What if the all-changing Westsun came while I was out of my body?

What if a stone fell upon me?

All of the what what-ifs struck with the instantaneous speed of thought. But the sense of fear exploded through his body with the force of a tree-height fall. The sense of fear was within his body faster than the thought. It made him roll aside as if in self-defense. But faster than the lash of fear, three things happened in his body.

His Radiant Body was jerked back and slammed into his body. The force was great enough to make him gasp with pain. Instantly his body felt as if all the nettles and needles of the planet struck and whipped him from the inside and outside at the same time.

His physical body was momentarily aware of an incapacity to move, yet a maddening urgency to do so.

His conscious mind reasserted its control with fear, dread, and a sense of humiliating failure—of worthlessness, and stupidity.

The stone crashed to the floor. Splinters pelted his body as if thrown Warrior-strong.

He rolled aside and to his feet in the stance for hand-to-hand combat. Before the noise of the crashing stone had stopped echoing in the vault, his eyes had scanned the room. All the stones except three had been moved to the inner wall. Splinters of stone lay around the floor, and the fallen stone was broken almost at the centerline across its width leaving sharp and jagged edges.

He shuddered. The what-if was clear. If the stone had fallen on his prostrate body he would have been seriously injured, perhaps maimed or possibly killed. He felt the shivers in his flesh and the anger in his mind. A fury at himself, at the room, at the stone, at the circumstances. It was that searing anger born of helplessness and frustration that had flooded him earlier. But now it was capped with dread and fear.

Fear. He had been afraid of failure. Now he was afraid of trying. So he was sure to fail.

He attacked the pile of stones, moving them swiftly from the inside wall to the outside wall. When they were arranged with the neatness that Thoth's discipline demanded, he carefully lifted the halves of the broken stone and fitted them together tightly on top of the pile.

"Holy Atl..." the cry echoed in the vault, "...help me."

There was a slight stir. He turned swiftly to see Thoth seated placidly on the broken stone. Thoth ran a finger between the close-fitted broken stones, the full length of the crack caused by the break, back to front, then front to back.

"Where'd you come from?" A-Sar-U felt the harshness of fright in his voice, fright caused by Thoth's sudden presence.

Thoth ran his finger again along the crack in the stone, back to front, front to back.

"Ah, A-Sar-U, when you do divine things you can never be alone. The gods all stand await to help. I felt your desperate call and came the nearest way, through this stone wall."

186

A-Sar-U felt the struggle of doubt and faith for control of his face. Doubt because his training had assured his conscious mind that such a thing was impossible. Faith because his Master had said it was true. The battle raged within him for several breaths. Thoth sat, his eyes fixed placidly on A-Sar-U's.

"You saw the mess I made, the dismal failure?"

"I saw," Thoth's tone was filled with authority and yet gentle, "a beginner trying and almost succeeding in a saintly exercise." After a long silence he continued, "It may be that I did not explain clearly enough that when you try to do divine work you do the best you can and leave it to God to make it good. It is certain that I did not explain clearly that in sacred things, if your disciplines are not perfected, if you allow doubts or fears into your physical mind, or tensions in your body so much as the crooking of your little finger, it interferes with your Radiant Body. That is why so many cannot do this sacred work."

"Help me, Holy Thoth. Tell me what to do and how to do it."

"Beloved of the Gods, no one can tell you how you must do it. What you must do your greater mind knows." Thoth rose and stepped halfway into the stone wall, then turned back. "Help you? You don't need help, you need practice. Practice. Discipline. Doing it over and over, perfectly."

Thoth stopped and was still for a moment, then smiled. "I broke two stones in my practice before I learned, truly learned, that fear in sacred things, even as small as a mustard's seed, looms larger than mountains in the way of your success. So? Go ahead. Smash a few more. But don't cry out until you get into real trouble.

"And don't doubt. For doubt of self is a seed of fear higher than the mighty Atals."

The stone closed over where Thoth had been, leaving A-Sar-U alone again.

Alone, and once more determined to try to achieve union with Ast-i and Virgin Birth. Alone, determined first to send his Radiant Body through stone.

20

Ast-i's Flight of Soul

Ast-i paced the length of the room and back again. She longed for the open air, the feel of a breeze upon her skin. She had always been athletic. At least in a mild way. Running and scuffling with A-Sar-U and all the boys. She missed such outdoor activity now. Her mind would not stop in its busy work of going over and over useless ideas and half-formed passions. A hundred thoughts came with each breath. And each thought caused a nagging question before it skipped away.

Was she beautiful? Was she beautiful enough? Bes, her kindly father, had taught her: "Woman is the beauty that draws all men, she is the heart of the heart of heaven." Oh, was she a beautiful heart of the heart of heaven that could draw the fecund and wonderful—oh, so, so wonderful!—A-Sar-U across time and space? So long now, surely almost a whole Westsun, she had visualized him coming to her in a glorious form. She had visualized holding his dear head to her breast and opening her person to him. The thoughts made her breasts rise and her breath come swiftly in anticipation of joy. Such joy!

Was she—small compared to the beautiful, strong, long-legged Ama-Sones who guarded her in her apartment in the Temple of the Virgins—was she big enough to be A-Sar-U's heart of the heart of heaven forever? Her hair was long enough to reach her waist. It was reddish-golden blonde, the color of sunlight glancing from honey, and it floated on a breeze or when she ran. Did he like her hair? He had never really said so.

The hair of most of the Ama-Sones was dark, curled tight, and short like a helmet tight-fitted. They were so strong, with force and grace in movement. She was...

She was a Chosen Woman!

For six breaths she felt the up-flowing of elation. But with the seventh, she tumbled again into doubt. "But what if *they* wanted to be chosen? There are other women. Any girl in all the beauties in the Temple of the Virgins' School for Virgins would want to be A-Sar-U's chosen. Was she beautiful enough to hold him? Or kind enough? Or gentle enough?

She had often been rough in play with him and hurt him a little. Did he remember? *Would* he remember at some time and decide he did not want to come to her? She had been a little punishing cruel to the very one she loved. Why? Why had she wanted to hurt the only man she ever loved? Why? Was she...?

Why did she dwell upon her own emotions and doubts when she knew there was much happening beyond the walls of the Temple that could be important to the planet? She could sense them and their importance and urgency. Yet she made the little things happening to her so much more important.

Was there something really wrong with her?

When the Mother Goddess came into the entrance, she ran into her arms, sobbing.

"Oh, Mother, why am I such a mess? Why did I like to hurt A-Sar-U when we played? Will he remember and not want me? Will he want me enough? Really, really enough? Am I beautiful enough to be his heart of heaven? Why do I dwell on me and my little world while out there rebellions are being formed and the Empire is under threat from man and nature, and we all may die and...?"

God-ette clamped her fingers over Ast-i's mouth. "What in the name of Atl are you babbling about?" She walked Ast-i to the far end of the room, beyond earshot of the Ama-Sones. She shook her. "Don't babble. What makes you think there might be rebellion, that the Empire is under threat human and natural, and that we all might die?"

Ast-i looked up into the troubled eyes of her Goddess Guardian. Did she read fear there? Was her Goddess filled with human worry?

"I don't know why I think that. Nor why I *know* it. But when I try to reach out and pull A-Sar-U to me, I pull in knowledges, certainties..."

The expression of harsh concern on God-ette's face gave way to her usual softness. "Oh, intuitively you *know*. You have not heard talk?"

"In here, Mother, where only you may come? Where only you may speak to me?"

"Good! Rumors are more dangerous than slings in affairs of Empire. Of course the Empire is in danger. There are always those who wish to rebel, and many do. That is the real problem of all authority. For authority cannot function unless the people accept it. But Thoth lets all have their say. Anyone may grab the sword from his helmet and try to best him.

"Yet, Beloved of the Gods, this period in the history of our Government on this Pleasant Planet may be one of the most peaceful times. Well, at least, on the surface. Empires, like people, have inner conflicts that may destroy them if not understood and dealt with.

"To set your mind at ease concerning the things you sense. Yes, as usual, there may be rebellion. Yes, as usual, the Empire is under threat..."

She stopped speaking for a moment and stroked Ast-i's hair from her forehead and temple. "Yes, Ast-i, as usual, all humanity may die. Will die, sooner or later. Whether it is sooner or later depends on you and my Godly son."

There was silence for ten breaths. When God-ette spoke again her face had regained its beautiful composure, and its ready and gentle smile.

"Now, to the harder questions you asked. Why are you such a mess? The answer is as simple as it is important. You have thoughts and passions, ideas and experiences racing through your body because you are Chosen of God. You are to be the symbol of all womanhood, all motherhood. You are given the pains and reactions of all of the womanly, feminine emotions and problems."

"But why?"

"So that all women may come to you with their fears, problems, and tears and be understood and helped. They can come to you with their unfounded dreams and not be ridiculed or rejected. They may come to you with their emotions and not be reasoned with. They can come to you with their petty dislikes and unfounded jealousies and doubts and be accepted and loved. They can bring you

their unfounded doubts, and feelings of personal inadequacy, and find acceptance and love. So that any woman,
now or forever, night or day, alone or in a crowd, may turn
to you and find physical and spiritual community, belongingness and assurance. How can you be fully prepared to
help them unless you have been helped with the same
problems by the Supreme God?"

"Are you beautiful enough? Well, no. No, in the way
that no woman is ever beautiful enough, not really, to satisfy herself. Her criticism of herself is really an insult to
the God who fashioned her.

"Any woman who doubts her own beauty is sacrile-
gious. She should dread the points with which God will
wound her in return for the darts of doubt she has thrown
at Him and His wisdom. Any woman who criticizes her
own beauty says to God, 'Hey, dummy, I think I could
have done better than you did!' Do you want to go on
throwing darts at God?"

Ast-i was giggling at the ridiculousness of the thought-
picture. "No, Mother of God, I am throwing away all my
darts."

"Good. With the looks you have you do the best you
can, and leave it to God to make it good. Alright?"

"Alright, Mother. Of course."

"Now, are you beautiful enough that my son will want
you? As his mother I often thought he should at least look
at other women. But from the moment you two held hands
and walked to your anointing by the Great God-e, Priest of
God Eternal, at the Golden Fountain of Life, his eyes have
been only on you.

"Oh, at times I saw you be gently cruel with him, and I
worried. But then I realized it was because you loved him
so much, and it was the only way your young heart could
devise to make him aware of your body. Even in play you
were telling him two things. 'I want you to want me as
much as I want you,' and 'I want you to know I am strong
enough to fight for you, and I'm jealous.' "

"Oh, Holy Atl!" Tears were flowing when she asked,
"Then you do not think I was really mean at heart?"

"Mean? Is it really mean for any woman who loves a
man to stir his longings? Face it and be proud. You've
really been seducing him in your body contacts since you

were able to walk. And that's a very acceptable feminine employment, young lady."

"I thought...oh, I don't know..."

"That's why we women almost always win. Usually we don't know, we only feel. And in feeling we hit it right."

Ast-i sat on the edge of her sleeping platform, her knees weak from the load of wisdom placed upon her. "If only I could be all that I know I want to be and should be!"

"Darling, and chosen of the Gods, Just *be*. Don't worry the past and don't harry the future. You cannot borrow from either without injuring the present. Yesterday's problems have formed your personality and character. Tomorrow's problems cannot be solved until they appear. Today, only, is yours.

"Today is yours. You may want to use it to bring your Golden Radiant Body out of your flesh body."

"I'd like that. Will you teach me how?"

"Of course not. You do not need to be taught. You are a woman sensitive. You are a Divine Mystic. You have inherited Cosmic Wisdom through thousands of generations before As-Tar. You have imbibed the Universal Knowledge of Bes. You can do it. Just do it!"

21

A-Sar-U's Pathway of Glory

As the lights of the Eastsun went by, A-Sar-U came to almost love the very stones he carried from one side of the room to the other twice each Eastsun. He did not know why he was assigned to do it, except that it was strengthening to his muscles, and his Master wanted it. He no longer fought the stones, and found that as he performed the accustomed task of moving them, he entered into some deeper form of mentation.

It was as if movement itself, purposeful movement and effort, the results of which he could immediately see, helped to calm him and take him deeper into a kind of walking peace.

At times he found it almost as deep as true meditation. He realized in some far place in his consciousness that action need not disturb meditation, but might add to it by moving it into a special place in his mind.

But he did not relax his search for the most perfect disciplines leading to meditation. And for the fastest and surest way to get to the deepest peace. Again and again he rushed himself into the depth of meditation, put his mind in that joyous limbo, threw energy into every part of his body.

He began to recognize the extra energy delivered to his body when he accurately touched each of the secret places along the sacred Pathway of Gold.

It was a Pathway of Radiant, Resplendent Glory! When he was suspended between the antipodes of mind, held in the warm cradle of divine energy and peace, floating in a radiant form in the inner visions of his minds in all the places of his body, he felt a rising Glory.

The feeling was satisfying and also humiliating. It was as if he had become Thoth, or in some way risen above the quality and worth of his own physical body to some resonance with all time and all things that equated him with The Good. Each time he did the Sacred Exercises, he arose with more assurance of the Divinity within, and less ego about the physical shell.

Pondering upon the things Thoth had shown him, realization began to light his waking mind to the imponderables. He was flesh that could be divinized. He was divinity that could be flesh. Thoth spoke of the Sons of Atl, the Children of God-e, who were really the Sacred Children of Thoth, the natural-born or trained and disciplined Godmen of all Ages. It bothered A-Sar-U much that he did not fully understand that concept. His conscious mind wondered at how man could be God-e, that is, God in human form.

Je-Su had preached to him, to all Warriors, that man could know the will of the Supreme God-e only by faithfully accepting that Je-Su was the Only Begotten Son of God-e through the body of a Virgin. To know the will of God-e, one must submit to the will of Je-Su. Je-Su who considered himself alone able to know God and God's will. Je-Su said that he alone was the father of mankind, the Great Papa. The power of God's will was made manifest in Je-Su and enforced by Warriors under Set.

Belief in the concept, and submission to the will of the Vast Papa (or his righteous Warriors and Priests!) was the only way to salvation of life and bliss in Divinity. Je-Su and Set were so proud and boastful, as if they were trying to shout down their own doubts of themselves, of their worth, the worth of God himself.

Je-Su and Set held power over a large number in the Empire. Those who believe in Je-Su and Set were a potent body. Potent enough to be a worry to Thoth. Ah, ha! Why did not Thoth remove Je-Su from office? Bes would fight Je-Su, or his chosen champion, Set, in the Lists. Bes would win.

A-Sar-U was certain that knowing God was not possible through the mind or opinion of any other person than one's very self, but only through the experience and discipline of one's self. One could not entwine with Godhood through mind alone, or through faith only.

194

One must first work and clean, prepare the Temple of Flesh for the entry and residence of Divinity. Then, and then only, True Divinity would come into its Holy Temple.

And Divinity did not possess man. Divinity served man at his will. Yet, not because of man's will always. Sometimes Divinity's will enwrapped man's will and allowed it to choose more justly and perform more perfectly. Man could not accept any other between himself and his Divinity, for each man must reach Divinity through his own efforts and by himself. He thought of Ast-i and added, "Or herself."

A-Sar-U laughed aloud. "You are becoming a little Je-Su," he said aloud to himself. "You'll be preaching like Je-Su if you don't watch yourself."

He lay down in the middle of the room and disciplined his mind to allow his Radiant Body to move all the stones. But cautiously he had them taken around, not over his body. He had moved all the stones to the outside wall and was moving them back to the inside wall when it began to happen.

His Radiant Body began to weaken. It did not hurtle back to his physical body, pulled by the command of the silvery cord. The Radiant Body grew weaker and weaker, like an overworked muscle, to lose some of its enormous strength. He could feel even his physical body being exhausted as if by a too-long run.

He thought to bring back the Radiant Body into the physical body. But he could not make his will work against the ever growing, increasing weakness. On the inside of his physical eyelids, he could see his Radiant Body bearing a stone equal to his physical weight, but unable to go further toward the outside wall. It seemed suspended, unable to move, as if impaled on a thousand invisible spears held by invisible Warriors.

Then, without rousing to consciousness, as if floating in the cocoon of an unpleasant dream, he became aware of things of sense. His physical body was hot. His breathing was shallow and fast. His heart was thudding. His mind was dulled. His will was without focus. His ears were roaring.

Strangely, his Radiant Body was feeling the same things. It was as if some fluid connected the energy of his two separate bodies, letting...no, no, making them fully *conscious* of identical feelings and sensations in each.

The fluid interconnected the feelings and sensations of his two bodies, but it did not connect the energy of muscles and will. It did not connect the way to respond to such terrible stress. The breathing was not deeper. The strength was not returned. Both radiant and physical bodies seemed incapable of long sustaining life.

The thought thundered in his consciousness, "Is my Radiant Body dying? Can it not sustain life forever under any circumstances?"

As if to show him, to reassure him, to make him ashamed of his weakling faith, a jade-green glow began to brighten in his Radiant Body's heart. It grew until it filled the vaulted room with its intense radiance. He felt the power of divinity flow again into his Radiant Body. It placed the stone it held, and then the others, in perfect order. It was functioning in the debilitating fluid.

His physical body was not functioning well. He felt sweat rolling down his cheeks and from his chest down his sides. He could not seem to gulp enough air into his lungs. His body hurt.

His Radiant Body, unaffected by the fluid or by his physical stress, continued its work. The work his will had set it to doing. To test his command power, he willed the Radiant Body to return to his physical body. It carefully placed the last stone against the outside wall, rose in the air above his physical self, turned over so its back was down, and gently floated toward his physical body gathering speed until it slammed into his flesh. He joyed in the feel of nettles stinging his body from the inside. He joyed. It meant that he had not lost control over the Radiant Body of Divinity.

He roused himself against the life-sapping lethargy and focused on the roar. It seemed to be the sounds of a million grains of sand flung one after the other against the Temple and the suffering earth. He knew then that the Westsun had come to punish the Pleasant Planet and all things upon it. Twenty-eight Eastsuns he had been working. Twenty-eight Eastsuns! A large part of the time permitted to achieve fecundation for Virgin Birth or forfeit his hope—and perhaps his and Ast-i's lives.

Though he continued to work at his disciplines and exercises, A-Sar-U found himself waiting impatiently for Thoth's next appearance. Many questions kept echoing in the void of his knowledge. He rehearsed them as he waited out the seemingly endless Eastsuns:

"What is the meaning of the Jade Heart?

"Why did it come only when I felt death was in my physical self?

"If you can go through stone walls, how is it that you can lift stones on your hands without your hands going through the stone? And sit upon stone without your body going into the stone?

"Will I have the Jade Heart forever?

"Does it symbolize eternal life? If so, is it eternal life for the Radiant Body only, or for the physical also?

"How can I learn to send my physical body through stone walls? I tried as soon as you left me last time and it did not work. What should I do to make it work?"

22

Ast-i's First Soul Flight

Ast-i twisted fretfully on her bed. She was not able to sleep. She was letting her mind wonder about time, and why things took so long. So very long!

By the calendar of the Pleasant Planet, it was 3001 Westsuns since the people arrived from That Other Planet. No, more! And it was now twenty-eight more Eastsuns.

Why had she lost her ability to raise her Radiant Body?

Holy, Atl! It had been...it had been twenty-eight full Eastsuns since Ast-i had been able to (or first began to) raise her Golden Body from her flesh body. She knew it was possible to do it. But try as she did now, she was not successful.

Oh, true, as she was drifting into sleep she would feel her Golden Body uncouple from the physical. But she was not able to send it out at will. To send it and to know when it went, where it went, what it did, and when it returned.

She was worried. The Lady Mother, God-ette, had said Ast-i should be able to raise her golden self easily—well, more easily than any man—because she was a woman and had the marvelous energy of the mystic's intuition to help her.

"Perhaps," she said aloud. "But if intuition fails me?"

It had. It was failing her. Would it do so forever?

She twisted forcefully under the sheepskin covers, and forced her body more deeply into the deerskin cover to the padding of reeds on her bed. She lay listening intensely to the slight sounds of the Ama-Sonian guards being changed, the swift, soft, careful words that passed from one to the other the duty and responsibility of guarding her.

"Halt! Who moves there?"

Ritual words, repeated by the Ama-Sones every thousand breaths. They had purpose. They had footing. They had place and known relationships. They had authority to guide them in their rounds of duties. They had clearly assigned duties which they shared with and passed on to each other.

How lucky. Her own duty was not clearly assigned. Just a general, "Bear a child as a Virgin." And then, what?

Would she do it all over again like the changing of the guards? Or would she say it over and over again?

"Bear a child
        As a Virgin."
"Bear a child
        As a Virgin."

The ridiculousness of it made her giggle, but the rhythm of the words caused her to say it over and over in her mind. Over and over.

Then what? There was some hope that a great good would come to all mankind. But what would her future be?

She sighed deeply. She knew it was the fourth watch of the dark. In another thousand breaths it would be light. But she could not get up and weave, not now. With nothing else to amuse her, she let the rhythm of words and ideas run through her thoughts.

"Soon be light.
        It's all right.
        Bear a child
    Soon be light.
        It's all right
        As a Virgin.
        Bear a child..."

The feeling of expansion began in her heart. It was as if it swelled slowly. In some cavern of unconsciousness she had the thought that her heart was swelling with pregnancy. It was filled with a feeling of growth, with warmth, like a touch of Eastsun through breeze kissed leaves. A lovely, lovely feeling. Lulling, lovely...

The warmth and swelling spilled out of her heart into her body. It raced downward into her being and upward into her brain. Her head, body, legs, toes grew warmer and swelled gently. Gently, but so much that she could not

199

breathe, until the pressure was a gentle pain crying for release.

Ast-i wanted to cup her head in her hands. She could not. She could not move. Yet she could feel. She felt every small particle in her body as if it was thistle-down blowing out and away from her body.

She felt a blow, a gentle but quite distinct blow at the back of her head. Or was it, inside her head?

The blow was gentle. But the noise it made in her brain shook every bit of her body with sound. Loud, loud sound.

Then there was light.

A brilliant glow of beautiful, intense light filled her body. It was warm, bright, and seemed to glow from inside each smallest particle of her vibrating body. Vibrating, like an aspen leaf in a wild, wild wind. Vibrating! Every little bit of her flesh vibrating to that joy-filled, inner light. Her body was over-filled with pressure, with joy, with light, and every smallest particle seemed to dance with the happiness of its potential.

She was not certain how it happened. Suddenly she was two.

Yes, two!

The girl huddled and immovable on the deerskin bed.

The wraith of warm, brilliant light that moved away from that body, wobbling and struggling, as if standing in a wind-tossed boat.

Something was pulling upon the wraith-like, light body. It was a great pull that seemed to come from a silver cord that ran from the back of the girl's body to the head and heart of the light body. With the instinct of will, she forced herself to go away from the body. At first it was very difficult, but with each step that was taken the pull became less, and the light body was more steady.

Her senses then seemed to transfer into a glowing, pink body. She was near the door and very distinctly heard the new guard say, "The guard of the fourth watch of the dark to replace the guard of the third watch of the dark." Then she was away, outside, in the fresh air, the cool, delightful air of the dark on the Pleasant Planet. How free she was. How good it was.

In some way she willed to be on the porch of the Temple. She was there. She did not go there, she was there. She could see the circling curves of rivers, interlocked with canals, all feeding at last into the bay of the Ancient Sea. Turning, she could see the giant Atals with their sides covered with green and their peaks covered with the white-cold.

She could *see* it, although her conscious mind could have told her it was too dark to see with physical eyes.

She looked beyond the dikes, across the rivers to the Fen's Land. There, she knew, were tracts of marshland jungle where life went on among a peaceful and powerful people. She turned and saw—yes, she saw, even in the blackness, the Temple Guard. It too was being changed to the fourth watch.

In that strange way, with that pure will, she willed to be in the quarters of Bes. She was there. Bes was asleep, his great arms and chest bare and uncovered. His blanket of tiger skins covered his short legs and the children sleeping cuddled near him. They were children of all tribes. Tribes that fought each other! Now, in the assurance of love and protection, they slept in confidence and peace.

"No wonder you are called the Lor'd One of Children and Love," she said to Bes.

Bes opened his eyes and looked through her. His huge hands touched each child to be certain of its comfort, and he went instantly to sleep again. A smile made his face quite beautiful, even with its many battle scars.

"How great is strength tenderly used," Ast-i thought. She was to remember that thought when she found dreadful strength foully used.

The idea occurred to her that she could go to A-Sar-U's quarters. She was not certain where he might be. Surely not in a Warrior's cubicle. Yet she willed to see for herself. Instantly she was standing at his cubicle, but a strange armor was hanging on the ready-pegs. Someone had been assigned his space. Where was his armor?

She willed to find his armor and was instantly moving. She was over low hills looking down upon a Line of Twenty Warriors running through the dark. She could see his crest, his sword, his shield. She could see his helmet and breastplate on a big body moving at swift pace through the dark.

It was his armor. It was not A-Sar-U.

She fought against the pull to go back to her body and willed to see what lay ahead. She opened her eyes slowly and saw the Warriors go to a small river, narrow and shallow, then stop.

"Halt here. Post guards. Make camp. Eat. Sleep." The orders came from within the helmet belonging to A-Sar-U. But it was not his voice. No! Not at all the voice she loved so dearly!

What was the meaning? Again she felt the pull trying to return her to her body. She fought against it. She fought hard. She wanted to find A-Sar-U. Instantly she was above the Temple of Po-Si-Don. Intuitively she knew she was near her beloved.

She willed to be in his room and moved a few arms in that direction. She felt herself stopped by an energy. A soft, yielding, but impenetratable force. It allowed her to move, even to lean against it, yet not to penetrate into or through it.

She felt a sense strange to her. She knew that the energy meant her no harm. But it was more powerful than even her desire to see her beloved. She tested it by willing to come into and through it from different directions. She made tries around a circle. But there was a ring of energy through which she could not pass, an invisible, inviolable Ring-Pass-Not.

To test the strength of her will, she willed to be in the quarters of Set. She was there. He lay asleep under a lion-skin, his face in a scowl, a sword gripped in his right hand, a dagger in his left. Some dread of the future, a sense of fear, rippled through her, and she was drawn backward. She was hurtled backward by—a sense registered a reaction, a thought—by the same gentle but unyielding force she had found in the Ring-Pass-Not.

She slammed back into her physical body with a force that almost rolled her from her bed to the stone floor. She came to her feet, stinging inside her skin from the speed and force of the recoupling of radiant and physical bodies.

Her senses were fully alert. She saw the guard pass the tasseled, ceremonial spear of authority, and heard her say, "The guard of the third watch of the dark gives into your hand the authority of the Empire to guard one of its treasures, and the duty to guard it as faithfully as you value your life."

Ast-i moved slowly, as if in a trance. In a trance! A trance of dry-eyed tears and joyful confusion...and some fear of the unknown future and the unexplained things that had just happened to her. No. No. What she had done was through the use of techniques taught to her out of love and through her strange will.

Unspeakable! Bewildering! Impossible! Yet she knew it had happened.

"It was not a dream," she said, so loudly that her guards glanced into the chamber to be certain she was alright. "It was not a dream!"

Numbly, and a little chilled by a strange fear of the unknown, she loosened the clasp of her coton and felt it slide to the floor. She ran her hands slowly over her body, from the top of her forehead down over her firm breasts, to her thighs, her ankles and her feet. It was not unpleasant. In fact, she approved of her figure, soft but vibrant. She enjoyed the sensation of touch, and knew how very much she would enjoy the questing touch of her beloved. Sighing, and dreamily, she moved toward the pool and almost tripped over the white marble which was her testing block.

"Oh, no," she sighed. This was the light of the coming of the all-demanding Westsun. Like every other woman on the Pleasant Planet, she would sacrifice to her femininity, and the white block would tell the Lady Goddess that she had not become pregnant. For she had to sit on it all the light of two Eastsuns. But only after the Westsun blazed its path across the sky.

She stepped around the testing seat and eased herself into the pleasant water. Floating in the pool, she let her mind search for peace, for release from tension. But the usual blessed peace would not come.

Questions. Questions. Questions! They pounded inside her head and clamored for answers. Answers now.

"Why doesn't the Mother Goddess come?"

But God-ette did not come until after the Westsun had roared by, thrown its punishing, garish red light through the translucent light of the Eastsun, burning and shrivelling, and demanding its tribute, which sent her to sit on the testing stone and fume at the problems of being a woman.

23

A-Sar-U and Thought Reading

A-Sar-U was impatient for Thoth to come to answer his many questions but was mildly surprised when, after infinite numbers of Eastsuns, Thoth came physically through the stone door. Once again his broad face was lined with the marks of obvious worry. He walked with that swift assurance and slow movement that marked his great strength and simple dignity. When he sat on a stone, A-Sar-U saw a momentary sag of his shoulders, and heard a slight sigh of fatigue. His amazing voice made A-Sar-U think of the song of birds, the fragrance of trees, and the taste of sun-warmed honey.

"I come late. Affairs of the Empire have grown heavier than these stones. They multiply almost as fast as Je-Su and his followers, his powder children, as Bes calls them, can contrive. Set's army is moving toward open rebellion."

A-Sar-U wondered: "Thoth is Supreme. Set's Warriors are a danger. Why does Thoth not remove him from leadership and power? Why?"

Thoth sat still, very still, and slowly went through the cycle of breaths. His face relaxed, his body seemed to gain strength. When he opened his eyes, the laughter had returned to them.

"Ah, the Westsun. The Mother Goddess reports that Ast-i is paying her dues to the Lord of Nature, as are all other non-pregnant women. How are you faring? You, who are the hope of the Empire, the salvation of thousands of generations of mankind in the future, if the plans work well."

A-Sar-U poured out his questions with all the passion of his frustration, doubt, and despair. Thoth thought for a long time and then smiled.

"You have asked questions that should take a lifetime or more of training to prepare for and receive the answer.

But I hear in your voice and see in your behavior that you have mastered your disciplines well. You have grown from boy to man and from Warrior to Candidate for Initiation in a very few Eastsuns."

Thoth stopped and again seemed to be deep in thought. "But," he smiled broadly, "you did not ask aloud the one question that flashed through your mind as I was speaking just past. It is a question that shows you have also grown toward understanding the problems of Empire, authority, and rule. You wondered in your mind: 'Thoth is supreme authority in the Empire. Je-Su and Set threaten the Empire's future. When is Thoth going to take them from their positions of leadership and authority?' "

A-Sar-U felt his breath catch in astonishment, and saw the merriment that spread on Thoth's face, even before the merry laughter reached his ears.

"You read my thoughts..."

"Sometimes I read thoughts. Unfortunately not always accurately, but usually swiftly enough to help in combat. You will soon be doing it as well as I. It is a skill that comes with Initiation, unless you are born with it. It is not a high skill that requires that you develop the Jade Heart."

A-Sar-U felt the urgency of curiosity that he always felt when Thoth spoke of such things. It was a feeling that made him want to urge Thoth to hurry the information. To hurry, for he could never get enough or fast enough to satisfy his racing mind.

"I will answer your question expressed in thought. I, Thoth, Supreme Physical Power on this Pleasant Planet do not remove Je-Su or Set from power for two reasons. A temporary reason is you."

"Me?"

"Yes. You. A long-range reason is the obedience I owe to my Master, Ra. His orders, when he was hurriedly leaving were simple: 'Until my return, make no changes you do not have to make.'

"Ra did not expect to be gone beyond one or two Westsuns. Besides, you and what you are doing are more important to the Empire and to future humanity than a few disturbances that are meant to show contempt for authority or even a threat to overthrow it. If I order Set's removal, it means immediate war between the Empire and the

Sethian forces. Of course I could order the Combats be reopened. That would mean that all Warriors, including you, would, by Empire Law, have to report to their duty station. Either way your project would be interrupted. That is exactly what Je-Su and Set want.

"Again, you ask in your mind. Why? Because if you and Ast-i succeed in proving Virgin Birth by Thought-Force, it will be considered by all to have been accomplished by Divine Grace from Thoth-Khnum, Mut, Atl, or Amun, or one of the ancient powers. You two will be thought of as God and Goddess.

"Ah, that is, by all but Je-Su. Je-Su will never allow a Goddess in his religion, or a mere woman to become a Goddess. Nor will he allow you, a mere man, to be known as a God in the Empire. He will prevent it if he can and hopes to kill you if he cannot.

"You see, it would disturb and might prove false his claim that he is the only spokesman for the Supreme God, that he, Je-Su, is the Great Papa, the beneficent father of all mankind."

Thoth was silent for a long while before he said, "I think I can hold out long enough. Bes suggests I let him challenge Set to a duel. Then one would have to be killed, and I think it would be your twin. But...ah, you see why there is urgent need for you to accomplish...and little time. Too little time."

Thoth rose and approached the inward wall. At his knock, a small gate at eye level was opened, and two flats of food were passed through to him. On the flats of willow-wood were plantain leaves. In small mounds spaced on the leaves were mounds of food. A savory and onions, a slice of roasted venison, a mound of boiled rye with chunked tomato, a mound of wheat with red chiles. A heap of millet in a paste of simmered milk and cane juice. A large slice of cheese of that tawny color that bespoke of goat's milk. He placed the flats on the stone on which A-Sar-U sat and returned to the small gate to accept two large ram's-horn flagons filled with a liquid savory of fruit juices, powdered cinnamon, cardamom, and ginger, with jasmine flower petals floating on top.

Thoth sat on the other end of the stone, smiled, and nodded in a most companionable way. Realization of how very much he missed the companionship of communal meals came to A-Sar-U so strongly that his eyes misted.

Without seeming to notice, Thoth said, "The punishment for leadership is to miss companionship. The punishment for men at war is not only the threat of death or dying, but to miss the joys of the presence of women. Especially the woman's way with food and man. In the struggles of our tribes we must never forget that powerful feeling of community. It is our unspoken acceptance, by ourselves and our companions, of our place in a cause. This acceptance is important in ultimate victory.

Also, we should not forget that women are a spice to life as ginger is to a savory. And they are as fragrant as jasmine. Women are wiser than men and, in the long run, hardier. Not as strong, mind you, but more enduring with their strength. They are shorter, softer, warmer, more desirable, and more desiring than men."

Thoth ate with complete attention to his food and did not seem to note the flush of desire that rose in A-Sar-U's face. A desire that racked his body and emotions with visions of Ast-i, her warm little body, so soft, warm, rounded, yielding...

"To desire a woman is next best to desiring God. Fortunately it may also be more quickly and repeatedly rewarded."

A vision of Ast-i's body and the reward it could be to his desiring flushed through all the places of A-Sar-U's being.

Thoth was silent while the meal was finished, the flagons drained, and the flats returned through the small gate. Then, as was a habit of his, he continued to speak as if the words were continuously connected to those that had gone before. "Also, and this is important, women are the cause of true Initiation. One major part of the Initiation of man is to awaken in him the softer, more feminine part of his nature without weakening his masculine side.

"In ancient days in our tribes, women were denied Initiation because it was felt they did not truly need to be more feminine. They are already perfect in that way. Women are more sensitive to the impulses of sacred things. They know without reasoning, succeed without effort...at least it seems so at times. Man may need to go through extreme tests of will and determination. Women, in their gentle way, are born determined and of strong will.

But enough of goddesses. Now to your five questions, which are in fact questions about Initiation.

"There are truisms about Initiation. That suggests that in sacred things certain experiences are repeated from one person to another and seem to be true in all cases. Some of these are:

"When the student is ready the Master will appear.

"A Master wants a student as strongly as a student wants a Master.

"A Master is not allowed the privilege of dying until he has passed on to a willing student his accumulation of Divine Wisdom.

"All of these are false, and all are true. True, as is the statement that no one becomes a Master until he is willing to accept the responsibility and declares that he is a Master. False as this shows: Masters are of many levels, many grades, and many degrees of ability.

"Truly Sacred Masters, those who change civilizations, not only individuals or groups, do not need students.

"Divine Masters change planets and all that is on them. These Divine Masters never are without physical bodies unless they wish to be, for they can disassemble, transmute, change, and reassemble physical flesh.

"Other Masters can send forth their Spiritual, or Radiant, Bodies and clothe them with flesh at any distance. But they cannot reassemble their own bodies. They use an energy to create anew, but cannot reassemble their own bodies.

"Don't ask me why. I do not know why or what. The 'why' may have something to do with the Jade Heart you asked about. Some Masters can teach, heal, and create marvels, even project their Radiant Bodies, but cannot make the Radiant Body solid like the physical, only make it not solid, like the spiritual is expected to be.

"You asked the meaning of the Jade Heart. It means that Divine Grace has entered into a clean, pure, and deserving body and blessed it with the service of at least five of the nine bodies, or souls, which one may eventually come to possess and control for eternal life.

"Will you have the Jade Heart forever? And does it symbolize eternal life? If so, is this for the physical or the Golden Body? The answers are: You may have the Jade Heart forever, for both the physical and the Golden Body. This depends on whether or not you develop the remaining four souls, or bodies, to reach your ultimate Divinity. Only the ninth body can give you eternal life.

"Why did it come only when you felt death in your physical body? Because you are being Initiated into sacred things and death is an ultimate Initiation. You must risk physical death, for in any Initiation something must die. Or if it cannot die, must forever change.

"Death is the ultimate change. Initiates through all time risk death, and sometimes will die, to be restored to a higher, more wonderful life. They must risk death to have life more abundantly. There is a reward for even being willing, as you were, to risk the death of the flesh in order to make the Radiant Spirit more certain. The reward is to be born again in spirit."

A-Sar-U found he had been listening so intently he had almost forgotten to breathe. He moved ever so slightly and the rhythm and beauty of Thoth's voice stopped.

"Let's walk," Thoth said and rose.

A-Sar-U fell in with Thoth's pace as they went slowly, but in very rhythmical steps around the room. The steps and pace were like the beat of a small drum. Their bodies moved in rhythm. The beat, beat, beat of the silent drum was like sleep dripping into an attentive mind. A very attentive mind. A mind so fixed on the unvarying rhythm that it held the mind to that cadence which moved it toward peace, lulled peace, gentle peace, and to a walking sleep. Then, Thoth again began to speak in the same slow but definite rhythm.

"Each of your nine bodies has a mind. You have nine minds in your body and brain, and even the smallest possible grain of your flesh has its own mind, its own special use of energy from your brain and body. By breathing in the special way you have learned and sending energy to those special places on your Pathway of Gold, you have used all your minds. The smallest particles—ah, Atl said they were to the human body what the cells of the priests are to a temple, and he called them 'cells'—of your body have taken energies sent to them by your minds and made them into a force for growth, for life. This Life-Force is fecundating. It has slowly made you younger, more spiritual, and more and more sacred. Life-Force has caused you to be born again in spirit."

Thoth stopped speaking, but his body and pace continued to beat a muffled drum in the consciousness. After many paces he continued:

"A-Sar-U, you are acutely aware of the rhythm of our steps? Yet at the same time you are acutely aware of what you are thinking? Good. Without losing either of those, imagine what it would be like to be in the Temple Guard compound. You are stripped to the waist. The sun is warm on your skin. There is a gentle breeze. But the sun is warm. Very warm. And the practice fencing sword in your hand is flashing against the sword of your instructor. You are in a forward attack. You feel the strain on your legs, the weight of your body as you lunge, recover, and lunge again. It is fast. It is hard. You can see your instructor working hard to fend your cuts. You can feel the jar of the sword in your hand, the extra weight of the training sword. You feel the sweat on your forehead and body."

Thoth stopped A-Sar-U in mid-stride, the left foot still in the air. A-Sar-U felt the sweat on his forehead, the sweat on his body, the need for air in his lungs, the strain in his legs, and the jolt of the blows in his arm.

"Lor'd One, I was out there. In mind, I was physically out there!"

"Favorite of the Gods, you were out there in your minds. In your imagination you created a vision of reality. Reality is potential actuality. If you hold all your minds forcefully enough and long enough on any thing you can imagine, it will become actual.

"If you hold your mind and will forcefully enough and long enough on raising your Radiant Body out of your flesh body, it raises. This you know. This you have proved. If you are fully adept, your Life-Force is obedient to your will. If you are not fully adept, your Life-Force leaps to your aid when you think you are dying. Every little bit of you throws its strength into keeping you alive. When all works together, that is, when all minds are one, when all eyes see as one, you have changed your physical self to

211

Golden Light and given it opportunity to function outside your body. You have transmuted your flesh at least a little. You have become a Master. You have the ability to create phenomena, to make strange things happen, to read minds, and time and distance. To heal.

"If you rise above the thrust of death, you become a Radiant Master. A Radiant Master has the abilities of a Master, but uses easy, unassuming spiritual skills. Such a one heals by Thought-Force, which is always available, and therefore heals by physical presence only those who want to be healed and feel they can be.

"This is the problem. Even impure persons may have these abilities and are capable of doing much good, but also much harm because their minds and hearts have not been attuned to the sacred. If one is pure in motives and selfless in desire, one may be graced by the symbol of potential highest bliss, the Jade Heart. This is a sign that one may progress further, that one has caused at least five of the minds of man to function as one."

A-Sar-U let the rhythm of words and the drum of the steps lull him to a deeper and deeper quiet. He found that in not fiercely directing his conscious mind he was in fact more conscious.

"There are levels of Masterhood above the Radiant Master. First, Master of Men, then Sacred Master, then Divine Master. And finally, Divine Master of the Jade Sun.

"All these you will be permitted to study, as avatars of the future, as the Children of Thoth. You will, in that future time, serve by breaking the minds of mankind out of molds of civilizations.

As Krishna, out of disrespect for and love of women.

As Christ, out of the iron grip of religious law.

As Ram-Tha, out of accepted limitations put by cultures on those not of high birth, also out of limitations on the natural reach of mankind toward *again* becoming personally divine, and showing that low-born man may become divine through freedom of thought and force of will.

And as A-Sar-U, or Osiris, to demonstrate that Gods become men to serve mankind, and men become Gods to change destiny.

"All this and much more you will do later, in lives and on planets, and in times of your lives yet to come. But first

212

you will succeed in this assignment. You will be the savior of the lives of the seven million persons on this planet."

A-Sar-U kept the pace, felt the beat of the drum of his mind, and the deep, accepting peace of his being.

"Now, you may prove to yourself that you can move through stone in your Radiant Body. As we pace, let your will send your Radiant Body around the room ahead of us."

A-Sar-U focused his thought and will on projecting his Radiant Body. Through his closed eyelids he could see its brilliance and knew it was pacing before them, leading them around the room.

Thoth pulled to a stop at the pile of stones. "Put a part of the broken stone on the floor."

As A-Sar-U reached for the stone Thoth commanded, "By your Radiant Body."

A-Sar-U willed the stone to be moved by his Radiant Body and it was instantly moved to the very place he visualized.

"Now you are ready to have the answer to your questions, 'If you can go through stone walls, how is it you can lift stones on your hands without your hands going through the stone?' And, 'How do I learn to send my Radiant Body through stone walls?'

"Focus your eyes, your will, and the will of all your bodies upon the broken stone. See it in every granule, and see those granules moving at a very high rate of speed. Now, imagine that your physical hand is made of particles moving *at the same speed.* See this as a reality and then visualize it as an actuality in all your minds. Now will, in all your bodies, to let your physical hand pass through the stone. Know it will pass through. Now in your mind see it passing through the stone. See it in all your minds!"

A-Sar-U passed his hand through the stone, and back again. He could feel only a hint of resistance. He would have turned away, but Thoth said, "Now ask your Radiant Body to put the broken stone back where it was."

A-Sar-U willed, and the broken stone was lifted back to its place.

"Now, ask your Radiant Body to sit on one part of the broken stone, and pass its hands up to the elbows through the stone several times."

He willed it. It was done.

"One last test. Ask your physical body self to rejoin your Radiant Self. Sit on one part of the broken stone and pass your hand through the other part."

A-Sar-U did so.

"You have done well. Now, Beloved of Gods, I have questions for you:

"What has all this to do with impregnating your beloved Chosen Woman for Virgin Birth?

"Before you can answer that you should answer this:

"How is it possible that you sit on one part of a stone and your body does not go through, yet you pass your hand repeatedly through the other part of the stone with little resistance, if any?"

Thoth stepped up on the stones and grasped A-Sar-U in mock drama, fondly on the shoulder and smiled. "And to think! I knew you a long Westsun ago when you were just a kid. Your progress proves that one who desires strongly enough achieves swiftly, if it be the will of God."

Thoth stepped to the wall, and as he disappeared through it, he left the sound of gentle, loving, yet self-satisfied laughter echoing through the vaulted room.

24

Mystic Ast-i

Ast-i sat in dejection until God-ette came and allowed her to move to a more comfortable seat and clothe herself. She then sat dry-eyed in total confusion and the shock of fear, and told God-ette in detail what had happened to her and the strange power that kept her from A-Sar-U.

God-ette listened with a bland expression so different from her warm, personal self that it told of deep and growing concern. "Thank you, Beloved of the Gods for telling me the things that have so disturbed you. Now, please, let me go over your..." she paused to find the exact word, but Ast-i gasped and grabbed her hand hard.

"Oh, please don't. Don't say it was a dream."

"Oh, darling." She took the distraught girl into her arms and rocked her gently. "I was searching for the words I intended to say. They are *your Spiritual Adventure*. And I feel that your spiritual adventure has been extremely upsetting to you. Can you please go over the details again with me?"

Ast-i nodded and wiped tears from her cheek.

"Thank you. I know it is a strain. But some of the important parts both Thoth and Bes will be curious about, and will ask me questions about all sorts of details. You know how they are for details?"

"Yes, Beloved Mother."

"You did it all in less time than it takes to change the guard, although it takes five hundred breaths to repeat it in words?"

"Yes. Yes! I know it is impossible but..."

"Shhh. Don't imagine something bad, or borrow from the future, because you do not understand it all yet. Frankly, Beloved of the Gods, I don't understand it all yet, either."

Ast-i swallowed hard and nodded her understanding.

"You left your physical body in a Radiant Body that was pinkish? Could you tell me just what shade of pink? Is there anything you can compare it with?"

"It was a shimmering pink, almost like silver, but pink. It is very hard to describe."

"They will be interested. Very deeply interested, Ast-i."

"Oh? Well, if you can imagine seeing the palm of your hand under the surface of almost still water. That would be the color with highlights on the water."

"Oh, I can imagine that."

The look of concern in her eyes, the concentration on her forehead, and the slight pursing of her lips almost escaped Ast-i's occupied mind.

"Is there something wrong in that?"

"Why, Darling, I don't think you'd do anything wrong, not after your long training. Do you?"

"Well, it is all so confusing, but, but...I hope not, Beloved Mother."

"Good. Now, in your pinkish body, with highlights something like silver, you traveled to Bes's chamber, to Set's chamber, and over the mountains following A-Sar-U's armor. This you could do at speeds as great as thought. But when you tried to close in on a part of the Temple of Po-Si-Don..."

"No, mother. When I willed to close in on the place where I thought A-Sar-U might be..."

"Oh, yes. That part of the Temple where you were guided to think A-Sar-U might be—although you had seen him, at least his armor, ten thousand paces away over a mountain. But when you tried to close in on that part of the Temple you came up against a power, a soft and yielding but impenetrable power, in the form of a ring you could not pass. A Ring-Pass-Not, so to speak."

"Yes. That is right. Does it seem strange to you, Sacred Mother?"

God-ette thought for a long while. "Blessed One, it seems to me to be all quite confusing, splendid, and wondrous."

"Then I should not worry?"

"Oh, Ast-i, we should never worry. You especially. You are a Chosen of Heaven, and a Chosen Woman. But...well,

I might, just might, have a suggestion to speed up your readiness to receive A-Sar-U's spirit-child."

"Oh, oh. What should I do?"

God-ette thought for twenty breaths. Then she smiled, and Ast-i thought it was a little forced, a little too bright for the cloud in her dear eyes and the tiny furrows of concern on her forehead.

"You might teach me again the Sacred Exercises that raise the Radiant Body. Begin at the very beginning. Teach me as you would a new student. Leave nothing out. Not even the smallest thing."

"You mean, all 257 exercises that become one? All, absolutely all you have taught me?"

"Yes. All 257 that become one. With complete explanation so that I, the new student, cannot fail to understand. And then make me do each one correctly."

"Very well, Divine Mother. If I do it well enough will you tell me how to go though the ring I could not pass and visit my Chosen Man?" She heard the sudden intake of breath as if God-ette was startled, but the smile was still on her face though the veil in her eyes was darker.

"Oh, you must never do that. Woman is the creative, generative center. The passive matrix. She pulls all creative seeds to her as Mother Earth. Does Mother Earth go to the seed, or does the seed come to her?"

"But, Mother! Mother Earth can wait."

"I hear you saying that you feel you cannot wait."

"If my Radiant Self can visit my beloved before his Radiant Self can visit me, why should I not go? Mother Earth is so big and important. I am so small. And he is so slow. Slow! It has been all these Eastsuns. I thought he would come before the first Westsun. I would have!"

"You would have? What do you mean?"

"I have been able to dark-travel since I was...can remember. Doesn't every one? Don't men?"

"No, everyone does not. And men tend never to believe easily in spiritual things or in non-physical things."

"They're dumb! It is so easy."

"Yes. True. Men are dumb and slow. I told you they do not easily use intuition as much as women do. But aren't men wonderful?

"Again, I say, you must wait your time with patience to become the most important woman on this planet. Wait. I will go tell the guards to bring another bed, and food for a full-light for both of us. Then we can work and work."

She went to the door and spoke softly to the Ama-Sone. "Anet, please tell A-Thena to double the guard. Say to her, 'our jewel is more precious than we thought.' Bring a bed and food for two for the next two or three Eastsuns. Personally take this exact message to Thoth and also to Bes. *Double jewel. Physical red. Spiritual pink. Mental green. Suggest past-dark conference, Som if you want.*"

She had the puzzled guard repeat the message four times exactly. "Now, as soon as you can, go and deliver my message. But go slowly. Stop and talk to several Warriors. About anything. Deliver the message only in low voice to the attentive ears of Thoth and Bes. And take that puzzled look off your face. Go as if you were at ease and having fun."

God-ette went back to her sacred duties with open smiles and complete attention. But she suspected much and knew that if her suspicions were true, the planet would soon be changed forever in one of two ways.

218

25

The Message

When Thoth heard the whispered words of Anet, the Ama-Sone Guard, his smile of welcome faded only slightly.

"Repeat, please."

When the Ama-Sone repeated the message, he then repeated it as if to himself and shook his head as if he could not understand it. Then he thanked the guard with a smile.

"Is there a return message, Supreme Lor'd One?"

"Yes." There was laughter in his voice. "To God-ette say: *Thank you. Double message heard. You women do complicate things don't you?*"

Anet did not like what she thought was a sly dig at womankind. But his laughter was so gentle, and his approval of her so obvious, that she instantly forgave him, even if he was a man. She had thought maybe she bore a message of importance. But Thoth's reaction seemed to tell her that it was only moderately important.

Then, for several breaths Thoth spoke to her about her job as an Ama-Sone Guard, her duty hours, her food rations, her quarters, her companions, and her general satisfaction with the events of the Empire. It was like one Warrior exchanging views with a companion. Before she left him, he had made her believe her message was not greatly important, but that she and her ideas were very important to him.

After Anet left Thoth, she glowed with pride. The Supreme Lor'd of the Pleasant Planet had taken time to find out what she thought. She thought he was wonderful! He roused in her such an adoration that she thought it might not be the right thing for a young Ama-Sone to mention to her superiors.

Bes was not hard to find. Everyone told Anet to listen. Where she heard children having the most fun, there would be Bes. She found him on the steps leading up to the top floors of the Temple of Po-Si-Don. A hundred children played on the steps below him. How could she whisper a message to him?

It was as if he read her thoughts. He spoke, not loudly, but every child stood quiet and still.

"Good! You are very good." Bes's voice was pleasant, although filled with authority and command presence. It was not at all what Anet was expecting from such a big and famous Warrior. "Now, here is a treat for you. You young Warriors, look at this Ama-Sone. See how straight and proud she stands. You young Virgins, see how firm and ready she is, how womanly she looks though we know she is one of the swiftest and most powerful fighters on the planet.

"Detachment! Form a square and guard of honor. Do it!" The tight square formed around Anet in a most Warrior-like fashion and promptness.

"Detachment, escort her to me here. Do it!"

Anet knew it was a form of play for the children, but the praise of her person and her people made an unaccustomed and very warm place in her heart. As she began her climb inside the determined square of honor, Bes commanded:

"Neith!" A young girl stepped forward smartly. Bes took his sword from its scabbard and held it by the blade across his left arm, hilt to the girl. "Take this sword and guard these steps. No person comes above you after the Ama-Sone passes. Is that clear?"

"Clear, Lor'd One!" The tiny Neith could hardly heft the sword, but she held it firmly in both hands as the Ama-Sone walked up the steps past her. She then stood spraddle-legged in the very center of the steps.

"Neith!"

"Lor'd One?"

"You guard a treasure of the Empire."

A movement of pride went through the little body and a look of determination came to her face.

"Guards! You guard Neith. If you fail her, she fails the Empire."

As Anet came up to his level, he surveyed the ranked children. "Good. Very good!"

Then Bes turned eyes filled with love to the Ama-Sone. He smiled at her. As Anet leaned close and whispered her message he blinked. "Please repeat."

Again Anet spoke the words that seemed to mean so little. He smiled at her, and some unaccustomed warmth touched her Warrior-trained heart. "Do I hear you say: *'Double jewel. Physical red. Spiritual pink. Mental green. Past-dark conference. Som, if you wish?'* "

Anet nodded yes. He smiled again. "Thank you. Oh, before you go, would you be willing to talk a little to my darlings? They may climb all over you."

"I'll try." Anet wondered about being close to male children. But if the Commander of All Temple Guards suggested it, she'd try.

"Neith!

"Have your guard escort our honored guest to the third level. There, stand easy and she will visit with you. Do it!"

The piping voice repeated the instructions to her guard. As soon as she had formally surrendered the sword back to Bes, she changed instantly from a fierce guard to a laughing child. She raced down the steps to cling to the Ama-Sone's fingers, and with the other children ask a hundred questions, and touch her muscles a thousand times in awe and approval.

The Ama-Sone enjoyed the children much more than she thought her superiors would approve, and found they were fascinated with her stories of discipline harsh and long, and drills repeated for a thousand breaths without pause, as was the custom of the Ama-Sones. Anet enjoyed the day, adored Thoth, loved Bes, and felt drawn to the children, oh! even the male ones. She felt a greater pride in herself and the Ama-Sones. As she walked about the compound, talking with Warriors and others in the Temple forecourt, she wondered how it was possible that delivering an apparently unimportant message could have made her feel so admired, important, and...and...well, yes, even loved.

26

A-Sar-U's Failure

A-Sar-U blinked, glazed-eyed, at the place Thoth had disappeared through the stone wall.

He had seen it. Stone gave way to human flesh. Stone! Stone that was strong enough to support thousands of man-weights gave way to a gentle push. Then it became again as solid and strong as before. Stone that could hold the weight of the body on one part, yet permit the passing of a hand through its other similar part. How could it be? He considered the thought with open-eyed fascination.

What has that to do with your impregnating your beloved Chosen Woman for Virgin Birth?

What indeed?

The ability to think logically, in fact to think at all, seemed to have left his head. He felt empty of ideas and a clutching in his belly, a tightening fear that he might never pass this examination. He always had belly-knotting in combat or contests. But this was different. In combat the solution was obvious—kill, incapacitate, or allow himself to be killed or incapacitated. Now the solution was not obvious. It was as if now he had to kill or allow his beloved, himself, and the whole planet to be destroyed.

So much depended on him. Thoth had called it "the weight of responsibility." It was the awfulness of making decisions for so many. Doing it swiftly, with so little knowledge, and less understanding. And with a brain that walked backward like a hard-pressed, confused, retreating Warrior. A Warrior whose legs were locked by fatigue, whose sword arm was of wood, whose brain was of stone, but who could not escape without fighting.

He felt the grip of fear like mounds of snow from the High Atals packed into the space of his heart. Thought, with answers to his questions, would not move in the frozen uplands of his brain. Yet, one idea came to him.

Thoth, or was it his mother, or was it Bes, had said, "When in doubt, act."

He was in doubt. Oh, was he ever in doubt! He should act.

He mounted the stones to the broken stone on top and sat upon one part. He thrust his hand to pass it through the other part of the stone. The pain of the blow reached from his finger tips to his shoulder, for it did not pass through the stone.

He sat for a hundred breaths, his finger on one hand pressing on the surface of one piece of stone, the fingers of the other hand drummed in impatience on the second piece.

"But it works," he said aloud, and heard the disgust of self that echoed in the vault of the chamber. "It works. It works!"

Did Thoth make it work, he wondered. Can I do it only in Thoth's presence?

The thought echoed in his head. Surely not!

No. Always the training must be obedient to my will, to my wish, to my level of wisdom. Thoth, as my Master, helps me. He never hinders. Never. Never! Then why...?

An idea flicked though his brain. A constructive idea. There must be some magic in what Thoth had caused him to do just before he was able to perform the impossible of passing flesh through solid stone!

What was the magic?

Seemingly there had been none. None! Thoth had simply explained the nine bodies. Straight teaching. Oh? Or was it only teaching? Was there something in the facts that...?

No. No more than there was magic in the mere "facts" that he had heard whispered in derision of the theory that such things could be done. Not facts.

Then what?

Blank.

"You know the answer!" he shouted aloud and to his brain and clamped his sweaty face into the palms of his cold hands.

If not facts, then what?

What had Thoth done, exactly? Exactly!

He had caused A-Sar-U to imagine, to visualize. Then he had told him facts that created great wonder. Wonder! What was wonder but a state of mind that held the thoughts still and fixed? Fascination! Was it more?

Yes. It was heightened emotion that roused some deep response beyond the conscious mind. It stirred some most primeval emotion, some race inheritance in the belief that there was a great and wondrous presence, far greater than man, who allowed all things. Wonder, an emotion akin to and as strong as love, or...or worship. But not an emotion that focused the mind on one single person or concept. Call it emotion without individualization, akin to love, but universal love.

But why? And again, why?

Radiant Divine Masters like Thoth did not do things without purpose or before the student was ready. Radiant Masters could speak only Truth. Their word once spoken could never pass away and must echo down the ages to the benefit of man. This was the teaching. The true teaching.

Then what was Thoth doing?

After twenty breaths he sighed. "Holy, Atl! Who knows what a Divine Master like Thoth will do. He always has a plan, but..."

A-Sar-U stopped. "He always has a plan for the future. Yet he never demands more than the student, with personal effort and God's grace, can understand and apply."

After a hundred breaths of twisting thought, he sighed deeply again. "I have God's grace. Thoth has spoken. It is therefore true. Now, how do I apply the personal effort?"

After long reflection he said wryly, "That's how students miss their path. It is not for being unwilling, nor for lack of desire, but from lack of knowing how to apply their personal effort."

Exactly what had Thoth done, or caused him to do?

He came down to the floor of the room and started pacing. Pacing to a repeated rhythm, a drumbeat that echoed through his head so full of wonder. He stepped along the walls, hearing his Master's glorious voice and the increasing pace of the rhythm.

Firmer. Firmer. Steady. Steady. The beat was in his mind, in every smallest particle of his body. His steps were measured by it. His body was buoyed by it. A beat. A rhythm. An all absorbing beat of rhythm and wonder. So that even in action he was in complete and deep meditation.

Meditation in action! Meditation by action. For a purpose! No wonder Thoth was called the creator of learning and wisdom!

A-Sar-U found that he could consider, think, and stay in deep meditation. Meditation was not, then, a sweet feeling of peace and bliss only. It was a more intense activity of mind and body. It was as if the conscious mind passed through the human body into another mind beyond. And that mind, beyond even the great unconscious, but as powerful, developed a new body beyond the physical, including the mind of the Radiant Body, but again more powerful.

In that mind he asked his Radiant Body to walk in front of his physical body in the circuits of the room. After about three paces he felt a rhythmic pulsing in his body. It grew more and more intense until his Radiant Body burst forth from him and walked the circuits ahead of him. The rhythm, the drum in his head, seemed now to beat in two places. It pleased him to see that the Jade Heart in the Radiant Body beat its own steady rhythm.

Perhaps he had become a Radiant Master, he thought. He was very greatly pleased.

He asked the Radiant Body to sit on the broken stone and run its hand through the other part. It did so. He then climbed up, coupled with his Radiant Body, and saw himself sitting on one part of the broken stone and running his hand through the other.

He was elated. He felt he could now attempt to pass his body through the stone wall. He stood by the wall, willed it to give way, and turned through the stone wall into open space.

Terror assailed him. Terror! He was standing on a ledge two spans wide, looking out upon the west courtyard of the Temple of Po-Si-Don. He was seven levels or more in the air, and a dreadful wind was lashing all things. He could not seem to go further, and longed to be back inside the vault.

Forcing his way back in was difficult. The stone seemed to reject him, to be hardening fast with each breath, like Warriors' porridge cooked too fast for too long. At last he forced himself back into the room.

He stood on the top, on the broken stone, and looked fondly into the chamber.

But the terror still beat its horror into his conscious mind, and he was aware of questions pounding upon his brain.

"What have I not done? Why have I failed?"

The weakness in his knees invaded his body, and he sat upon the stone. But it invaded his head, and he lay on his back upon the top stone, feeling the broken cleft gouging his body in what seemed just punishment for failure.

He may have dozed. When he was fully conscious again he was aware of the question burning in every smallest portion of his being. Why had he failed?

What had he not done right, as Thoth would have done it? Thoth often said: "In sacred things there is no right way. There is only the way that works *for you.*"

"What is the way that works for me?" A-Sar-U heard the words echoing in the vault of the chamber before he realized that he had spoken his thoughts aloud.

Words, even those spoken aloud by himself, created some sense of comfort that began to warm the cold terror he had undergone.

Slowly he began to move down from the piled stones and into the center of the room. The movement was slow, deliberate, and important to his mind. He let his mind dwell upon it. He thought hard about each movement, and about what caused his body to move. What caused it to balance on his two feet? What fed his legs with power and strength?

In the same slowness of mind and body, he began to carry the stones from the outer to the inner wall. Slowly. Ever so slowly! He analyzed and questioned every bending of his body. What made the body bend? He questioned every flexing of his arms. What caused the so-little-noticed spreading and grasping of his hands, his fingers? What gave the power to his shoulders, to his hands, arms, body, legs, feet? Why was he able to lift and carry twice his body weight?

When all the stones had been moved, he placed one in the center of the room, near the Mound of Desire.

"Why did I do that?" he asked aloud. It stirred thoughts of primitive desire, but also thoughts of a primitive sacrificial altar.

His concentration on why he had done this was so intense that the cause of his terror was eased in his mind. It had not revealed the cause of his terror. It had not even answered the question, "Why?"

Why had he set up something that might serve as a sacrificial altar?

He sat upon the stone and felt his body slump with the weight of his thought. His useless thought, useless thought...

He lay back upon the stone, stretched his full length on his back. Why? Was it because in the dimness of memory he knew he was re-enacting some ritual, some ancient myth? Some rite important to mankind, and most ancient in the memory of his race? Was he the sacred victim, the one who was to suffer and die that all men might have life ...life abundantly? And joy. The joy of knowing that man was indeed so close to God that he might become divine and rest in Everlasting Memory by Ceremonial Death.

What was the ancient folk tale so much told among the Fenmen? That the Savior of Mankind in every age must die, the hero of ten thousand deaths. That he must be buried, and on the Magic Day marked by three, must rise again. Then he could rivet the attention of men, and aid them, and then go again into spirit so that he would be remembered fondly and for ages be used as an example.

Was he, A-Sar-U, to be that holy sacrifice? Was he unconsciously preparing the sacrificial stone, driven by some pre-knowledge and tacit acceptance? Thoth had said that he, A-Sar-U, would be the Savior of Mankind through worlds to come. Had he also been the Savior of Mankind—in some mysterious way that only Gods could fashion—in worlds past?

Was the internal uneasiness which all persons felt, the dreadful insecurities that haunted reveries and turned dreams into nightmares, the feeling of never quite being of this *here* and this *now*, but of belonging to some other place—?

Was this the result of being forced from worlds to worlds through times and times, and its effect upon race memories?

"Stop!" His mind thundered at his mind. "If I am the Savior and destined to be the cause of the Initiation of mankind into a better life, or a new and safer world, my Master will guide and protect me."

For twenty breaths he felt justified and true. Then he smiled wryly and then laughed aloud. "Yes, he will! After I have worked out my own problem, Thoth will give me greater ones. And I will love it!"

He settled more cozily onto the stone and then sat bolt upright. "But, what will they be?"

He lay back down and began again to do the Sacred Exercises. In his mind he knew he had not been able to think his way to a satisfactory solution. His mind had roamed. He had not been able to come to a single satisfactory conclusion. Why?

The answer was clear. He had not asked for a single solution. He had thrown a handful of arrows into the air, but none directly at the target. He had scattered his desire and allowed it to be incomplete. He had wanted to go through the stone! He should have wished to go to his beloved Ast-i. He wanted phenomena, the magic of walking through stone. He should have wished to be in the presence of his Beloved Chosen Woman. He desired many things, but they were only learning steps toward what should have been his true and only desire.

What had Thoth said: "Women are a spice to life as ginger is to a savory, and as fragrant as jasmine. To desire a woman is next best to desiring God. Fortunately it may be more quickly and repeatedly rewarded. Women are the cause of true Initiation. Women are more sensitive to the impulse of sacred things. They know without reasoning, succeed without effort, it seems. Men may need to go through extreme tests of will and determination."

A-Sar-U remembered the vision of Ast-i's body. Her delicate coloring. The floating gossamer of her hair. The pent-up longing for her that seemed to have been his from birth, or before. All the loving, exciting touches and prodding. But, oh, those glorious moments of yielding. The promise of all in the yielding of a finger. The assurance of success in a reluctant denial. So very much he had desired her. To be her Chosen Man. To be enfolded in her warmth, cradled in her arms.

To be her all...

He felt a push, a rush as his Radiant Body rose out of his physical body. He was able to see his physical body from above, his Radiant Body from below. He could feel with all senses and in both bodies, he could feel! The desire for Ast-i was doubled. The will to succeed was doubled. With some puzzling twist of will, he threw energy into the Radiant Body *and set it free to do with that will what it needed to do.*

He felt, and enjoyed, the slight pressure as the stone of the outer wall gave way before his radiant force. The caress of a new Eastsun, slightly dew-tinged, was on his skin. He looked down across the courtyard onto the sacred Temple of Virgins. He looked to the left, to the scurrying of drilling bodies in the courtyard of the Temple of the Warriors.

In his physical body he felt the movement of air around his Radiant Body as he moved across the space, approached the Temple of Virgins, and let his Great Unconscious Mind guide him to the apartment where his Goddess was. He moved through the stone wall and, even as the pressure gave way, he was pleased by the fragrance of jasmine. Yes, and more subtle, more gentle, more exciting, the fragrance of his beloved. His joy was wonderful. His delight was intense. His desire was unbounded.

27

Committee of Concern

A thousand breaths before first light, three hooded figures glided from the main entrance of the Temple of Virgins. They did not speak. They had no need to do so. Their plans had been made and discussed most carefully beforehand. A-Thena, the supreme Ama-Sone, and Anet, her brilliant and beautiful young assistant, moved through the coldest part of the dark with only the slightest whispers of their steps to mark their swift passage.

At the same time, Bes moved out of his apartment. At each of his elbows moved a trusted Warrior whose weapons were cloth-wrapped to make no sound.

Som walked indolently, yawning, between two young Warriors from his apartment guard in the north end of the Temple of Po-Si-Don. He was grumbling in his mind. "Oh, Holy Atl, what is it now? For what simple puzzle in the area of science must I get up so early? They will listen. They will question. But no one will really understand and no changes will be made." Angry at the lack of personal ease, and at being requested by Supreme Lor'd Thoth to attend, in silence and in dark, he padded heavily and grumpily.

Som's heavy, incautious footfalls were heard by the Captain of the Fourth Watch of the Guards in the Warriors' Temple who noted to report to Je-Su that someone moved through the dark along the north wall and then the east wall of the Temple of Po-Si-Don.

This, the Captain knew, would be enough information to make Je-Su grasp both sword and dagger, and fume and curse because the Captain had not been able to see clearly and get more information.

Finally, his rage evaporated like water on glowing coals, Je-Su would conclude that he knew Thoth held meetings of all kinds of crazy people at all hours of the dark deliberately to keep Je-Su, only Begotten Son of God, from having full knowledge of what was happening. Probably this was something about that false Virgin Birth Thoth was arranging. Hah, he, Je-Su, Only Begotten Son of God, could not be denied knowledge of what was happening. For he was the only person on this cursed planet who came of Virgin Birth. He was the only...

And as his mind raced, he would stride from end to end of his apartment, a dagger in his left hand, a sword in his right hand, a towering rage in his brain, and treachery in his heart.

The Captain thought of not mentioning the sounds, and then shivered. If Je-Su ever found out about them, he would blame the Captain, believe he had joined a conspiracy against him, was guilty of apostasy against the First-Born Son...and the punishment would be as horrible as it was devious.

Anet, in full armor, stopped just inside the entranceway of the long passage that led inside the Temple toward Thoth's quarters. Two Warriors, in battle dress, took their stations beside her. She set before them the Ensign of the Empire, a jaguar and a thunderbird, stitched in gold and silver on a blue field filled with yellow stars and an exploding planet. The ensign was to assure the curious that things of Empire were occurring and could be disturbed only by force. And that the use of force would lead to the usual punishment by the Empire, death by crucifixion on five swords at the front edge of the Window of Ra.

The others in the gathering party moved onward down the passageway to the opening to Thoth's quarters. Here A-Thena and two other Warriors took their positions facing the entrance. They were not in parade dress with its wild colors and gleaming metals. They were in battle dress with bows strung and slung, grey feathers fletching the arrows which were held in an earth-colored quiver, in full armor, with helmet visor at combat-ready, and equipped with a shield, dagger, short-sword, and metal-tipped trident spear.

The three Lor'd Ones turned inside the apartment passage, passed through two short halls, and came into the inner chamber lit by a dozen tapers. Four steaming meals awaited them, set out on flats of willow-wood, covered with

231

plantain leaves and placed on individual jaguar skins. Thoth greeted God-ette by name and as he did so, signalled by his giant hand where they might sit. He then turned to the sleepy-eyed Som who was yawning behind clenched teeth.

"Som, Lor'd One of Science. Sit here." Som began to seat himself, and Thoth continued, "As you eat, tell us the meaning of a pink Radiant Body."

Som was almost seated when the words lifted him to his feet, the yawn frozen in his gullet, and a new tension on his face. He looked at Thoth in doubt. "Surely, Lor'd One of the Empire, it is too early for one of your famous jests." He laughed lightly and began to seat himself again.

"Yes. Much too early for a jest. Possibly too late for truth. What is the meaning of a pink Radiant Body?"

Som's almost too slender hands flew to his belly as if to recover from a blow. He stood straight again to his full but slender height, and his sensitive face betrayed the confusion of ideas that crowded his brain. Slack-jawed he nodded to Thoth that he now had registered the question in his mind and was thinking on it.

Slowly, as if bemused, he sat cross-legged on the jaguar skin and absently reached for food. As soon as his eyes fixed on the food he put it down. He had lost his appetite. He breathed heavily several times as if throwing something heavy from his chest. Five times he looked at Thoth, God-ette, and Bes. Five times he tried to speak. Either voice or mind failed him. He shook his head and retreated into deeper thought.

Thoth, Bes and God-ette ate slowly, glancing at Som between bites. They saw his struggle and the confusion on his lean, long face. They waited patiently.

Som was brilliant. Not a good Warrior, but a good thinker. He was small, slender to a point of emaciation. He was so hesitant that even with all his quickness of mind, eventually, he always responded slowly as if his mind thought through ten things when it had time only to think of one. They knew his memory was phenomenal, almost never failing. But it seemed to pick up his ideas in layers, examine each and discard it, if it was not what he wanted. But when he found the one he wanted...

"Lor'd Ones—forgive...my mind cannot grasp...surely not pink...?"

Thoth nodded to God-ette. She spoke in her short, clipped way. "Lor'd One of Science, we may help. You know of course of the test for the Registered Virgin Birth."

"Yes. Lor'd A-Sar-U, your son through Lor'd Ra? And Goddess Ast-i—or does she call herself by the more modern name, Isis? She is the daughter of Bes and As-Tar, isn't she?"

"Yes. You should know something else that may be most important. All of us, and you and Set were born by Virgin Birth, but not official, not registered."

"I have been told so by my parents. But Je-Su assures me that only he is Virgin Born. As a scientist, of course I believe him—almost." He seemed to relax at smiles at his jest. "You know that it was common in our people on That Other Planet? But not since our people arrived on this Pleasant Planet."

"Why not on this planet, Lor'd Som?"

"Oh. Perhaps—possibly—maybe—most likely—because when we had to leave That Planet we lost the effect of our sacred disciplines in learning to control our hands as well as our minds. Also, too, because there is more pull on things on this planet. Our swords are heavier and harder to wield. So, though our Radiant Bodies seem nothing but radiant light, they are heavier here. Being heavier, they are harder to control."

"Ast-i, or call her Isis if you must be modern, has come out in a pink Radiant Body."

"Really? Not golden at all?"

"Pink."

"Ah? The reasons. Endless. Endless!" Som thought for a dozen breaths and said, "Endless!" He thought hard for twenty breaths. "Oh, a point of information. Are you certain her techniques and disciplines are adequate?"

"Adequate. More than adequate. She talked me through them all, and she knows and practices them exactly. Exactly!"

Som sank into himself and put his head into the palms of his hands. He rocked his head gently, almost as one might rock a fretful child, Bes thought.

"Pink! Exactly which shade, do you know?"

"I asked her. She said, 'like the color of the palm of your hand with water standing in it and light that reflects from the water.'"

Som seemed to sink further into himself. Bes liked to show his children the way the leaf of shamy-weed curled inward on itself when touched or prodded. Each new fact seemed to make Som close in more. Was it from shame that he did not know?

"Lor'd Ones, I cannot give you your answer today. The possibilities are too numerous. Lor'd Bes, was Ast-i very wise when young?"

"Lor'd Som, she was never young. She was born with the ability to talk to the eternals. She reads minds, and time and distance, and knows more than most women. We have let her grow as she will without calling her attention to her exceptional burden and skills."

"Sacred Mother, do you think she meant that her Radiant Body was silvery pink, or a patina of silver over pink."

"A slight patina of silver over pink."

Again Som turned further inward, folded into himself and seemed to compare thousands of ideas. After three hundred breaths in silence he said, "I will give you something inside ten darks." He picked up his food and began to eat.

Thoth stirred slightly and said, "We must make plans. Little rebellions are always afoot in the Empire. We know Set's posanga eaters plan to discredit our effort. It may be they will claim the conception through Thought-Force was invalid for some reason, and try to prove it before the people at the time of re-testing."

Som put his food aside and sighed deeply. "Lor'd One of the Empire, I will not worry if they try to prove the conception false. I have a deeper problem. A worry. You know and I know the Virgin Birth is possible. My worry is greater. She comes forth in pink with a patina of silver. One of three things may—I tell you, may—I will know more later—may be true. She may be a Bride of God able to conceive only of the highest and purest God.

"No offense, Lady Goddess. Your son, A-Sar-U, may be such a God. But..."

"No offense possible, Beloved Som. We deal with the future of the Empire. Little lives have no place. Speak truth as you see it."

"Well. If so, she may respond only to a Son of God-e, the First God." Som was silent for several breaths, then spoke, his long head lying to one side as if too heavy to hold upright. "It may be that Isis may never bear a child she conceived through Thought-Force."

There was a dreadful stillness after the imperturbable Bes sucked in his breath as if recovering from a blow. Thoth's eyes grew a little more solemn and bleak as if his mind was seeing great pain and death.

"Finally...well as final as I can say now...her inner energy may be locked into an invisible drain through space— much as a leech locks into one's energy and takes one's blood."

The quick look that passed from Thoth to Bes and God-ette would have betrayed much to Som. But he was too inward turned to notice.

"Like what kind of energy drain?"

"Oh, like...like...well, there is a story told of Ptah, a planet traveler whose ship was trapped and in trouble. His mind locked into the mind-energy of Ethera, Daughter of Thoth-Khnum out of Mut. She told Khnum, the inventor, exactly where Ptah was, and what his trouble was. Thoth-Khnum was able to put into her mind all information on how to repair the planet craft.

"Ptah read it, fixed his machine, and came safely home. Of course, Ethera became his Chosen Woman. And, of course, that is a non-scientific myth from That Other Planet.

"But is not important here. For we do not now know how to build Planet Travelers or to power them. So the Pleasant Planet has no one stranded. But there'd be danger if we did. The drain on energy could kill. Rather quickly, too! That's all now. More later."

Som picked up his food and ate with delight. He finished and looked expectantly at Thoth. "You have affairs of State?"

"Yes, Lor'd Som. Thank you. You can be back in your quarters before first light. No one should know of our problems."

Som moved to the entrance as if floating on quiet feet and was gone.

Bes rose, his huge body strangely solid on his short, powerful legs. "By Atl, for a breath I thought someone had betrayed the Cabal. Could it be that Ra is reaching for her. He is so long past due and..."

"Ra alone could not. But As-Tar, her mother, might. She and Ra went together. You know how long ago your beloveds disappeared without a trace," Thoth said, rising easily to his feet.

"Thirty-seven Westsuns and a few Eastsuns. Too long. If they do not return soon you must open the Lists and let me joust Je-Su," Bes said matter-of-factly.

"You know I wish I could do that, Lor'd Bes. It would solve one problem of the Empire. But Ra, my Master said, 'make no changes until we return.' "

"I know, Lor'd Thoth. I heard him say those very words to you. But Lor'd Ra expected to return within twelve Westsuns. Perhaps he, they, are..."

The unfinished thought hung on a hint of dread until God-ette said, "Lor'd Bes, you know that your Chosen Woman and my Godly Chosen Man will return, or in some way take up their bodies again to serve the Empire. Now, let's get back to our own quarters before first light betrays us."

28

Som, Lor'd One of Science

Back in his own quarters, Som sat disconsolate on his own rug made of eagle feathers woven into a double-reed mat. He was an Eagle-man and proud of it. His mental powers supported his spiritual skills as the reed mat supported the colorful eagle feathers. Thoth and Bes were Jaguar-men, Tiger-men, of the tiger clan and ilk. Warriors, swift and fierce. The Eagle-man was always smarter. Always. But this light, the new-come light, shone on one of the hardest problems, and possibly the nearest failure, he had ever had. That the science community had ever had.

Thoth, Bes, God-ette were all stalwarts of this Empire on the Pleasant Planet. By Atl, why would they be so concerned with the lore and science that came from That Other Planet?

Why?

He had noticed their fascination with the story he told of Ptah and Ethera. Frankly, he thought it was untrue, just a tale, a myth as were most of the facts of science. But they had loved it. Were they...wait! Some thirty-seven Westsuns agone they had asked him to tell them all the science lore of a probably mythical planet called Ayr Aerth.

Yes! The great Atl had—oh, another myth?—visited Ayr Aerth in a Planet Flyer, they said. Ha, the indefinite *they.*

Well, he had told them all that the Science Lor'ds before him had passed on to him. But was his prodigious memory failing a little? At times he found it necessary to be a little inventive. Ah, but only adequately inventive to meet the question.

Ayr Aerth! Atl had named it in the language of That Other Planet. In the old language, Ayr had meant 'sweet, productive, rich.' Aerth had meant 'heaven, refuge, haven.' Ayr Aerth meant 'safe haven,' or 'rich heavenly land.'

Atl had spoken, they said, of a bountiful island (or was it a continent?), which he called Atl Antis. Most of the Lor'd Ones of Science thought Atl was showing the usual, expected ego of the Jaguar-men, and attached his own name to a continent. But Som knew that Atl, the Planet Adventurer and one of the best-known Lor'd Ones, was also Atl, the Lor'd One of Science. He was both a Tiger-man and an Eagle-man, scientist, inventor, and savior of many from That Other Planet.

Too, Atl, who undoubtedly knew that the word meant water, had called the continent "Atl Antis," the "Water Mountain." Was the continent Atl Antis the Safe Haven? Or was it all of the planet?

Som did not know. Nor did any other Lor'd One of Science know. But, ah, here was the point, neither did Ra, As-Tar, Thoth, Bes, or God-ette. But...but...but...no, it could not be! It could not, but...(Damn, was there no other word but "but" to serve the mind in a quandary?) Yet... some 150 Westsuns agone the order had come from Ra. Ah, there was a God-man, a Lor'd One of Science, of Culture, of War. A fierce and busy thinker as well as a fierce and strong Warrior. Of course he had been given a large, strong body, a good body. A body much like Thoth, Bes, and...yes, even Ra's son, A-Sar-U.

Ra! Back to Ra. Ra had asked—a request from the Supreme Lor'd One was an order—the Lor'd Ones of Science throughout the Empire, at selected places in each of the fourteen temples, to set up a specially shaped obsidian pillar on the porch of the Temple.

It was hush-hush, as all science projects should be.

But this pillar was to have sharply defined edges and taper upward to support on a narrow stem, three spans long and one palm square, a cube. A perfect cube three spans in each direction. The pillar was to be of the transparent, golden obsidian from the North End Volcano. This Golden Pillar was to be placed on a square of the purest, newly mined, white marble. Pure white, unlined! Those were the orders...ah, suggestions. . . . And in one piece.

Foolishness! Any scientist knew that the Westsun would darken the fresh marble a little each time it passed. Ra was...why am I using the past tense? Ra is, wherever he is, a scientist. Maybe not as well-loved as Thoth or as

238

inventive or good at words, but a scientist. He knew the marble would darken. Knew...and yet gave very specific instructions as to materials, measurements, leveling and... and...

"Som!" His voice was loud with some bitterness. "Something more important than you know is happening to this Empire. That is not a religious monument, as we have all supposed. It is a...a what?" He drove his left fist into his right palm so fiercely that he winced. "And what has it to do with the disappearance of Ra and As-Tar?"

Som pulled himself into himself, as if he wanted to shut out all sight, sound, and feeling, and incubate a new and marvelous idea. He pulled himself into a ball around his head, as if to put his mind into a protective incubator to cause his ideas to grow.

"Remember, think. Remember, think. Remember, think." He repeated the words like a lullaby, rocking his head slightly like a baby in swaddle. After a long while he was absolutely still. Absolutely still, except for the Golden Body that rolled out of his physical body and moved swiftly away.

In that Radiant Body he went to the Window of Ra, on the porch of the Temple of Po-Si-Don, to the Golden Pillar on the gleaming white marble base. Carefully he examined the obsidian, measured the taper, the neck, the cube.

Then he measured the marble base. With the passing of the Westsuns, as he knew they would, the punishing rays were putting a shadow upon the marble. It was growing darker and darker. As expected! Everything was as expected.

The eyes of his Radiant Body glanced at the marble on the south side of the pillar. At first his eyes could not register the meaning of what he saw there. When they did, the shock struck his physical body, and his Radiant Body was jerked back and slammed painfully into his body. He sprang to his feet. So overwhelmed he could not breathe, he stood, struggled to catch the air for life into his body too filled with fear and awe...and horrible dread.

After he was able to breathe his mind was blank and in shock for a hundred breaths. He could not even think. The implications of what he had seen and at last understood stunned the mind. He must think. Think! Good God-e, he must think.

The more he tried to think the more he could not do so. His mind went uncontrollably its own erratic way. His will was gone. He could not control his words. He could not be certain of what was happening to him. Dimly he felt himself stripped of his cotons, put upon and held down on his bed, while he screamed and screamed.

He felt the Mother Goddess and her ministering hands. He was dimly conscious of Bes and his loving touch. He was aware of Thoth and his healing presence. But it seemed that Eastsuns spun fast. Too fast. For he was talking to himself, telling himself over and over that what he had seen could not possibly mean what he knew it meant. Then he heard a voice, not his, not Thoth's.

"Som. Som! Yes it does. It does Som. Accept it, friend."

Som, Lor'd One of Science, felt himself sweaty and nude. He heard his breath coming in labored ways as if trying to escape the smell of his own sweat. Then he felt the gentle balm of water in a soft sponge cleansing his body.

"He's waking." It was God-ette's voice.

"Good!" Was it Thoth?

Som opened his eyes and looked into the concerned eyes above him. "We've been waiting for your recovery."

Som's gaze drifted to the room and saw three beds. They must have been in constant attendance.

"Why?" His eyes indicated the beds.

"You were shouting, and you might have betrayed some secrets of the Empire. So..."

"Oh, Holy God-e! What was I shouting?"

"At the top of your voice, 'I can't accept it. It cannot be. That is not the Secret of Ra!' "

"Is it Thoth? Is it Bes, God-ette? Is it . . . ? Holy God-e, from your faces I know, it is the secret of Ra."

"First we could not tell you. We are under sworn obligation not to tell anyone. But we knew if you once got a clue, your mind would reach the right conclusion. We had not been sworn to keep from you all clues, and we need your help."

Thoth was silent many breaths and then spoke gently and matter-of-factly. "Som, what you have seen is not the full secret of Ra. It is only part of it."

Som blinked and recoiled almost as if from the unexpected threat of a blow. He sat solemnly waiting and finally broke the silence with, "How many know? I mean, absolutely know?"

"Six," Thoth said.

"Ah," Bes inserted, "Ast-i suspects and possibly knows. She reads minds."

Som nodded approval. "I understand the need for secrecy. Holy God-e, the shock! The awful helplessness, frustration, and despair. What can be done?"

"We have a long-range plan. We need your knowledge and help to make it work."

"It must involve A-Sar-U and Ast-i and Virgin Birth."

"To start with. Then more, much more, Som."

"Now I'll do everything I can to help. I've known you wanted...but I thought...how many Westsuns until...?" He left the unfinished question hanging like chill in the air.

"You tell us. Gather information from all your Lor'd Ones of Science, and then you tell us."

"How accurate must we be? How close?"

Thoth's smile was grim, like a Warrior happily closing in combat. "Oh, fairly close, Som. Say, within half a breath ...or less."

"No room for human error, Lor'd Thoth?"

Bes laughed. "Sure. Say an eighth of a breath."

Som looked at the Lor'd Ones with eyes newly filled with understanding and admiration. "Long ago I heard of a Great Cabal. We scientists agreed that it was for the good of mankind through the ages. A way of civilizing mankind. A plan for raising saints or gods from common men and endowing them with everlasting life. But it was not a scientific plan. Of course, therefore, it could not possibly be that it would influence mankind for all time." He swallowed hard, and looked slowly and deeply into the eyes of each of the three. "But, Lor'd Friends, if you three were part of it, it could be that it will change destiny. And I would be highly honored if you would count me in. Is that possible?"

"Som. Friend. We have been with you for six Eastsuns. We'd better get back to the problems of the Empire and you can now go about even more important things. We will have more to discuss immediately after we know A-Sar-U and Ast-i have succeeded. At that time will you please give us a very full, very accurate, and very complete scientific report?"

Som gazed at them from large, rounded eyes in a face too long and narrow. And yet, somehow, there arose from him an aura of a resolve, new and firm, of heroic proportions. His nod was a promise.

29

JE-SU'S REPORT

The Captain of the Watch of the Warriors' Temple reported to Je-Su almost as Thoth, Bes, and God-ette left Som's apartment. He could not say why they were there, but they kept all persons away, even Som's own servants. And they were there, one or all three, at all times for almost six Eastsuns.

Je-Su dismissed the Captain with an imperial wave of the hand even before his full report was made. He could not be bothered with guessed-at details.

He paced his apartment. So they thought to keep him in ignorance! But he knew. He, Je-Su, Papa of the Empire, Only Begotten. He knew what they were planning. Som had screamed, so it had been reported to him, "That which I have seen could not possibly mean what I think!"

Of course it could not. Som had seen the horror of what Thoth, that clever fiend who stripped heros of their rightful deaths, was planning to further humiliate Je-Su.

It *was* unthinkable, horrible. Horrible that minds could conceive a plot against the honor and dignity of the Great Father of the Land, he, Je-Su, Only Begotten Son. Horrible!

But he knew it was true.

More. They planned to weaken his legions in the provinces. They planned to find and destroy his posanga manufacturing camps, hidden as they were in the most inaccessible places. Ah, ha. He would not even think where, lest they read the powerful thoughts of his mind.

Also, they planned to open the Lists again. Open the Lists to see if anyone would dare try to beat him in the Combats.

Ha! He would be ready. He was ready. Now. And the Great God-e would see to it that His Only Begotten, Most

Beloved Son won. Won! Got all the things he wanted. Got whatever he wanted.

He would hurry his secret negotiations with that impossible Chief of the Shumen, Africanus. His Warriors were strong. Undisciplined, but strong. And after Je-Su had trained them, their dirty, untrustworthy leader would...no, no, he must not think what he would do to dispose of that one when his value was gone.

He would get whatever he wished. With his well-trained legions he would see that all people obeyed his slightest wish. For he would wish only for what the God-e wanted. He, Je-Su, alone could tell the people what Divinity wanted. He alone could bring through the true message.

And he would be true to his duty. Any rules he made were made only because they were part of God-e's law. It was the God-e's law that His Only Begotten Son should be Emperor of the Empire, worshipped and obeyed. Obeyed. For when he spoke, God-e spoke, and had to be obeyed. He spoke for God-e. He was God-e.

He shook his fist at an imaginary throng and cried, "And you will obey, you bastards! You will bow down in worship and obey the Great God-e come to rule you. To lay down laws by which you are to worship and conduct your lives. To rule you against your desire to sin, sin, sin.

"Oh, why must you sin and make me punish you? It hurts your dear leader. But you will obey. For I come to bring peace and truth. I am the Supreme. I come to speak for God!

"You will obey!"

30

True Love of God

A-Sar-U entered the Temple of Virgins through the stone wall. He was inside the room of his beloved Ast-i. He could feel her presence, but he could not see her. The chamber was alight with the new Eastsun, glowing with a pale pink color reflecting from the stone walls. There was a bright blue-white spot of Eastsun reflected from a small part of a pool of water.

Even the heart of his physical body back in the Temple of Po-Si-Don beat wildly as he saw the clothing she had stored neatly in niches, the raised platform bed covered with the fawn-colored skins of highland deer, the flagons, promises of happy feasting, serving now as vases to hold bunches of fresh flowers. There was a pile of dried reeds. Some were partly split and stripped, and made into fronds with which she was weaving. Weaving baskets. Small, tightly woven, to hold food and drink, and large, loosely structured baskets to hold large amounts of fruits, berries, and grains.

For a dazzling, exciting moment his eyes rested on a basket some four spans long, three spans wide, and four spans deep. It had a hood over one end. It sat on a frame with legs that fitted into curved rockers. It was, it had to be, a cradle woven from the wicker of the reeds.

The thought sent a thrill through his being. It was an invitation that was a delight. He felt the surge of creative joy through both his beings. It spoke of her determined hope, her expectation of success, and her readiness and desire. And it inflamed him and fanned his expectations. How, he wondered, could there be a greater message or thrill than that mute invitation?

Then he saw Ast-i. She had been in the spot of light reflecting from the water of the pool. Now she was rising slowly out of the water. The sunlight seemed to surround her little body with a holy halo, and to glance from her face as if touching her skin made it skip for joy.

The light reflected in her eyes. To shield her eyes, she raised a hand with tapered, pink-skinned fingers on a slender alabaster arm. Her movement scattered jewels in the water and almost exposed her breast. As A-Sar-U's eyes were fixed upon the near exposure of her beauty, water rose and fell along the smooth surface of her bosoms as if tantalizing his eyes by half-revealing, half-concealing her beauty. This was the first time his Warrior's eyes had rested upon such femininity uncovered. She turned fully toward him and spoke. His heart beat faster with each joy-filled, throaty word.

"Oh, welcome, welcome, A-Sar-U. I know it is you though the sun's reflection blinds my eyes. But my heart knows you. Oh, come, come to me."

She walked slowly up an incline toward the edge of the pool. With each step a little more of her breath-stopping charm was exposed to his eyes. Her full, pointed breasts. Her small waist, and then the feminine flare of her hips, her thighs, and then her feet. Small feet, small and beautiful. And so very exciting to see. He thought, "Too small to carry all that beauty."

Ast-i smiled as she moved up out of the water. Droplets ran down her body as if they did not want to leave off touching her.

"They are large enough to carry my body to your body. Large enough to carry your child, and oh, Beloved of God, I do so want to."

She picked up a spun-flax, woven towel and draped it over her physical body. As she did so, her Radiant Body stepped toward him, arms outstretched in joyful welcome. At last he could try to take his fill of caressing her, of holding her, of exploring all those secret places where passions dwell, creativity begins, and an unspeakable femininity turns woman into Goddess. Where joy mounts on joys ever ascending. Where moments of pleasure grow to delights a hundred breaths long and unendurably sweet. Followed soon by a longing to explore that same emotional pathway again, to reach again a sacred moment of Godhood.

When at last he lay under the soft covers against her warm physical body, he wanted to be absorbed into her very flesh. He felt that he could penetrate to the very core of her beings, physical and radiant. He did so and revelled in her willingness. He came out of her flesh and her Radiant Bodies with a realization that she was his wife, his daughter, his sister, his mother.

She was all womankind. For in her, he knew, as if it were his Initiation into the Wisdom of Eternity, that he had found the eternal woman, the earth mother, the Lady Goddess, the Mother of Mankind, the Mother of a new race of God-men.

Folded in his arms, she smiled happily and dozed. Her fragrant breath was gentle on his cheek. After a hundred breaths, but, oh, so short a time, her blue eyes were suddenly open and glowing warmly into his.

"Unto us a son is to be born and we shall call him Horus. He shall be the most Lor'd of All Men except his Divine Father."

"Ah? If unto us a girl child is born we shall call her...?"

She stopped his lips with a kiss. "You of little faith and some doubt." She cuddled close to him, warm, exciting, and fragrant of jasmine. "It shall be a son. We shall call him Horus. Horus! Because we know he is the first of those Virgin Born under law. But men shall call him Horus because he shall be a link between his father, the God of Mankind, and men who strive for eternal life. He shall help you become the Savior of Mankind in all ages of times to come and on all planets where you shall be found."

"How do you know, Beloved One?"

Her eyes opened wider in surprise. "Why, because I am a woman." She nestled even closer to him and whispered, "Oh, yes, *now* I *am* a woman!"

A-Sar-U lay in some sweet rhythm of joy until she opened her eyes again.

"You make me very proud."

"Why?"

"The Lady Goddess says that Thoth told her that you are the brightest man and best Warrior on the planet."

"Oh! What do you think of that?"

She squirmed closer. "Old news. I've know that for almost two hundred Westsuns."

"At times I feel so slow and dumb. You called me dumb, remember?"

"Sure. About some things you are. Because you never see negatives, or the badness in anyone, or think anything bad about anyone. You love everybody, even your enemy. But you defeat them. You never worry about anything, even what may happen to us on this planet. Or the danger to us from Je-Su or from Set. The Mother Goddess says Thoth should remove them from Lor'dship. Why doesn't he? Why doesn't he? Everyone can see, and the whole planet is asking."

A-Sar-U lay quietly, but his mind was racing. He was moved to speak several times but did not. Finally he asked, "What do you want to happen to us?"

"That which, and only that which, God wills. But, I hope He wills that we do this again and again for at least ten thousand Westsuns." After a long silence she shuddered slightly and said with a resigned sigh, "At least as many Westsuns as we have left."

"Don't we have ten thousand?"

She burrowed even closer to him. "Oh, yes. Maybe more. But only if you fix it."

"If I can't fix it?"

She spoke as she was gliding into sleep. "You are the Beloved of God. You will fix everything. Forever."

He looked down upon her beauty and said to himself, "I'll try."

In his mind he heard a voice either from an ancient experience in ages past or from the future saying:

"Life carries in it the hope of eternity,
And the possibility of annihilation or death."

31

Puzzles from the Past

Confidently, Som, Lor'd One of Science, began in his mind to unroll the memory chain of the Lore of the Sciences from the early times. He knew he must soon answer questions involving the techniques and wisdoms of the ancient days. Ancient days! How wonderful it must have been to live on That Other Planet. There man had knowledges of how to melt the fierce metal, and had equipment in which to do it. Yes! Yes! And fuel that would burn hot and long.

Ah. Those were the days of magicians, mechanical and mental. In that former time they had ships that could travel through air and space. They built *things. Great Things!* So the Lore said, and he believed it. They built men. They built minds. It was said they did so through careful selection of the mating pairs. They could travel in their nine bodies through time and space and had in themselves *generally* the power to create.

Creation! Lore said they went back to the beginning and changed the very nature of mankind. It was said they found human animals, very primitive, wild and mean, on planets where they went, or were driven, and made them into God-es by special, secret, and Sacred Exercises. When those exercises failed in the creation of God-es, Lore said, they at least created super-men and super-women. Persons of health, strength, endurance, knowledge, wisdom. They raised most primitive men to civilized and thinking men.

There was the Lore of the Champion of Man...ah, ha! That might be a myth. He would consider it later.

The magnificent magicians, the God-es of his race, taught the primitives all the arts of learning and building. Also, the greatest art, that of worshipping. The sacred longing found in all persons, the glorious wonder, those ancient magicians turned into worship of a higher *some-thing.*

He, Som, did not think it mattered what that some-thing was. It could be a Supreme God-e or it could be a concept of science or maybe even a leaf or a moment of beauty or a man or a woman—did it really matter, if the worship was awe-filled and accepting?

This was the basis of the God-es' ability to heal. They taught that man was capable of being pure and God-e-like; that man could become one with the Supreme God-e, that is, with the source of an energy, a Life-Force. The great healers were the first to use Life-Force. With it, used in a specific way, they could help tissue right itself.

More! They could do more, for they could make Life-Force renew itself. And some, Lore said, could make Life-Force and all the elements of personality change from one human body to another. And still more! They could make their own body change to energy containing Life-Force and personality, travel through space and time, then change from energy to flesh again.

In trying to breed those who had the greatest ability to handle Life-Force, those ancient magicians found that cer-tain individuals were more akin in mind than they were in lineage, though sometimes lineage gave great energy to the minds.

"So!" he said aloud, "Two such minds could speak through space and time."

Yes, he was right in that! That was the Lore! Two minds could speak through space and time even though they had never met physically or practiced.

Yes! By Atl, that is the point of *now.* The problem with Ast-i. It is possible—no, more, I believe that someone is trying to reach Ast-i through mind alone. I think, if the Lor'd Ones have reported correctly, that it must be a mas-culine mind, well mainly. It may be, it appears, that both masculine and feminine minds are trying to reach her mind and come into consciousness.

Why do I think that?

Ah, ha! Lore has it that the masculine pulls the femi-nine radiant energy toward silver and away from pink. Feminine energy pulls the radiant from silver (or gold, they said) to a ruddy pink, deeper than the pink color of the palm of a hand.

His mind trailed aside into indecision. He felt he needed more of the ancient Lore.

Som could not bring to mind the Lore he wanted. He tried very hard, very methodically. His mind would not recall that which he wanted.

This was impossible! It could not be! He was Som, Lor'd One of Science, entrusted with the Lore because of his memory.

He was so annoyed with himself that his long fingers picked feathers from the Eagle Wing design of his pad. When his distracted, distraught brain focused on what he was doing he jumped to his feet. He was angry with himself. Angry at his absent-minded stupidity in destroying a work of art. But far more angry with his mind for being so slow to bring to memory the Lore he wanted to recall.

All he wanted was an insignificant detail, a simple fact. He knew it was important, though he was not certain why he knew it or why it was important.

The Lore said that long ago the race that became the God-es, had been quite wild and had invented many special devices. But that was not the Lore he wanted.

It had to do with the myth that Thoth as the first God, or Khnum, Mut, Horus the Elder, Atl, Ra, Thoth as the Beloved God of mankind, Po-Si-Don, Africanus (but how could that be?) and all the others who had such God-powers, had come from a place called Ayer Aerth. Or was it that they had visited Ayer Aerth? Anyway, a long time since, maybe over five thousand Westsuns agone, they had come, or was it gone, in one of their Cosmic Schooners filled with specialists, people and their families. They had come...well, they had to come before they could go, didn't they?...for the purpose of planting colonies to serve as a place of refuge, for they knew they would have to leave the planet they were then on. Ah, the fact he needed was this: Was that planet actually That Other Planet that had exploded only three thousand Westsuns agone?

And exactly how long ago had that pilgrimage been? How long before Atl's most recent trip? Or was it the same trip?

That Lore was fuzzy in his mind, but...

He sat down again and slowly sank into himself. His shoulders folded down, his knees came up, his arms wrapped his knees to his lanky chest. Mentally he turned inward until his mind was all blackness except for one tunnel of light. Through this he traveled to a time and space his memory desired.

He was back in time to his training. He felt the bare granite floor upon which he sat and felt the tremors of the surface of That Other Planet. He wanted Lore. He could get Lore only by penetrating the then-mind of one who knew. He chose to enter the then-mind of Thoth-Khnum and search for the meaning of the myth.

Before he could even finish the thought he was seeing as if through the eyes of Thoth-Khnum. He was hearing and feeling with the incredible speed of a spider spinning its thread in air.

He was in the Cosmic Schooner with six thousand others as it came into the roughness of its approach to Ayr Aerth. It put down on a river which was called Hindus. There Ram, and his co-regent, Ram-Tha, the Spirit, or *Life-Force,* of Ram, led five hundred couples and were off-loaded. Ram was the Lor'd God-e. Ram-Tha, who had risen by his own technique and pristine will from man to God, and taught mankind life-enhancing techniques for acquiring Universal Knowledge and Cosmic Wisdom, was the stalwart hope of his race.

Again they set down, on the island (or was it a continent?) of Atl Antis. Po-Si-Don was off-loaded with five hundred couples.

The Cosmic Schooner then turned toward the rising day-star into a vast continent with high and treacherous mountains and lowlands and deserts. There Africanus (Oh, no, surely the First, not this Africanus) was off-loaded with five hundred couples.

The schooner then went to the right of the setting sun to an island near a delta, near a vast inland sea. The island was called *On.* There all the remainder were off-loaded and were set to work building a secure colony for the future of the race. Among those who worked beside the Beautiful River were Thoth-Khnum, or Teheuti (the old name for Thoth), Amun, Re (the old name for Ra), Ptah...

252

oh, and many, many others. Of these others, one special one was to be important to all time and all races.

Thoth-Khnum shielded this mysterious, powerful priest of Amun from recognition. But it was this marvelous priest who built the temples of Amun, Re, and Thoth on the Island of On. It was this man of Wisdom who built twenty-seven giant stone tents along the reaches of the Beautiful River. Some of these were a full 150 arms in height, with a square base of almost 150 arms. They were built after the model of tents with four poles that sloped upward to meet each other at the top. The shape alone was said to cause miraculous things to happen. Perhaps this was why the tents and their stone copies were so popular with the people from That Other Planet. But the tents along the Beautiful River were made of giant blocks of stone, not poles and fronds, for they were to last forever and be Initiation Temples and also beacons, or signals, to other space-travelers.

In each of these great stone tents, at the center, was a small chamber where the Lor'd Mystics of Science were placed out of harm's way, out of curiosity's unintentional disturbance. For when these specialists were in full peace and complete silence, they could communicate by Thought-Force with those from the Schooner who were in other places, and through space with those on That Other Planet.

This shadowy, mysterious, powerful architect, builder, and priest (at least in the myth) seemed to be in nine places at the same time. Some said he occupied the bodies of each of those who sought Initiation in the mystical chambers. Anyway, when Africanus claimed he had deliberately been assigned to a barren continent and with his Warriors assaulted the Temple of Amun on the Island of On, the shadowy Man of Mystery stood in buckler and shield and defeated Africanus and eight of his henchmen and held the gateway until Re and Thoth could bring fighters to drive back the contenders.

The Mystery Man, sometimes called Ge-en-us, taught, fought, and built. Though he held and would accept no office, he commanded workmen, Warriors, priests, and even all the Lor'd Ones. He seemed to fore-know everything, *even what individuals thought and wanted to do.*

It was he who showed how to build the canals that took water from the Beautiful River to irrigate the desert ten thousand paces on each side of the river. He taught workmen how to quarry stone and build beautiful homes in a treeless land; how to make and play instruments of joy and worship; how to snare game and tame it; and how to catch and raise fish.

He taught the priests the exact details of their duties as servants of the Great God-e and, therefore, of the people. He deposed those priests who sought to control the beliefs of the people and make them all believe as the priest wanted them to believe. He taught wisdom concepts and rituals that freed the minds of men and would allow no one to impose restrictions upon the thinking of good men.

It was said that Ge-en-us was the nine radiant bodies, or Spiritual Children of Thoth, for he never used the word "I" to refer to himself. He used the word "we" and in modest truth really believed others had done what they knew he had done. To him, the others deserved all the credit.

This Mysterious One established the healing Temples of Sleep in the temples built along the Beautiful River. He developed and used *neter neter neteru*, the rhythmic chants (which Lore said was a way to cause men to know they were one with God) to heal diseases and minds awry due to imagined or actual stress. Later, Lore said, this hard-to-say name became *ekachignosis.*

He instituted the great ceremony of Initiation that made his race of men into a race of God-es. He used, and taught mankind how to use, the *Hekau*, the words of power, and the *Meket*, the energy of God. Using them he established sacred rituals, especially the *ashemu*, in which man ate the symbol of the Flesh of God and drank the symbol of the Blood of God. When this ceremony was performed, magic happened in the minds of humans, and they thus took on the aspects of Divinity with many of its powers!

Especially, also, the ritual by which one who lived purely in *Maat* might be Initiated into the Eternal, Sacred, Secret Order, be put into harmony with the universe, and be able to take from his Master Teacher the powers and sacred wisdoms to use in the service of all mankind.

The Mystery Man helped Thoth conquer with love all the people of Hindus Land, Africanus Land, the Tribes of the Beautiful River, and the continent of Atl Antis. These people all gave love. Fealty was not required since man was best ruled with love. Peace was known on Ayr Aerth.

The myths and the teachings of the Mystery Man were remembered with love. He brought civilizations, agriculture, medicine, priestly wisdoms, initiatory grandeur, writing, handicraft, science, and the Law and Order of Divine Worship.

He invented marvelous machines. He showed how channels within the body carried blood from the heart to the extremities and back again to the heart. Also how nerves caused muscles to move when stimulated, and that muscles could be stimulated through the brain, and the brain could be trained to stimulate them exactly on the breath desired. And that in the body were little receptacles, rooms or cells. Each little room of flesh, or cell, had its own will, or functions. He taught the words that showed the brain and the little rooms of the flesh, or cells, how to more swiftly heal the body. This, Lore said, was truly *ekachignosis*, the knowledge of being one with God and able to use His power to heal and for service to man.

He taught music, instrument, and dance, and how to use the human voice, the most beautiful instrument of all, to sing. He taught how to breathe the Divine Breath and how to live the purified life.

Then, this Champion of Man, this Ge-en-us, said he was to leave. And when he had left the people found that there were no mystics in any of the stone chambers. Then there was confusion, and strife, and the languages began to vary. But all the people loved and worshipped the Mysterious One who founded their civilization and their concept of the Good.

Slowly, Som unwound his body and stood up on the eagle-feather mat. He stretched to relieve the tensions of his muscles, and as he did so, realized that there was still tension in his mind. There were questions which his scientific, incisive mind had not answered to his satisfaction.

Why could he not be certain who the Champion of Man really was?

Why could he not be certain whether there were two separate visits to Ayr Aerth, and if there had been, how far apart in life-spans they were?

Was there truth to the Lore that time was a circle, the serpent that eats its own tail?

Was he, Som, or Thoth, or Ra actually the recycling of Thoth-Khnum, the most ancient god?

Was Thoth the recycling of Ge-en-us, the Champion of Man?

What had what he'd observed to do with the immediate problems of the Pleasant Planet, and especially with the test of Virgin Birth now in progress?

"Holy Atl," he cried aloud, "Science is chancy at best. Ancient Lore is filled with details. Each detail is a new confusion. At times, I'd really rather be a Warrior."

32

Ast-i's Secrets of Ra

Ast-i awoke from a tantalizing dream and restless sleep with first light bathing her chamber with cool indifference to her hot face. She rolled from her bed, her head spinning. She felt strange pressure in her stomach. She had a desire to vomit. There was a terrible, whirling, cruel heat and pressure in her stomach and head.

"Oh, Holy Atl," she thought. "I'm sick. Yet I feel so wonderful."

She attempted to stand, sank back to sit on the side of her bed, her hands thrust outward and holding hard as if to steady a swaying of the bed itself. She sat for several breaths and again tried to stand.

She was wracked with a feeling of nausea. It was as if too much blood had got to her head and was pressing hard to get out through her skull.

Her head hurt so much she dropped her face into her hands. This was a huge mistake, a giant mistake. The bed began a slow spinning to match the fast turning inside her head. Oh, more! The wild go-around of every little particle of her whole body. She felt as if she, the bed, the room, the whole planet was spinning.

Sweat was suddenly over her whole body.

Again she flung her hands outward to grasp and hold the spinning bed. That, too, was a mistake. She hurt in the head, and then all over, and her blood seemed to run fast and hot within her.

She was dizzy. She was nauseous. She was sweaty. She was a mess!

And yet she felt so wonderful!

It was as if every nerve in her body, except those making her nauseated, was calm and placid, and—and *happy!* *And satisfied!*

Every nerve and muscle seemed to know in its own way that she was whole, healthy, perfect. Her surface mind was involved with the physical feeling of sickness. But her Great Mind was calm and placid, and—yes, purring. Her Great Self was purring with gentle happiness and inborn joy.

"How can it be? I'm sick at my stomach, achy in my head, spinning in my mind, yet I feel so wonderful." She spoke aloud as if to assure herself that she was not crazy with her loneliness.

Perhaps she reassured herself. Within thirty breaths the sweating stopped, the dizziness passed, the bed did not spin. She rose and walked toward her morning dip in the pool and marveled that she had never before in her whole life felt so very, very *right*. She released the shoulder straps and her coton slid to the floor. She noticed with some delight that her breasts were plumper and nipples more defined and pink.

"Oh, good," she thought, "Men notice such things with delight."

Then she remembered. This was the day of the Westsun. Oh, damn, she would have to sit on the white proving stone when the Westsun had passed.

She eased down into the water of the pool, taking a special and personal delight in feeling the water gradually involving her body. It was as if her skin was being hugged into contentment. She lay back to float in the water, breathing in the way of the seven breaths and allowing the warm, clean water to caress her body. The clear, warm golden light seemed to fill every grain of her being inside her body.

As she floated, she thought how very lucky she was. Yes, so very lucky. She had the best of all planets. A strong man to love, a high duty to perform, a cozy place to enjoy, and a beautiful belief to worship.

"Ah, yes, I have the best of all planets!" She said so aloud, in joyful voice. The chamber echoed with her words.

In the faint, fading echoes she felt a tremor, a pull, a drain upon her energy. Another voice strove against her happiness. Not to destroy, but to right and clarify. She listened hard.

Was it imagination? Or was it a voice? A voice so faint that imagination was stronger? So slow that heartbeats brought few words. So insistent that her body responded to the message as if it was present somewhere else.

She was somewhere else. She was in that faint voice. It was her voice. Her voice in pain.

Yet, somehow she was separate from that voice, straining hard and listening to it with frightened fascination. What was being said was so important. But it was so faint, so faint!

"Speak louder," she thought.

The voice seemed to hear and obey. It became clear, and thoughts turned into words. Words that reached her conscious mind with wisps and scattered bits of meaning.

It was as if her mind spoke the words of another into her head and not into her ears. As if another spoke in her voice, yet silently. A silence that roared with dying echoes in her consciousness.

The meaning of what the voice spoke she experienced in an intense, internal vision. She seemed to be transported out of her Perfect Planet into a strange world. Not dangerous, except there was such a great pull upon her body that she felt as if bound in stretchable gauzes. She was bound down, not by cords or strings, but by some strong, invisible pull that was tiring. Very tiring to her muscles. Draining to her body. The force allowed her to move upon the surface but held her firmly down to the place.

"What place?" The sound of her voice echoed in the chamber. "What place?" she asked in her thoughts.

What place! It did not seem to be on the Pleasant Planet, yet is was much like! So very much like, and yet very *heavy* in feeling. And on its surface she seemed to be living many breaths in the passage of only one breath. Even breathing was heavy under the invisible pressure upon her body. She saw, as if she held it all within her head, a world of strange vistas and wild aspects. A world of indistinct views and mysterious sounds.

It had three suns. One very great day-sun, with many other planets of which her planet was only one She was on a planet that had one very hot day-sun, and two cold night-suns. [*Editor's Note: The Aymara legends, probably the oldest myths of humankind, hold that once there were two moons circling planet earth.*] The pressure upon her body was almost unbearable and fiercely held her to the planet.

She tried desperately, again and again, to break away from the pull upon her. Even though she knew she was in her Radiant Body, she could not break away. Even her Radiant Spirit was captive to a monstrously powerful pull.

Then, in that confusing way daydreams have, she was no longer Ast-i but was As-Tar. She was the mother of Ast-i on a strange but wonderful planet. Oh, but it was a very big planet. As big as Atl had claimed the (quite probably mythical) planet he called Ayr Aerth to be. He had said it was forty-four millions of arms around. Of course people did not believe him, since the Pleasant Planet was only a few thousand arms around. Atl had said that the larger the planet the stronger the invisible hands were that held any object to it and the more power a Cosmic Schooner needed to break free of its clutch. She was Ast-i on the Pleasant Planet, but she was also As-Tar on the enormous Ayr Aerth.

On the Pleasant Planet the temperature was almost always the same both in the light and in the dark of the Eastsun. It was uncomfortable only when the Westsun burned its path across their peaceful sky. Yet, she was As-Tar on the planet Ayr Aerth where the light of the day-sun was uncomfortably hot, and the dark of the night-sun was too cool for real comfort.

She was Ast-i in the comfortable pool on the Pleasant Planet. *At the same instant,* she was also As-Tar in a Temple on the continent of Atl Antis. She knew and could feel the conditions on both planets at the same time.

With a strange type of overall vision she could see the persons on each planet and realized that the hairy faces of some persons on Ayr Aerth were normal. So was their inability to talk. They were human, not animal, and in a way they were advanced. They were active, had very powerful bodies, but minds that could not easily be concerned with the spiritual aspects of life. They had ability to reason abstractly, but not to reason without emotion on things of the spirit. And no ability to talk.

She knew she was in the water in the Virgins' Temple in the compound of the Great Temple of Po-Si-Don on the Pleasant Planet. She knew she was in the Priest's Quarter in the Temple of Poseidon in the Citadel on the continent of Atl Antis on the possibly mythical planet Ayr Aerth. She knew she was with Ra, that she was As-Tar, and that she was in Radiant Body.

Then she became aware of Ra's radiant energy. It gripped her in a swaddle of power. It was so powerful, so demanding that she twisted and moaned in the water of the pool on the Pleasant Planet. She felt Ra's Radiant Body was filled with desperation, frustration, and even anger...or possibly it was fear.

Her mind in some way was turned into Ra's mind, and his thoughts seemed to burn a special message into her consciousness. A message not at all like that of a God-e or a Lor'd One, a message that was filled with desperation, frustration, and anger. No, not anger, it was worry. She was Ra's mind. She felt the transfer from his mind to hers. She felt she received and held the precious secrets of Ra, the secrets of the Great Supreme God-e.

She knew the secrets of Ra!

She knew the feelings of Mother As-Tar.

She knew they wanted her to tell! Oh, No! No!

She knew she would not dare to tell anyone of this crazy time. She knew that she had waked feverish and upset. She knew that in the reassuring pool of her delight she had gone into one of her daydreams. Those waking dreams that seemed so natural to her. But once when she mentioned such dreams to one of the friendly Virgins, she had been shunned and called weird, and many of the Virgins talked behind her back.

Besides, she knew that the Westsun was beginning to curve its burning path from northwest to above the Temple and then northeasterly. She could hear the high-pitched whine of the fore-wind, the sound of millions of grains, as if blowing sand, hitting the Temple and the ground.

As the light turned to garish red, she thought that she would soon be required to sit on her proving stone and be very uncomfortable for hours, hours, and more hours!

She listened to the mounting fury of the Westsun, felt the oppressive heat, and the feeling of helplessness and frustration. Yes, and worry or anger.

She had only been feeling the onrush of the Westsun.

Ha, ha. By Atl *that* was the binding of oppressiveness she had seemed to get when she imagined she was in contact with As-Tar and Ra. So much for the Secrets of Ra. Ha, ha, ha!

Her laughter turned into weak gasps of near hysteria as she walked up out of the water toward her proving stone. She laughed at her girlish foolishness. She laughed at herself for imagining she could read the thoughts of the Great God-e, Ra, and of As-Tar, her Divine Mother. From another planet way away she knew not where. She? Ha! How presumptuous she was! How foolish. How girlish. How immature. She must never mention it to anyone and...

Yet. Holy Atl! And yet, she really felt she had done it. She had read the disturbed thoughts of the God-e and the Goddess! She had. She had!

Oh, God-e, had she? Had she really?

She sat in great physical discomfort on the white seat. Alternately laughing and crying. Now sure she had read time and space inside her own head. Now equally certain she was a foolish, prideful child who had girlish upsets because she was so bitterly lonely and so in love. A small, insignificant child of 203 Westsuns, who hoped, oh how foolishly, to influence destiny for millions of Westsuns to come. A mere child who got stomach upset from nervous strain.

She was sitting on the white stone weeping hysterically when God-ette came, a thousand breaths later, and put her immediately to bed. The Lady Goddess then gave her a tea made of chinquona bark to stop her shivering chill, and a tea made of the flowers of chamomile to calm her nerves.

As Ast-i drifted into sleep she said, "Oh, Mother of God, I should give up this trial. I'm not worthy, and you know I'm not."

God-ette leaned her body over Ast-i to warm her, and held her against the shivering chills. When Ast-i had relaxed a little, God-ette stroked her damp hair from her forehead and said, "You know I do not know such a thing! We'll talk about it all later. Rest now and get over the fierceness of the Westsun."

As Ast-i drifted into sleep, she saw God-ette glance at the uncomfortable proving stone gleaming white and baleful in the sky light from the dark of the Eastsun and heard her mutter, "Now begins the dreadful time of waiting."

33

The Annunciation

The Drum!

The head-throbbing voice of the giant Drum of the Empire talk-talked often through the long dark. Ast-i slept fitfully, waked groggy. But she revelled in the joy she felt throughout her lethargic body. She was drained, tired, and she didn't know why. But she felt so very good. So whole. So pure. So loved and feminine.

She worked at her mat and basket weaving. But it was a peaceful time, not the frantic thrusting of her nervous and unsure efforts Westsuns agone that tore and bloodied the flesh of her fingers. She was settled in her mind, full in her swelled body, and so in love with everything. She had no doubts, no dreads. She was certain that she bore divinity within her body.

"Eleven Westsuns, oh, really, almost I think, of idleness makes anyone lazy," she mused. "And a little fat. And tired. I wonder why I am tired. How can I feel so wonderful when I am so tired?"

She was so attentive to her pleasant musings that she startled as the Empire Drum sent its deep command across the land. It caused the water in her bathing pool to ripple. She felt the beats through the floor on which she sat.

The voices of her Ama-Sonian guards added to the sound of hurrying feet on the stones of the hall way outside her room. There were firm orders, excitement, and many questioning voices.

"What is it?" She called out, although she knew not one of the guard would dare answer her question or lessen her sudden anxiety. She sat huddled, hugging her knees, and bent so far over that her hair fell across her face and breasts, making golden strands lay upon her white arms.

"I'm so pale. Too pale." The thought came as if from within herself.

Again the Drum spoke. She knew it was being heard and understood by other drums and relayed to every corner of the Empire. It was as if the drums were alive.

"What is it?" she cried.

Her answer was sudden silence. Silence! Holy Atl, silence can be so ominous. Silence could be so much more threatening than the sounds of hurrying steps, low urgent voices, and sharp, half-heard commands. All was silence.

Then the Drum spoke again, sending its messages across space almost as fast as frightened thoughts could fly.

Then there was silence. Silence. No voices. No movement. No sound of Warriors' weapons or leather uniforms.

A-Thena's voice came through the door in peremptory, official tones. "Ast-i-Ankh, Beloved of God-e, scion of Bes, Lor'd One of the Realm, hear! Lor'd Thoth, Supreme Lor'd One of the Pleasant Planet, sends his felicitations. This is the command he also sends to you:

"'Ast-i-Ankh, candidate in the Ordeal, prepare yourself and appear under triple guard at the examining stone on the Window of Ra, Temple of Po-Si-Don, at first light of the next coming Eastsun to submit to examination before the people of the Empire. You will be examined by three women from tribes, as you were before. You will also be examined by Isi-Ankh, Lady Lor'd One of Eternal Life, by Lak-Shi-Mi, Lady Lor'd One of Population, by Ram, Lor'd One of Population, by Brahm, Lor'd One of Knowledge, and by Som, Lor'd One of Science.'

"Ast-i, Beloved of God-e, do you hear? Will you obey?"

"A-Thena, I have heard. I will gladly obey." She knew that she might as well obey gladly, for obey she must or she might die in great dishonor.

Ast-i could not read the Drum well. But she knew that Thoth ordered a sudden run of Warriors through the dark of the Eastsun according to a plan called Bold One. Also, that the Temple Guards of the Empire were alerted to combat-ready. Also, that all citizens were invited, and urged, to run to be at the Temple of Po-Si-Don at first light for the examination.

She felt a deep concern when she heard that the Empire was instructed to watch for A-Sar-U, and if he appeared at any temple, to command him to appear at the examination. This was followed by answers from the Temple in Africanusland, the Temple in Fenland, and the Temple in Northwestland that A-Sar-U, in his full dress uniform, had been seen there in the past two Eastsuns.

Her concern was deep. For she knew he had not been away from the Temple of Po-Si-Don. For every dark of the Eastsun he came in blessed spirit, and they knew such tenderness and love. Oh, it made her long very much for the time that the radiant contact could be turned into real flesh, into passionate man-body straining to drain the universe of creativity and at the same time yield up ecstasy.

She hugged herself, her mind whirling in a dance of imagined pleasures.

She inspected her cotons, chose one of bright emerald. To this she added a belt of turquoise with little pouches of embroidered gold. For a sash she chose a golden color in a broad band from her left shoulder to her right hem, with a raised sea-green insignia of rank at the shoulder. (Holy Atl, it was the first time she could publicly wear the insignia of Chosen Woman!) It had tiny tassels hanging like rays of Eastsun reaching hands of love to the planet. The sandals she chose came high over the instep and ankle, were gold in color with raised emerald colored lashes at the instep, and had an ankle band of golden-colored doeskin.

As she laid each garment upon the other, to see what visual effect they might make, she smiled. She liked it very well. She let her gaze wander through the apartment. It had seemed so confining during all those Westsuns. Now it seemed such a place of security. If she lived to return to it she would be joyful indeed. If she did not... "Oh, Atl, I am sure in my mind that I will return. I don't want to be dead."

Again, all through the dark, the Empire was filled with messages from the deep throats of the Temple Drums. She tried to read the talk-talk at times. A glimmering of orders for Warriors to prepare for call-out to combat; statements that Africanus and Je-Su were fomenting overthrow of the Supreme Lor'd One, Thoth, followed by hot denials from the drums of the Warriors' Compound and the Temple of

266

Africanus; statements that A-Sar-U had been seen in temple areas to the East, West, Northwest, and Mountain areas. Again and again, an invitation from Lor'd Thoth to all the people of the planet to be at the Examining of the Ordeal.

And the chilling news that in the fourth watch of the dark the Temple Guard at Africanus Temple had successfully defended the Temple from takeover and had killed over three hundred dirty, grass-covered persons who seemed to rise up out of clumps of grass and fought to the death chanting happily, "Je-Su. Je-Su. Je-Su, Only Son of God-e."

Ast-i also felt the usual pull of Ra and As-Tar. The heavy, exhausting pull. But she put it aside as usual. Yet, she slept very little. She wakened to find again that she was tired and yet felt good. Long before first light she was up and ready.

God-ette appeared in early first light and swept into the room like a small whirlwind. She was in a flowing coton of gold-colored cloth, with threads of pure gold from hipline to hem, spaced about a thumb-width apart. She had chosen a bodice of pure and gleaming white, and a sash of the Lor'd Ones in flaming scarlet, belted by the same color, with a gold ankh woven into the cloth, and a piping of white. She was stunning to see, with her beautiful hair and clear, bright eyes.

"Oh, Ast-i, you are so beautiful! So beautiful."

"Holy Mother of the Virgins, I was about to say the same about you."

"Good. Say it to me on the way back. Now we must hurry. The Drum's call to formation has already begun. We will be ordered out soon. A-Thena and your triple guard are ready, as always."

"Yes. As always. Oh, if I could only be as beautiful as you, Mother, and as dependable as A-Thena."

Ast-i made fidgety adjustments to her dress. But when, after a short silence, the Drum spelled out her name and then fell into a slow, measured, four beats for the march, she found she was trembling and her breath was hard to take in. The weight of dread was so upon her that she felt a cramping, a very great cramping, in her stomach. The weight of secret dread was in each muscle of her body,

267

gripped her stomach and even her brain, like a heavy, squeezing and angry hand.

"We march for the Empire!" God-ette's voice cracked the message into the darkness of Ast-i's bemused brain and jerked her attention from the pains in her body. Her head came up and her body became more erect. In cadence with the drumbeats, the two swept out and into the hall, and immediately into place.

The Ama-Sonian guard stood three rows in front, three rows behind, and three rows to the left. As soon as the two stepped into place the three rows to the right fell into step and place. The three rows behind them closed them into an almost impenetratable box of fiercely protective, highly trained, deadly female Warriors.

Each Ama-Sone carried a short spear at ready, bore a short-sword inside her shield hung on the shield-rest strapped to her left shoulder, a long-sword belted at her left side in a leather guard, and a bow with a quiver of twenty arrows slung beneath the shield over her left shoulder. Each helmet was of gold-colored Oricalchum lined with leather, with three large battle feathers inserted into a band of Oricalchum alongside three metal spikes two spans in length, deadly in hand-to-hand combat.

"A-Thena, Commander of Ama-Sones, deliver this precious jewel of the Empire to be examined for the Ordeal and behead her if she fails."

A-Thena spoke firmly, and the guards seemed to march more at attention and in perfect rhythm to the Drum. Mercifully, in shortened strides for the tall Ama-Sones so that Ast-i could keep in step without ungainly forcing her stride.

Ast-i could see little beyond the Ama-Sones, but she was aware that ten arms in front of the triple guard, Ama-Sones carried a beheading cradle attached to a sleeping platform, and a curved-bladed axe with a handle a full arm long. They also bore a body tent in which she must lie awaiting the decision of the three judges, the Lor'd Ones' report, and finally acceptance by the people.

"Beloved Mother, you said the way to Virgin Birth was over dead bodies. Is this the last body we must go over?"

"Oh, Holy Ra, no, Beloved of God-e. We must born the child, protect it from enemies of the Empire, train and educate it to have your inner sight and A-Sar-U's great strength and knowledge and wisdom."

"Oh, life looks so long. So long!"

"Yes, yes. Looking ahead. But looking back, it seems too short. Smile. Soon you will be the most honored woman in the Empire."

"Oh, Holy Mother of God-e, though I tremble and hurt in my body and doubt and fear in my brain, I march on glee that the God-e has bestowed such honor on me. For I am blessed above all women."

As they marched along the north side of the Temple of Po-Si-Don the hedgerows of the fields suddenly rose up. A-Thena's shouts of warning and command was almost drowned by piercing shouts that echoed from the wall of the Temple. Ast-i saw the outside line of the triple guard wheel into a phalanx, shields and short spears at the ready. The shields of the Ama-Sones formed a wall around her and God-ette. All Ama-Sones were facing the threat, marching side-step, and never missed a beat of the cadence of the Drum.

"Kill the witch. Kill the lying bitch. Kill the illegal child. Kill. Kill. Kill."

The hedgerows broke into about a hundred chanting figures in long, filthy robes, spears in hand. Some spears were hurled but fell short. The figures racing toward the guards were figures of white in shrouds of dirt.

Ast-i heard the running feet on the second and higher levels of the Temple above her. A flight of arrows struck the white robed, screaming figures, in a pattern of incredible accuracy. One arrow pierced the gullet and stopped the screams to a gurgle. Another pierced the lungs and heart, and another pierced the groin.

Some in the front rank stumbled and fell, exposing the figures behind them. Some ran forward about thirty arms before falling. As soon as the body behind them was in view of the archers, arrows picked the chosen targets. In twenty breaths all of the attackers were gurgling, writhing, and dying. And Warriors sped among them carrying out the orders to cut away their private parts and force them into their mouths.

Ast-i felt a strange sickness clutching at her insides.

God-ette snapped, "The path to Virgin Birth is over dead bodies. Don't let it bother you. They are posanga zombies, recruited to die, and trained by Je-Su and Set. They must have lain there for ten or more Eastsuns, just to rise and die. They knew they could never reach us."

Even as God-ette spoke, the outside rank formed back into the Guard. Ast-i saw A-Thena glance upwards to the Temple Archers above, smile, wave a thumb-up salute, and bow thanks. Then she was again all dedicated Warrior with no apparent feelings.

"Why did they try to reach us, those zombies?"

"They are fanatics. We must be stronger than they to protect against such fanaticism. They have been told that Je-Su is the Only Begotten Son of God-e. We know that all persons are potential heirs of God-e. They try to kill us to enforce their beliefs. We must defend ours, even if it means unfortunate killing. It is a shame, no, more, it is a crime to waste human life and potential, but..." Her shrug was eloquent with frustration.

"Thank you Mother. I feel reassured. One is more bothered by the unknown than by the known—even if it is incredible!"

The Guard mounted the incline to the second level of the Temple. The tempo of the Drum increased as Ast-i came out upon the porch and into view. The Guard opened ranks, so that she was visible to people below, and a cheer—a chillingly short cheer—arose. As she moved out onto the Window of Ra, she was startled to see so many thousands of eyes staring at her from unbelieving, almost hostile faces.

The wild and boisterous pleasure with which they had greeted her eleven Westsuns ago was now a judgmental quiet. Ast-i could feel the doubt from their minds like an accusation.

"Oh, Mother, what have I done? They are so...so hostile."

"No, Beloved of God-e, not quite hostile. They are confused. Je-Su has spread rumors. The people need to be reassured that you and A-Sar-U are not part of a plot to deny Je-Su his rightful place as the Only Begotten Son of God-e, entitled to rule the world. They are only confused.

Soon they will be reassured. Smile. Stand tall and wave. They love you."

The Guard wheeled into place. The outer rank took stations along the edge of the Window of Ra. When in place they took their shields from the shield-guards long enough to bring forward their bows. They fixed an arrow at notch.

The Guard placed the beheading stand, and the beheading axe was handed to A-Thena.

Ast-i stepped forward to the edge of the porch, smiled, and waved down upon the people standing. There were answering waves, but no lusty cheers. She waved both hands, and then placed them on her swelling belly, and mimed hugging the child she carried there. And her reward was a small cheer from the crowd, a firm kick from the child, and a slight gripping pain.

To the mounting cadence of the Drum, groups already on the porch of the Window began to move into place. Each took its assigned place. Je-Su's guard swept into place, with Je-Su bowing proudly to the few cheers from the people below.

Thoth appeared with A-Sar-U on the fifth level. They descended the stairs past the fourth level, down the steps to the Window and moved into place at the edge of the porch. The people began to cheer wildly.

As they stepped into place, Bes appeared at the fourth level, flanked by about twenty Temple Guards carrying large, trailing banners.

The Drum came to a crash stop. Thoth said:

"Citizens and judges of this Pleasant Planet. I swear to you that A-Sar-U has not descended those stairs since he ascended them some eleven Westsuns agone."

"But he has been seen at temples throughout the Empire," Je-Su challenged.

"No, Je-Su, Lor'd One of War. His armor has been seen. But it was worn by a son of the Ama-Sones called Big Warrior. Here is Big Warrior."

The Temple Guards lowered the flags. Big Warrior stepped to the edge of the fourth level landing. "I swear to you that I have worn A-Sar-U's armor for the past eleven Westsuns. A-Sar-U is big like me, one of the few men of the planet whose armor I could wear."

271

The sounds of approval came from the people.

God-ette moved to the edge of the Window. "I am God-ette, Mother of A-Sar-U, and Mother Supreme of the Temple of the Virgins. I swear to you that we have kept pure as a treasure of the Empire, this Ast-i, child of the Lor'd Bes, and Lady Lor'd One, As-Tar. She has been isolated in her chambers for eleven Westsuns, fed by me, and at all times in sight of and guarded by the Ama-Sones. To all this I swear, and that no flesh man has touched her flesh since last she was before you here and you loved her for the risk she took for the good of the Empire."

A-Thena turned her head and said: "I am A-Thena, commander of the Ama-Sones and guard over this Treasure of the Empire, Ast-i, Chosen Woman of A-Sar-U. She has been isolated in her chamber for eleven Westsuns. And so all my guard will testify."

A-Sar-U stepped to the edge of the Window. "I am A-Sar-U. I swear to you that I have not bodily come away from the chambers assigned to me in eleven Westsuns until this very morning. I swear that I used the techniques taught me by the Lor'd One of Wisdom, Thoth, and did impregnate Ast-i by Thought-Force only when in a projected Radiant Body. I believe that in a few Westsuns we can teach all of you how to do this magical thing."

Thoth stepped to the edge of the Window. The people applauded him wildly. "Thank you. Thank you. All things needful to assure the purity of this maiden and the impregnation by Thought-Force alone in a Virgin's body have been done. These two young ones have risked much and worked hard to pass the Ordeal. Virgin Birth is imminent. To this I pledge you my sacred word.

"I know you have heard rumors. There are those among us, each of whom would like to be known as the Only Begotten Son of God-e and therefore entitled to rule the planet. Each of you knows that you are the offspring of God-e, the glorious God-e Indwelling. Is my word enough to reassure you that this is the cause of the rumors? Shall we proceed with the examination?"

Je-Su and his contingent shouted, "No." But the people below began to shout "Yes." It grew into a roar of approval. They reaffirmed this by an ovation of applause.

Ast-i was placed with her head outside the tent, resting on the beheading stand. She waved at the crowd and blew kisses. They laughed, but did not cheer. Her body was inside the tent, and the touch of the three examiners was swift and practiced.

She felt the hands of Brahm, then Som, then Lak-Shi-Mi exploring the outline of her swollen belly, and palms testing the size of the child within.

They all came from within the tent, and approached Thoth at the edge of the Window.

"How do you find?" Thoth demanded.

Brahm stepped forward. "I am Brahm, Lor'd One of Knowledge. I have examined this woman and find her with child. The child is well placed."

Ram stepped forward, "I am Ram, Lor'd One of Population. This woman is with child. The child is large. It kicks when it is pressed."

Ast-i felt the kick that sent her into a spasm of pain.

Lak-Shi-Mi stepped forward. "I am Lak-Shi-Mi, Chosen Woman of Brahm, and Lady Lor'd One, serving this day as Lor'd One of Life. It is my belief that Ast-i is with child. That it is more than eight Westsuns in growth. That it is well placed, but so big that a small woman will have difficulty in birthing it. It kicks when her stomach is pressed. My experience says her time is well upon her."

The three examiners solemnly walked forward.

"Lady examiners from the tribes. Is she still a Virgin?"

Three thumbs up sent the crowd into pandemonium, and only A-Thena was close enough to hear Ast-i's scream of pain. She tossed the axe aside and dived into the tent. A moment later she called, "Holy God-e, she is birthing."

God-ette shoved into the tent, and a moment later called, "Bring cloths, hot water, and Lak-Shi-Mi and Som. She is birthing. The spasms are two breaths apart."

A-Sar-U ducked into the tent. As the Lor'd Ones moved to their tasks the crowd surged about until someone shouted. "Lord Thoth, what is it?"

"Lor'd Som, report to the citizens of the Empire."

Som's head came out the front of the tent, a big smile on his usually dour face.

273

"Unto you, People of the Pleasant Planet, a child is being born. Excuse me now. On my honor, I must slit the hymen."

He ducked into the tent and then his long neck and head popped out again. "So you know it is a Virgin Birth."

34

Beginning of the End

Ast-i felt the pain at first like sharp blades cutting the muscles of her stomach. Then she felt the pain as if she were in a daze, confused and stunned by the pain.

She was annoyed. Very annoyed. Some girl kept grunting, groaning, and sometimes screaming in pain. She was annoyed at that girl, for the woman in her joyed at the strain and gloated at the pain. It was her feminine duty. Only a silly girl would think it such an ordeal that she needed to cry out in pain.

A-Sar-U was kneeling at her side and held her shoulders in a firm, tender embrace. It gave her comfort. It helped her squeeze against the lashing pains. She felt Ra and As-Tar, and she thought someone called to Thoth who hurried to her side.

She felt a flood of liquid on her lower parts and the pains all ran into one pain so great that her senses were squeezed from her brain. She heard someone say, "She's unconscious!"

She knew she wasn't. In her bright consciousness she began to talk to Ra and As-Tar. She asked them to let go their grip on her mind. For the grip was painful and her whole body was being pulled apart. She cried out for them to stop. But they kept up their demands on her energy and mind. They were draining her, stealing her senses. She would not do what they wanted. She would not relay their messages. She would not tell Thoth where they were, or how they were caught and held by the invisible hands of planet Ayr Aerth.

She dared not tell anyone. No one would believe her. They would despise her. They would shun her. Please leave her. Leave her. Leave her! Holy God-e, just leave her alone!

Suddenly she was conscious of the people below. They shifted and swayed impatiently. They also talked and laughed in low, urgent, respectful tones. She saw—yes, saw—Je-Su motion Set to get close to the tent and listen to what was being said. The Guard motioned him away with a spear, yet he signalled that he had heard something important.

She floated in time, wandered in space, until one giant spasm of pain rammed her back into full consciousness. There was a down-rushing feeling. She heard Lak-Shi-Mi, God-ette, and Som cry with delight, "It's a boy. A big boy! Warrior size!"

Moments later the warm, squirming, fragrant child was lying on her breast and she was crying for joy. The strange joy she had been feeling for so many Eastsuns.

A-Sar-U caressed her and the child, and Thoth riveted her floating attention by his deep voice.

"By what name shall he be called?"

She fought to be certain her spinning senses had heard aright.

"Horus."

"Then Ast-i, for the good of the Empire, may I borrow your divine son, Horus, and your Chosen Man, A-Sar-U for a hundred breaths?"

"Yes, Lor'd One. Your wish is my command."

"Bring your son, A-Sar-U."

Thoth walked beside A-Sar-U, who was carrying Horus, out of the tent and over to the very edge of the porch. "Hold him high," he whispered.

With the child held high on the palms of loving hands, its legs and arms waving as if swimming through air, and its voice cooing its contentment to the awed crowd below, Thoth began to speak. His rich voice thundered out across the masses.

"Fellow Citizens. Unto us is born Horus, a son and our Savior. Behold Horus, the Golden Falcon."

The crowd was jubilant and cheered endlessly. Many wept openly with their joy. Some called bawdy, Warrior things up to A-Sar-U that were compliments to his prowess. Bes signalled the Drum and it sent Thoth's words by relay to every part of the Empire.

"He is a Divine One, of Registered Virgin Birth. There are those who threaten him. They do not wish such a birth. But he is to be our Savior. For the planet we love is

276

in great danger, greater danger than you will at this moment believe. We need the help of the God-e, the miracle of the Birth of Horus, and the teachings of A-Sar-U to prepare us to meet our unspeakable danger.

"A-Sar-U and Ast-i have risked much for the good of the Empire. It is my hope that soon they may come among you, in all your tribes, risking their lives upon your protection.

"They must come and teach you much that you will want to know and be delighted to learn.

"By my orders and by your will he shall teach in your temples that which may save the peoples of this planet.

"Right now, he will speak to you. For I must return your youngest and dearest treasure to his anxious mother's arms. He is a divine treasure, born because of the use of Thought-Force through the Radiant Body. He is your Savior, and mine, and ours to cherish and protect against all dangers."

A-Sar-U waved at his former companions in the Line of Twenty, then at the entire crowd. His voice, younger and fresher than Thoth's, and almost as deep and pleasant, reached across the distance, from the banks of the canals to the rim of the inland sea.

"Lor'd One of Wisdom, the Divine Thoth, has told you that we face great dangers. You may think that it is to be a contest of arms against an attempt to overthrow the Empire.

"It is more important than that. It is your very lives.

"The true force, the great strength of the Empire lies not in its Warriors alone. Not in spears, shields, swords, arrows. The true force of Empire is in assuring each citizen of their individual safety, place, and liberty with personal dignity. No man is a leader, no man is a king, no woman is a queen, who people serve out of fear.

"Though the Empire has given a Lor'd One final say over property, servitude, life, and death, remember that the sword that pierces the heart may bring death yet not bring conviction. The idea that pierces the brain will serve the Empire better than the sword that pierces the flesh.

"Within the cocoon of safety which the Empire weaves around each of us, and all of us, each one must feel personal freedom. Remember, too, that each citizen has the right to say and do anything that does not threaten to burst the cocoon.

But if any individual exercises his right to such a degree, or imposes his thought in such a manner that it threatens the cocoon, is it not the right and duty of each of us in the Empire to restrict his actions, words, and concepts?

"It is the swiftness and severity of this restriction, and the force with which it is applied, that determines the difference between a benign Empire and a tyrannical State. The tone of Empire may be set by the impatience, ego, will, and inflexibility of the great leader. And the leader at any lower level is but the shadow of the arm of the great leader.

"I am proud to be the shadow of the powerful arm of our Beloved Thoth. He has asked me—not ordered me, mind you—to come among you and teach you in your temples what he taught me while I lived inside this Temple, with nothing to do but achieve.

"He knows you are busy with duties of field, forest, home, and life. He knows it may take longer to teach each of you busy citizens.

"But he sends me among you to teach you a Divine Skill. It is how to build inside your physical body a golden duplicate of yourself that may know eternal life; that may travel through space and time; that may know how to transfer all your physical senses and Life-Force, your creative fire and your divine essence across time and distance.

"It is not a secret skill. On That Other Planet it was in common use. On That Other Planet Virgin Birth was almost commonplace. But it is a skill that requires rigid discipline and personal, pure living, complete relaxation of body and complete effort of pristine will.

"Please welcome me to your temples."

A-Sar-U was pleased with the ovation he received and blushed deeply, to the great pleasure of the crowd.

It was Ast-i who heard, and later told A-Sar-U and Thoth, that Je-Su turned to Set in anger and declared:

"We must kill that so-called Divine Bastard, destroy his father, and take his mother prisoner, and starve out of her the things she knows about Ra and As-Tar.

"Send to Africanus the word to attack, and I will order all Warriors into the field. Je-Su's army can then overrun all the temples. We must teach the people the Creed of Je-Su and enforce it with the thrust of the sword:

> I believe in one God-e, Supreme Lor'd of the universe. I believe in and adore His Beloved Only Son, Je-Su. He is God-e in spirit, mind, and flesh. Of him he is the very likeness and essence. I will submit unto these two my will, my hope, my fortune, and my bodily self. They are one in essence and identical in will. I swear on my honor and hope of salvation that I will be obedient to their holy priests. For the appointed priests are the earthly heirs of the powers of God-e and his son, Je-Su. They are rulers of the spiritual and temporal domain. I will accept their wishes as the will of the God-e, the two bodies in one. I know that therein lies my only possible salvation and hope for eternal life."

A-Sar-U and Thoth were not certain that Ast-i had actually heard Je-Su's words. But they did not doubt the words were spoken and were the true thoughts of Je-Su. For they were now certain that Ast-i had powers of knowing that were beyond the usual. Only later were they to find out how much beyond the usual her powers really were.

35

Prelude to the Death of A-Sar-U

Thoth sat quietly in his large room. Bes stood near the entrance, apparently indolent, but Thoth knew he was keenly alert to the possible dangers that might invade through the outside hallway and was ready for them. Godette sat near Thoth, her fair hair and blue eyes highlights of beauty. Som sat beyond her, his slender face and dark eyes looking almost ineffective as keepers of his copious brain powers.

"Lady Goddess, how is the Divine One?"

"Horus is fine. A-Sar-U is as good as a nervous father can be. Ast-i is not yet well. She still has times of almost complete unconsciousness. Her energy is being drained and the why is beyond my skills."

"Will she now talk to me, tell me what she imagines Ra and As-Tar want me to know?"

"Lor'd Thoth," Bes said gently. "Ast-i does not imagine things of the spirit. She knows. Ra and As-Tar speak to her, they pull upon her."

Thoth nodded his appreciation. He then got up and walked about the room, his big body moving swiftly and seemingly without effort. But inside his mind was racing. He was perplexed. He needed time.

"We know Je-Su is readying his Warriors to attack. We don't know where, or how strongly he will attack some Temple Guard. We don't know when. He moves his Warriors almost every night. And his armies of posanga zombies continue to harass and threaten the Empire. Perhaps we should let the dreaded secret be known."

He glanced at Som, Lor'd One of Science, and shook his head in disappointment. "But we do not know for sure that there is a secret. Som, the Lor'd One of Science, and all his helpers in the Realm cannot assure me that what we suspect may be about to happen will, in fact, happen. And we must not tell the populace that this monstrous thing is to happen until we are absolutely certain.

"We should move, yet we cannot do more than we are doing. We are limited to warning the people of possible dangers unspecified and sending A-Sar-U among them.

"We dare not let the people know of the possibility of a catastrophe that may soon destroy this galaxy for hundreds of millions of reaches about us."

"Not until we are sure," God-ette said. "To do so would remove hope from the minds of men."

"True," Thoth said. "Man's ingenuity is honed by hope. When hope for the future dies, mankind must wither, shrivel, and die. Life on this Pleasant Planet will then virtually stop. The old ones will not mind. They have known the joys of life and explored the mysteries of mind and the happiness of love. But the young cannot live without hope. If they are suddenly bereft of hope, they will rebel and virtually bring civilization to a stop. Life would not continue in its peaceful cycle if all mankind were to be deprived of the light of hope—hope in the inexhaustible attractions of the unpredictable future.

"Oh, a few might continue for a while. But like flowers past their time, they would slowly fold and molder, languish in lassitude, and fall away in simple despair.

"Man progresses by ingenuity. If hope for a future for him and his beloved is denied, man would slowly die though he sat upon a mountain of unending energy. For without hope for life, without the taste of Life-Force, without possibility of escaping his doom, man would not care to prepare for the adventure of his future. Man does not build the house he knows in advance will be burned down tomorrow. He does not beget the child of body or of mind he knows will be destroyed by nature in a few short years."

Bes spoke softly, but the room was filled with his conviction. "You are right! We must give the people some hope. Without it the young will turn upon society in madness, take revenge on individuals for what nature has done. Anarchy comes from hopeless frustration, chaos comes from struggles against hopelessness."

"I agree," God-ette said. "We must give the people some hope or we will be destroyed before we can ever know if horror will come upon us...and when. Without hope the future will not be permitted to be. For we are the future."

"Thank you for reasoning with me, my dear companions in fear and distress. We have a sickness in our bowel. It is the acid juice of fear."

"True." Som spoke so quickly it startled the room with sound a little too loud for so thin a frame. "But more. We are crushed by the dilemma of the inexorable."

"Lor'd One of Science, do you have a suggestion?"

"Yes. No. Well, maybe. I do not have facts. My Priests say the Westsun is coming south each time it passes over the Pillars of Ra. But they do not know that it is coming closer to the Pleasant Planet. We cannot tell."

"Then, I don't see..."

"Perhaps. Perhaps I do not see either. But let me apply the mental tools of science and reason and see if...maybe there is just a glimmer of hope."

"Good." Thoth strode back and sat upon his rug. "Apply!"

"It may take us further into the dilemma of the inexorable"

"To know the worst is to look toward the better."

Som tried to sit straight, but as he talked his tall, thin body curved inward upon his head. "In the tent at the borning we all heard Ast-i in her delirium talking to Ra and As-Tar, telling them why she could not relay their messages to Thoth."

"I did not hear it," Bes said. "But I know my daughter and her fear of not being accepted by her peers."

"Then, even in delirium of pain she would not lie?"

"My word on it, Lor'd Som."

"Would she fantasize?"

"I doubt it," God-ette said. "With all she is young, she is a very firm thinker. She is emotional, but not to that extent."

"You said that she was so distraught that you were afraid at times she might lose the Thought-Force child."

"Yes, at times she was so weak that I was afraid she might not have the strength to carry it to term."

Som's long arms shot out, his palms toward her in almost a defensive gesture. "Lady Mother, Lor'd Thoth, Lor'd Bes. I may have had enough information all the while. Let me give you my reasoning based on scientific Lore and see if it fits her condition.

"She dared not sleep or rest, for she was tormented by visions of Lor'd Ra and Lady Goddess As-Tar?"

"True, Lor'd Som."

"She felt as if she was on the planet Ayr Aerth, held there by invisible thongs, pulled down by invisible forces."

"Exactly her words over time."

"Then, Lor'd Thoth, Supreme Lor'd One, I can tell you where the Radiant Bodies, or spiritual doubles, of Lor'd Ra and Lady As-Tar are. But you, and only you, can tell me where their physical bodies are to be found.

Thoth did not flinch. But his green eyes opened wider. "Where do you think their Spiritual Bodies are?"

"And why do you think so?" Bes added.

"Oh, Lor'd Thoth, I do not think. The logical process of science tells me unerringly. Lor'd Ra and Lady As-Tar have been strangely 'gone' from their very important and essential duties in the Temple for several Westsuns.

"Ra and you, Lor'd Thoth, are deeply Lored in science. You and he have built and placed the Pillars of Ra on the temple porches of the Empire. You have built an exact, measurable grid by which to measure the rate of the movement of the Westsun to the south. From these exactly placed pillars they read that the Westsun was coming closer to the Eastsun at High Light. They suspected, but could not prove, that the Westsun was coming too close and would be pulled into the Eastsun. The result would be annihilation. Utter and complete destruction."

He paused, and Thoth nodded. "You have a theory there, Lor'd Som. It is a good theory."

"Rather than wait in desperation for the probable death of all, you decided to search for some possible way to save the people.

"You had heard the myths of Atl, and too, too many myths of the mythical planet which he called Ayr Aerth. And you researched it. Thirty-six Westsuns agone you probed my memory for all the things Atl had told. So did Lor'd Ra.

"You wanted to know if it is true that Ayr Aerth is, as Atl claimed, six times bigger than this Pleasant Planet. You wanted to know if, as Atl claimed, it was the nearest planet, and, in general, a pleasant one.

"In remarkable courage born of desperation, you decided to try to find out. But since Atl had accidentally destroyed the last space cruiser from That Other Planet, you had no way to travel physically through space."

"Obviously true," Thoth smiled. "What would you have done?"

Som smiled, and his dark face became pleasant. "Exactly what you two decided upon, Lor'd Thoth. I would have traveled through space in my Radiant Spiritual Body. Ah, that is, if I had been taught the skill in spite of my inflexible scientific mind. I would have traveled through space and tried to find the planet by the reverse attraction of thought, just as I am sure you planned, and Ra did.

"Ra and As-Tar went through the cosmos to find and examine Ayr Aerth. They found it. They examined it. They found it habitable. But it was in fact six times bigger than the Pleasant Planet. Its invisible hands were many times stronger than those on this planet. They could not then project their Radiant Selves out of the grasp of the invisible thongs. They could not escape the binding of the planet upon their Spiritual Bodies in order to return to the Pleasant Planet.

"This they are desperate to tell you through Ast-i. They have contacted you, but they know the message is not clear to you. They are trying to get a message to you through a natural mystic of incredible sensitiveness. She is terrified by the pull upon her, and by the terrible, unaccustomed things she sees that she thinks she knows cannot be true. So she refuses to let the messages come through. They desperately try, and the pull upon her is taking a great toll of her vital Life-Force."

Som was silent for a long time, and began to unwind, raising his head from within the fold of his body.

"Lor'd Ones, I have spoken."

"And well. Very well, Lor'd Som. Lady Mother, what do you suggest?"

God-ette fitted her actions to her word. "That Lor'd Bes and I go to her apartments and waken her. Tell her what we suspect, and that you and Lor'd Som will come in a hundred breaths. Then we will get her to describe in full detail, for the good of the Empire, all the things she is afraid to mention for fear of ridicule. If you reassure her at every breath, you may at last get the message from Ra."

"And if you do, you may be able to send through her mind a message to Ra," Bes said. "She is powerful."

"Can we do it all before Je-Su attacks?"

"We can try," Bes said.

In a hundred breaths the four great Masters of Time stood in the apartment assigned in the Temple of the Virgins to A-Sar-U and Ast-i. Ast-i lay upon her sleeping mat with Horus nestling her bosom. Her face was pale, drained. Lines of pain etched her eyes toward dark shadows, and her lips toward an old-woman's pursing. Her eyes were over-bright and she seemed to want to retreat into the mat. Her voice trembled slightly when she attempted to be gay and bright.

"Lor'd Ones, welcome to the house of Lor'd A-Sar-U, His Chosen Woman, and his Divine Son, the Golden Falcon."

Thoth waited through the pleasantries and then spoke decisively.

"Lady Goddess Ast-i. Sometimes for the good of the Empire we all must do that which we would prefer not to do. We now must ask you to do that which you have sworn you could not do. Emergency and our entreaties may persuade you of your special ability and of our dire need of your help. Be sure that this is an emergency or we would not come so soon after your Ordeal to ask so much of you. Will you help us?"

Ast-i pulled unconsciously at her cover as if trying to escape by hiding. Her eyes were deep with fear and confusion.

"As you command me, Lor'd Thoth."

"I do not command you, Ast-i-Ankh, Beloved of God. Genius such as you possess cannot be commanded like trained Warriors. It is a priceless gift you have that we need turned to our aid right now. Will you do it? Do you have strength enough to do it?"

"Lor'd Thoth, I fear it is the thing I least like about myself, the thing I least want to do."

"Perhaps it is the thing you and you alone can most quickly do to aid the Empire in its needs. Should you, then, give weight to your personal aversions or the needs of the Empire?"

"The needs of the Empire—at least, I think."

"You will do it?"

"I will try."

"Will you relay to us all you can remember of the contacts you have had with Divine Ra and Lady Goddess As-Tar?"

"Oh, no, no..."

"And then will you let Lor'd Ra and Lady As-Tar speak through you to us, and from us through you to them?"

Ast-i's eyes closed as if to ward off a blow. She breathed deeply and painfully. Tears welled out from under her lids.

"All I ever wanted was to be like other girls. Not to hear voices and know things beyond sense. I just want to be normal."

"The duty of those who bear the blessings of the God-e is to use and develop those blessings."

"Even if spurned and ridiculed?"

"Especially if spurned and ridiculed. The award of a gift always requires that you be able to carry the burden of the gift. Would God-e make you more wonderful than most to be bound by the opinions of most?"

Ast-i began to weep, but through her sobbing began to tell all that she had experienced. The horror of being bound by invisible thongs in strange places. The oppression of trying to reach the Pleasant Planet with information vital to the future. Her realization that she had the Wisdom of Ra, but dared not use it. How she could not shut them out of her mind, and the dreadful drain upon her body.

As she talked, she seemed to be relieved. The dark shadows left her eyes, the lines left her lips. Color came into her cheeks, setting them alight with beauty and youth. When she had finished, Thoth, Bes, and Som knew she was receiving the true pictures of Ra and As-Tar. Each was trapped in the extended spirit in a willing body on Ayr Aerth, without hope of returning to the Pleasant Planet.

286

"Ast-i," Thoth said, "You may have aided, possibly saved, the people of the Pleasant Planet. I trust you are as pleased with yourself as we are pleased with you."

"Lor'd Thoth, it is happy-making to please. I feel so very relieved. You all have made me feel so loved and special."

"Can you talk to Ra and As-Tar through your mind-force projected?"

"I don't know how."

A-Sar-U kissed her. Holding her hand, he said. "My Goddess, you can do it. You must go into the deep peace of yourself. You must reach a place beyond time, a space where only the beginning may be known. It is not enough to go where time is not nor ever was. You must go beyond time, where it does not exist. There you must speak the word that is the first syllable of divine energy. To you it may sound like the baby-prattle of the giant universe. But there, in that bright darkness that is all silence, you must see the light that is all sound. There, as an echo of all sound, you must speak the silent words that go on forever. Into that sound which is silence you put the breath of energy that grows until you can force your will upon all matter. Every little particle of your body will sing the joy of sadness, the beauty of creation, the happiness of destruction. And the things you think will be like inward, muted, thunderclaps of sound to the ones you want to hear you."

All eyes were fixed in astonishment on A-Sar-U, for he had spoken in the voice of Ra.

Confused, and as if coming out of sleep, he let go of Ast-i's hand. His voice instantly changed to his own as he said, "I wonder where that all came from."

"The Wisdom of Ra," Som said. "The Wisdom of the Eternal One."

36

The Idyll Before the Storm

A-Sar-U, under Thoth's wisdom-guidance, prepared for his visits to all the fourteen Temple Centers of the Empire. He was stressed on the physical level by the task of training seven million persons in techniques that might save their lives. He knew he might run into extreme resistance, even physical violence, from the followers of Je-Su or the Warriors of Set. He was to have a retinue of servants, and a bodyguard of a Line of Twenty with a commander and leader. For these he chose Luflin and Big Warrior.

In the spiritual, he was filled with joy. His body was out from confinement in a single room. He could feel the fresh and changing winds of each Eastsun upon his face. His being seemed to expand to meet the glorious moments. Life, because it possibly had only a few remaining Westsuns, became extremely precious in each moment.

The most glorious moments he knew were those he spent with Ast-i. Her lithe little body beckoned him often to prove again it could and did give all the physical delights it seemed to promise.

Some magical energy exchanged in their contacts. That energy turned a physical act into a sacrament so sacred that it raised the physical act to the level of Divinity. He mused to himself: "Loving a woman truly is the nearest most men ever come to divinity."

In a sweet moment Ast-i said, "Is it true as Ra has said that the Lover's Touch is a Serpent of Wisdom that eats its own tail?"

"If Ra said it, it is true."

"But Goddess Lak-Shi-Mi says women must be careful of the Lover's Touch. It may turn the Serpent of Love into a snake in the grass."

A-Sar-U laughed and held her close. "Lak-Shi-Mi is not touched by the lover she wants. What do you say?"

She pulled back in surprise to look at him. She studied him closely. "You do not jest. I'm glad. You see, I think you say wonderful things through me. So does Khnum, Ra, Mut, God-ette, As-Tar, and Thoth especially, all the time. I'm a relayer for wisdom. But that does not mean I am wise."

"You are the wisest one I know."

"I'd like to be wise. But I'm very like those who speak with the dead."

"You are what?"

"I'm very like those who speak with the spirits of the dead."

"So?"

"Ra's Wisdom says they are channels through which the spirits of the dead may speak to the living. But that I am more, ah, uh, more valuable to mankind.

"Oh, even in saying that I feel a little ashamed of such boasting. Do you think I am boastful?"

"I think you are wonderful and too modest about your great gifts. Why does Ra say you are more valuable?"

"Oh, he says I am a...a co...conduit...that means something that something else can run through and not be changed.

"Did you know that, A-Sar-U?"

"I know it now," A-Sar-U was smiling.

"Ra says that I am a conduit for the Eternal Wisdom of those who have never died. That is, not *really* died, after they were created by Divinity to experience the problems and joys of, well, of the flesh. Like, well, you, Thoth, God-ette, Bes, As-Tar, all those who have been Virgin Born. Do you understand?"

"Yes. Oh, yes! And that makes you very special, for you are Virgin Born, you know."

Tears came to her eyes. "Oh, A-Sar-U, I know you mean to be kind. But that makes me very scared and not like others. Not just normal. Oh, darling, hold me, hold me. Hold me! Make your strength flow through me, make me feel warm. Make me feel safe and needed and normal. Make me feel normal!"

"Darling, you are normal!"

"You know I'm not. I hear things beyond hearing, feel things beyond feeling, see things beyond seeing, and know things beyond knowing. I'm not wise, I am a conduit for special wisdoms.

"I want...oh, I do so want to be normal. Like you! Oh, I know you have those great powers, those divine wisdoms, and those enormous strengths. But you are so calm. You accept what you are. You are content with you, for you belong. So with all your greatness you are normal. You are a normal God-e."

He held her close. Her fragrant hair spread across his bare chest and her warm body seemed to try to burrow into his for safety. It made him feel so wonderful that she turned to him for comfort.

Carefully he tried to separate his thoughts from his emotions. "Oh, God-e," he prayed silently, "give me the wisest answer."

The answer came. He relaxed and let his other mind speak. "Beloved of God-e, you are wise. Far wiser than most. You are wiser than I am...though face it, Beautiful, at times I'm pretty smart for a big, gawky, bumbling kid. At times great energies pour through me like rays of the Eastsun making little suns in a billion billion particles—Atl called them *cells*—you know, the little rooms priests live in—in my body. When this happens to me, I accept it. Then I am blessed and filled with wisdom. Almost the same things happen to you, don't they?"

"Yes. Very like."

"But when you are filled with such wisdom you hold it in. You do not want to empty, lest people think you are not normal. Maybe this is the difference. I know I am not normal. I know people will never accept me as normal. They tease me. I think they tease me in love, for when I tease them back it is in respect, love, and laughter. They pay me respect and, I hope, love me. But they do not accept me as normal, as one of them."

"The same with me. But it bothers me and it does not bother you."

"Oh, yes it does!"

"Oh?"

"In a way it bothers me very much. We all want to belong, to become a part of the others. To be at one with

290

all humanity. But some of us are different. We do not want to be different, but the others force us to be."

"Yes, they do, don't they?"

"Yes. But it has bothered me less since the day I saw the old woman carrying a basket of food."

"You tease?"

"No love, I report something very important. I saw an old woman carrying a basket of food along a path on which I was making a training run. She was on the hill above me. She stumbled and the basket fell from her head and rolled over and over on the stony ground until I stopped it. I picked it up and handed it to her. Her gnarled fingers trembled as she undid the sisal-grass thongs that held the lid on the basket. She lifted the lid and looked down upon a basket full of unbroken eggs. Lovingly she touched the thongs, proudly she touched the basket, gently she touched the lid. Then she squinted up at me and said:

"'Good thongs. Good basket. Good lid. Good eggs. Thankee, good youth. Took y' all t' save me my sev'n East-sun's eatin.'"

"Maybe we are different. But all of us are needed to give mankind the feast of love and greatness the Supreme God-e has gathered and bound into baskets of wisdom with thongs of love."

"Oh, A-Sar-U. That was beautiful. But what part do you feel you are?"

"The thongs were different than all the rest. Yet they saved it all. I think we must be thongs of love intended to bind mankind to a basket of fragile wisdoms. Maybe the Great God-e has given us the privilege of being His thongs."

Ast-i sighed. "It doesn't bother you...I mean, you don't ever ask the Supreme God-e to—to make you the basket—to, to use you in any special way?"

"Oh, yes. Each Eastsun rise I thank him for using me and ask him to use me in the service of all our people."

"Without reservation? You don't ever want some special thing, or to serve in a special way?"

"Only to serve in His way, in His time, in His stead."

"I want to serve the Supreme God-e. But in my way, in my time, and how I wish. The Blessed Mother of God-e,

291

Goddess God-ette, says women try to force men and God-e to their will. And are unhappy when they cannot. Do you suppose that I want secretly to have all the great gifts of God-e, yet want to appear normal?"

"It is quite possible. Experience speaks, you know."

"Thank you. I think I will no longer ask to be normal or a part of the basket or of the feast of wisdom. I will ask to be a good thong."

She melded into his embraces. When passions were spent, she lay contentedly beside him. Suddenly she raised on her elbow.

"Yes. I'll be different. A good thong. But, please, can I be a Golden Thong like you?"

A-Sar-U had heard that very young women were sometimes awkward mothers, but when Ast-i held Horus, or gave him her breast, they formed a picture he wished everyone could see. He said so to Thoth. The very next East-sun fourteen stone carvers visited their quarters to study Ast-i and Horus, even make many measurements.

They went away. But at all temples in the Empire, a statue appeared. It was a statue in pure white marble, fixed near the base of the Golden Pillar of Ra on the porch of each temple. Ast-i, in all her beauty, cradled Horus lovingly in her left arm and gave him her left breast. She looked down upon him with divine love, the love of divine woman for a divine son. Above her right shoulder was the face of A-Sar-U beaming his love on the Divine Pair.

When first he saw the statue tears flowed. For in stone, the carvers had managed to show what he had longed to say.

At temple after temple, as the Westsuns sped by, people went first to view the statue before they came for training.

A priest said reverently, "The Eternal Feminine. Truly the Eternal Mother of God-e."

"Mother of all, and of our Savior," another said.

Wherever they went as they toured from temple to temple, it became a place for rejoicing and praising the Supreme God-e. The people were coming eagerly to learn that which might save their lives, and this gave A-Sar-U and Thoth great pleasure.

Horus was almost six Westsuns and growing well when Ast-i asked for a conference with Thoth, Bes, God-ette, A-Thena, Som, and Ram. "This I must tell you. For Ra and As-Tar have found a dreadful thing. But we will let Ra speak."

Ast-i reached and took A-Sar-U's hand. Both seemed to go into a trance, and then the voice of Ra echoed in the room.

"On Ayr Aerth there is a tribe of advanced humanoids who would gladly lend their sound, strong bodies to be filled by what they conceive as better minds such as ours. For some reason, perhaps a fault in their throats, they cannot speak easily. They look on us as their 'Gods from outer space,' and will help us. It would be a good combination. Each race would improve the other. But there are only a few more than four million of them. They are scattered over seven continents. Each continent is as large as the landmass of the Pleasant Planet. If dire necessity drives us to it, we must transmute, send through space, and reassemble at least three million bodies from there to here."

"How can that best be done?"

"Thoth knows. It is the same method you were taught in raising your Radiant Body. You learn that first. Then you must be at the verge of physical death, or your Other, your greater mind must believe you are. At that moment, another energy comes into activity. Some deep and wonderful energy! By using that energy you can transmute flesh. You can change flesh, bone, blood, and sinew into energy. Into a sacred energy that is the radiant double of the Golden Body. You can then send that energy through space and time to any place you will and wish. Then you can turn it from energy back into flesh. If you think it sounds easy, recall that you must die to the flesh to be born again in the spirit.

"Thoth knows how to do this, and he can teach how. It requires more discipline than raising the Radiant Body. Remember, you do not go toward peace, you go toward death.

"It is an Initiation in which you risk all to gain all. In Initiations, many, many die in the flesh before they can raise the Energy Body that can transmute flesh."

"We will train for it," Thoth said, but he appeared to be greatly disturbed.

Brief as the contact had been, Ast-i was trembling with fatigue.

Som looked solemn-eyed at everyone in the room. His head seemed to pull down to rest on his narrow shoulders. It shot up again on his long slender neck. "Lor'd Thoth, you are confused, as I am. The scientific reports of Lor'd Atl said there were thirteen million humanoids on Ayr Aerth, another million on the island of Atl Antis, and yet another million on the Island of On or along the Beautiful River that waters the land."

"Thank you, Lor'd Som. I remembered. I was puzzled."

"Another thing. Every God-e must train for the transmutation of the flesh, and in extreme cases, for the teleporting of other physical things. Is that so?"

"Yes. That is true."

"Then, how could Lor'd Ra forget?"

The silence was long and deep.

"Lor'd Thoth?"

"Yes, Lor'd Ram?"

"Our dependable records on population shows that there should be at least fifteen million humans on Ayr Aerth. If there is not, something is wrong. If something is wrong, we may have no place to go to from this planet. No place that is safe."

Som's head shot up again. "Lor'd Ram is thinking rightly. If we go to Ayr Aerth and it is wrong...we all die anyway. Could not someone fresher and stronger than Lor'd Ra go and see what the true conditions are?"

Ast-i felt the chill of dread creep like freezing water over her skin and up the back of her neck. "Someone might go to see. But the invisible hands hold one firmly to that planet. We might not be able to return once we reached there."

Again silence was the battle-zone of thought.

"If one must go, I will," Thoth said.

"But who then would be strong enough to hold these battling tribes in the Empire? Who would be the Supreme Lor'd One if you were gone?"

"Ask Lor'd Bes."

"Not I, for causes a-plenty, but which you may not know. Not A-Sar-U yet, for he is known as a spiritual master, not a physical master, as he will be known in the future. None of the God-es, for they are of the mind, and our planet must yet be ruled by Warrior might."

"Then who?" Ram's dark face was showing strain and concern.

"In dire emergency, and for a short time, Thoth might bind Je-Su before the Empire and upon his honor, to accept a temporary appointment, subject to Thoth's return. He could bind Je-Su just as Ra bound Thoth. But make him Supreme Lor'd One by Temporary appointment, not by contest. And bind the Empire so that the Combats could be opened at any time Je-Su did anything not seemly and in the interests of all the Empire."

"The Combats and the Drum are solely under the control of the Supreme Lor'd One, or one appointed by the Supreme Lor'd One who serves for life. Like Bes. He controls the Drums for life."

"True. But Je-Su might not accept that they were to remain outside his control. I, Bes, must hold control over them. Therefore I must be able to open the Combats at my will. If Je-Su proves too cruel and inhuman, or the tribes grow restless under him, I will open the Combats, challenge and kill him, and regain control."

"Then you would become Supreme Lor'd One."

"Ah, for so long as it took me to appoint someone. I have no desire for place or power. I'm quite content being Lor'd One of Nothing."

Thoth spoke slowly, "It is a possible plan to be used in dire circumstances. Meanwhile we must continue as we are. Except, A-Sar-U, you and I must work together. I have much more to teach you, just in case."

37

The Nine Energy Bodies

A-Sar-U was preparing to begin his second series of visits to the Temple Centers to train the citizens. Now, however, he felt the rush of time, the press of circumstance, like an attacking eagle. Little was said of the impending dangers; yet it was always in his mind.

Thoth began a daily series of teaching sessions for him. Attending often were Som, Lor'd One of Science, Ram, Lor'd One of Population, and Brahm, Lor'd One of Knowledge. Lor'd Bes often attended, and "the Lor'd Horus," now forty-eight Westsuns, sat quietly, listened carefully, and remembered.

Horus's mind was a sponge for knowledge. He had been talking and running with playmates since the time he had reached eighteen Westsuns. Large, gentle, and full of laughter that was quick and catching, he spoke knowingly of wise things and taught his playmates. His coming to any of the temples was a cause for celebration.

"The Golden Child is come," the citizens would say.

Horus was golden haired, with large blue eyes that were level, steady, and unafraid. He was beloved by all.

All, that is, except Je-Su. His reputation caused Je-Su and Set to plot and plan to destroy Horus. Whispers were abroad that they intended to kidnap him. But the love of the people for Horus was so great that they were afraid to attempt to harm him.

A-Sar-U was glad to have Horus in the teaching sessions where he was safe. And also where he learned.

Thoth began one important session on science:

"You must now learn of the conflicting theories of energy and life held by the Lor'd Ones. Why? Because you must decide which theory you can and will use to change the destiny of individuals and the Empire.

"There are nine levels of energy, some crass, some subtle, that seem to be in each human body. They are powers that built bodies, some physical, some energy, some spirit. These are:

"Ren, the energy of a pure life; Khat, the energy of human life in the animal body; Ka, the subtle energy of life able to project itself from the animal or human body; Ab, the subtle energy of the heart; Ba, the energy of the heart turned to spirit; Sekem, the repository of energy found in the physical, mental, psychic; Sahu, the energy of the Sekem intertwined with the more radiant energy of the spiritual; and the Khu, the transcendent, radiant energy of spirit with everlasting life.

"Those are accepted. Lor'd Som will now summarize his own scientific theories on energy."

"Energy," Lor'd Som's head bounced on his long neck and he looked as if embarrassed by not agreeing fully with Lor'd Thoth, "is that which goes from one particle to another as they grow or change.

"It is the primitive force which forms the universe. Energy is a fundamental flow of the most primordial essence. But I believe it shapes the world. For matter is nothing but a series of little whirlpools of energy. It is that uncomprehendable thing or force that forms the material of all solid and substantial matter.

"Thought is energy." Som stopped, let his head pop up from between his shoulders on his long neck while he looked at Thoth as if expecting argument. "Thought is a subtle, substantial, primordial force. Thought is an act of consciousness combined with an act of mind.

"When will is added, thought becomes a new, or nacent, force, naked and pure and unencumbered by visible material essences. The energy of such a force must not be ignored; even though it may not be immediately apparent to the five senses. It might be less dangerous to ignore the burning rays of the Westsun just because they cannot be seen with normal human eyes." Som again looked about the chamber, licked his thin lips, nodded as if congratulating himself.

"Consciousness is an active form of energy alive in every particle of a being and is not limited to the so-called higher life forms. Consciousness stirs in the most primitive

297

life forms and, I believe, in the seemingly solid material things, like this marble floor we sit on. Consciousness may possibly be the direct descendent of the unifying stresses of the particles of matter.

"Thought is a process for materializing the energy of mind, the unification of many forces. It is a put-together thing called a synthesis. Every synthesis costs energy, even the synthesis that takes place in the most spiritual realms of being.

"Thought mounts on thoughts, like steps on the stairs of a temple. The more energy of thought that comes into the world, the more it is consumed, and the higher the synthesis may be of further thought, and the higher our citizens may mount on the stairs of the temple of science.

"How does this apply now, as we race the Eastsuns to outrun what we all believe is to be certain disaster?" Som squirmed uncomfortably and shrugged helplessly.

"As Lord Thoth has pointed out, man consists of nine bodies, each an energy, each a spirit, each with a destiny. The Ren lives forever as a thought-form in memory; the Khat may change form and go from tissue to energy, from matter to energy. The Ab, the sacred heart, seat of life, may go from material to energy in a new form. But the Ka, Ba, Sekem, Sahu, and Khu all have the potential of energy that can have everlasting life, and exist as an almost-distinct force field, as a drop can exist in water.

"Lor'd Thoth does not agree with us scientists that all energy is crass and material. He will assure you that we can, when adequately trained, bring forth from our living body each of these several energies and make them exist in time outside of the human body.

"But mark me, each energy is held near to the being that has been its host, by a force that is given to each by the human body.

"Lor'd Thoth thinks the human body, therefore, is the seed-ground of many specialized energy forms, spiritual essences, that can take on life and activity of their own. They can exist outside the human body once they are formed and grown there. These, Thoth believes, may be called special servants of the Supreme God-e. They are energy forms that seem to have wings. Lor'd Thoth calls them angels. Scientists call them energy whorls.

"Lor'd One of Knowledge, Brahm, will explain further some of our doubts and our opinions."

Brahm was a visual contrast to Som. His small stature seemed to belie his knowledge, and he looked as if he were angry about it. He was so nervous that he swallowed several times before he said:

"Lor'd Thoth and Lor'd Som have explained that there must be nine energy levels in the one human body. Some, when grown, may live forever.

"In a like manner, it is my opinion that there must be three or more universes. Three!" He looked hard at each person searching for doubts. All faces seemed to be accepting, so he nodded and continued.

"We can easily see and be aware of the physical universe. That is one, but there must be three.

"These three must be made of the one, the many, and nacent energy. Why? Because these are the three faces of the material sphere.

"The one increases as human consciousness expands.

"The many increase as the material increases.

"Nacent energy increases as thought-forms pile one upon another. This may be like Lor'd Som's temple steps."

He smiled and the usual anger of his expression turned to charm.

"Yes. There must be three, or more, universes. One is in the visual realm, the physical world of the five senses. There must be another universe, the realm of the unapparent.

"This invisible realm may then be divided into the spiritual realm and the all-important realm of the new-mind which we might call NEO-mental.

"Here any form of energy seems to be multiplied. The energy of spirit seems to be small yet indeterminately powerful.

"The physical dimension seems to have no being at all in the NEO-mental realm. However, it cannot be resisted, even though its energy cannot be seen. It is in this NEO-mental realm that the energy for the salvation of humankind from cosmic destruction may be possible.

"We must realize..." He stopped and glanced at Lor'd Som and his face eased back into its accustomed mold of anger. "We must make the material-minded, like Som, Je-

Su, and Set, realize that there is NEO-mind in all material systems—if only as potential.

"By the subtle energy of thought constantly applied, the material universe may be turned into the higher spiritual universe in its time and place.

"Especially if NEO-mental forces are applied!

"In every smaller particle of energy, there is a next-larger particle in its birth pangs. In every particle a potential pebble, in every pebble a potential stone, in every stone a potential mountain, in every mountain a potential continent, and in every continent a potential galaxy, and in every galaxy a potential universe.

"We must have confidence that in every universe there is a cosmos of universes. This requires faith—until we can know it positively.

"But this must be true in every dimension. True in the physical universe, the spiritual universe, and also in the NEO-mental universe.

"To save our people, we must solve two problems. The first is how to understand the interplay of energies within these universes. The other is how to transfer the energies from one universe to the other and back again with full control. We must be able to go from the physical to the spiritual universe. From the spiritual universe we then must go into the NEO-mental universe, traverse space, and then return again down to the physical universe.

"Subphysical must be raised to physical, then mental, then spiritual, and then NEO-mental. We must develop a divine radiance which is the energy of light traveling at the speed of thought."

Lor'd Brahm's face began to glow with some inner radiance. His eyes glazed and his speech began to be staccato as if he were reciting his inner beliefs. A-Sar-U saw Thoth's fleeting expression of disapproval, then the smile of resignation. Brahm continued, almost chanting:

"For safety in times of danger, and for training in spiritual and NEO-mental ways, we must have a single social and economic system on this planet. This system must search for a single solution as to the best way to work for the salvation of mankind, a way to keep all people from eternal physical destruction.

"In our hope for help, we must have faith in God-e and submission to the temples and His priests. We must also develop a new physical death. We must teach everyone to reach safety in the NEO-mental frame in order to endure.

"You may think, 'But Brahm, you suggest an existence outside all physical essences. It would be a spirit without life or purpose.'

"Almost true.

"It would be a living spirit with mind and will and a most uncertain future. But it would be a spirit free of matter, matter that is most certain to be destroyed.

" 'But this is against religious teachings,' you may think. Religious, philosophical, realistic, mystical—define such teachings however you wish—still leave you short of eternal life. There is and will be only one way anyone can be saved."

Thoth stirred. Brahm startled and came out of his trance-like state.

"But we now get into the more refined spiritual aspects of our future. Lor'd Thoth will give you that Wisdom and its practical application."

Thoth spoke quietly, but his resonant voice brought a new brightness to every eye, a new attentiveness to every mind.

"Eternal life of the spirit, with mind and will, must be defined as metaphysical. We must be able to pass from the study and control of details, facts, and logical conclusion to a wide synthesis of all concepts. This we must do for seven million citizens with only limited time in which to do it.

"We do not have time to follow the course of evolution, letting the forces of nature and time form that which is desired. In the physical and material realms this requires endless time. Evolution is random. It is hit or miss. It is test and try. To escape the certain-and-future fire hotter than we can imagine, we must develop a new, speedier process.

"This new process must take man from the physical to the spiritual quickly and then burst forth instantly with a new type of mankind. It must give rise to higher orders instantly. It must be a metaphysically oriented mento-social organization readily developed and acceptable to all.

"In the past we have had cooperation with toleration of a diversity of opinions. Now, instantly, we must have a new and more highly concentrated organization. We must rise above the cooperation we now have for practical control, education, life improvement, and enjoyment. We must have a citizenry that moves, thinks, and breathes together. It is not enough that we become skilled, disciplined, and wise.

"It is not enough that we become our brothers' keepers. We must become our brothers' saviors.

"It will require a new social order, a new organization of universal political scope. It must be a metaphysical society in which, without exception, the will of all is the will of each. It must be formed instantly or our race is doomed to physical death.

"We must have planet-wide unity of thought, systems of learning, and knowledge. Yet, because of our many indigenous tribes, we must allow great diversity within that concentrated unity. In time of greatest possible stress we must have kindness, love, and goodwill—and more, we must have emotionally oriented co-operation.

"Each person must be fully informed so that each can be internally at ease and at peace. Each must be taught to be in full harmony with oneself and with all others. Each must have a driving, burning desire for knowledge and techniques. Above all, each must have an overwhelming love of God-e and a desire to live eternally.

"Each must have no fear of pain. No fear of death. No fear of heat. Otherwise one cannot reach the relaxed peace of mind needed to save one's life in the NEO-mental realm.

"We must expand all consciousness to the ultimate limit. Oneness, the unity of souls, increases as consciousness increases.

"We must start with the physical senses and build a series of experiences that leads all our peoples to the new-mind.

"The trouble is that sensory experience as a basis for faith or fact is only a little more dependable than a column of smoke for the foundation of a temple.

"Yet it is our job. We must do it. Nature has closed down our hope for the future. We may end in a clash of suns that will obliterate this galaxy. The fruits of our upward struggle and progress may abruptly come to be a deadly stillborn in an absurd and fickle universe.

"But I know there is a higher destiny for me and the people of this Pleasant Planet. For they are high-souled, super-souled, mega-souled people.

"A-Sar-U must lead as we teach a cadre of our people the highest secret of all time, the most sacred skill of the Supreme God-e."

Thoth stopped almost in mid-thought, and smiled. "But lest we talk and not teach, who among you would like to tell the others what Lor'd Som, Lor'd Brahm, and I have said? And what it means to mankind?"

A-Sar-U sat in deep concentration, recalling the details of the information. Suddenly Horus left his side and stood.

"Lor'd Thoth, Lor'd Som, Lor'd Brahm, Lor'd Father: You have spoken from the spiritual and the scientific side of energy. It all fits together to help us know that we may raise Radiant and Eternal Bodies from our physical bodies, and each Radiant Body has special power."

"That's right. We discover that mankind can go into NEO-mind by raising the right body. We think the right body may be the Sahu. We know it can dependably be raised only when dire threat of physical death is upon one.

"When this body has been raised, one can transform one's own material body to energy and send it through space and time, and then change it back again to one's material body."

Thoth stopped speaking and the implications to the welfare of all mankind rang in the minds of those present. "Who would like to repeat what we have just said? Horus, can you, exactly?"

"Yes, Lor'd One.

"But first will you answer the unspoken question in the mind of Lor'd Bes?"

"We'll try. What is that question?"

"Can one in any universe, if in the NEO-mind, transmute and send the physical bodies of others through space and time and change them back again?"

"Why that question, do you think?"

"Lor'd Ra and Lor'd Lady As-Tar! If we must leave this planet, can we take their bodies with us?"

"Yes, with enough training and skill, and enough love and energy. At least we hope so."

"Thank you. In your brilliant lectures you said..."

Horus began and repeated what Thoth, Som, and Brahm had said exactly, word for word, stumbling over some of the bigger words.

After Horus had repeated the talks, he was applauded and called "Little Lor'd One of Memory."

Even as Horus was talking, tattered-robed bodies were multiplying along trails and hiding in grass or clumps of bushes near the fourteen temples of the Empire. Je-Su had ordered that Horus be captured or killed, and issued a secret order through Set to all the posanga zombies.

Only later was A-Sar-U to be sure that his feeling of the onrush of time and oppression of events had been picked from the minds of others.

38

Flight From Slaughter

It became needful that A-Sar-U visit and train citizens in the Northwest, Northern, and Northeast Temples. Ast-i did not respond well to the constant travel. The heart-rending decision was made to place her where she would need little travel, although she would not be with A-Sar-U. At Thoth's suggestion, she decided she could help most by spending time with the women of the Fentribe.

The Fen was a tribe that lived in the difficult marsh-land. Though the people were brilliant, their lives were hard. Perhaps harder than the lives of any other tribe in the Empire. But they were inordinately proud as individu-als and as a tribe. Each individual echoed the pride of the tribe in bearing, attitude, and skills.

It was arranged that she spend a Westsun at each of the three southernmost Temple Centers, and A-Thena was to be with her to see that she kept a light schedule and rested to regain her strength. She would, of course, take Horus.

Her desire was to stay with A-Sar-U. To be like the Fenwomen who would bear any difficulty to be with their men or to protect their family.

The Drum spoke of the parting of the Holy Family and announced the destination of each.

Weeping, Ast-i clung in the last twenty breaths to A-Sar-U. "Oh, darling, I shall not know what to do without you."

"I shall miss you, Beloved of God-e. It will be only three Westsuns until I can hold you in my arms again."

"Three Westsuns. You say it so easily. But I fear it may be three forevers. For three Westsuns can be forever to a woman in love. And I have such foreboding. I am afraid."

"Afraid? Of what? A-Thena and Big Warrior, each with a Line of Twenty will be with you. And Horus. He and his memory will be a good addition."

"But in the dark when quiet terror assails me, I take courage through my fingers from touching you. Even though you may be asleep!" Her tears flowed. "I take my very life from touching you in love."

"Darling, each dark I shall come to you."

"Oh, A-Sar-U, I know the joys we may have of each other in the spirit of radiant mind. But I have more happiness in your flesh-self than in a radiant God-e."

"Then I must quickly learn to transmute my flesh as Thoth is teaching me, and then I can come to you each dark in an alternate energy body and turn it into flesh in your arms." Laughing, he kissed her trembling lips. "You are cold. You are shivering."

"I am cold with dread. This is my first assignment alone for the Empire. If I fail, all women will be scorned because of me."

"True, Beloved. But you will not fail. You must not borrow from the future."

"Oh, how I wish I were normal and did not see the future." She seemed to be gazing into the future with eyes fixed and steady and quite brilliant. "It is lonely without you. I see, I feel the terror of a woman lost in space. I see, I feel the abyss that separates our bodies but causes love to grow beyond all containing and burst out over all the planet. Oh, no, over all the universe.

"I see you as the Lor'd One of Life and Death, as the center of love from all the cosmos. And I see me, torn from you by circumstance, and then by the demands of the cosmos.

"And I see our son, a source of eternal life as you are, melding in energy with you, and yet being separate as ages pass.

"Oh, my beloved God-e, I see you in changed form through our son in changed form, serving all the tribes of men in all the universe."

A-Sar-U said, "Of course, Beloved Goddess. Then you see yourself as the center of love and the example for all women, as the Mother of God-e and of all mankind."

Ast-i continued as if he had not spoken, her eyes staring, fixed on the future. "I feel the pain in myself of being torn from you and on that far planet with the fierce bindings. I see the Pleasant Planet consumed in flames with all the things on it.

"I see that I am to be the Goddess of Love.

"But, Oh, A-Sar-U. I see myself commanding fighters. I see me, fleeing. I see for me and Horus there will be no place of ease or safety."

"I know how intuitive you are and it may be almost as you see it. But I promise you a place of safety. Always in my heart and often in my arms."

Soon the two contingents moved out of the Temple Compound. A-Sar-U turned north at Warrior speed. Ast-i turned south toward the Fenland Temple at walk speed. On Ast-i's face was a smile for all to see. In her heart were stark fear and unwept tears.

Horus took her finger and strode beside her. Along the trail he said, "You must not be afraid. You are a mother. Mothers can solve every problem."

Ten ears buried in weeds beside the trail heard his words. Within a thousand breaths they were reported to Je-Su by Set. Je-Su rubbed his pudgy hands together in delight.

"Now! Good! We can give her a problem she can't solve. People disappear forever in the Fens. Capture her. Capture or kill that bright little bastard. Do it!"

Ast-i noticed a change in A-Thena. The Ama-Sone who had such great strength, fighting skill, and no apparent emotion, changed even as they marched. A-Thena, not a man's woman, became tender toward Big Warrior.

Ast-i saw A-Thena as she looked down upon him resting during a stop beside the trail. Ast-i saw the puzzlement on A-Thena's face as she bent closer to examine whatever it was she saw on Big Warrior.

From that moment on A-Thena became tender toward Big Warrior, and less brusk with all around her. She looked at him with hidden, sidelong glances, and touched him on his broad shoulders and powerful arms fondly and lingeringly. To others she was neutral. To some indifferent. To all more kindly than before. Ast-i wondered why.

Her sensitivity might have solved the puzzle had she had time to dwell upon it. But excitement ran through the party, and anticipation. The Fenland Temple Complex came into view.

The Fenland Temple was on flat land, west of the Fen River and below a range of hills. Low hills, compared to the giant Atal Mountains to the northeast, but considered the last barrier before entering the Fens. Below the hills, the Fen River became sluggish and wide, then spread into nine arms, or branches, that seeped a thousand fingers toward the sea some seventeen thousand reaches away.

The low, moist, treacherous swamplands were called the Fens. The fen was a reed-like plant on a stalk rising usually from mud at the water's edge. Its heart was like a sweet cane. The stalk, dried to form a water-repellent shell, was used for baskets, for boats, for barges, and for mats or beds. When the wet husk was pounded it spread into sheets, limber and pliable. Sheets pounded together and dried—especially in the strange light of the Westsun—remained flexible and soft, like woven flax or deer skin.

Big Warrior was explaining this to the curious Horus who sat astride his neck when he stopped so suddenly that A-Thena bumped into him. He put Horus down. "Go back to the Lady Goddess. As you go, whisper to the line to be alert. I smell them!"

As Horus ran back along the trace he kept whispering, "On alert."

Ast-i's guard closed around her. "Big Warrior smells them," Horus explained.

"Zombies," Big Warrior said to A-Thena.

Ast-i moved up to him.

"We can't stay in the open through the dark," A-Thena said. "We must get to the safety of the Temple."

"No." Ast-i was motionless, and seemed to be listening to the inside of her head. "Something is wrong up ahead."

"We can fight through. We have to get to the Temple," A-Thena said.

"Wrong move, no man's woman." The voice was soft but filled with authority, yet no one was seen beside the path.

"Sounds like the voice of the woman who has no name but Chosen Woman of Da-Na the Fenman."

"Same." The leaves of a broad leaf fern moved toward them from two reaches beside the trail.

"We meet again, man-loving woman," A-Thena said.

" 'Yealp! You knowed we 'd, fight lovin' woman." The voice changed from icy-hard to kindliness. "Beloved Goddess, I wisht we cud welcome y' prop'rly t' our wonerful Fenland." The Fenwoman fell on her knees before Ast-i. "Holy Mother of God-e, bless me 'n min'."

"I bless you in the name of A-Sar-U, Horus, Myself, and the Supreme God-e."

"Thankee, Moth'r o' God-'. Th' zombies un'er Set hav' tak'n th' Temple. They 've stol' 'n hid th' drum so 's we caint sen' messag's. They got Warriors 'long th' tra'l so 's we caint sen' fer he'p. In th' Eastsun past, they made Fenlan' a pris'n camp."

"How could they do that?" Big Warrior asked, "In one Eastsun?"

"S'prise, 'n tre'chry o' som' Fenlan' Warriors. They o'whelm'd th' Temple Guards. Th' killin's. Oh, Holy God-e!"

Her voice broke. After six breaths she continued. "They hol' Da-Na 'n all the trib'l Chiefs. Set prom'ses t' mak' th' one that captur's 'r kills the Little God-e, Horus, a full command'r of Two Lin's o' Twen'y by 'pointmen' f'r life."

"They must want him badly," Big Warrior said.

"Yealp. Say he mak's a lie 'f Je-Su's Virgin Birth and his d'vin' right t' rul'."

"How many of them, Loving Woman?" A-Thena's voice was brittle, but tinged with admiration and wonder, Ast-i thought.

"Don' righ'ly kno' fo' shor'. 'Bout Twen'y, Thirty Lin's o' Twen'y 'n a passul o' zombies, lik' maybe Two 'r Three Lin's o' Twen'y." After a pause she added frostily, "Fightin' woman."

"What do you suggest we do?" Ast-i's tone indicated that she was assuming command of the impromptu war council.

"Disappear."

"Disappear? More than Two Lines of Twenty!" A-Thena growled. "Loving Woman, make sense."

"Holy Mother, wil' y' bless them bushes ther', pleas' Mam? If'n y' do ev'r one 'll turn int' a lovin' Fenwoman."

"Of course I bless them, in the name of A-Sar-U, Horus, Myself, and the Supreme God-e."

"That's real fin', Mam. Cou'd you bless 'em in th' Holy Name o' Ast-i, Mother of God-e? 'Cause ever' Fenwoman wan's t' be lik' you. Bein' blest by you is nex' bes' thing. They love you 'bove all others."

Ast-i's voice was choked and her eyes filled with tears as she raised her hands toward the sky and said: "In the name and with the love of Ast-i, Holy Mother of God-e, I bless you, all Fenwomen, and all women everywhere now and forever."

"Thankee, Holy Mother. O.K., girls, y' ast f'r it. Yo' got it. 'N you, Fightin' Woman, git them tears outten yo' eyes and yo' feet amovin'. We got fightin t' do. Yo' gotta teach us how. I don' think much o' yo lovin', 'n mabbe less o' you livin', but yo damn fightin' is th' very bes'. Com' on, girls!"

The bushes of broadleaf fern, elephant ears, broadleaf willow, hickory nut, and lily pads moved. Two at a time. Each two carried a fenreed boat.

"Holy Moth'r, y' caint stay on lan' in the dark. We brought fenboats f'r 'bout fifty, 'n fenreed cloth fo' y' all. By scramblin' dow' n'is bank we c'n get on th' river ' fore them zombies get wis'."

Ast-i looked for agreeing nods from each of her Commanders before she ordered, "Do it!"

In two hundred breaths some sixty bruised and sweaty people wore a new cape of fengrass cloth camouflaged with fen leaves. Under their weight, twenty fenboats floated low in the sluggish river. Those who chose to stay behind and were left on the bank saw a clump of fengrass that seemed to hang up on the river bank and then slowly wheel out into the current again.

By full dark the clump began to move more swiftly than the current, and the low sound of many paddles wielded by skilled hands could be heard. All through the dark the clump moved. By first light the clump had disappeared into a broad slough. At mid-sun the clump was anchored near a grove-like line of willow trees. Fengrass-clad figures were sleeping, while lookouts and guards signalled safety in the tones and calls of the marsh birds and a straying flock of ducks.

Two Eastsuns later, deeper in the marsh, the clump came to what seemed to be an impenetratable barrier of swamp grass, water lilies, and ferns blocking the ever narrowing slough. The clump broke apart into boats. Most of the boats stayed near the barrier. A few boats went back up stream, and from them individuals got to shore and tramped deep into the brush and trees. They moved like sunbeams among the tall mahogany and the gleaming, grey-white hearts of the stonewood trees that stood pale and ghostly long after the outer tree had died and dropped away.

At a signal, the sound of a duck calling to a mate, the barrier opened just enough to let through one boat at a time. In a hundred breaths all boats were inside an enclosed pond of the slough. To an unexperienced eye the village that floated on reeds there would not have been visible. Each reed matting looked like the foliage on the river.

It was thus they came to the first of many camps to which they were to flee in the thirty-three Westsuns of desperate escapes from Set's Warriors and the insidious and filthy zombies who combed the fens for them.

Ast-i grew in health and strength and became a true Commander of her tiny force. She thrived on command and on activity and gave Horus ample attention and training.

Early, she gave orders that no Warriors or zombies were to be killed needlessly. No combat would be joined if escape was possible. Even those Warriors taken in swift raids to destroy supplies, or for intelligence, were treated well and released after being many breaths on the water, blindfolded and constantly whirled in a boat so they lost all sense of direction.

They were repeatedly told: "We are not your enemy. The Empire will conquer. You cannot keep the Commander's post promised you. I command you to return to Set and tell him this. Je-Su is your enemy. He will cause your death, now or later."

Je-Su was bestially cruel in his rage. With surprise and his long-sword, he killed some of the messengers who brought him unfavorable news. He came personally into the marshes, captured a village of about twenty adults and

311

eight children. He had the parents tied to poles and made them watch. Then he penned the eight children on a large flat rock and built a raging fire under it.

"Now, tell me where Ast-i and that little bastard are, or your brats will fry." Rubbing his chubby hands, and laughing in a way that sounded oily and slightly insane, he danced around the fire singing, laughing, and shouting lullabies.

For three full Eastsuns the children suffered, and a few of the very young cried and begged for help. They suffered much before the last one fell from stubs of burned legs and died.

But no Fenlander would tell that their Goddess, Ast-i, her divine son, and her little contingent was blocked in a slough only three thousand reaches away. The death cries of the roasting children only made the Fenlanders hate Je-Su more.

As his flotilla of some two hundred boats left the village, Fenmen came from the reeds and forest, swam under water, and clung to a boat until they could capsize it in deep water. They drowned many heavily armored Warriors. They almost succeeded in drowning the squealing, floundering Je-Su, but were driven off by a swarm of Warriors.

Yet, some swam ahead, dived down, and again clung to the boats. They cut small holes through the reeds so that the boats slowly sank. Je-Su was so terrified—because he had never learned to swim—that he left Set in charge and rushed back to the comforts of his quarters on land. He contented himself by assuring all his inferiors that he was doing magnificent and important work by commanding the Warriors on the siege line that cut off Fenland from the remainder of the Empire.

Using the Drum, Je-Su sent messages that Ast-i and Horus were being held in the high Atal Mountains by the Altmen.

Tricked, A-Sar-U led a relief column toward the place his beloved family was said to be held. He and his Lines of Twenty were cut off and pushed higher into the mountains by the army of Africanus.

Thoth was unsure of the intelligence gathered and given to him on which to base decisions of war. He was also unsure of the loyalty of the Warriors stationed in the

Temple Centers. He chose, with Bes' advice, not to risk the last line of defense, the Temple Guards, in an open campaign. He and Bes alternately led raids that destroyed Je-Su's and Africanus' supplies and starved their Warriors into desertion. The conflict settled into a war of slow, slow attrition.

Ast-i's expected three Westsuns grew into thirty-six Westsuns before Je-Su was convinced that Set's Warriors and Africanus' Warriors combined could not win the Empire for him.

Je-Su began to negotiate for peace by blaming Set and Africanus. He even began to withdraw Warriors from the Fens, but sent in a horde of zombies to find and kill Horus.

As the frequency of Warrior patrols lessened, Ast-i moved her contingent out of the deep Fens, slowly and with much care. At every camp they dug body holes, called redoubts, or laid up barricades against surprise attack.

The contingent had reached its last intended camp before they expected to reach the Fenland Temple. The posanga zombies made an all-out assault chanting: "Let me die for Je-Su, Only Begotten Son of God-e. In him I have faith. For him I will die."

Ast-i picked up their chant rhythm in changed words. "Let me live for Horus, spirit begotten son of the Supreme God-e. In him I am well pleased."

"Thankee, Mam," Da-Na's Woman said with a grim smile on her face, "I lik' th' tho't o' livin' bett'r 'n dyin'. That I do!"

After flights of arrows, the zombies attacked in arrow-point formation, frontally in lines of spears. They had archery support from trees behind them and on both sides.

As directed by Ast-i, Big Warrior's Line of Twenty waited until A-Thena's archers sent arrows into the onrushing zombies. The arrow-point attack was blunted. The zombies were staggered by the loss of Six Lines of Twenty. When they faltered, Big Warrior's line pursued them, relentlessly cutting them down with spear, sword, and shortsword.

Routed, the zombies abandoned arrows, bows, swords, and everything of weight to outrun the Warriors. At least

Eight Lines of Twenty reached the shelter of the forest and the protection of the archers in the trees.

Big Warrior's line closed behind shields. As they returned, many stooped to pick up quivers of arrows and cut bowstrings. When they regained the trench redoubts, they set up shields to protect the wounded from arrows, and the Fenwomen began to dress wounds.

Big Warrior had taken an arrow through his upper left arm. A-Thena hurried to work on him with strong, skilled, and strangely tender hands. She seemed so concerned that she spent more time than Da-Na's Woman thought necessary.

With a slight smile on the faintly yellow-skinned face the Fenwoman said flatly:

"Liss'n, Fightin' Woman. Git t' others. He aint t' on'y one got nipped."

A-Thena straightened quickly and turned. Her eyes were starry, a little misty, and her voice soft: "Yes, Loving Woman, you're right. You're right."

As the two worked side-by-side, the stocky Fenwoman leaned her yellow-skinned face close to the tall, fair-skinned Ama-Sone and whispered, "Liss'n, Fightin' Woman, y' 'r unsettled. Y' got trembles 'n teary eyes."

"I know. I know. And I can't help...oh, maybe I'm unfit for a fighter. After all, I'm just a teary, maudlin female. I've . . . just realized my life is full of loneliness, my heart is full of tears."

"Yealp. Noticed how much y' 'n Big Warrior fav'r."

"Oh, Holy God-e! Has Goddess Ast-i...?"

"Yealp. Nothin' 'scapes that l'il Goddess. She ast me firs' off."

"Oh, Holy..."

"No use swearin' 'bou' 't. She kinda thinks y' shou'd remmem'r, som' timz its marv'l'us t' be maudlin'. Tears flowin' out o' yo' heart through yo' eyes sure clean out yo' brain. When'd yo' kno' he was yo' son?"

"First ten breaths out. Strawberry mark behind his left ear. Very unusual shape."

"He was a boy baby in a woman on'ey world. Custom mad' yo' set 'im inna basket."

"Custom should change a mother's heart. I had to float two away before I get a girl baby." A-Thena's voice became hard. "Three times I had to go into that Temple and sub-mit."

"Submit? Whas'sat?"

"To men."

"Yo' had three men? Ain't yo' lucky. I just caint submit offen 'nough an' I on'y got one man."

"You're a sexy wench."

"Yealp! Yealp, yo're right. My Da-Na says so. An' ain't that gran'?"

The tall, fair Ama-Sone and the broad, black-haired, yellow-skinned Fenwoman worked well if testily together, and Ast-i was pleased with them. The wounded were put low in the trench. Some were badly wounded, and she knew they would die of wound fever unless more medications could be found. As she was thinking hard on what could be used, the Fenwoman turned large brown eyes toward her and nodded.

"Yessum. Yo're right. We gotta gie 'em fas'. On'y things near 's fengrass leaves f'r stoppin the bleedin', papaya f'r cleanin' out the wounds deep down, 'n chichonny bark f'r chasin' 'way th' fev'rs 'n stoppin' t' agues. Jes' 'n a breath I'll go get 'm."

"How did you know what I was thinking?"

"Oh, unnerstannin' thinkin' 's easy, Mother of God-e. Y' thinkin' 's lik' homefolk talkin', on'y clear'r. Thinkin' ain't got no funny di'lect."

"Let's go get..." Ast-i began.

"Beloved Mother, yo' sh'd stay..."

"We will go."

"Yessum. We'll go."

A-Thena came too. Three fencapes, almost invisible in the last rays of the sun, edged into the forest. Two hundred breaths later they came back into the trench with emergency medicines which the nearby forest had yielded.

The fen leaves staunched the seepage of blood in a few breaths. The papaya meat ate at the dirt and foreign bodies in the wounds. Those who chewed the bark grew drowsy and soon stopped shivering.

Near first dark Big Warrior said, "Flights of arrows. They're gonna attack again soon."

The repeated flights of arrows sounded like pelting rain after the Westsun. Arrows embedded in the edge of the trench and thudded into the shields. A wild cry from Eight Lines of Twenty, a desperate and goaded cry, accompanied the pounding of feet as the zombies charged.

"They ain't askin' t' die this time. Wonner why?"

A-Thena and her Ama-Sones sprang to position and she commanded, "Save arrows. First dark confuses distance. Hold till you see both their eyes. Hold. Hold. Aim. Hold. Now!"

The twang of bowstrings and the flight of arrows sounded like doves in flight. The entire front line of zombies fell. Each one cried as he fell, "Thank you. Thank you for helping me to die for Lor'd Je-Su, Only Begotten Son of God-e."

The fifth line fell a dozen reaches away. The sixth line fell almost at the lip of the trench. The seventh line retreated into the eighth line, and confusion soon turned into riot. As soon as the line faltered the Ama-Sones stood up to see better and to fire faster. The slaughter was swift. Few of the Eight Lines stayed on their feet. Big Warrior rose to lead a charge.

"Hold," Ast-i commanded. "Hold, I say."

"Lady Goddess, there's a whole Line out there we can get!"

"Yes. And Seven Lines of wounded and dead they will want to take away. We don't want them. They do. Let them live to do the work. We'll rest. Each Eastsun has need to be heaped only to the side-boards with pain and sorrow. We have filled ours for this light of the Eastsun."

Meager rations were passed, the wounded rechecked, and the contingent rested in that half-sleep, half-awake way of Warriors under fight conditions.

Almost with full dark, a small figure eased silently up the side of the trench and crawled away. Several times in the next two hundred breaths it came back to the trench and with great care for silence dropped something in.

About mid-dark the watch heard the sound of bodies being dragged away, and the moans of wounded zombies faded into the forest.

At first light Ast-i missed Horus and whispered her concern.

"Horus is here," A-Thena said.

Ast-i hurried to A-Thena who stood looking down on the figure of Horus sleeping amid a cluster of bows and quivers of arrows fletched in the way of the zombies. She stood looking at the collection for several breaths with uncomprehending eyes.

"Ain' 't th' dam'est!" the Fenwoman said.

"He got 'em in the dark."

"Risky. Took lot'sa nerve."

"That it did," A-Thena said in a voice filled with admiration.

A-Thena stood looking down on Horus, wagging her head. "By God-e, sometimes boys seem almost as brave as Ama-Sones." Her eyes fell on Big Warrior sleeping a few arms away. Her face softened as she turned to Ast-i. "Beloved Mother of God-e, mothers must be proud of having brave sons."

Ast-i followed the gaze of the Ama-Sone. "Yes, A-Thena, we mothers are proud when we have brave sons." She touched the tall Ama-Sone lovingly on the hand. "Aren't we?

A-Thena swallowed hard and smiled ruefully.

The Fenwoman drawled, "'Gin a moth'r borns a chil' the God-e ties h'r wi' three thongs, all magic. Love that mak's h'r se'fless; mem'ry that mak's h'r wise; an' honor that mak's h'r divine."

A-Thena smiled through her tears and said, in loving mimicry of both Horus and the Fenwoman, "Yealp, 'n neces'sty that mak's h'r solv' ever' dam' probl'm inna world."

39

The Treaty

Thoth kept his broad face looking pleasant. But it was difficult. Deep hurt and frustration showed in his green eyes for God-ette to see and read. For they were assembled on the porch of the Temple of Po-Si-Don to ratify the agreement with a defeated enemy.

The enemy! Thoth thought, "It cannot really be the tall, indifferent, indolent, and swaggering Africanus. He could have been beaten easily by half the Warriors in Je-Su's command. It cannot be the craven, almost cringing, dark-skinned twin of A-Sar-U, Set. His rampage of horror and destruction in the Fens could have been stopped by a third of the Warriors available to Je-Su's command.

"No! It was Je-Su, the egoist, who even now is strutting among the colorful uniforms of his personal guard, with a swagger worthy of a conquering hero."

Bitterly, Thoth mused aloud to the attentive ears of God-ette and Bes. "Maybe Je-Su is the conqueror in this, after all."

He stopped, for even with his command of his emotions he felt that he was beginning to have a chest full-to-aching with anger.

"Could be. When Je-Su knew he couldn't win, he turned on his co-conspiritors in the rebellion he started against the Empire," Bes said.

"Je-Su now makes it look as if he had rescued the Empire."

"Please open the Combats so I can challenge and kill that insufferable fraud."

"Bes, you know I cannot. I am bound in Honor to Ra." Thoth's voice rose in frustration.

"I was there, I heard." Bes said. "But when Ra limited you as Supreme Lor'd One of the Empire, he did not expect to be away as long as he now has been. One hundred twenty Westsuns!"

"Ra's conditions were that I make no changes and permit none in the positions of the Empire."

"That restriction was without cause!" Bes was emphatic.

"I do not know if there ever was a cause or if one now exists. But cause or no cause, no cause at all, I am honor bound. As will be anyone who follows after me."

"Even if the Empire suffers?"

"But for the honor of its officers and the pledges given before the citizens and held as sacred laws, the Empire would suffer much more. Honor is the basis of trust. Trust helps guide all activities of man, and in a physical sense is mankind's final salvation."

"I agree. But, by God-e, I wish I didn't."

The half smile on Thoth's face slashed to a full grimace and then to a sardonic smile at Bes. "Old Friend," he said, "both you and I wish I didn't!"

"You are right, as usual!" Bes smiled

Thoth let his thoughts settle down. He breathed in slowly and deeply and sent energy down into his huge, muscular body through the Pathway of Gold. In seven breaths he had calmed himself to the point that he could think clearly—could be attached to the end results but detached from the personalities that helped reach those results.

All who knew the policy of the Empire—declared when those great Lor'd Ones from That Other Planet first established benevolent control over warring tribes—knew that a negotiated settlement would end any conflict. Always on the edge of conflict, the Empire policy was an option, always as available as it was final.

When Je-Su saw that he could not get his Warriors to willingly kill enough of the citizens to force the others to submit to his terms of total and complete surrender, he turned on Africanus and attacked the Warriors that held A-Sar-U and Luflin in the high mountains.

Je-Su sent zombies to attack his own zombies and apparently relieve the threat to the Temple of Po-Si-Don. Then, proclaiming his victories as Lor'd One of War, he attacked Set's Warriors in the Fens and put onto them all the blame, hatred, and calumny for having pursued Ast-i and Horus.

All this Thoth and the Lor'd Ones of the Empire knew. But they didn't know that Je-Su had sent a secret detachment of zombies to attack, capture, and kill Ast-i and Horus as they came up out of the Fens toward Po-Si-Don.

Thoth knew of Je-Su's treachery, which he was sure Je-Su termed 'clever maneuvering for advantage.' He wanted to take an action against Je-Su, but he was bound. Also, he had a special purpose, a hidden agenda created by the pressing need to rescue Ra and As-Tar from the grasping energy of Ayr Aerth. Bes would not accept appointment as Supreme Lor'd One. It took a very strong person to be Supreme Lor'd One to such an Empire.

Thoth knew that Je-Su was resourceful and strong. If his ego could be satisfied—a big 'if'—he was strong enough to hold the fragile, seething Empire together—at least for a while. Hopefully, until A-Sar-U had trained the citizens more adequately. It was, therefore, to assure his own plans and be ready for any emergency decision, that Thoth seemed to accept Je-Su's stories and lies, and negotiated toward peace.

Thoth watched Je-Su whisper to Africanus and Set and could read his thoughts and words. Je-Su said to each: "Don't betray me. I had to do it. We lost this one. Trust me and give me time. Trust me."

The conditions and stipulations of the peace was given to the assembled citizens and sent by Drum to other temples. It was a slow process, for they had to wait for transmission and for answers. Slowly, the people accepted the terms, with a sullenness that disturbed Set but not Africanus or Je-Su.

To Thoth the slowness and sullenness was worrisome. For if the citizens refused to accept the treaty, Thoth would be compelled to continue a war that disrupted the Empire from preparing for a much greater and more important event.

Finally, late in the third watch of the Eastsun, all temples had responded and the citizens had accepted the conditions. They were not harsh conditions. "More like a slap on the wrist and 'now you promise to be good,' " Bes said through gritting teeth.

Africanus solemnly promised on his honor, but with a sly wink at Je-Su, that he would stay in the Southeast with a base at Africanus Temple, keep his Warriors beyond the Crags in the swing of the East River near the Eastern Sea.

Set was obviously relieved when he was detached from Je-Su's command and made Commander of the Northwest, with Four Hundred Lines of Twenty and a base in the Northwest Temple Compound.

When all the items of the treaty had been formally accepted, Thoth rose. His raised hands brought instant, respectful silence. For this, Thoth was thankful. A riot of sullen groups could have been hard to handle with the few Temple Guards he had available.

"Beloved Friends of the Empire. I wish to come among you to thank you each for your part in putting down this unfortunate incident. You controlled the riot. You have earned and deserve this peace, this rest from shortages, doubt, and strain.

"But I ask your indulgence and generosity. Lady Goddess Ast-i, with the Golden One, Horus, will soon come from the south to be united with that Lor'd One so Beloved of you and the God-e, A-Sar-U. They are not yet arrived. When they do arrive they must be back to the Empire's duties.

"I know your love for that Divine Trio. I know they would like to be with you to share their love with you. I know they would like to be with you to celebrate this peace. But they ask that you celebrate yourselves and victory and they send their love to you.

"So, in your name, and using the stores you own, I have ordered that all people in the Empire shall have this Eastsun for feasting and celebration. If you approve, I will tell the Drum to speak to all your friends of the Empire. The Divine Trio will know, and in spirit will be with you here to celebrate."

The people wildly cheered. The Drum spoke. And a joyous time on the Pleasant Planet ran its course. But not everyone was joyful.

Je-Su was angry because Thoth had not told the people of all the wonderful things he, the Only Begotten Son of God-e, had done to save the Empire.

321

Africanus was angry because he could not base his Warriors in the temple that bore his name; which meant that the Temple Guards would really control his territory.

Da-Na, the Fenman, was angry because he could not get close enough to Je-Su to take revenge for the destruction of the Fenland Temple and avenge the eight children Je-Su fried to death on the stone.

40

Ambush

Da-Na's Woman wanted to be with him. Da-Na was detained at Po-Si-Don Temple, negotiating details for the settlement of the peace. With Ast-i's permission, the Fenwoman took a Line of Twenty and set out from the Fenland Temple for Po-Si-Don. This was four Eastsuns before the main part of Ast-i's battered contingent would be rested enough to make the same march.

A thousand breaths' walk from Fenland Temple the contingent of Da-Na's Woman was attacked from ambush by zombies. Most of her Line of Twenty was killed and she was penned down.

The others threw up brush and logs to form a redoubt and settled in to fight. Two slow Eastsuns passed before A-Thena, leading her Ama-Sones back toward Po-Si-Don, heard the sound of a zombie group chanting.

The instant she saw the conditions the Fenwoman faced, she raced across the open space and plunged into the redoubt.

The Fenwoman paused long enough to gasp, "Thankee! Fight lovin' woman, we got plenny o' 't here. To t' ri'ht han' side o' yon'er bush, in t' tree! Can get arrows down on t' us. Get 'im."

As A-Thena moved into place she saw seven Fenwomen, dead, but propped into place, the tips of their bows showing.

The twang of a bow string was followed by a yell from a zombie.

"Got 'm!" The Fenwoman nodded her head in the direction of the tree. "Not 'im yet? Shoots, then hides. Good, too." Her bow in her left hand waved toward the arrows in the dead. "'ny he'p commin?"

"No. I left two days early."

A momentary fatigue showed deep lines on the Fenwoman's face, then she shrugged and smiled. "'s ok. We c'n tak' 'um. On'y twenny an' that squirley bastard..." Her bow came up and the twang of the bowstring told of a hurried shot from a partly pulled bow. A quick shot. But there was a cry, almost at the edge of the redoubt.

"Wa'ch 'um. They's a li'l drop, 'bout twinny steps out. He ain't hidin' b'hin' 't no mo'."

A hysterical battle cry came from several voices. "We are the Sons of Je-Su, we cannot die. Charge!"

After a few breaths, ten voices shrieked, "Death to the infidel. Death to all unbelievers."

"Mus' be out 'a posanga. Workin' themse'ves up."

A-Thena watched the tree in which the sniper was hiding. She saw a slight shift of light on the leaves as a white-robed figure leaned out on a branch from behind the trunk of the tree, to the left. His arrow was released left-handed. It thudded into the redoubt a half span below her chest, but in a direct line with her heart.

"He's good," she muttered. "Another try and he won't be short on range. Not one that good."

She raised her body slightly above the redoubt to tempt him to try such a shot again. She held her bow flat, but the arrow was notched to the bow-string. The slight change of light came on the leaves behind the trunk, and she released her arrow at the spot where the head should appear.

The head came out as her arrow reached past the trunk and sank through the base of the nose. She heard the thud, and then a squeal of horror. The body turned slowly and she could see the tip of the arrow sticking out of the back of the skull of the falling body.

She had no time to enjoy her victory over one more man. "C'mmin'. Ten! Two lin's o' five"

The Fenwoman spoke as if to herself, in a low, calm, almost joyous tone.

A well trained archer is able to shoot an arrow accurately from a full-pulled bow once each breath. A-Thena stepped up and loosed her first arrow at the man closest to them. In amazement she saw the Fenwoman's arrow strike the chest of the one furthest from her.

"Damn. You're an amateur," she said under her breath.

"Dam'. Smart hun'er," the Fenwoman grated, "allwa's kills t' last in a lin' so 's not t' spook th' game. Her second arrow sank into the chest of the last man in her line.

A-Thena downed another. The three left in her line charged at a dead run. The line of the Fenwoman did not speed up. She dropped them all and picked off the last one in A-Thena's line as he pulled his arm back to launch his spear down upon her. He fell almost in her arms. She stripped him of his quiver of arrows and let him slide open-mouthed to the earth.

"Thanks. He came on fast."

"All 's do 'n y' get 'm riled. Pic' off the'r leaders an' they try hard'r."

"You're one cool bitch, Fenwoman. I trained for years for this. Been in twenty engagements. You never trained."

"By Atl! I trained. Y' think a woman ain't trainin' fo' war when she's 'bout her hom' duties. You jes' don' know 'bout keepin' cool wh'n birthin', weanin' tit-bit'rs, trainin' 'm t' go outside t' go out, livin' through kids wit' sniffles an' real sic'nes'. 'N turribl' things like puppy love. Gettin' work done, findin' mates f' girls an gettin' 'em chosen up.

"Then y' start gettin' old'r 'n slow'r. Y' kinfolk gets real ol' 'n die. 'N y' frin's too. That's hard'r than trainin' f'r war. That's trainin' f'r life, 'n that 's no lie! Motherin 's harder 'n fightin'." She paused and smiled and said, "Cept so'time in fightin' y' need mo' arrows. So I best go an' git som' those."

She nodded toward the fallen bodies before them, and slipped out of her own quiver. "They'll yell up a lot, then charg' us. Giv' me plen'y time."

She crawled up, scrambled forward and stripped the quiver of arrows from five dead bodies before the yelling started. She then ran back and dived into the redoubt as flights of arrows thudded around them.

"Hep y'sef to arrows, Fight Lovin' Woman. Got plenny now."

"How long you been holding out here, Fenwoman?"

"Two days."

"Food?"

"Wha' ' that?"

"Hungry?"

"Havin' too much fun t' think on 't."

The battle cry went up, "We are the Sons of Je-Su. We cannot die. Death to the infidels."

"Looks t' me lik' they ain't count'd them bodies out ther' 'r they'd know they c'n die.

"Ama-Sone, y' fight t' prov' y'sef better 'n any man, tho som'tim's y' know y' ain't. Y' fight for admir'eation, tho som'tim's y' don' 'mire y'sef." She took a half-bow shot that brought a yell of pain. "Now me, I fight t' prov' man 's worth fightin' f'r, tho som'tim's I know he ain't. I fight f'r love, tho som'tim's I don' 'love m'sef. Is one better 'n th' other?"

"I don't know. But here they come. If we don't stay alert we can get awful dead for either reason."

"Yeah. Us women, we got al' kin's o' crisus, ain't we?"

When the charge had been stopped, she relaxed against the side of the redoubt.

"Look 't. Temple Guards comin' a runnin'. Bef'r our chat gets mess'd up, 'cause we're rescu'd, tel' me, what's a infidel?"

41

Thoth's Decision
to Visit Ayr Aerth

Ast-i, A-Sar-U, and Horus were celebrated and worshipped in every family in the Empire excepting those influenced by Africanus, Je-Su, or Set. They became the symbols of God-e, and considered the physical manifestation of spiritual God-es serving the people.

This pleased Thoth, for it gave him more time against the inevitable revolt fostered by Africanus, Je-Su, and Set.

Thoth knew that Warriors faithful to him, Bes, and A-Sar-U should be able to contain the coming revolt by the enemies of the Empire. But he needed time.

Time! So many things to do, so little time. The pressing need was to train each one of the seven million citizens more deeply in the spiritual skills—including those who refused training out of misplaced loyalty to one of the rebellious three. The need was urgent for something to be done to help Lor'd Ra and Lady As-Tar in their duress. Tribal frictions to placate. So much to do, so little time!

To keep abreast of the swiftly changing, dangerous events, he asked Lor'd Som, Lor'd Ram, Lor'd Ma-Nu, Lor'd Brahm, Bes, God-ette, and A-Sar-U to report to him each Eastsun on the Science, Population, Information, and Knowledge of the Empire. Bes was in command of all Temple Guards, God-ette in charge of all Compounds of the Virgins, and A-Sar-U was filled with intelligence valuable to decisions.

After each meeting, Bes, God-ette, A-Sar-U, Ast-i, and Horus joined Thoth for a meal, during which they worked upon or discussed problems of the Empire.

Thoth was most disturbed by the circumstance of Lor'd Ra and Lady As-Tar. For his own knowledges were exhausted and he felt totally out of contact with his mentor and benefactor.

"Ast-i, Beloved of God-e, have you contacted or been contacted in mind by Ra or As-Tar since your return?"

"No, Lor'd Thoth. But remember, I receive when Ra wishes to send. His messages I relay immediately."

"I know. I know. My senses disturb me greatly. Recently I have not been able to feel Ra's strength and protection around me."

"Do you fear for Ra and As-Tar?" Bes asked directly.

In the flickering lights from tapers and grease-tub candles, Thoth's face showed anxiety...even fear. All were concerned, for Thoth's usual impassive countenance was for them a constant assurance that their inner emotions would have a stable place to return to. Thoth rose swiftly and paced the room. In the wavering light, his face took on a crag-like appearance, in hard, flat planes, with eyes in deep-set, dark pools reflecting sparkles of green.

"Yes. Yes, I fear for Ra and As-Tar. But my fear is wider than that. Atl said that Ayr Aerth has fires in its navel. We know that fires in the navel of That Other Planet caused it to shake itself to pieces and almost destroy all of our race. Only the detachment of our ruling class, the God-men, escaped to come here. We live in primitive circumstances because all of the good things of physical life were destroyed. We began telling time by Westsuns and Eastsuns. But Som has said that on That Other Planet, and on the Space Schooners there were little time-telling machines that would fit into the palm of a hand.

"Ra is the last one who knows fully the Wisdoms of those scientists and mechanics. I, Thoth, know much. But not mechanical details.

"We have been too involved with training and equipping Warriors to defend our safety to have time to train and equip skilled mechanics. We have, by our inheritance, as the scions of the Supreme God-e, natural, innate, and immense wisdom in the spiritual and metaphysical world. Ra trained me in those skills, but did not have time enough to train me in all the Wisdoms of the Mechanics.

"Without Ra we do not have anyone who is a Metaphysician, a Mechanic, an Administrator, and a Warrior. Ra has gone to Ayr Aerth. Ra has grown weaker and weaker.

Ra does not contact me in force as has been his wont since he became my Master.

"Yes. Yes. Yes! I fear. For Ra's own great self, for As-Tar's great learning and sensitivity. For the Pleasant Planet's future. For the very existence of the planet Ayr Aerth. For without all of these our race faces more than a disaster, it faces ultimate and final extinction. It will be as if this great race of God-like beings had never been.

"Even if we can get all the training done, are we to have a planet to take our citizens to? Will there be willing bodies our spirit-formed citizens may enter just in case they cannot learn to transmute their bodies? Is Ayr Aerth a place where our people can live for a long time? Remember, we have been on this planet for less than three full lifetimes!"

Thoth's worry was cosmic. Instantly all were concerned.

"For a moment at least, Bes assures me, we can have peace to turn our energies and minds to preserving our futures not just our lives. Also, it gives me time to think about Ra. Ast-i, have you tried to contact him?"

"Not since before our flight to save Horus from murder by Je-Su."

"He seemed to you to be growing weaker?"

"Yes. But sometimes my contact was not as good. Maybe because of my stresses or worries."

"Do you think we—you—can contact him?"

"I can try, Lor'd Thoth. But...it is he who sends, I who receive."

"If he is strong enough to send!" Thoth's voice rose slightly and he stopped in mid-stride. "Forgive my emotion. Ra is my beloved teacher, mentor, and friend. Usually, he is present with me in a cosmic way, in a subtle energy. In the past nine Westsuns I have not been conscious of him or his energy."

"I hear you saying that if Ra, with all his divine energy, wisdom, and power cannot live on Ayr Aerth, no one of us can."

"Not for long, Lor'd Bes. Not for long."

"Then, plainly said, we face annihilation here and disaster or death there?"

Before Thoth could answer Ast-i caught her breath sharply.

"Even if we reach there," God-ette said matter-of-factly.

"Beloved Mother, we can reach there. We will reach there, everyone here, almost everyone on this planet. Thoth's techniques work," A-Sar-U said.

"But once there," Ast-i said, her voice trembling, "Oh, I have felt the pull, the binding on a Spiritual Body there on Ayr Aerth. How much more awful must that pull be on a physical body? When we get there, if we cannot stay on Ayr Aerth, can we escape the dreadful pull and get away from that planet? Ever? Ever? Ever?"

"Ast-i, that has worried me more than even the recent conflict," Thoth said. "I can fight in a conflict. But in this I am powerless..." He let the words trail off.

Horus asked, "Should one—some—of us go to Father Ra and Mother As-Tar on Ayr Aerth? Can we do that?"

"We possibly can go there, My Golden Horus," Godette said, "but can we come back?"

"Beloved Goddess, would we need to come back?"

"Yes. If we could not stay on Ayr Aerth."

"You have an idea you have not expressed?" Ast-i asked.

"Yes, Beloved Mother. If physically, we can not stay on Ayr Aerth we may as well die like physical heroes. For there is no place else in the cosmos we know where we can keep our physical selves. If we need to, can we, not all—but at least some—stay in a spiritual world in the Radiant Bodies we know we can develop and will have to develop in order to leave Pleasant Planet...does that make sense?"

"Good sense, Golden Horus. We are in certain danger here, and possible danger there. We might stay in our Radiant Bodies forever. But we should not lead seven million people from physical death to another physical death, not if we can help it."

"Then someone must go to Ayr Aerth. An advance scout, so to speak."

"Two." The voice rang with overtones of Ra. "To send back to you, two energies are needed, one male, one female. Two must go to Ayr Aerth."

"Which two?" Thoth asked

330

"Thoth and Ast-i." No one in the room knew who spoke those words. Each thought some other wise person had done so. But the wisdom seemed so good that it should not be denied.

"Why?"

"Thoth to use his knowledges and lore of science. Ast-i to use the Wisdom of Ra and send back to you."

The word spoken was the word decided. The council turned its attention to plannings for the future. Not one doubted that disaster would strike the Pleasant Planet. Exactly when they did not know, but soon.

In preparing for leaving, Thoth asked Bes to accept appointment as Supreme Lor'd One of the Empire.

"Good friend, do not ask me to do that. I would suggest appointing A-Sar-U but he cannot be spared from teaching. Not yet. Soon. Meanwhile, I would support appointing Je-Su temporary Supreme Lor'd One. But with limitations. Many limitations and restrictions, sworn to on his honor before the populace on the Window of Ra.

"I repeat to refresh your resolve. These powers reserve to me:

"I, Bes, alone may reopen the Combats at my will. Je-Su may not order any executions or make any changes in the officers of the Empire, appointments of priests, Warriors, or chiefs. I alone may command the Drum. I alone may command the Temple Guards. On his life he may not change any laws of the Empire, or imprison anyone, or punish anyone for religious reasons."

"Thank you," Thoth resumed his seat, calm and efficient in action. "Ast-i, A-Sar-U, what do you feel?"

Ast-i's eyes filled with tears that dimmed the blue and made them sparkle like distant stars. "I feel that in times of disaster even the weakest of us should be willing to volunteer and risk."

Through tears in his eyes and in his voice A-Sar-U managed to say, "Then I, the weakest of all, volunteer."

"Lor'd Bes, please arrange all things so that we may depart at any time. No one will know in advance. Arrange especially secure storage for our physical bodies in case we must leave them behind. Let us know when all arrangements are completed to your satisfaction. Do it!"

331

So much to do, so little time. Bes moved swiftly. In three Eastsuns Je-Su, on the Window of Ra, before the citizens, and with Drums and Cryers relaying to all the Empire, accepted the temporary appointment with all restrictions. All was ready for Thoth and Ast-i to leave when they judged it wise and essential.

A-Sar-U was at training in the temples. When he returned a few Eastsuns later Ast-i was gone. Horus sat dry-eyed. But there were signs that he had been weeping.

"Ast-i-Ankh, Mother of Mankind, Beloved of God, is gone."

A-Sar-U fought down the tears that formed in his eyes. "Until she returns...oh, Golden Horus, you know, and I know, she will never return to us here. We must go to her on Ayr Aerth."

"Yes, Lor'd Father, we must. For without her, you are only half a man and empty of joy. Without her, I am not a God-child. I am only a frightened little boy."

42

Discovery of Doom: Thought Control

A-Sar-U agreed when Bes muttered that Je-Su would violate his oath and contract within six Westsuns. Je-Su did.

He imposed mind restrictions and punishment on any person. Cleverly! First he got Africanus to declare them. He then imposed the same laws "for equal justice to all" and enforced them with all the might of his armies.

He imposed his creed. And if any citizen protested against excessive laws of cruelty, that citizen disappeared.

The Lor'd Ones met in secret. Lor'd Bes stared at their grim faces hollow-eyed, as if sleep was not his recent bed companion.

"Three things: First, Je-Su has ordered Two Lines of Twenty in each Temple District to find the bodies of Lor'd Ra, Lor'd Thoth, Lor'd Lady As-Tar, and our divine Ast-i. They will soon ask each of you if you know where those bodies can be found. Do any of you know?"

No one answered.

"Good. I declare to you that I do not know where they *may* be. But to be safe they must be where the soldiers have already searched. For they will turn every crevice in the Temple District and every cave in the Empire before they stop searching.

"To the second subject: We should be preparing for the time we may have to leave this planet in spiritual form. We should know how to transmute our bodies and take them with us, too."

Lor'd Som's head bobbed up on his long neck and twisted about. Then it began to draw inward as he went into a deep study. After a while his head shot up again.

"Lor'd Bes, when we transmute our bodies we take the vital elements of the flesh self."

"I know. Do we leave anything behind?"

Som thought deeply. "Nothing of feeling or value. But in living we create around us an aura, a force field resonant with our dispositions and natures."

"Yes, Lor'd Som?"

"We do not take the artificial, self-made part of *that*."

"Then, what do we leave behind that is visible?"

"A cast-off force field of skin, a copy of all the energies of emotion and thoughts that have been allowed into our auras. It is visible to the eyes, but it has no reactivity or feeling."

"Simply put, it is a useless shell based on energies generated by past experiences and emotions."

"Simply put, yes."

"Then, as we leave with our transmuted physical bodies we can seem to be leaving behind a useless, feelingless shell?

"Yes, like the body reflecting from a still pond. Visible but not actual."

"If some of us cannot transmute our flesh and must go only with our Radiant Bodies—what do we leave behind?"

Som's head bobbed, his lips pursed, the brows knotted. At last he replied, "The best of ourselves. Some of our precious memory. Some of our reasoning ability. Some of our greatness, all of our physical cleverness."

"You are saying, to be ourselves truly in the future state, we must not only raise and take our Spiritual Body, we must also transmute and take our physical."

"Yes. Although, some may take physical bodies from the willing humanoids there. The ancestral history may not be the same. Some ease and confidence may be lost, some nervous behavior may develop."

Bes turned slowly as he looked into the eyes of each of the Lor'd Ones. "This is what Ra is relaying through Ast-i and God-ette."

A-Sar-U leaned forward. Then we must know where the physical bodies of Ra, Thoth, As-Tar, and Ast-i are. We must find a way to transmute their flesh and send them through space."

"Exactly, Lor'd A-Sar-U."

334

"No." Horus's voice was firm. "Before they left I heard Lor'd Thoth teaching Lady Ast-i how to transmute her flesh. I believe they took their bodies with them."

"But you are not sure?"

"No. But Lor'd Ra and Lady As-Tar expected to return to their bodies here."

"Two bodies. We must transmute and send two flesh bodies."

"Yes."

"Who can do it?"

"My Lor'd Father can."

"How do you know?"

"Lor'd Thoth told Mother Ast-i, 'A-Sar-U knows how to transmute our bodies if we fail and will do it at the last breath. He has Cosmic Wisdom when he is forced to use it.' "

"How will you do it, Lor'd A-Sar-U?"

"I don't know. But if my Master said I will know at the time of final and desperate need, then I will know."

"Good," Bes said, "now to the third subject. Because Je-Su has broken his contract, his word, and all the promises of honor, I plan to call all citizens and let them know that the Combats are to be reopened."

"Good!" A-Sar-U said.

"Not Good!" Bes said. "I have talked with the Chiefs, High Priests and Priestesses, the Commanders of the Temple Guards and the Ama-Sones. They will not let me challenge."

"How can they stop you?"

"They will vote against reopening the Combats unless I promise to stay in charge of the Temple Guards. They say that as vicious as Je-Su has become, they have sure knowledge he would be worse if he could get me out of control of the Guards."

"Good thinking," A-Sar-U said.

"Who are our choices to beat Je-Su and his Champion, Set?"

"Luflin, Big Warrior, Da-Na the Fenman," Brahm ventured tentatively.

"None can take Set on the sword. Certainly none could take Je-Su if he decided to fight for himself in the List."

"My father can."

"Horus, you are volunteering A-Sar-U. Why?"

"He can win, or I can be his Champion. Lor'd Thoth has said he is the greatest Warrior alive, save maybe Lor'd Bes. That if Bes could take him in the first bout, Bes might win. But A-Sar-U is younger and can stay longer at combat."

"Too true," Bes said. "Since I cannot, A-Sar-U will enter the Lists?"

"Of course. And I will be his Champion. Lor'd Bes, have I your permission to be my father's Champion?"

Bes smiled fondly and winked at A-Sar-U.

"I'm sure you'd make a good Champion for any man."

Horus turned to A-Sar-U. "Father, may I be your Champion?"

The smiles of the Lor'd Ones were hidden behind palms.

"Any son of mine can be my Champion. But, we start training at half the first watch, next Eastsun, and will train every Eastsun until the Combats are called."

"We must, by law, give notice of fifteen Eastsuns," Bes said. "I will call the leaders of the Empire this dark, and set the time exactly as soon as they will agree."

A-Sar-U began his training even before the dark ended. In full armor he slipped from his rooms and began his endurance run. He crossed the Lion Gate Bridge, swung back and headed toward the hills to the northwest.

After three Eastsuns, A-Sar-U found that he reached a sense of peace, a euphoric point, in his training runs. At this point his body took over and automatically performed, and his mind was freed for thought and reflection.

This Eastsun he had chosen to race up the mountainside to the Marble Arches. They were arches on the side of the path as it went through a white marble cut in the trail. His path was clear, and he could yield his mind to revery, reflection, anger, frustration—and work them out of his system by running ever harder.

He was much concerned with the repression in the laws lately proclaimed by Je-Su through Africanus. Especially those that declared that no one could think—even think—that which was proscribed by law.

Thought was not controlled in those ancient days before the people of the planet decided to flee terror.

A-Sar-U let his mind pound on this series of thoughts as his feet pounded ever faster up the steep side of the mountain toward the Marble Arches. He was to be a contender for the office of Supreme Lor'd One in the Combats, newly opened by Bes and delayed by Je-Su.

But the citizens of the Empire had risen in protest. Now the contest was set. He must win or die. He knew he faced certain death or triumph. The battle was to be between him and his twin brother Set, Commander of the Armies, and fighting as appointed Champion of Je-Su.

Should Set win, death was certain for A-Sar-U. Only thus could the people of the Pleasant Planet be brought effectively under Je-Su's complete control.

The lifetime post of Lor'd One was not easy to win, for almost all soldiers would risk their lives for a chance at it.

He would win the Combat. He had many reasons to drive him on. He must control the armies of the planet and resist with force the edicts of the half-mad Je-Su and his Commander of Armies.

He had to win because the freedom of the peoples on the Pleasant Planet waited upon his success.

At a sharp switchback A-Sar-U concentrated on the trail. The footing was jagged and dangerous. Past the steep, dangerous turn he let his mind drift again into its mode of meditation in action.

The citizens had a right to religious freedom. He must obtain it for them. How beautiful and meaningful had been the old Creed! It had stood in effect for more than three thousand Westsuns by count in the planet's history. It was beloved by all peoples on the planet. He let the Creed murmur in his mind:

I believe in one Supreme God-e, Supreme Lor'd One of our universe. Through His will we have bounty and happiness in this life. Through His grace we have joy and the eternal life we earn and deserve. I believe that all who live truly are heirs of His body, mind, and spirit. By purification of the body and mind of the Temple of Flesh, by true

337

discipline, all men may become one with Him; of His body, of His mind and of His soul and raise the Radiant Self from the flesh self to live with Him forever. They become Him in very essence. This joy is denied no one who strives to live in Eternal Truth and serve his brothers in this holy place.

A-Sar-U's breath whistled into his nose halfway in his run up the mountain trail. His lungs ached. His legs ached. The heavy scabbard of his Oricalchum sword repeatedly beat upon his left thigh. The shield, spear, and combat helmet were heavy. But he had to train his muscles to respond to the weight and movement of his combat gear by wearing it on his training runs.

Each running step reminded him of the need to work, to harden, to grow, to increase his strength, endurance, and skill with weapons. He had to be better than any other person on the planet, or die.

He must win or he must die in the Combat. Je-Su, sure of winning, had made laws that imposed the duty on the victor to kill the vanquished.

"By order of Je-Su, Lor'd One of Wisdom.

"Only the strong and the brave may remain as citizens of our great country."

A-Sar-U thought that the lucky might remain without being strong or brave. But Je-Su had even decreed that it was treason to the Empire to have such thoughts.

Truly, only the strong, the brave and the very, very lucky would be left alive once they had entered the Combats. No man was required to seek to progress to any level. Once he had chosen to strive for a level and declared his intention, he must achieve that level against all contenders—or die. It was not success or failure. It was success or death, by the will and order of Je-Su.

Ignoble death! For to the victor belonged all the spoils of conquest—properties, persons, men, women, children, and all other spoils of war—to the limit of the possessions of the vanquished and his dependents. If the victor did not pronounce anathema upon the family and offspring of the vanquished, he might assign them to a virtual slavery of dependence upon the goodwill and charity of the victor. Wives, women, and girls were always torn from their male kin. Most heinous act of all, the victor might proscribe the girl-child from belonging to the Daughters of God-e and becoming a Virgin of the Temple of God-e.

Here only could she be educated and trained in the necessities of society. Here only was a girl-child protected.

A-Sar-U pulled his mind back from its euphoric rambling. He had to do that often when he ran steadily for a long while. His mind became as if under the power of the posanga fruit. It floated in a world all its own, thought only upon subjects it chose. When his mind reached this condition, he seemed to use very little physical energy. He could run up the mountain as if his muscles felt no heaviness. It was as if his mind entered itself and began to float on its own bed of energy.

The sound was slight, not much louder than a sigh. It was almost lost in the pounding of his feet and the clanking of his armor. It was not clearly more than the hiss of the wind vibrating around his shield. He did not slow or falter in his steady pace, but his mind was suddenly back in the physical and he was alert.

Every sense seemed to focus upon the sound. The muscles of his right wrist swelled under the forearm guard and his hand formed itself into a sword-claw. But he did not slow. Many opponents tried to interrupt the training of those they must face in combat. If they did it often enough, they gave themselves a better chance to win. A-Sar-U ran on, wary and alert.

The sound came again. The muscles in his face twitched slightly under the tan. His eyes fixed upon the small stone that struck the trail five steps in front of him. It rolled straight across the trail indicating that it came from his right side, high up, and had been propelled with accurate force. He raised his head slightly to fix the place from which it had appeared to come, a ledge above the trail apparently in the rock of a sheer mountainside.

Strange! The sheer face of the wall of the rugged canyon was not all visible. He could be wrong. But he fixed it as a ledge. Anyone on it would be invisible from the trail. Why? What did it mean?

He did not slow his pace. Wind, he thought, in the narrow ravine might dislodge such small pebbles. He increased the driving power of his legs.

He heard a different sound. It zipped like a wasp past his helmet and struck the trail some four paces in front of him. He saw it as it bounced, spun and lay still. It was a golden-colored ring of Oricalchum, the metal only the God-e might use for ornament.

A-Sar-U did not look up. He knew that whoever was above him, hidden in the crevice in the sheer wall of the canyon, meant him no personal harm. He knew, too, that the person did not want to draw attention other than A-Sar-U's own to the hiding place.

The risk of throwing a ring of Oricalchum, a ring of such great value, was a calculated risk from which either great harm or great benefit might come. This was a trail often traveled by citizens and sometimes patrolled by the Warriors of Je-Su.

Without breaking stride, A-Sar-U stooped and grabbed the ring and with it a handful of pebbles. He then launched the bits of gravel as if he were practicing throwing a spear while running. One he threw up to the ledge to signal his awareness.

He did not know what he was being involved in. He did know that it was secret and therefore dangerous. But everything was dangerous under the despotism of Je-Su, even thinking as he was thinking.

In a planet ruled by the tyranny of Je-Su, even the canyon walls had eyes and ears. Each turn in the steep trail could hide observers. Perhaps only to watch and observe his training and conditioning. But, perhaps, also, to look for the slightest breach of the many rules spewed out by Je-Su.

Or imagined breach! For the slightest infraction in thought or action of the detestable rules was cause to destroy the individual and claim his property. As Je-Su had ordered, 'to reclaim for God-e what has been the property of those who do evil.'

Sanctimonious drivel. It was a way to claim the property of any person or group of people who might in any way have power to overthrow that tyranny of Je-Su over body, mind, purse, and spirit.

As he ran, A-Sar-U slipped the ring upon his finger, but did not look at it carefully. Even a swift glance at the

intaglio-crest sent his sent his heart racing. It was the sig-
net ring of the God-e.

His breath caught in his throat and was released with
a grunt.

The ring had been on Thoth's finger when A-Sar-U last
saw him. The message it sent was clear. Those secret persons in charge of protecting the bodies of Ra, As-Tar, Ast-i,
and Thoth had seen fit to change their hiding place. Probably to escape the searching of Je-Su to find and destroy
them! Oh, Holy God-e! It was a another reason to win the
Combats.

A-Sar-U's spinning mind grasped at many possibilities,
and these drove him to even greater effort.

How long he ran in his bewilderment he did not know.
When he came out of dwelling in the chaos of his inner
mind, the rim of the canyon was threatening with the glaring light of the Westsun.

A-Sar-U knew that as soon as it rose above the rocky
lips of the canyon, it would pour down an intolerable heat
for a hundred breaths.

He must find a crevice to shelter him from the direct
rays. He ran now in desperation. He remembered the tall
Marble Arches, like a steep V in the canyon walls, so steep
that the rays of the moving sun could not penetrate to its
bottom. There he could lie and escape its direct rays. It
was sometimes called "sunstreak crack," for the white
marble walls were streaked with marks said to have been
caused by the heat of the Westsun.

The winds in the canyon were beginning to rise in answer to the demanding heat of the onrushing Westsun. He
bent his head low, turned his shield, and raced hard. This
was a contest to test his strength.

The breath whistled in his nose as he forced himself
into a ten-step one-breath rhythm in a burst of speed. He
pounded air into his aching lungs as his feet pounded the
trail. His energy was even higher now. He had a goal to
reach in limited time. He had motivation.

He reached the gap between the marble half-arches
and flung himself down in the shadow made by the north
arch.

The brutal rays of the Westsun were glancing from the
rock less than three spans from his head. His helmet crest

was catching the rays and beginning to become hot. He crouched to make sure his entire body and his armor were protected from the burning red-purple light. But he could not get completely in the shadow. The crest to his helmet was cast before him on the base of the arch. His eyes focused on the pattern that the shadow caused in the white rock of the pathway.

Where the shadow of his helmet's crest had been, before he crouched lower, was lighter in the stone. Around it, but elongated northward, was a blackened, burned arc curving inward toward him. Slowly as his breath began to ease from the hard run up the hill, his mind began to try to interpret the meaning of these marks burned into the white stone. He felt his heart give a sudden jolt to his whole body, and gasped as if struck fiercely in the pit of his stomach.

It was there! It was clear! It was unmistakable. Ast-i had been right, he was dumb! Dumb and slow. He had seen the marks burned into the marble base of the pillar on the Window of Ra on the porch of the Temple. He should have interpreted and understood the meaning, the unacceptable, incredible meaning.

The marks on the marble before him curved in graceful arcs. It could be seen that the Westsun had come many times. Many, many times. But the past few had a very critical variation, an ominous reverse dip. The pattern in the stone showed that for many passes, the Westsun had burned the white rock in an even, almost identical sweeping arc. Then—Oh, Atl!

He began to shiver even as the sweat poured from him.

Then the marks showed ever-increasing sudden dips toward the north as the Westsun reached its nearest approach to the planet. It was a dip that grew ever greater as the number of passes increased. The marks of the dips made it appear as if the Pleasant Planet *bowed* to the Westsun and allowed markings to be burned into the white stone.

Or...

Again he caught his breath as he felt the surety of an impossibility sear its inescapable certainty into his brain.

Or, at the nearest point in its passing, the planet had been pulled toward the Westsun. And, if the markings were true, with each passage the Westsun's pull was greater and lasted longer, and it pulled the planet closer, speedily closer!

It was all there in the stone to read. Sweating and benumbed, he read it many times.

Yes, the Westsun came out of its curving orbit as it approached the planet. Each time it came closer and stayed for a longer time. And the question in his mind was like a signal fire.

"How much longer before the Westsun will not return the planet to its usual path? Still more important, what will happen to the planet if the Westsun does not resume its usual path?"

The Westsun roared away. He rose to his feet and continued his training run up the mountain. The thought struck him:

"The Westsun is going to pull the planet into it much sooner than we have thought. The two suns will not collide as the scientists thought. The vast energy they expected will not be released to give speed to our Radiant Bodies."

He gasped to himself: "The burning Westsun will destroy the Pleasant Planet and all persons on it.

"It will be much sooner than any of us thought. The Westsun is now rushing us to our doom.

"Je-Su will not accept that the planet is in danger. He is convinced that he alone has the power and will to save us.

"Another good reason why I must win the Combats and control the destiny of our citizens."

A-Sar-U reached the top of the mountain, and turned for the easy run down. Fifty steps behind him, Horus came up the trail like a barefooted waif, pounding the trail with Warrior speed.

"Sorry I was late," he said, "Explain later. Race you down."

Horus almost won.

43

A-Sar-U's Capture

A-Sar-U liked to run to the Marble Arches. He did it as often as he could. This Eastsun he ran at Warrior speed along the trail, forcing his training. For in three Eastsuns he was to meet Je-Su's Champion in the Combats. It was to be an honor match to death or surrender, the winner to be Supreme Lor'd One of the Pleasant Planet and Chief of the Empire.

He had prepared for treachery. Horus was at the arches, Big Warrior at the foot of the hill to watch for Set's Warriors. He had run twice up and down the mountain, and was nearing the top again. Horus stood tall for his 130 Westsuns, was in good training condition, and was waving A-Sar-U on to greater effort.

Then it happened.

Set seized Horus with a hand over his mouth.

A Line of Twenty Warriors rose up out of the very dirt of the hillside and surrounded A-Sar-U. He was able to kill six with the sword and the skills Thoth had taught him, disarm and break the fingers of two more.

He felt a great exaltation at joining combat. Too long had he sheathed his sword. To see flashing steel, feel it bite deep, and see the terror on the faces of his many enemies made him feel good. Good! He knew that he might tire, that a stone beneath a foot might throw him out of balance and open him for a sword thrust. He knew that death could be near. But he enjoyed hacking down these minions of Je-Su.

Somewhere in his mind he reasoned, even as he fought, that he fought by instinct. He was aware that he seemed to have many minds, and that each of his minds seemed to function in some strange way for its own separate purpose. With one of his minds he protected himself carefully. With another he was joyous, and reasoned with himself that man risks much because he enjoys danger, revels in being on the very edge of safety. The possibility of quick death gave savor to life.

As soon as Set's Warriors realized that even twenty could not conquer him with combat weapons, the nature of the fight changed. They formed a ring around A-Sar-U, almost dancing, and began to throw at him an almost invisible powder.

He dodged aside, cut through the ring, but was surrounded again. The powder was hurled over his head from many directions so that it fell all around him and all over him. He felt a searing heat inside his nose. His mind was incredibly active, very alert.

But his muscles would not obey his own will. He stood frozen in action considering what to do.

Behind him he heard the harsh laugh of his twin. Set held Horus in his arms and grated in pure hate: "Now, you little bastard, you'll see your 'Divine' father in a new light, for what he really is. A-Sar-U, surrender your sword."

A young Warrior held out his hand.

In spite of the anger he felt, and the realization that it was all wrong, A-Sar-U handed his sword to the youngster, handle first. The youngster took the sword, slapped A-Sar-U soundly on the backside, and then kicked him. The Warriors whirled him about, struck him, and spat in his face. His anger mounted, but he could not make his muscles obey his will.

"Now, A-Sar-U, show this *supposed* son of yours how much you *truly* love him. Hit him in the face as hard as you can."

In spite of the anger that caused his chest to ache, he found himself curling his fingers into a hard fist preparing to strike.

The young Warrior holding his sword dropped it, cried out, spun, and fell to the ground, an arrow sticking through his neck.

Thirty arms down hill, Big Warrior was fitting another arrow and instantly shot another Warrior.

"Hold Horus in front of us. Retreat. Retreat." Set screamed his command. "Don't get caught here. Get away. Get away."

A-Sar-U was spun by a Warrior and he saw the anger and contempt on his son's face. At the top of the ridge, Set put Horus on the ground and kicked him into the opening of the arch. A-Sar-U felt himself being shoved along at a run, past the Marble Arches and along a trail almost overgrown with dwarf oak brush. He was spun away into a series of trails, with long waits at the tops of passes while his captors looked back for pursuers. All the while his mind—no, his many minds—worked wildly but could not make his muscles obey.

After a run of at least two thousand breaths, Set seemed satisfied that no one followed them closely. He turned angrily upon the young Warriors.

"You stupid, incompetent fools. You left seven dead back there. The enemy will try to tell the public what happened. To save your fool lives, I have a plan. Bang each other up and take a few sword cuts. Then speed back to your barracks to spread the word that A-Sar-U's personal guard of Three Lines of Twenty tried to ambush me as I was preparing for the Combats. They surprised us and killed—make much of the corpse with the arrow through its neck and his sword not drawn from its scabbard—and killed seven. Say we killed more than a Line of Twenty, then, outnumbered had to withdraw and escape into the hills.

"Wait. Three of you, the youngest, for this posanga zombie won't be able to do anything until the first day of the Combats, take him to the ravine camp beyond the Field of the Combat. Tie him to the Pole of Honorable Death. That is, tie him by the right hand to a high pole, or the branch of a tree. Draw him up until just the toes of one foot touches the ground. Keep him without food or water until near first light of the Eastsun of the Combats. Then, bring him, in full battle dress, to the Lists. When the trumpets sound at sunrise, force him out onto the field.

"I will meet him there. Then we'll see how long he can stand to my sword.

"Now go. Tell everybody you meet of his cowardly attack. Do it, now!"

Chuckling with self-satisfaction, Set strode away.

A-Sar-U was shoved along for another two thousand breaths, often struck, unable to defend himself. At near first dark they clambered down into a ravine, and the three young Warriors made a line of green sisal fibers. One climbed into an oak and dropped the line. It was knotted around A-Sar-U's right wrist, his sword arm. He was told to stand on his tiptoes. It was hauled taut and tauter still until only the toes of his left foot could reach the ground. Then they tied it off so that he dangled awkwardly.

"He doesn't look divine to me," one young Warrior mimicked Set's voice so well the others laughed.

"They say he is the symbol of love throughout the Empire."

Another laughed, "Who could love that?"

"Millions do," the third boy was almost crying. "And if we fail, they will..." He signed being skinned alive. "I've never heard anything bad about him except from Set and Je-Su. Maybe we don't know..."

"Maybe you'd better shut up. You do know what happens to those who cross Set or forget to call Lor'd Je-Su by his title."

"Oh, stop yelling, both of you. Let's get some sleep. At new light maybe we can get a buck at the ravine pool."

"And eat it raw?"

"We'll build a fire and roast it."

"Smoke from the fire will..."

"Aw, it will never be noticed. Anybody'll think it is Warriors on a two-dark run. Come on."

"Should one guard him?"

"Why. We'll be ten arms away. He can't get free and couldn't go anywhere anyway unless we told him to. You know how posanga zombies are."

"Zombie or not, after a dark, a light, and another dark hanging by his sword arm like that, without water or food, he won't be able to hold a sword, much less fight. Hardly seems fair."

"Who says Je-Su or Set have to be fair? They make their own rules. They are winners."

44

Combat of Set and Horus:
First Test

Je-Su let his pudgy hands settle comfortably on his big belly. There was a glint of self-congratulation in his eyes, and a smile of contentment on his usually dour face. He was pleased with what he had arranged.

Of course, of course he knew nothing about the kidnapping and drugging of A-Sar-U. He had cleverly arranged to have Set, twin of A-Sar-U, announced as his Champion, to fight in his stead just in case A-Sar-U or his Champion should appear on the field. If an unexpected Champion did stand forth, Je-Su could not be harmed. If Set won, to Je-Su would go the victory and the rewards.

Yes, yes, he was pleased. The posanga powder in A-Sar-U's face had made him helpless. Now, somewhere in the land he was tied by the right hand to the Pole of Death. A-Sar-U could die the honorable death with a short dagger in the sinister hand against the sword of some young ambitious Warrior sent to kill him. Or he could swear allegiance to Je-Su.

Or, if he managed to escape the young Warrior's full sword, he could come into the Lists groggy and slow and die on Set's.

Ah, yes. A-Sar-U's severed head would lie in state on the shield and be borne amid the populace so those stupid ones could say farewell to the soft-hearted, pig-headed fool. The crowd would be sorrowful. Oh, of course, so would he, Je-Su.

Yes. Yes. All would be well. All would be as it should be. For no champion could arise to challenge Set in combat. Horus, the son, was only 130 Westsuns, surely not strong enough to win over a warrior fully trained. He was a mere child, no match for even the youngest warrior.

348

Je-Su smiled at Set. They exchanged nods of pure delight.

Both looked down upon the field of the Lists, the place of the combat, surrounded by tiers of stone seats on all sides. The field was about one hundred paces long and seventy paces wide. No Warrior was there. Soon, in another hundred breaths, the Eastsun would be fully risen. After that, no one might challenge him, for he knew A-Sar-U could not appear, and he had no possible Warrior to be his Champion.

He was looking at Set when he saw the tension and unbelief. Je-Su looked back upon the field. All was well. Yes, yes, all...but wait: A waif of a boy came out into the Lists. Purposefully he approached the combat block, mounted it with some effort, and stood small and insignificant on the big slabs of stone.

Je-Su would have laughed, but the voice was clear, though still piping. The crowd in the Lists fell into a sudden, astonished silence.

"Lor'd Ones of the Realm. Beloved citizens of the Pleasant Planet. Blessed priests of the Eastsun and the temples of the Empire, I swear to you on pain of death that I am Horus, son of Lor'd One, A-Sar-U. Under the laws of the planet, one of blood may choose to be Champion at any time.

"I further swear to you that I saw those in the livery of Je-Su kidnap my father and bear him away and that I cannot find him.

"I further swear that I am his Champion and have freely chosen to fight the Tyrant, Je-Su, or his Champion, Set.

"I further swear that Set did not defeat A-Sar-U, but caused him to be given posanga powder which weakens the knees, the eyes, and the will, and overcomes with drowsiness until it robs one of purposeful action.

"So all will know, this is Combat to death. I call Je-Su a liar to the people of the Empire, a cheat on the field of honor, a coward afraid to fight a Warrior in competent mind, a betrayer of God-e, and a frightened bastard afraid to fight me.

"I challenge him to three days of the Combats, with any weapons he may choose to carry, and according to the

349

laws of the Lists, with this stipulation: The loser and his Champion shall be put to death by the Empire."

"Don't be a fool, Horus. You pledge the death of yourself and your father."

"If I lose, yes. But if I win I assure that those sniveling liars, cheats, frauds, and bastards shall be destroyed from control in the Empire."

The cheers from the crowds brought a flush of anger to Set's face. The crowd sat in silence for twenty breaths, while Set hoped they would exert the citizen's choice and refuse to let the Combat proceed as obviously unfair. But slowly the crowd began to cheer and shout its approval.

"Fight him, Je-Su. Fight him yourself." The taunt of the crowd made Je-Su flinch because the chant was picked up by a thousand voices.

Set saw Je-Su's confusion, and stood up, tall and splendid in full armor. It was a command of the people. A summons inescapable to Combat, that Je-Su dare not enter, and his Champion could not win with honor. Yet he could not escape it. Oh, he could drive a spear through the child, but his Warrior's honor would be forever tarnished.

"Fight him. Fight him. Fight him!" The chant grew to a roar. The crowd could not be denied.

Set pulled his sword and, smiling, held it aloft. "I am the Champion of Je-Su, your Beloved Supreme Lor'd One. I ask you to reverse your order. If you will not, and force me to slay that child, will you grant me full Warrior's honor?"

There was a storm of jeers. Set's smile faded.

"If I refuse to fight in this uneven match, will you deny me honor?"

The boos and jeers gave way to shouts of "Yes!"

"Then let the needless death of this foolish child be on your swords. You cannot plead innocent of the slaughter of that child. As Champion of Je-Su, your Beloved Lor'd One, to clear my honor, I accept his challenge and your orders. The fight shall be to death of Champion and Sponsor."

"Choose your Weapons!" Horus called, his voice clear and firm.

"Why, the weapons of a Warrior defending the honor of a Beloved Lor'd One of the Empire. Armor, shield, three spears, bow and a quiver of twenty arrows, sword, short-sword, and the kepesh knife to cut off your stupid head. What Weapons do you choose?"

"Why," Horus mimicked Set's ponderous tones and speech pattern, "the weapons appropriate to a youth defending the betrayal of his father by a liar, a cheat, a fraud upon the Empire, and a coward afraid to fight in his own behalf although present in the Lists. Thirty-six eggs and thirty-six flintstones, granite stones each of small size. Also six handfuls of dirt, and this flowing long-robe for my armor."

There was a stunned groan from the thousands in the Lists. Then shouts of advice and warning.

"You mock me," Set cried, his face livid. "You mock the Warriors of the Empire."

"I mock Je-Su, false Lor'd One, and I mock you, false and lying Warrior. I do it to restore honor to the Warriors of the Empire. You have denied the greatest Warrior of the Planet the use of arms in fair combat, and you have done so by treachery and kidnapping. I will deny you the honor of conquest by affront to your insufferable ego."

Set felt the anger as a sour-tasting lump in his throat. His huge hands clinched in the imagining hope of crushing the stupid boy and ending this ridiculous, unjustified assault upon his integrity and his service to the Empire.

The priests of the Temple of Po-Si-Don began their usual flummery to which Set did not listen. He knew! Everybody knew the rules of the Combat of Honor. Battle was joined at the blast of the trumpet, ran for 1200 breaths, stopped for 360 breaths, then ran for another 1200 breaths and then stopped for the dark of the Eastsun. Contestants could not leave the Lists. They slept in the open and were fed by the priests who guarded them. No article of combat could be reused after once discharged, abandoned, or knocked from the grasp. He who was defeated gave his life to the will of the winner. Flummery! Put up by priests who had nothing more important to do.

Set walked stolidly down the stone steps into the field. His armor, spears, shield, and bow and arrows were not as heavy as his goaded pride. He chose a spot of advantage and fiercely stabbed the spears into the earth to enjoy the shock that ran through his body as an outlet for his anger.

The fury of his will made him toy with the idea of hurling a spear across the field at Horus, who mocked him by walking aimlessly in a circle and kicking at imagined clods of dirt. He could thread three rings at fifty arms. Surely he could find the back of a broad child at seventy arms.

He fought down the urge, for the moment. But at some time he knew he would strike unawares to justly punish those who besmirched his honor. Spawn of the Westsun! Evil loose on the Empire! Doubter of the Divine Right of the Only Son of God-e.

Set picked up his shield and one of his spears and waited the sound of the trumpets. Even as the trumpets were lifted to the lips of the trumpeters, he charged toward Horus who was squatting beside his mound of the huge eggs of the Fenland crane. He rose as Set thundered toward him, an egg in one hand, some stones in the other. For a moment Horus stood as if undecided, then ran as if confused or frightened, seeming to be able to stay only an arm or two in front of the spear tip.

The crowds in the stands roared with laughter and with jibes at Horus. "He of the flying robe," they called him. He looked so funny, his robe blowing out behind, his bare legs and feet churning through the dirt, apparently just able to outrun his enemy.

Horus looked ridiculous and vulnerable to Set, who was confident of reaching him with just a small additional burst of speed.

Set put on that burst of speed and his spear point almost touched Horus. But Horus ran even harder, yelling at the top of his lungs as if already punctured. Set ran even harder, at top speed, his armor clanking, his arrows jittering in the quiver on his left shoulder, his shield turned slightly sideways to lessen the pressure of the air against his passage. He was within a few hands of thrusting with the spear when Horus cut to the left.

Set was unable to stop the weight of his full armor, and ran three strides further before he could turn. He raised the spear to launch it at the child ten arms away.

As the spear neared its mark, Horus stumbled, sprawled in the dirt, and then scrambled to his feet again. The spear had passed only thumb-lengths from Horus.

The angry explosion from the crowd let Set know that attempting to spear a child in the back was most unpopular.

Set was confident that he could overrun and subdue the boy. Again he ran at full tilt, spear at the ready. But Horus lumbered away, and managed to flee just beyond reach of the spear or Set's crushing hands.

The second time along the length of the side of the thousand arm-length field began to drain Set's energy. His breath came heavily into his lungs and burned. He saw that Horus apparently was slowing down and was winded.

Set knew he was in top condition for combat. He was always ready for he was one of the greatest Warriors of the Empire. As he began to tire, sweat formed in rivulets inside the armor. But he saw Horus falter and lag back, and stumble slightly as if from extreme fatigue.

Set gritted his teeth and ran on at full stride, hopeful of overrunning the child, overpowering him, and thus saving himself from grievously injuring a child in front of thousands of witnesses.

Three more times around the field at full exertion. Each step, Set felt, was the last one needed. Yet the spry one managed to just barely outrun him.

He dared not take off his armor, for he could not then use it again. Doggedly he ran, barely hearing the jeering crowd and the derisive epithets above the clank of his weapons.

Three times down each side of the field until his muscles ached beyond bearing and his lungs burned as if from Westsun heat. Three jolting steps he took for each breath. Three thousand, six hundred steps he ran until he was a steaming bath inside the armor. His head spun with the effort, his knees ached. The hand that held the spear and shield trembled as he ran.

Tears of frustration came to mingle with the sweat that rolled down beside his nose.

When the trumpets sounded he thrust his spear into the ground and flopped down. He had never before known such anger, frustration, and exhaustion.

Horus slowed to a walk, then lay beside his mound of eggs and instantly fell asleep.

Set dropped into a daze while planning his surprise strategy for the next 1600 breaths. He smiled to himself as he dropped into an exhausted half-sleep, too tired to really sleep. He knew he would start the new combat with a spear thrown with his usual accuracy. He was tired of insults. He would kill the brat.

At the sound of the trumpets he bounded to his feet and grabbed his spear. Horus was running directly toward him, as if bent on impaling himself on the spear point. At less than five arms length, Horus hurled an egg at Set, who instinctively caught it on his shield.

Even as Horus ran by, just beyond spear reach, he hurled another egg against Set's helmet. The contents of the egg spewed up and fell down upon his shield, arrows and even the up-turned visor of his helmet. The fumes of knot-oil assailed Set's lungs and made him cough.

He swung around. Horus was directly in the sun, running away. Through tears in his eyes, Set fixed the figure and flung his spear.

Horus fell forward and the spear passed above his back and buried itself into the land. Horus was instantly on his feet and running straight down the sun toward Set. At five arms he stopped, planted his feet and with all his might flung a small stone against Set's shield.

He danced backward up-sun as Set advanced with the measured tread of a Warrior now confident of the kill.

Horus danced backward almost the length of the combat field before he again planted himself. Set lunged at him.

Horus again flung one of those insultingly small stones. This time he dived beneath the shield, and kicked Set's armored ankle just enough to make him stumble.

Before Set could regain his balance his shield was ablaze. He swung it wildly around, holding it away from himself in the air. But splattered flames into the fletching of his arrows. The choking smell of burning feathers assailed his lungs and caused him to gasp and cough convulsively.

He reached to unbuckle the quiver of burning arrows from his shoulder and let it fall. His concentration was so great that he did not realize that the metal arm-hold and palm-grip of the burning shield had scorched through the gauntlet and his glove, and seared his left arm and palm beyond bearing.

Even as the quiver of useless arrows fell, he thrust his shield from himself and abandoned it. It burned with a fierceness that rivaled the Eastsun's light, with billows of smoke that rose on waves of laughter from the crowd.

Flames lapped up from his helmet, and his head began to feel the burn. He thrust the helmet from his head. The anger that swelled through him was dammed in by confusion and frustration. Even as he reached for his longsword, Horus dived at his feet, pulled the ankle guard away from the shin and heel, and dropped a small egg into the gap. He then kicked the guard, and rolled aside as Set kicked viciously at him.

Even as Horus rolled away from his kick, Set felt the first burning sting in his heel. It shot fire-like pain into his leg, that clawed at his heart. The second sting was at the bone of his inner ankle and caused him to utter a non-Warrior like groan.

He knelt, pulled the shin guard aside and saw two small, transparent scorpions scurry downward from the light. As he brushed them out of his armor, they stung his fingers, and sent the pain through his chest and shoulders. He stomped the scorpions fiercely as they fell to the ground, and his body pained from the effort.

His heart pained at the howls of derision from the crowd.

He lunged toward Horus, rage tearing at his body almost equal to the fire that ran its mad chemistry through his blood. Lighter by the weight of the shield, spear, and arrows, he sped at his taunting adversary. His fingers closed cruelly toward the neck of the brat. He was met by a handful of dirt flung into his mouth, nose and eyes, and his fingers closed on air.

He tried to run. His leg was swollen and filled him with pain. He could not make his ankle bend or his foot obedient to his will.

Horus danced backward before him, tantalizing him with the nearness. Set broke off the pursuit and limped toward his two spears. He seized one and whirled to throw it. As it neared the mark in its flight, Horus raised the blackened shield and deflected the strike.

The fools! The fools! The crowd stood and cheered. For whom? A true Warrior who could launch a spear two arms long over a distance of more than seventy arms and hit a target? No! The fools! So little judgment. So little reason.

Horus dragged the shield, arrows, and spears to mid-field and fashioned a rough corral by forcing them into the ground so as to form a circle. Set pulled his sword and hobbled toward the brat who worked on, seemingly unconcerned with the oncoming danger. He formed a circle with objects so close together that Set could not get into it without touching an object he had used and abandoned, and so high he could not leap over it. The circle was complete before Set could hobble to it. Horus stood serenely in the center just beyond the reach of the sword.

Set stopped in disgust. "Surrender so that I do not have to kill you," he grated.

Horus' voice carried to the last reaches of the tensely quiet audience. "I will not accept your surrender until you confess to the Empire that you tried to kill me as an infant, tried to murder my mother with serpents, drown my father by deceit, and poison him with posanga powder so that you would not have to face him in these honorable and supervised Combats."

"Unless you surrender you force me to kill you." There seemed to be gravel in Set's low growl.

"Unless you surrender, you force me to disgrace you in the eyes of the Empire by showing the truth. You would prefer death to dishonor and disgrace. Confess and I will then accept your surrender."

Set grabbed his short-sword and hurled it like a javelin at the boy's chest. Horus calmly stepped aside and the knife buried itself to the hilt in the land.

"Thank you," Horus said calmly as he picked up the short-sword and held it loosely in his hand. "Three more to go and then your confession. Or would you prefer me to kill you with your abandoned weapons?"

"One is enough to kill you. One bare hand can do it."

"You lie to me as you lie to the Empire."

The trumpets sounded to end the first Eastsun of the Combats.

Set swung his long-sword in a wild, whistling arc. Such treachery caught Horus by surprise. He was able to

356

deflect it with the short-sword, but the force knocked Horus to the ground, stunned. As Set fumbled in his effort to stretch enough to reach the boy without touching any of the arrow fencing, the citizens set up such an accusing and violent clamor that the trumpets were sounded the second time, a reminder that the Combat had been ended for that period.

Set swore and stood trembling in his passion to kill. But he dared not break the code or all the forces of the Empire would be against him. Damn rules! Made to protect the weak and the incompetent!

Sullenly, he crippled back to his spear, threw himself down. The stupid crowd hissed him continuously. He looked at them through red-rimmed eyes filled with the will to kill. He would make them pay. All pay.

He felt the poison from the scorpion stings flooding his body with a chemical fire. He let his aching and shaking body slump to the ground limply.

With the coming Eastsun he would kill. Kill. Kill!

45

Je-Su's Plan to Destroy A-Sar-U and Horus

Je-Su sat on his tiger-skin and knotted and relaxed his fists faster and faster as he worked himself into a rage.

That damned Set, he fumed, why didn't he loose an arrow through that bastard son of A-Sar-U? Why had he foolishly risked the Empire in trying to look good in the eyes of his fellow citizens and the Warriors of the Realm? The purpose of the Combats of Honor was to win. Win. To show that one could win. Even by trickery as Thoth had won over him, Je-Su, Only Begotten Son of the Supreme God-e.

Set had lost the prestige which Je-Su had so carefully won over the many Westsuns of wise management. Stupid fool! Stupid! He might lose the Combat. Even worse, he might draw the Combat. In case of a draw, the laws said that the two principals would be forced to take the Lists.

Great God-e! He, the Divine Je-Su, born the Son of God-e, forced to fight A-Sar-U. It must not be! The Son of the Almighty grubbing in the Lists like a common Warrior. No. No. No. There must be no chance of that. None!

Yet Set, the bumbling, conceited fool, stood to draw the contest. A-Sar-U might be released from the Post of the Death of Honor by some means. He could then insist on fighting Je-Su. No! No matter how the Combats came out between Set and that Bastard Demon in a child's skin, Je-Su must be rid of Horus and rid of A-Sar-U.

He had planned for this. But all his careful plans had to be rethought, replanned. Some backup plan had to fall into place...just in case.

Oh, yes! Then his careful brain work would again have to be placed in the incapable hands of fools. Of persons who could not see that all the Empire must bow down to

Je-Su, Son of God-e, who bestowed his personal benediction upon all the land.

Why did they not see his Divine Right? Why did they not accept his creed more joyfully? Why did they resist his rule for their good?

He would force them. Not now. Later. He would make them accept him, bow down to the righteous might of Je-Su. Now, he must replan the way to get rid of A-Sar-U.

Set, by careful planning, had imprisoned A-Sar-U on the Post of Death. He was hung by his sword hand, with his toes just touching the earth. Perhaps he should order them to poison...no, no, no...the priests of the Temple knew all the poisons and how to treat them with herbs.

An arrow? An arrow from an unseen archer could pierce him through and end his miserable life, his interference with the application of Je-Su's divine wisdom to the control of the bad people of the Empire.

No. An arrow at such a distance might miss a vital spot. Injured, A-Sar-U's body might not be of service. But his brain . . . his addled, foolish, interfering, non-revering brain would still plague Je-Su and mar his plans.

Somehow, A-Sar-U had to die. But die in a way that could be explained.

A passionate partisan might assassinate...no. Even after the passionate partisan was justly killed, as of course he would have to be to stop his mouth, there might be questions. Investigations. Delays.

How?

Ah, yes! The lucky young Warrior, eager for his first kill, would approach A-Sar-U tied to the Post of Honor. Sword, shield, and freedom to move would be more than adequate defense against A-Sar-U's left arm with a short knife in the left hand. As they all did, A-Sar-U would back away from the sword until he wound himself tight against the pole.

Then the inevitable thrust! Yes, the end, with the slash of the sword through his damned neck.

Oh, how he'd like to be there to see it in person. It was nice to savor it over and over as he visualized the scene. A-Sar-U first, and then all the lovely, lovely things he could do to Ast-i. Or perhaps he would give her to Set who was, he knew, secretly in love with her. Stupid man. And then, the joy of graciously tending to that bastard.

No, he must not let his mind visualize such pleasures. He must plan now the immediate fate of A-Sar-U.

That was most important. It could not wait.

It might be that no one would dare challenge A-Sar-U, the greatest swordsman of all time—except Je-Su, of course. The plan had to be made, prepared, assigned, and executed by first light of the third day of the Combats—in case Horus was still alive.

Ah, yes. He must send one of his worshipping priests to aid Horus in losing the Combat. By high sun of the second day, the Eastsun coming.

Plans! Good plans. Honest plans, for the good of the Empire.

He could not fail. Of course not. Was he not Je-Su, Son of God-e, born to rule all the Empire?

46

Combat of Honor:
Second Test

Purple shadows, in places as deep as the swollen patches on the body and face of Set, were cast by the Eastsun on the tip of rising. Where rays touched the top of the highest stones in the List seats, it was red as the rims of his deep-sunken eyelids. But nowhere did it leave a scowl of pain as deep as that on Set's face as he hobbled from his safe place onto the field. His left palm hand and left shoulder were blistered. The flames that had destroyed the feathers on his arrows had singed his ear and cheek. His ankle was swollen so much that his *sanapu* straps were almost buried in flesh. He obviously was sick. But he carried his long-sword, and in his belt was thrust his curved beheading knife.

Horus came from his safe place walking as sprightly as he could. His right arm was swollen at the wrist, and he tried not to limp in spite of pain in his left leg. All had come from the blow Set aimed at him after the trumpet sounded last Eastsun, which he had fended almost totally with the short-sword.

The morning ceremony had to take place. When commanded to do so by the officiating priests, the combatants faced each other at five arms distance near mid-field.

Horus noticed a most familiar face among the priests. It was a haunting face, gaunt, drawn, and chalky-white. The priest kept his cowl up, seeming to be ashamed of that face and the long, buzzard-beak of a nose on it. The priest also kept his hands thrust deep in the sleeves of his robe, except when he raised them above Set's head in the Morning Blessing. Horus could see that the right palm was lined with white. He saw also that though he was supposed to rub his palms together, in token of washing the spirit of the combatant with forgiveness, he kept the palms a thumb-width apart, and only pretended to rub them as he intoned a blessing and forgiveness in case of death. He thrust his hands deep into his robe again and came swiftly, purposefully toward Horus.

He raised his hands above Horus' head, and began to rub his palms together. Horus saw the almost invisible powder that began to fall toward his face.

A gust of morning wind blew most of the powder aside, but a stray amount entered his nostrils before he could hold his breath.

He instantly felt the heat the powder caused in his nose, and swung around so that the wind blew into the priest's face. Instantly the powder ceased to fall. The priests narrow-set eyes gleamed angrily down his long, crooked nose and he turned away with the blessing half spoken.

Horus heard a short command. All the priests whirled in military precision and moved away. They seemed to be unaware that they were in the march step of trained Warriors. Also they seemed oblivious to what had happened or chose to ignore it for their own safety.

Horus' senses were dulled. The inside of his nose stung with a heat that seemed to sear into his brain and eyes. He worked hard to focus his eyes, and saw the raised area at the left shoulder of each priest that made him think crazily of a shield holder. He was so sleepy.

"Do you surrender?" Set's voice echoed like thunder in a canyon.

Horus fought to hold onto his reeling senses. From some distant place he heard a childish voice say angrily:

"Yes, I surrender your miserable carcass to the crocodiles. Your scorpion-swollen leg to the time you put scorpions in my crib. Your fire-singed face and hair to the time you set fire to the Fengrass in which you thought you had trapped my Goddess Mother and me. I surrender you and Je-Su, Lor'd One of Liars and Frauds, to the mercy of an enraged public."

"You are a child and a fool. You force me to kill you."

"Kill me? Hah! You have tried many times in my lifetime of 130 Westsuns. You are not very good at killing me or any able-bodied Warrior."

The trumpets blew to announce the beginning of the combat. Set lumbered painfully toward him and was aiming a sword strike at his head. Horus knew he should run. His mind told him to run. But his muscles seemed not to obey his mind.

"Run!" The crowd roared its warning. The order, from an outside source, gave will to his muscles. He dodged the descending sword and ran.

How he ran. Time and again he ran when the crowd bellowed its command at him. And after a thousand breaths there arose a great anger in him. A desire to kill. He had never felt such anger before. It was choking, cloying. It seemed to come from a belly so filled with frustration and hatred that it was ready to burst him.

And the thought came to him that he was not capable of such anger. The powder had made him sensitive to the orders and the feelings of the crowd. He was feeling the pent-up, destructive frustration and anger of the crowd!

The anger ate at the compulsion in his mind. Yet he was not able to move as Set hobbled slowly and painfully toward him, the long-sword at kill-thrust ready. Again the cry of the crowd put will into his muscles. "Run, Run, Run," gave him will from outside himself. He ran. His mind was clearing, and this time he ran in a circle, again at a deliberate and teasing distance in front of the lumbering, sweating, grunting menace pursuing him.

After a thousand breaths of running, his mind was clear. He could trust himself to move at the command of his own will, not as a zombie at the will of others. He circled by his stack of eggs.

He chose a large crane's egg and four smaller eggs, the shells speckled brown, red, and blue-green. He planted himself until Set hobbled within distance and shattered an egg into Set's face. He sidestepped and danced in a circle and crushed a second small egg into Set's right *sanapu*. A moment later he crushed an egg on Set's right hand. Then he danced away and let Set come at him in a straight charge. He threw the large egg against the base of Set's throat, above the collar of his armor. It shattered, and small worm-like serpents wriggled to get into the armor.

Set grabbed his throat and screamed, "You bastard. You've put adders onto me."

"Yes. Just as you put adders on me in Fenland. You know and I know that the bite of any adder that can move is death unless my Divine Mother uses the Wisdom of Ra and the Words of Thoth to save you. Do you surrender?"

"No. Never. I'd rather die!"

"Then move and the adders may bite. From my experience I can tell you, the bite is painful, the death is mean."

In obvious terror, Set eased out of his armor bodice and struck the adders from his chest with a single swipe. He stomped them into the ground and swung at Horus with the long-sword. He groaned with pain, for his right wrist was swollen and red and stiff.

"You're welcome. I have returned to you some of the powder of the black hornet's poison you put on me in Fenland. That powder takes a while to get through your skin. Then it works a shrieking pain in you. But you should know. You put it on twenty of my friends in Fenland to make them tell you where I was hidden. They could not stand it and told. I barely escaped you. Can you stand it? Or would you rather confess you did all those things?"

Set tried to shake his head, but groaned. The right side of his head was swollen and red. Flaming red.

"Oh, standing in the sunlight makes it more painful. After you confess, I will take you to the cooling shade and apply a cooling ointment."

After a few breaths Set's knees began to bend. He thrust the long-sword into the ground and leaned on it. But it was obvious he was about to fall.

Je-Su signalled frantically and commandingly to the trumpeters. They sounded the end of the morning contest.

"You are two hundred breaths too soon!" the crowd yelled in rage.

"It is an official count," Je-Su screamed, livid with rage at being challenged. "It is official."

"It saved Set," the crowd screamed back in equal rage.

At a signal from Je-Su Twenty Lines of Twenty ran onto the field and stood with swords drawn facing the screaming, milling crowd.

"How dare you doubt my word. I am the Son of God-e, Supreme in the Land. The Combats are now at rest time. They will resume again. Anyone who disputes this shall meet my Warriors who guard my impeccable honor and my divine right to rule."

Set tried to grin, but collapsed where he stood. The priests with Shield Carry Guards beneath their robes rushed onto the field and carried him to his safe place. They applied ointment, gave him water and food.

Though they were charged by law to treat each combatant equally, they ignored Horus. They gave him neither water nor food. He walked back to his safe place, lay down, and fell asleep.

He was awakened by the sound of steps approaching.

Through the fence of arrows, Horus saw the buzzard-nosed priest approaching. His right hand was inside his robe. In the left he carried a water basket. He was not concentrating on it, Horus knew, for the water was sloshing out with each step.

Instinctively, Horus slipped the short-sword under his left arm and filled his right hand with sand and gravel. He stepped through the arrows, and approached the priest with his left hand out as far as possible and awkwardly holding the short-sword. As he came within two arms of the priest, he flung the gravel and sand with all his strength into the eyes of the priest.

He followed through and slit the robe from neck to hem and threw it back to reveal a Warrior's leather bodice.

The crowd gasped. And then cheered.

Horus struck the priest on the forehead sharply with the flat of the sword and knocked him to the ground stunned. He then grabbed the hidden right hand, pulled it from the robe, dripping white powder. He thrust the hand over the nose of the priest and held it there until the priest had gasped for breath twice.

He then stepped back and waited for the powder to work its dark ways into the mind. Then he commanded: "Stand up!"

Obediently the priest stood up.

"Face the official stands"

The priest faced Je-Su.

"In a loud voice tell us who you are and who sent you to impersonate a priest of the Temple of Po-Si-Don and for what purpose."

"I am Mas-Pa-Ro, Captain of the Personal Guard of Je-Su, Lor'd One of Warriors. He and Set sent me to dribble posanga into Horus' face, as we did into A-Sar-U's last Eastsun, so he would lose the Combats."

"Kill that lying bastard!" Set's command was desperate, but ten Warriors swung about and sent arrows into the false priest.

He fell smiling, and cried: "Thank you. Thank you. Thank you. You make it possible for me to die for my Lor'd, Je-Su, the Only Begotten Son of God-e. Thank you. Th..."

Horus was so absorbed by the pitiful statement of belief that he failed to see Set until his sword was starting its swinging arc. He ducked down and parried the swipe upward. The force of the blow thrust the hilt of the sword he held into his right temple. He was knocked down.

He wobbled to his feet, and moved away. But he knew his steps were slow. Too slooooowww. He tried hard. But his senses spun out. His vision was down to a tube through which he saw Set rushing as best he could, intent on kill.

Intent on kill.

His senses spun out and he felt himself sliding backward and he felt the overwash of blackness. Deep, endless, spear-filled blackness from which he might never waken.

The last thing he heard was the fury of the crowd, the uproar, the cheering...

He floated downward and away into silent blackness.

47

A-Sar-U'S Death
and Resurrection

When the young Warriors were gone, A-Sar-U hung listlessly and without will. As the dark passed, the pain in his arm and shoulder became like fire in all the muscles. "I can reason," he thought. "Can I do my Sacred Exercises? Thoth said I must be able to do them with logs rolling over me."

He stopped his mind and thought only of the sacred exercise of the Pathway of Gold. In three breaths he was calm. In seven breaths he was able to pay no attention to the pain. His will could not move his muscles. Would it move his Radiant Self?

How did he move his Radiant Body? It was not by conscious will. Thoth had said it was by pristine will, the will force gathered from every little particle of the millions of particles of the body, gathered into a river of energy that assaulted his consciousness.

He calmed himself with many breaths and let his mind go free. No thought moved. No pain was felt. No muscle had will to move. A moment later he was in his own chambers watching Horus fill empty eggshells.

And then he knew nothing.

When A-Sar-U returned to consciousness he found himself drenched with water, It ran down his body.

"Throw some more water on him!"

A basket of water struck him in force and he sucked some into his mouth. "He's drinking it."

"Holy God-e! Who cares? He's dying. You know that. And we have only the last watch to get him to the Combats as Set ordered. So let him drink all he wants. He's still had no food for...oh, God-e, he's gone again. I think he's dead."

A-Sar-U was aware of pain. He was also aware that pain could be so intense that the mind would shut off—to keep it out—and with that act shut out all apparent consciousness. He might seem dead to the bumbling young Warriors. But he was vitally alive in another mind, in another consciousness. It was lack of control in one mind. Was it control in another mind?

"Slosh some more water."

"We've got to get him to the Combats."

"You said that. We can carry him!"

"Cut him down."

"No. No. No! He might be tricking us. Lets leave him swing."

"O.K. But I'm hungry. Let's go eat some of that venison. It's cooked enough."

"Yeah. Good idea. Condemned men enjoy last meal."

Thoth had taught A-Sar-U that when he was close enough to death in his own mind, and willed to do it, he could transmute his flesh and project it as a Radiant Body, then project the Spiritual, Radiant Body and clothe it with the transmuted flesh body. As the young Warriors turned away he fixed his desires on the venison. Using pristine will, he willed himself into his Radiant Body, willed it to be clothed with the transmuted energy of his flesh body, and go to the venison.

Light burst through every particle of his body, and he felt the out-rush of energy. And he was standing beside a low fire on which three pieces of venison were roasting on spits. He took one, and stood back and began to eat it.

The taste of the venison was wonderful. But the joy and wonder at the wisdoms of his teacher ran in all his minds and bodies.

As he ate, the frightened and confused youths came to the fire, walking slowly, quarreling. He heard:

"What if we can't get him to the Lists?"

"We'll puncture him good and claim the posanga wore off, he escaped, and we had to kill him."

"We three kill A-Sar-U? Nobody'd believe it. He's the greatest Warrior since Atl."

"But he's unarmed."

"No matter. He could take all of us, tied up as he is if the posanga wore off."

"Then let's kill him where he hangs, then cut him down."

"They'd know if the posanga hadn't worn off."

"So what!"

"So to lie to Je-Su is to become a posanga zombie, and you know that's worse than death."

"O.K. So, O.K! We'll just eat and wait for him to quit breathing or regain consciousness. Then we'll…"

"Who took my meat?"

"Maybe a wolf. Here, take some of mine."

A-Sar-U consumed the venison. It was as if he had created by mind and pristine will a body, a physical-spiritual body, that could move, feel, taste, eat, have emotions. He had created a duplicate of himself through mind and spirit.

Could he fight in this body?

He stooped to pick up a small branch of a tree in his right hand. The arm would move, but only slowly.

He felt despair. Perhaps he had not done the exercise correctly. Then he took the branch in his left hand, and it cut through the air with a whirr. He knew that the problems of the flesh were transferred through transmutation. He could not fight with his right arm. He needed to rest it. To get it free of the sisal rope, and rest it. And he knew it would take a full light and dark of the Eastsun to restore it. But how could he get his posanga riddled body to move at his will?

He heard the three arguing again. "O.K., it's agreed. You go puncture him, let him die for sure, then cut him down. We'll carry him to the Lists and claim he escaped and we had to kill him. They'll believe us. They have to believe us."

"Oh, all right. But I don't like it."

A-Sar-U returned to and reentered his physical body, and fought the clamping blackness of a mind that was unconscious. He worked in another mind. He found that the green sisal rope had stretched so much he could put both feet on the ground and back up three short paces.

He could see the bulk of the young Warrior approaching him, dimly outlined against the firelight.

Surprise was his weapon. As the young Warrior stood two paces away and began to draw his sword, A-Sar-U let the full weight of his body swing in an arc. He hit the youth full on the chin with his left fist, caught him between his legs, and squeezed the air from his lungs. He then eased the short-sword from its sheath and cut the sisal cord. As he fell, he turned so that his body weight crashed down upon the youth. He heard ribs crack, and a groan.

He rolled to his feet, took the long-sword from its sheath, and with the flat of the blade struck the youth sharply below the left knee cap. Quickly he grabbed the right foot, pushed the toes up toward the shin and struck the exposed tendon heavily with the handle of the sword.

"What's all that noise?"

A-Sar-U took the swords and dragged the Warrior behind the trunk of the oak. A moment later he was back on the spot where he had been tied, holding his right hand high. As the fire-blinded, incautious Warrior came close, A-Sar-U kicked his chin, grabbed him as he fell. He grabbed the sword, swung the flat of the blade against the left knee, and then used the handle on the right heel tendon.

He then ran along the trail and into the firelight. The third Warrior began to pull his long-sword. A-Sar-U drove his head into the youngster's face, kneed him in the groin as he fell, then struck his chin. He grabbed the sword, struck it's flat blade against the knee and then used the handle on the right heel tendon.

The youngster would have screamed in pain, but A-Sar-U knelt on his gullet. Terror came from the youth in waves tangible to A-Sar-U's tense senses. He let the knee up a little and the youngster gulped air.

"Silence!"

The youngster nodded agreement, his eyes wide with terror.

"Do you want to live?"

Again a nod.

"Then listen. Listen and obey and save your life. You have been bruised on your left knee and your right heel so badly you will not be able to fight for ten Eastsuns or more. You can hobble. Slowly, painfully. So don't try to escape for I can catch you in eight breaths and then you wont be able..."

He left the sentence unfinished, for what the youth could imagine was worse than he could describe in words.

"Your companions are hurt in the same way. One is injured badly. He may need to be carried. You must arrange to get me and him and your other companion to the Combats. First, make a carry litter for an unconscious man that two can carry. You are to carry that apparently dead A-Sar-U to the Combats."

"Why should we?"

"Because I am the risen guardian and friend of that dead."

"Oh, God-e! You are A-Sar-U. You have raised yourself from the dead!"

A-Sar-U nodded. "I can save lives, too. Yours, for instance."

By full sun, the carry litter was ready. A-Sar-U knew the Combats were already opened, but he had two Eastsuns to appear. He could never be in time to fight the first Eastsun of the Combats, but hoped to recover during the trek to the Lists. He ordered all swords placed in their sheaths, and his physical body cleaned, clothed in full armor, with spear and shield, swords, bow and arrows.

A-Sar-U's inert physical body was placed on the litter. Two Warriors carried the ends. The third Warrior moved painfully and slowly.

The young Warriors were convinced that the "guardian" lurked behind, that even if they hacked the physical body to pieces, the risen A-Sar-U would restore it to life and take terrible vengeance.

All the Eastsun they moved, well into the dark. About first dark, A-Sar-U's physical mind, which in his thoughts he called his body mind, began to reassert control over his muscles. By mid-dark he was certain that the plan would work out. When first Eastsun came and went he despaired of reaching the Lists. It was not until half into the second watch of the second Eastsun that the three Warriors processioned to the very center of the field and put his body down.

"It is A-Sar-U," the Warrior cried. "With Set we ambushed him. He killed seven. Then he was given posanga, became a zombie. We were ordered to keep him on the Pole of Honor. We did, but he had been given too much

371

posanga. He died. But he arose from the dead, defeated us, and ordered us to carry him here. Here is his dead body. His risen body hovers behind it. We swear it is all true on our honor."

Gladly the two other young Warriors confirmed it on their honor and the crowd was deeply moved. Some wept openly, others shook their fists at Set.

Je-Su bellowed, "Set, kill that bastard. Kill. Kill. Kill."

Set was driven to a greater revenge. He stepped over Horus and raised his sword to strike down upon the apparently unconscious body of A-Sar-U. The crowd screamed.

A-Sar-U rolled aside, grabbed Set's arm as it descended, and threw him three arms away, heels over. The sword appeared in his hand and its point was at Set's throat. A-Sar-U kicked Set into unconsciousness, placed his foot on his neck.

"Set is defeated. I now challenge Je-Su. Forfeit the Supreme Lor'd One of the Empire or come into the Lists and meet in combat one who has risen from the dead to avenge the Empire."

Je-Su jumped to his feet with an agility that belied the looks of his pudgy body. "I am the Only Begotten Son of the Supreme God-e, entitled to rule. Warriors, surround them. Kill them. Kill that little bastard."

God-ette, tall and splendid in her white uniform with golden braids, jumped to her feet, and her usually pleasant voice cut through the tenseness of the Lists like a trumpet. "Horus is of Divine Virgin Birth." All eyes turned to her.

"So you, the Mother of Virgins, would like us to believe. But we know the many men you smuggled in to make her pregnant."

A gasp of incredulity and disgust came from the people.

"Virgins, follow me." God-ette led her charges onto the field and sent them to stand facing Je-Su's guards, so close together no guard could pass between them without touching.

"Citizens, we, the Virgins of the Empire, are in revolt against the tyranny of arms. We hold that arms and lies cannot hold against law and truth. Law says that any man who harms a woman or touches her without her permission, shall be speared through the neck, his private parts cut off and stuffed into his mouth. We invoke that law. Virgins, take the swords of the Guard of Je-Su who stands before you."

"Kill. Kill. Kill. I command it. Do it. Do it! Do it, now!"

The crowd tensed and craned forward to see better, for they knew that the future of the Empire swung in the wind on the will and courage of young Virgins.

Slowly the white robed girls, with fitted bodices and flared skirts, moved toward the Twenty Lines of Twenty Warriors in full battle dress, armed with spear, shield, swords, bow, and arrows.

"Kill. Kill. Kill, They are nothing but common whores housed for the pleasure of men!"

The Warriors held their swords near the chests of the Virgins, threateningly. Slowly the white-dressed line of Virgins advanced. Very slowly. A thumb at a time.

The Warriors retreated until their backs were against the stone wall surrounding the Lists, and then they withdrew their arms. Slowly. A thumb at a time.

"My sister's a Virgin. She ain't no whore," a Warrior cried in despair.

"Virgins, take their swords," God-ette's voice made every Warrior tremble.

Four hundred slender hands reached out to take the swords of the Twenty Lines of Twenty. The Warriors stood in dismay. One Warrior, in turning to see if people from the stands were ready to pounce on him, pierced the breast of the maiden advancing on him.

Crimson came onto the white bodice, and a growl of anger rose from the citizens behind him.

The Warrior threw down his sword and fell on his knees as twenty citizens were poised on the wall above him. "Accident. Accident. Forgive. Forgive. Save me. Save me."

"Hold, Citizens," the Virgin cried. "I forgive him this one trespass."

The Warrior sank to the ground sobbing.

Almost to a man, the Twenty Lines of Twenty surrendered their heavy swords into feminine hands almost incapable of lifting them.

God-ette jumped up on the Combat block and called, "Horus and A-Sar-U have defeated Set and Je-Su in the Combats. A-Sar-U is now Supreme Ruler of all the Warriors loyal to the Empire. The Virgins have banished the tyrant Je-Su. A-Sar-U Supreme Lor'd One, what are your orders?"

A-Sar-U stepped up to stand beside her on the raised stones. "Citizens of the Empire. I will soon come again to your tribes and your temples. For great danger threatens our lives as you so well know. But much sooner than you know. But for now, I ask you to return peacefully to your homes, standing ready always to the call to arms."

As the crowd began to leave many filed out onto the field and stood looking at A-Sar-U. One Fenman, blocked by someone gawking too long said testily in that singing speech of the Fenlanders, "Mov' 'long. Aint y' nev'r seen a man com' bak from t' ded b'for'?"

"Cain't r'call 's I hav'. Not rightly, that is."

A-Sar-U lifted Horus gently in his arms. "Lady Goddess Mother, I have four who need your medication and tender care. This one of 130 Westsuns who stood against the anger of tyrants. These three of about 160 Westsuns have had my captive's crippling strokes and need to rest and recover. One has bruised and broken ribs. Treat them well, for they will be brave Warriors and love the Empire."

Big Warrior shoved near to A-Sar-U. "Boss, Je-Su's getting away. So's Set. They'r takin' them false priests 'nd some Warriors."

"Thank you, Big Warrior. Help them. They'll go to Africanus."

"O.K. Boss." He turned away and then turned back again. "Was you *real* dead?"

A-Sar-U shrugged and smiled noncommittally.

"Boss, I'm real glad you made 't. But nex' tim' ...I mean, don' you think you was jest a wee mite showy?"

Bes laughed behind him. A-Sar-U turned. "News of Thoth?"

"None. But Som has some news for you."

Som came forward. He was sweating profusely. His long neck was bobbing as if about to pull his head down between his shoulder blades so he could hide. "Supreme Lor'd One. We have plotted the track of the Westsun and read the tracks in the marble at each of Ra's Sundials. We can now tell you positively that the collision of Eastsun and Westsun will not occur as we scientists have said." Som almost folded into himself from embarrassment. "But...but...the Westsun is pulling the Pleasant Planet...the collision will be with the Pleasant Planet and it must take place. It cannot be avoided."

A-Sar-U knew, of his own observation, what the news would be, yet he felt the news like a blow. He knew he should react, but could not. Before certain doom (even though he had been certain it was coming) no reaction seemed appropriate. He heard his voice squeeze out, "When?"

"Twenty-seven Westsuns from next, if all continues to progress as it has been."

A-Sar-U looked at him and could think of nothing important to say, and said gently, "Now I know why you are sweating."

A-Sar-U felt the dread, the urgency and the frustration shown by Som's bobbing head. "Lor'd Som, any suggestions?"

"Yes. Tell them to begin a new calendar running backward. This will help keep them alert and learning."

"Explain."

"Make today, now, twenty-seven Westsuns, ninteen Eastsuns, second watch. Let the Drum send 27 - 19 - 2. And tomorrow will become 27 - 18. The countdown will continue until 27 - 18 from now will become Zero Time. Then all time will cease for this planet and we will be no more."

"Lor'd Bes, your opinion?"

"Do it. We'll all know and be prepared."

"Lor'd Lady Mother?"

"Ast-i has told me Ra's Wisdom says we must do it. So we must."

"If you please, Lor'd Bes, let the Drums speak. Four Eastsuns a-come all citizens assemble into the temples. Please, especially invite all children. Prepare a great celebration. Begin now to send the myths of Ayr Aerth, Ra's Wisdom, and especially the adventures of the great space explorer, Atl. Let the drum-talk be given each day to every

375

family in the Empire to prepare them for a great adventure."

"Wise," was all Som said.

Bes nodded.

It was high praise to the leader of an Empire who in less than three hundred breaths from taking office knew exactly how and when the Empire would end.

"Goddess Mother, why am I trembling? I've faced death before."

"Beloved Son of God-e, not for seven million."

The Drum began to talk almost immediately after Bes returned to the Temple of Po-Si-Don. All through the dark it rumbled its messages, with commands and advice, queries and assignments. Answers began to come back that the children were overly active, excited, and anticipated the coming adventure with confidence. Only the adults were filled with dread.

A-Sar-U was filled with his own dread. Dread that his planning would not be adequate, his supplies insufficient, his protection not good enough, and his messages not clear enough and forceful enough to convince a planet that action was essential and immediately required.

He called in all the Lor'd Ones, and all the Lor'd Lady Goddesses, and explained the problems to be faced and the solution Thoth and he hoped for. He then asked each of them to take any portion of the task of explaining it all to the citizens.

It was decided that Bes and Horus would explain to the children in the form of a myth, and get them to see how important it was to learn to project the Radiant Body and also to transmute the flesh body and freight it upon the spiritual. They would be taught to enter the state of NEO-mind. They would also be assured that if anyone was not able to transmute and transport the flesh body there were some three million human bodies on Ayr Aerth who were ready to receive them.

Brahm, Ram, Som, God-ette, and A-Sar-U would share the burden of meeting face to face with every adult in the Empire and explaining and having them practice projecting the Radiant Spiritual Body and clothing it with the transmuted flesh body.

The Mother Goddesses and Chief Priests at each Temple were asked to come a full Eastsun before the main group, so they could be briefed and then help with explanations.

Luflin, Big Warrior, and his Line of Twenty were detached to assist in training the Temple Guards assembled from all the land.

A-Thena and her Ama-Sones were pre-trained with knowledge of the impending collision of the Westsun at high Eastsun, Zero Time.

Each chieftain of each tribe and the leaders of each village were pre-told and helped to understand the shortness of time and the inevitability of the collision.

When all was done and the principles filed out of his apartment, A-Sar-U sat dazed with exhaustion. Bes and God-ette rose to go.

"Thank the Beloved God-e that there was so little bickering. We got so much done!"

"Lor'd One of Wisdom, humankind is a many-minded animal. When all goes well he quibbles and whimpers about whose flea is biting whom. When disaster in upon them, most simple citizens rise to the stature of cosmic giants," Bes said.

"Thank you, Lor'd Bes."

As God-ette moved away she looked back. A-Sar-U had rolled to his side, his knees pulled up to his chin. He was asleep. She tiptoed back and spread her cape over him and left him warm and asleep. She wondered if it was appropriate to tenderly kiss the Supreme Lor'd One of an entire planet. She did it anyway.

27 - 15—Last watch of the dark, A-Sar-U asked the Drum to order an inspection for sabotage all through the Empire. He inspected the Temple yard with Big Warrior and Luflin and the Line of Twenty. They poked into each clump of brush, drove spears into suspicious mounds, and caused each priest and Mother Superior to fall out and be inspected even beneath their robes. Then with A-Thena they inspected the Ama-Sones, the Warriors, and even the Virgins. All within the compound was secure.

They sent detachments of Twenty Lines of Twenty in all directions from the Temple of Po-Si-Don to be certain that no enemy was hidden close by. Then they inspected each tribe or individual that came toward the temples. Someone led the chief of each tribe toward the temple while preparing him for the details of what was coming.

"Chief, the Lor'd A-Sar-U, who has visited you and your tribe and thanks you for your kindness and hospitality, sends greetings of respect. He has asked that I inform you in advance, for he needs your help. The great disaster, only suspected when last he came to teach your tribe how to externalize the Radiant Body, has now been confirmed by all the scientists of the Empire. In 27 Westsuns and 15 Eastsuns, at high sun, the Westsun will collide with the Pleasant Planet and destroy all this planet. But do not despair. A method of sending your Radiant Bodies with your transmuted flesh body through space to life and safety on Lor'd Atl's famous planet, Ayr Aerth, has been perfected and will be taught to everyone. It is the method Lor'd A-Sar-U used to come back from the dead. It is tried. It works. It can be taught. And he commends it to you and yours on his sacred honor."

When the Drum began to beat the call to assembly, A-Sar-U moved out on the porch of the Window of Ra and took the place where Thoth had usually stood. The units filed into place. The drumbeat stopped. Leading Horus, A-Sar-U stepped to the edge of the porch. The thousands of voices shouted as one. Happy calls of encouragement and greetings. When silence came, he spoke:

"Citizens of the Pleasant Planet, our future is no longer in doubt. It is assured and short."

"So what's new? We've suspected it all along," Da-Na the Fenman called.

"Good. Listen then to my Divine Spirit-born Son, the Golden Horus. You named him 'The Golden Falcon.' "

"Hey, on the day of the Combats he was more like a screaming eagle!"

After the laughter and applause Horus said in a steady voice. "All children who have lived less than 150 Westsuns, answer me. If you do not, I repeat, do not want to be alive 27 Westsuns 15 Eastsuns and 100 breaths from now, please raise your hand and call out your name."

A startled hush was on the crowd.

"A great disaster is assured for our planet. It may lead to our deaths. But our forefathers lived through such a disaster which forced them to leave That Other Planet. Our forefathers, especially the great Atl, lived on the edge of death all his long life. He went to and came back from the planet Ayr Aerth. He says it is a good planet, much like this one. He lived through many assured disasters. Atl ran to grasp death but caught life and an eternal place in our memory. Atl has been our hero, our model, our guide."

"He aint n' mo'," a young Fen voice sang. "Y' ar', Horus. Y' 'n Lor'd A-Sar-U."

"Holy Atl, me?"

"Holy Horus, you." The Fen lad clapped his hands to the rhythm and chanted, "Holy Horus, you. Holy A-Sar-U, you." The crowd picked it up and chanted for several breaths.

Horus turned to A-Sar-U. "They don't want to hear me."

A-Sar-U gathered the boy in his arms. "Oh, yes they do. Sometimes people hear faster and better with their hearts than with their ears. They have already heard you. All ages have heard."

A-Sar-U and Horus stood hand in hand. "Citizens, you are more prepared than we knew and less worried about your future than we are about your future. But I want you all to hear from the Lor'd Ones. They will tell you why we have delayed so long. And we will have a suggestion on what to do. Lor'd One of Science, Som."

After the applause Som said: "Beloved of God-e, our people started from That Other Planet intending to reach Ayr Aerth. It is six or seven times larger than this planet. It has some fires in the navel and shakes at times. But, we want to go there. It is the only place we can go. Thanks to the Pillars of Ra on each of the fourteen temples of the Empire, we have been able to determine exactly when the Westsun will pull us into its path and collide with us. Then there will be fires in the navel of our cosmos, and Ayr Aerth will seem cool and safe. This planet and all on it will cease to be. The collision will come 27 Westsuns, 15 Eastsuns and 90 breaths from now. Then our physical bodies will be no more, that is, unless we learn to transmute them and take them with us. I give you this on the word of honor of every Lor'd One of Science on this planet. But we reserve the right to be wrong."

After the ovation, A-Sar-U spoke. "You have been readied for this long ago. Lor'd Thoth had a plan. Ast-i and I were to bring about Registered Virgin Birth, which can be caused only by raising the Radiant Spiritual Self and sending it forth to do the creative duties of mankind. This proved that all the ancient Wisdoms are right, and man can be trained by Thought-Force and pristine willpower to transfer the physical through the spiritual. He then sent me among you to teach you how to raise your Radiant Selves from your flesh selves. Most of you succeeded. Now, we must all train under great stress to raise our Radiant Selves freighted with the radiant energy of our transmuted bodies, and send them forth. We must be able to do this at the exact breath we wish. For as death is upon the physical body it develops a power that helps transmute flesh to energy so that we can save ourselves at the last breath."

A furor of voices broke out from many places in the Temple Compound. "You cannot save yourselves. Only faith in Je-Su, the Only Begotten Son of the Supreme God-e, can save you. Believe on Je-Su. Believe on Je-Su. Je-Su saves. Je-Su saves."

A tall Mountain Man shouted in a voice so commanding that the chanting stopped. "Lor'd One, do I got t' lissen t' 'em?"

"It is held that all persons are free to express themselves within the will of the people."

"You real sure?"

"Yes. Why?"

"'Cause that means that I'm free to tell them Je-Su freaks that if they keep up that clatter, I'm gonna lift 'em high b'fore I bust 'em down."

"I see. Do you have the will of the people to do that?"

"No, sir. But if the people let me through to get at 'em, I'll have the will of the people won't I?"

"Lets hope it is the will of the people to listen. We have many things to get done. The Lor'd One of Population, Ram."

Ram stepped to the edge of the porch. "To help you quickly learn all you must of this information, please listen well and remember. There are fourteen temples on this planet. There are seven million people, less those recently killed in skirmishes with the Africanians. A little less than

380

one million are near this Temple of Po-Si-Don and will be able to assemble to it. That means about four hundred and fifty thousand will need to use each one of the other temples. The priests and priestesses will be overburdened. We ask that every child of 150 Westsuns or less be taught by the elders of his tribe as soon as possible. Trained teams will be sent out from Po-Si-Don to help and assure. We have much to do in the next 27 Westsuns, 15 East-suns and 60 breaths. Please help us do it and save..."

"Believe in Je-Su. Je-Su..." The voices that started the chant all stopped with a grunt and a strangled gasp, as if a solid fist had struck in the belly.

"...your Radiant Selves and your lives," Ram completed as if there had been no interruption.

"What to do? We here will help all we can," A-Sar-U said. "You are responsible for yourselves and yours. Re-member, do the best you can and leave it to God-e to make it good. Remember also, that with your first breath you began to die. So what if death may come a little before our allotted span?"

"Aw, we're no' a scairt of dyin'," a Northman called. "'Gin we try, Horus will save us. 'Gin we die, A-Sar-U'll raise us to life 'gin."

The crowd took up the chant:
"We will do the best we can
"And leave it to God-e to make it good.
"'Gin we try, Horus will save us.
"'Gin we die, A-Sar-U will raise us."

"Thank you. Is that the voice of Annon, my running and fighting companion in the late campaign?"

"Aye. 'Tis. An 'a thank you f'r rememberin' so good."

"To you, Annon, and to all my good friends, we shall all win. We are the beloved of God-e. We are shepherded by His will. We begin this new thing, and we will all pro-ject ourselves to the safety of planet Ayr Aerth. There we will create anew our physical bodies. We are embarking on a new and glorious adventure for we all will rise from the dead to become living beings again. And the Radiant Bod-ies we develop shall live on through all the ages, using physical body after physical body. We are creating a race of the NEO-mind. We are indeed embarking on a new ad-venture, and creating a new race. We are creating the sa-

381

cred race of avatars, of metaphysicians, the greatest God-men the cosmos will ever know.

"The road we must travel is full of discipline and stress. The pathway we must take is as narrow and sharp as the edge of a sword, but we will tread it in confidence and joy as if it were as tender, fragrant, and beautiful as the petal of a rose.

"Now, we will plan to break into groups. Children, to the fourth level. Women, to the Virgins' Temple with God-ette and A-Neith. Warriors, to the Warriors' Compound with Luflin and Big Warrior. Scientists, to the quarters of Lor'd Som. Priests and priestesses, to the first level with the High Priest and the High Priestess. Chiefs, here on the Window of Ra, with me and Lor'd Brahm.

"And now let us practice." He signalled the Drum. "In a moment you will hear the Drum rise to a climax. When it pauses you will know the last breath is near. When it beats one time more it will mark in practice high sun at Zero. We must practice as if it were in fact only one breath before Zero. For then, under extreme stress, mounting heat and noise, and flashes of color, we will hear the same Drum call. At that last breath we all must leave in radiant flight for Ayr Aerth, taking with us our transmuted bodies."

The drumbeats increased to one loud final stroke, and A-Sar-U was pleased to see radiant wisps of energy ascending over many of the bodies.

"Lor'd Father," Horus cried, "Look! Many can do it now!"

When the stroke was past A-Sar-U held up his hands.

"Listen! Listen well! Many of you have raised your Radiant Bodies and possibly could leave for Ayr Aerth right now. But in spirit-form only. You need the power that comes with that last breath before physical death to be able to transmute your flesh. You need to transmute your flesh in order to take your physical body with you."

"An' if'n we caint transmute?"

"If you can't transmute, go to Ayr Aerth in your Radiant Spirit. Lor'd Ra and Lady Goddess As-Tar tells us there are millions of strong-bodied humans on planet Ayr Aerth who will be willing to accept our spirits into their bodies. For the good of the Empire and your own future life in your own body, or at least in a body you can call your own, stay and teach until we can all leave together in one flight at one final stroke of our Drum."

48

War Planning:
Africanus, Je-Su, Set

Angry and momentarily jolted from his euphoric belief in his own invincibility, Je-Su stomped from the Lists. He hurried to his quarters and ordered all his belongings taken to the camp of Africanus, in Cragshaven. He then shouted furious commands that all his followers must go there immediately.

With only the fighting-gear and things he could collect quickly, Je-Su hurried his personal contingent, his bodyguard, and his servants out upon the trail. He strode away fiercely, but looked back constantly over his shoulder, apparently expecting avenging forces to come after him.

He was focused totally on getting away, to some place of safety from A-Sar-U or the Empire Warriors now under A-Sar-U's command. Not Je-Su's command or Set's. The might of the Empire in the hands of his enemy.

He paid little attention to Set and his painful afflictions but sank into his own fuming mind, a bitter place to be. Bitter. Bitter!

"I'll show them," he fumed, "That A-Sar-U planned this to humiliate me. But he should know better than cross the Only Begotten Son of God-e, the rightful ruler of the Empire."

Set, obedient to his master's will and wary of his spite and anger, hobbled painfully through the dark. As he expected, Je-Su blamed him for everything and berated him endlessly.

"Why didn't you kill the little bastard? With an arrow at the first trumpet?

"Why didn't you keep him from hitting you with those eggs?

"By God-e, you looked stupid. You are stupid. Why am I surrounded by such incompetents? I am Je-Su, Only Begotten Son of God-e, destined to rule. Rule I will, in spite of incompetents. Hurry, Set, you are slowing the column. Hurry."

The war camp of Africanus was on a shelf of land, just east and south of where the broad East River broke through the Crags and emptied into the Eastern Sea. The shelf was of rich soil and was watered by the East River and a few rivulets arising in the sharp, mountainous Crags. No one knew the real source, for the Crags were so filled with sawtooth rocks and plunging ravines that no one had cared to explore.

The Crags circled the shelf for a distance of twenty thousand arms and stopped in a perpendicular bluff that was the shore of the Eastern Sea. It was a natural war camp, with fertile land, water. It was watered on the northwest by the North Branch of the Crags River, which dribbled its water over a rocky falls into the treacherous East River to the northeast and a sea to the east and almost impassable mountains to the west and south.

It was an easy camp to defend, with space enough for his Fourteen Twenty Lines of Twenty Warriors. All were well trained and fanatically loyal.

Africanus had reason to be proud of his following, his twenty Chosen Women, and his good looks. He was over a full reach and three spans tall. His hair was black, the pupils of his eyes the color of shined old leather, with rims a startling pink against skin even darker than Set's skin. His face was long. His chin was broad and square. In all, his face looked like a blunt-topped pyramid setting on his long, powerful neck. His body was black, the shined black of a healthy bull. His voice was a cultured, bull-like bellow that came out of a mouth that was abundantly filled with large, gleaming teeth. It all seemed to be locked into place by a pyramidal nose with a bulbous flare of the nostrils that invaded the space meant for his upper lip.

"Welcome to my land," he bellowed jovially. "Set, what happened to you?"

Before Set could answer Je-Su snapped, "He lost an Empire to a 130-Westsun little bastard which he refused to kill in the Combats."

"He is my nephew," Set defended weakly.

"I am your Lor'd One," Je-Su screeched. "Enough! Enough! Africanus, how soon can I attack Po-Si-Don?"

"We," Africanus emphasized the word, but Je-Su gave it no heed, "may be able to plan and attack within four Westsuns."

"Four Westsuns! Why would I wait so long?"

"We wait until the scouts we have sent can undermine morale. Then we can conquer, but we will lose fewer Warriors in the battles."

"I want to attack within two Westsuns. Forget the Warriors I would lose. I can get more."

"We will attack when all is ready and we are confident of our plans. We fight for an Empire."

"Yes. An Empire that is mine by Divine Right." Why, Je-Su wondered, could Africanus not see Je-Su's divine worth? Could he not clearly see that Je-Su was the Only Begotten Son of God-e, destined to rule the Empire? Could he not see that his wish was a command of God-e? Why did Africanus seem to bristle when Je-Su expressed a simple wish? Why did people seem to dislike him so?

"Set, my dark-skinned companion," the voice boomed, "Let me send my women to tend your hurts. Take him to quarters." At his word twenty women appeared instantly and carried out their duties with promptness and skill, and with many fond glances at Africanus. As Set hobbled wearily away, Africanus called. "How soon do you wish to attack?"

"As soon as we agree we will succeed, Lor'd Africanus."

Je-Su cringed within himself. Were these two plotting against his wish? Let them! He would have his way. They would see. Because it was the right, the divine way.

But three Westsuns and twenty-two Eastsuns were spent in planning strategy and movement of supplies, infiltrating Warriors into tribes, getting posanga zombies buried in clumps of grass along each trail and surrounding the Africanus and Po-Si-Don temples.

Then came news that Je-Su relished. It would help him get the attack he wanted, and assure that he would get his conniving enemies in a trap. Reports came that A-Sar-U and Horus, with a corps of specialists, were visiting each temple and staying for five full Eastsuns. Five

Eastsuns after Westsun coming they would be in Africanus Temple.

"Good! I've got them!" Je-Su gloated. "I'll take the leaders and the others will crumble. I've got them!"

"We've got a chance at them. But they are wily and battle smart."

Je-Su flew into a towering rage and his bellowing voice reached far out into the camp. "We will attack on the Eastsun they are leaving. We will let them settle in and have no thought that we will take them. Then we will attack. Or I alone will attack. On the fifth Eastsun after Westsun coming. Is that clear? That is final. We attack!"

49

War Planning:
A-Sar-U, Bes, Horus

The sacred training went well, A-Sar-U thought. He taught in the Temple Centers one after the other, then started over again. With each new visit he was more welcomed, more people came to be trained, and they worked more eagerly.

"When the doing is on you, the learning is faster," Bes said.

Horus and the children made progress most swiftly. "The little ones have not yet been convinced by the adults that they cannot do sacred things beyond the command of the five senses. They have little to unlearn before they can learn truth. So they do the sacred work easily, because it is natural to us all."

A-Sar-U was concerned about Africanus's war camp. It was reported to be on full war alert, with battle rations measured and ready.

Bes said, "Lor'd One, it is flat land, comfortable to possibly Fifty Twenty Lines of Twenty. It is reported to be almost full."

"Then they could threaten the Empire. Can we assault it?"

Bes's big face wrinkled in deep thought. "We could. Our Warriors would need to cross the swift East River and climb up a cliff twenty-five reaches high."

"With archers above it would be slaughter."

"Yes. Over land it would require Warriors to clamber over serrated, rocky crags that wrap around the camp from river's edge to Eastern Sea. We could do it...but at terrible loss of Warriors."

"Can we safely contain them, Lor'd Bes."

"They are trying to contain us. They have sent Warriors into the mountains, One Hundred Lines of Twenty. They have Twenty Lines of Twenty posanga zombies around Africanus Temple. Same around Po-Si-Don. And an unknown number along the major trails."

"Your information comes from?"

"Three of Africanus' Chosen Women. Also one of Je-Su's servants. They are all followers of Ra and Mut."

"Oh? Good."

"What do you suggest, Lor'd A-Sar-U?"

A-Sar-U found himself pacing back and forth as he had seen Thoth do in moments of important decision. So many things to be considered. To miss one of those many things was to lead the Empire wrongly. After a while he sat down again.

"Lor'd Bes, call to immediate council, Lady Mother God-ette, Commander A-Thena, Commander Luflin, Ra-Lu, and Big Warrior. And Horus and yourself, of course. We must plan. Oh, have food served for all. We may be some time in our planning. After the food, see that all servants are sent away, well beyond earshot. Je-Su freaks may be anywhere."

The meal was of Eastern Sea redfish, served under slices of lime, cutlets of mountain deer under papaya slices, cool green cucumber in curds of goat milk, goat milk cheese on piles of boiled millet and slices of stone-heated banana. During the meal they planned what the sacred training schedule was to be in the coming Westsun.

When the meal was over and the servants gone, A-Sar-U said: "Lor'd Bes assures us that Je-Su and Africanus are in an almost impregnable war camp. They have infiltrated Lines of Twenty into the mountains, around our temples, and have posanga zombies around temples and along trails. What do you suggest?"

"Can we surround and then starve them out?" A-Thena asked.

"Eventually. But not unless we control the East River," Bes said.

"That means we must hold the mountains at all cost," Ra-Lu said.

"Yes, Commander. How many Warriors would you need?"

"Oh, Twenty Lines of Twenty."

"Against Five Twenty Lines of Twenty?" Bes asked

"Mine must be mountain men, mountain trained. In our own world we can take one to ten and win. Can you spare me Twenty Lines, Lor'd Bes"

"Take Two Twenty Lines, Commander. Set one in the foothills to stop any surprise attack."

"That's wise, Lor'd Sir."

"How long until you can select your Warriors, train them, and get them into the mountains?"

"Five Eastsuns past next Westsun."

Bes nodded to A-Sar-U who said. "Then we must confirm our visit to Africanus Temple. We are all ready, if it please all of you."

"The zombies?" A-Sar-U looked at Big Warrior. "Spread out and hard to find."

"Give me Two Lines of Twenty at each temple, and one for the trails. We can be ready by the Eastsun you have set."

"That's a short time to find spread out zombies."

"Yes. We work the dark too. In the still of the dark we can smell 'em. In the bright of the light we can spot 'em. Either time, we get 'em. Same five days past Westsun a-come."

"Thank you. Commander A-Thena, would your Ama-Sones be willing to assume the duty of Temple Guards of the Empire for the next four Westsuns? This would free my personal guard to move out in campaign. Perhaps we can trap the forces of Je-Su and Africanus behind the Crags, or have the Empire's most deadly archers in place across their path of march."

"I'll ask the Ama-Sones. For you, Lor'd A-Sar-U, and Lor'd Bes, I think they'd agree to walk over fire."

"Thank you, and thank them. Last, Mother Goddess, how many Virgins could you prepare and send on a night run into the Southeast Temple, south of Africanus?"

"Virgins on a dark run?" Bes was surprised.

"They'll love it, my Lor'd Son. I can promise you Five Twenty Lines of Twenty from each of the fourteen Virgins' Compounds attached to each temple. Perhaps a few more?"

"That would be enough, Beloved Mother. A-Thena can you uniform and equip Five Twenty Lines of Twenty Virgins so that in the dark they will appear to be Ama-Sones?"

"Yes, Lor'd One. But why? They can not possibly win in a fight with Warriors."

"They must not fight at all."

"I can equip them."

"Lor'd Bes, can you equip Five Twenty Lines of Twenty Virgins from each of the other temples in the Empire so that on dark runs they will appear to be Warriors?"

"Yes."

"Then, what do you think of this plan:

Let the Drums command dark runs of Warriors and Ama-Sones to the Northwest Temple, the furthermost removed from Africanus. But, each dark send Virgins in Warrior gear to the Southeast Temple in the South. Forbid them to speak on pain of death. Be certain they are out of sight by Eastsun's first light.

"Why? The zombies will hear the movement of troops and report it. Je-Su and Set will think they know we are planning an attack from the South, and have left Africanus and Po-Si-Don lightly protected. I will make my appearance at Africanus at the agreed time. Ra-Lu will stop Je-Su's Warriors in the mountains. Big Warrior will uproot the zombies.

"Je-Su and Africanus may then be tempted to sally out of Cragshaven to try to trap us in Africanus Temple. We hope they will make the attack outside of their protecting crags. If they do, we can get at them without great loss. We will send archers into the crags to harass any retreat. Maybe we can defeat them so badly that we can rest from their constant threat to the Empire and turn our energies to sacred things. Time is short!"

"Good plan," Bes said. "It will depend on deception. I think we can do it."

"So do I," A-Thena agreed.

"Lor'd Father, it seems to be a wise and daring plan. But do you forget to use the children? Could we mount a crusade against tyranny?"

"How do you suggest, Horus?"

391

"Je-Su hates all children. But he sees them valuable as hostages. Set hates me, and eight of my former companions in Fenland. We nine bear both Je-Su and Set a grudge that aches to be filled. If children went to Africanus, would it make the temple more of a prize? Would Je-Su be more likely to attempt to take such a tempting prize?"

"He probably would."

"Then may I suggest that Ten Lines of Twenty children could picnic and swim in the East River?"

"Yes, divine Son?"

"The East River bends westward until it gets the waters from the North Branch of the Crag River, then southeast past the Crags to enter the Eastern Sea?"

"It does," Big Warrior said.

"After the river swings westward no one but those of the Crags drinks of the water?"

"Lor'd Bes, true or not?"

"True. But why?"

"We children love to splash and play in the water."

"But those waters are deep in places, and swift. Besides, you would be beyond the protection of the Temple Guard."

"Yes, Lor'd Grandfather. But children playing are not cautious. Are they not loud and obvious?"

"Yes. But they would be close to a war camp..."

"True. Children do not think of such things when playing with water-balls."

"Water-balls? Why?"

"Because they are hollow."

"They are hollow. So?"

"In the hollow you may put things."

"Such as?"

"Posanga juice."

"Posanga juice?"

"Yes. South Fenwomen keep it to threaten their men who are not kind. It is clear like water, and two drops in the water in a large gourd will steal a man's will for days. A water-ball, filled with posanga juice through a hole and then sealed with beeswax, can be opened on a signal by a little finger. The juice would then soon be floating in the water.

"Warriors in the Crags will not fill their combat bladder-skins until Lowsun of the Eastsun before the Eastsun of their attack. Five Lines of Twenty water-balls of posanga juice in the river will be more than two drops in a large gourd. Those who drink of that river water and then go into combat will not be able to fight. Many lives may be saved."

There was a long, long silence as each person weighed the benefits against the risk.

"We know when the attack is to come," Bes said tentatively. "But...if plans go awry, many children may be dead."

"Perhaps, Lor'd One. But many Warriors may be saved. The Empire cannot spend its last few precious Eastsuns fighting. We desperately need more time for sacred training which may soon save many, many lives."

"But the time you have is so short, Horus. Can you do it?" God-ette asked.

"Just barely, Beloved Goddess. We will have two Eastsuns to spare if I can run fast enough."

"Lor'd Bes, your opinion?"

"Guts and genius. I'm proud of him for both."

"Horus, who could supply you all you need so your Children's crusade can be in place the Eastsun before the planned attack?"

"Da-Na, the Fenman, and his Chosen Woman. If all children come from Fenland they will be good swimmers. They taught me water-ball. They are fast and sure with those reed boats."

"Do it," A-Sar-U said.

"Are all plans clear? If so, Lor'd Bes, after we ask the blessings of the Supreme God-e, will you send the needed runners and let the Drum speak, this time with forked tongue?"

50

The Children's Crusade

Horus felt the strain of the unrelenting speed of the night runs from Northwest Temple to Po-Si-Don and then on to Fenland Temple. His breath came harshly into his lungs, yet he pounded on. This was his first real commission, the first assignment. He was eager to do it right. Even as he ran he seemed to hear again the parting advice of his Grandfather, Bes.

"You get farther by asking questions than by making statements.

"Never cause anyone you want to work with to believe that you think you are better than they.

"Never, never say or think you are wiser than the dumbest kid in the line.

"Retreat if you must, but always attack if you think you know the moment is lost.

"It is better to die than to lose and become a zombie of bad fortune."

Near full first light, Horus passed through the Temple Guards and into the rooms of Da-Na and his Chosen Woman. She hugged him.

"By God-e you'v shot up tall 'n strong, Horus. Hardly kno' y'u, Chile. I'll fix som' vittles. Got t' git som' mor' meat on 'em bones us Fenmen ador'. Da-Na's lookin' t' th' Guards. Back soon."

Before he had stopped sweating from the dark run, a bowl of gruel steamed its savor and refreshment through his body, and Da-Na was looking at him with dark eyes, level and friendly. Horus quickly explained his project, his need for Five Lines of Twenty frolicsome and brave children, each with a water-ball containing posanga juice.

"We'll need ten reed boats to get them all into the East River above Cragshaven. And we have only eight East-suns."

"On'y four til Westsun."

"Je-Su will attack five after."

Da-Na grunted. "Dumb plan!" After a moment he burst into loud laugher. "Jes' dumb 'nough t' work, mebbe. By God-e, what a turn' bout on Je-Su 'n Set, if y'u c'n pull 't. But...doot th' South Fenwomen'll giv' up their posanga juice f'r so small a reason les' th' men git uppity. But we'll ask 'em.

What y'u think, Woman?"

Da-Na's Woman laughed. "'Gin y'u tak' way th' coconut wine fr'm their men, they'll."

Aye. But I'd druther they'll be pizzled 'n sexin at their women th'n chunkin' 'n shootin' at me. If we ask 'em, wine or no, Woman?"

"They'll."

"How 'd y'u know?"

"He's Horus, aint?"

"He's Horus, Woman, y'u c'n see."

"They'll. Agin' Je-Su, they'll. For Horus, they'll. So they'll."

While Horus slept, the planning went on, so at mid-light a reed boat started south into the deep fens. The Fen River grew sluggish as the growth along the bank grew thicker and taller. When, rarely, a flat glade came, the boat stopped and the people came. They were short, stocky, strong, with gleaming faces of laughter and good cheer.

Giant mahogany and stonewood trees and enormous banyans crowded behind palms. Elephant ears, cypress bushes, and ferns helped the thousands of orchids seem to make a pathway on land impassable. Lily pads reluctantly let the boat pass. And then the posanga trees and the water-ball trees blinded the view of the land.

At every turn in the river, the water-balls seemed to increase in size by a thumb-width. They had been small as a span at the start of the trip, and Horus observed the strange quirk of nature that produced the water-ball tree.

The rains and snows in the uplands of the mountains furnished too much water for the land at some seasons. At other seasons the Westsun scorched and the Eastsun dried too much water from the land. Then the water-ball tree was a treasure to the land.

In wet times they grew, filled with pure, wonderfully sweet water. When the dry season came, the stems seared, the water-ball fell from the tree, crashed, burst, and spread water and life upon the land. Horus wondered to himself if a child could lift one of those large water-balls if it was filled with water.

"'Tis no' t' fret, Lor'd Horus. Y' on'ey wan' 'um ha'f full 'r they'll no' float high 'nuf in'na seas."

Horus laughed and hugged the Chosen Woman of Da-Na. "You've been reading my thoughts again."

"On'ey learnin' I got."

"You've got learning for life."

"Why, thankee. Jes' wait'll I tell that t' my man."

At many glades the boat landed, and as if by signal many persons crowded around. Horus stood on the prow of the boat and explained to the Fens what he wanted to do, what was needed, and the great urgency. He had spent thirty-six Westsuns with the Fens, but had never really learned to read their inscrutable eyes peering out of the planes of their faintly yellow cheeks.

They began to argue among themselves, broke into smaller and smaller groups, and drifted away. Some broke into a dog-trot as they disppeared into the jungle. He knew it was not their custom to say good-bye, but somehow it bothered him and made him doubtful of himself that they didn't even look back.

When they had all left the glade, Da-Na's Woman said: "Ye'd's well make camp."

"Do you think they'll give us posanga and help?"

"Ar' y'u Horus?"

"Of course."

"Then they'll."

Something in the simplicity of her praise made Horus blink tears back from his eyes.

The mid-sun passed, and time with no activity wore sorely on Horus' nerves. He tried to doze and rest from his long run, but when the light slipped into the dark he began to count his tomorrows. He slept fitfully.

Sometime in the dark, long before fourth watch, he heard a gentle sloshing. Soft voices rose above the rasping together of reed boats. Then all was quiet, and Horus smiled and prepared for sound sleep.

"They'll!" he whispered exultantly to himself.

Before full first light there were sounds of paddles coming from all directions. Reed boats came, seeming to tow tall ships of river-mist with them. Slowly a chaos of mist, boats, oars, and people resolved itself into a flotilla of boats, each with ten children and ten waterballs.

Da-Na scratched his chin reflectively. "Y' kno', Horus, don' look lik' much 'f a' army to d'feat Je-Su's riffraff. Y'u look'd mighty puny down 'n th' List facin' Set, but y'u won 'n Empire. Why y'u lookin' worried?"

"If anything goes wrong they could all die." His hand indicated the children.

"Yealp. All us grown-folk know't, they all know 't. An' they know you'll improvise."

A tall youth came up the bank. Behind him lingered two identical youngsters, seemingly impelled by wide-eyed wonder, but restrained by ingrained courtesy.

"I remember you. Do-La, Da-Na's kin. You helped turn over Je-Su's boats."

"Thankee, Lor'd Horus. Oh, these 're my twin brothers. They're on'y seventy Westsuns, n' al'ready meaner 'n a hunnerd. But they're good swimm'rs. This 'u's Do-Ro, this 'n' Do-Ru."

Horus looked into four friendly eyes, so identical that they might have been in one face. He was certain that so much mischievousness needed four eyes and two faces to fully express itself.

He pointed at the flotilla of boats, children, and water-balls.

"Woman didn't hav' 'nuf posanga juice. We'll practice with water."

"Will they have enough by next Eastsun?"

"No."

Horus felt the jolt of that denial in his belly.

"But in two lights 'n' two darks, they'll."

"Good. Then let's give our children a chance to practice."

Water-ball was a game for training Warriors and creating endurance. Each person had a water-ball, assigned to him as supplies were assigned to Warriors. Ten 'home team' players would form a ring treading water, facing outward, with their water-balls inside the ring. Ten 'bad team' members would try to get the water-balls outside the ring. The usual way was for four or five to dive under and come up under a single water-ball so swiftly that they could throw it over the heads of those in the guardian ring.

If this could be done, one of the 'home team' was taken captive by the 'bad team' and had to leave the ring. But if the 'bad team' failed, or was touched by a player on the 'home team' before they could swim back outside the ring, they had to join the ring as part of the 'home team.'

One refinement was this: if any team member could 'walk the ball' on top of the water for thirty breaths, his side won the round. It was a very difficult feat. Very few could even stand up on the ball bobbing in the water, and those few could seldom manage to stay up more than two breaths.

The children organized themselves into ten boat commanders and nine assistant boat commanders. And the training began. They tested removing the beeswax plugs underwater with fingers only. It was hard but could be made to work.

Do-Ru and Do-Ro were like otters when in the water, like beavers in their busyness, and like hornets in the intensity of their excitement when playing. But, they wasted so much time, it seemed to Horus, for one or the other was always trying to 'walk the ball,' and neither could stay up two breaths. But their energy was so high and their laughter so infectious that others seemed to work harder because of the twins.

The following Eastsun the children had tired a little, and were more deliberate in what they did, careful in how they did it. They practiced righting capsized boats, swimming under overturned boats, paddling with hands, paddling silently. All skills they would need or might need as they swept into the turbulent East River.

Horus felt it was time for his War Council and for making final plans. He called the crews together.

"Come the new Eastsun, if the posanga arrives, we fill our water-balls halfway with it and we will be ready to start for Cragshaven and East River. We want to get into the East River, as near Cragshaven as possible. We will be under the arrows of Set's Warriors at times. If any want to back out now, say so."

"I wanna back out soon's Je-Su backs out." Do-Ru called.

Everybody laughed.

"We have food for five Eastsuns, and we will land near Africanus Temple. They'll be ready for us.

"We have these ways we can choose to go. Up the Fen, cross through the rings and canals, then up into the Loba and back down to the upper East River.

"Or, down the Fen, into the South Sea, eastward around the peninsula and back northwest into the mouth of the East River near Cragshaven."

Horus remembered the admonitions of Bes, "Never think you're smarter than the dumbest kid in the line." He added, "Or is there a better way?"

"Neither," a dozen voices shouted.

Do-La said, "Bes' go up th' Fen t' th' slough, east to the Eastern canal to the junction of the Crags Rivers, take the West Branch to the sea, around the peninsula and back up into East River.

"Why not up the North Branch right into the East River?"

"T'd be short'r. 'Ts a trickle with a fall right 'nto East River ov'r lots'a roc's."

"Then we'll be bordering Cragshaven for two whole Eastsuns."

"Yealp. 'N we'll hav' t' do 't inna dark 'r the zombies'll see us. Aint that fun?"

"How long will it take?"

"Three, mebbe four darks."

Although the pressure of time began to worry him, Horus took a vote, and that was the route chosen. He then put all his young charges to sleeping.

The supply of posanga did not arrive by first watch as expected. Horus put his charges back to rest. It was well into third watch that the posanga juice began to arrive, and it was not transferred until the beginning of the fourth watch.

By the time the children were roused and fed, it was beginning of the dark. The young Fens rowed through the sloughs with a steady stroke from first dark to near first light. All through the Eastsun light they hid in tall fen-grass or under large leaves. They slept, ate, and moved only when it was needful. Horus noted that in every way they behaved like fully trained Warriors.

"No wonder Fens make such great fighters," he mused to himself.

Again they rowed powerfully all the dark and behaved cautiously, seldom speaking above a whisper.

As they bedded down at first light of third sleep-time, Horus was feeling good. If all went well they would be in position with three days to spare.

But all went terribly wrong. Shortly after first light the air began to crackle with energy, and heat assailed them. And then the Westsun came. As it came over the horizon to the northwest the heat grew to an intolerable degree. By the end of the second watch the lances of red light were so great that leaves began to fall from trees. The large leaves behind which the children had hid began to curl like shamy-weeds and to crackle and split. Many popped. Some leaves exploded with a sound like a slap. The children were driven from crumbling shade to other shade. And it seemed to be endless.

The usual hundred breaths of punishment was extended to four hundred breaths of brutal torture, searing and drying and lancing with destruction. When it was all over, the children staggered from their seclusion as if they were battle addled. They wandered about, apparently unable to focus their thoughts.

Horus eased himself down into the river and found the water was almost too warm.

Slowly the children came together to help Horus survey the damage. The top runner-reeds of almost every boat was blackened and possibly weakened.

"Do-La, will they hold in the sea?"

"They'll. Mebbe."

"Can we replace them?"

"Yealp, with spec'al reeds, long dri'd. Tak' ten East-suns."

"At best we have four more."

Horus felt the weight of decision like a fist to his stomach. "As I see it, our toughest strain will be in the time we spend out in the sea around the peninsula. Do we need to go through pongos?"

"Not down. On'y up th' pongo from th' sea 'nto th' East River.

"Ever been up it, Do-La?"

"All 'f us hav'. Y' gotta pull lik' zombies. It's a four-reach drop in on'ey a thousand paces. 'Ts hard. A high'r tide hep's, so if'n we catch 't jus' befor' Eastsun, we'll make it."

"Mebbe," the children said in unison.

"Yealp. Mebbe," Do-La said. "We aint nev'r tried 't wit' ten, 'leven kids 'n each boat."

"If we don't get there at higher tide?"

For a long while no one spoke.

"What'd y'u think 't do, Lor'd Horus?"

Again the silence was long. "Then we'll...well, we'll just have to improvise."

"Like y'u done in th' Lists? 'Ats O.K. wit' us. Les go.
What'll we do if our boats break up?"

Two voices spoke as one. "We'll 'mprovise. We'll Tak' our water-balls 'nd swim up East River. Now, c'n we git back t' sleep?"

Horus decided to sacrifice one Eastsun for travel to help restore the energy of his obviously exhausted children. He would lose one full dark of travel, but perhaps they could make up for it.

They rested for the light and dark and the following light. Well rested, the children pulled strongly, and they made the entire length of the peninsula. They found a very deep mangrove cluster and stopped for the light of the Eastsun. Horus was not pleased because the river ran along the west side of Cragshaven. Though that part of Cragshaven was jagged and cut by impassable canyons, some stray person might hear them and alert Je-Su.

They left the mangroves at first dark, and pulled hard into the open sea. Waves slapped the boats. The boats creaked loudly, and some top-runner reeds began to explode from the strain and dryness.

"Put water on the top reeds. Maybe that'll help. Pass it to the next boat."

Soon the reeds were soaked and safer, and the boats were heavier and slower. They were not able to reach and round the tip of the peninsula until the end of the third watch.

And there was no hiding here. It was a desperate race to get up East River and out of sight without being seen by the lookouts on Cragshaven.

The sea had been rough. The moil of the water at the mouth of the East River was like a hundred hands dragging each boat in a different direction. Some boats were whirled by pools that tried to suck them under. One boat was swamped and had to be bailed out with cupped hands. And when it seemed impossible that they could make the five thousand arms remaining before the Eastsun light fell on them, the tidal bore roared in behind them.

Horus thought of the myth used to explain the tidal effects: "The Pleasant Planet is tilting as it bows to the Eastsun."

The boats were lifted several arms and thrust through the current of the East River.

They heard the falls of the North Branch of the Crags River and guided in toward the shore of the river. They went upriver and found a long, sloping beach on the west side of the East River, about three bowshots from the Warriors patrolling the rim of the bluff above East River. They rowed into the reeds, lifted their boats out of the water and seemed to collapse.

Horus knew his crew was exhausted. And he was tired. But something in his mind caused him to worry. It was an indefinite feeling that time was akimbo, urgency was great, and there was great hazard.

He tried to reason with himself. They had made it in time. They had all this coming Eastsun to recuperate, didn't they? The Fen children were accustomed to stress and hard work. They would not suffer long.

His mind would not be at ease

Cautiously, although he was not afraid of noise now, Horus saw to it that food was prepared and eaten, though many children seemed too tired to eat. He was not pleased to have to post guards from among children so exhausted, so he took the first watch.

He watched a benign Eastsun send its paintbrush of light into the blue shadows of the Crags and then touch the turbulent waters of East River with magic strands of golden light. He mused that he was too tired to think such poetic thoughts.

He had almost fallen asleep on his feet when Do-La relieved him and he staggered to his mat of reeds.

He could not fall asleep. Something was wrong.

After what seemed to be a thousand breaths he managed to doze. It seemed that even as he closed his eyes he was being shaken.

"Lor'd Horus, Som'one's come from Po-Si-Don Temple. Says he's a Temple Guard."

Horus rose quickly and hurried with heavy heart to where the Temple Guard was being held at the tips of three spears held by fiercely determined children.

"Lor'd Horus, Lor'd Bes commands me to find you and give you a message."

"Let him be, guards. But stand by."

The Temple Guard approached Horus and lowered his vioce. "Lor'd Bes commends himself to you and sends this message:

"'Best information is that a surprise attack on Africanus Temple will begin at the end of the third watch of this very Eastsun.'"

"End of the third watch, with this Eastsun?"

"It seems to be Je-Su's idea of a surprise that will give him great advantage."

"Holy Atl, what watch is it now?"

"Mid-second watch."

Horus's mind would not focus. He stood looking vacantly at the Temple Guard. At last his mind clicked onto the facts. He repeated them aloud.

"Then we have only about fifteen thousand breaths to get our work done. Do-La, wake all the children. We must move fast."

"Lor'd Horus, is there a return message?"

"Yes" Horus fought down the panic that was beginning to rise in him. Surely the Warriors would have begun to fill their combat skins from the East River by now, or would soon. His exhausted children were in no condition to frolic in the cold water. He forced his voice to stay calm. "Yes. Please thank Lor'd Bes for sending me the information, and say this: 'What is left to do when you know the moment is lost?' We'll improvise, do it instantly, and leave it to God-e to make it good."

The Temple Guard repeated the message, blinked doubtfully, and took a courteous leave.

Horus called the children to assemble. "Listen. Listen well. We are Five Lines of Twenty against Four Hundred Lines on Cragshaven. We thought we had two more East-suns and could play in the river to allay suspicions. But we have just been informed that the attack is to begin in about fifteen hundred breaths. The Warriors may even now be filling their water skins as they assemble for combat. What do we do?"

"'Mprovise," two sleepy voices said.

"How can we get posanga into the bend of the river and to Cragshaven fastest?"

The twins said: "Giv' us two water-balls, 'n we can slip over to the North Branch an' let 't go 'n to th' water. That'll be piddlin' slow. C'n we sen' couple 'f water-balls over th' falls so they'll crack on th' rocks below?"

"How would you keep the Cragshaven Warriors from getting suspicious if two waterballs suddenly appeared? If they get jumpy..."

"We'll 'mprovise," Do-Ro and Do-Ru said.

"Try. Now, the rest of us. How will we get the water-balls close enough soon enough. We don't have time to play games. If we take the wax plugs out this far up-river, it will be swept eastward. Besides, posanga runs slow through those little holes.

"Let's throw all the balls into the water, then play on the beach while they float down toward Cragshaven. Then we'll swim and catch them, release the posanga close in, then swim away." When silence had grown into heads nodding consent, Horus added, "Good luck. Be obvious! Do it loud, do it now."

The youngsters grabbed their water-balls and raced to the river shouting such playful things as: "Last 'n 'ns a sugar tit," and "If I beat y'u, y'u gotta kiss my goose pimples."

They threw the balls into the river, then began to undress. One youngster was grabbed and thrown into the river, coton and all. A raucous scuffle immediately developed at the water's edge which grew into a mass of writh-

404

ing bodies, and no one could get free to get into the river. The water-balls bobbed away toward the shore of Crag-shaven. When the water-balls had drifted half way to their intended object, someone yelled: "Look'it. Our water-balls."

The water threshed as the children plunged into the river, shouting and laughing, and swam toward the water-balls. Their fake excitement was momentarily halted by a scream from on top of the falls where the North Branch plunged into the inside bend of the East River.

The chunky twins bobbed nearer and nearer the lip of the falls. One arm of each waved wildly, and their cries of distress seemed to be real.

"Get back! Get back!" someone screamed at them, "There's a falls. They'll kill you."

"Caint. Oh, God-e, caint."

Horus swam as hard as he could toward the foot of the falls. All the children raced after him.

The twins rode the water-balls until they bobbed over the edge of the falls. As they began to fall downward the twins dove hard and far, screaming at the tops of their voices.

The water-balls crashed and split on the rocks near the face of the falls. The two young Fens soared outward and dived into the shallow pool formed by the falling water. After a few breaths they surfaced and swam into the East River, even further down river than the water-balls.

Horus swam even harder, for they were within bowshot of the Warriors coming down the steps of the cliff side of Cragshaven. The Warriors went on the alert, and then began to laugh.

Horus swam as hard as he could. The water-balls were now within bowshot of the Warriors.

"Get back. Get back," A Warrior called.

"Want our water-balls," Horus cried.

"We'll shoot!"

The children swam harder, and called, "We want our water-balls."

"Shoot them," a Warrior voice commanded.

A dozen bows came up, arrows drawn to the notch.

"We want our water-balls," the children cried and swam even harder.

The arrows were loosed and arced very little, so close were the targets. Twelve water-balls burst, and the Warriors laughed.

"We want our water-balls," the children yelled, and swam, perhaps with less speed but with much more splashing.

Warriors appeared on the run, and stopped on top of the cliff to laugh. Fifty arrows were fixed, drawn and released with the ruthless twang of bowstring and whistling arrow. Almost half of the water-balls burst

"We want our water-balls," The clamor went on, so loud the Warriors laughed at what they thought was childish distress. More Warriors appeared and joined the sport.

Within ten breaths the twins swam past Horus headed upriver, and the last of the water-balls were burst, many within ten arms distance of where Warriors on the steps were holding water skins to be filled from the river.

Grumbling loudly, the children turned and swam back upriver toward their camp area. As they climbed out of the cold water and shivered into their cotons, the twins came quickly to Horus.

"Y'u said t' 'mprovise. Did we do 't good?

"You did it good."

"Then, Lor'd Horus, Wou'd y'u bless us 'n 'a name o' th' 'Mpire?

"You took an awful chance. You might have been killed."

"Yealp. Had we failed, Horus 'd save us. 'N' had we died, A-Sar-U 'd raise us. Well, he wou'd 've, wouldn' he?"

Horus fought down the tears that came into his voice. "I bless you all in the name of the Empire." To the twins, who seemed to be disappointed he said, "Would you two like to see Lor'd A-Sar-U real close up?"

"You mean, the bes' Warrior inna 'Mpire? 'N feel his muscles? Holy, God-e, Yes, yes, yes."

"Take this message to him at Africanus Temple. When you try to go in, the Temple Guard will stop you. Just say, 'Lor'd Horus commends us to the Temple Guard. We have messages for Lor'd A-Sar-U in person.' They will get you to Lor'd A-Sar-U. Then say, 'Lor'd Horus sends love. The Children's Crusade lost their playthings to the arrows of the

Warriors of Cragshaven at river's edge. Please be happy, and let these two heroes of the Empire feel your muscles."

Wide eyed, the twins scampered away, running like true Warriors.

A-Sar-U and Bes, at war station in Africanus Temple, were constantly brought good news during the fading light of the Eastsun of Je-Su's attack. Few of the Warriors from Cragshaven could fight well, and the Temple Archers picked off many Lines of Twenty in each flight. Cragshaven Warriors were blocked, when they tried to retreat, by Temple Archers in the hills. When setback turned to defeat and defeat turned to rout, Warriors from Africanus and Je-Su surrendered to Bes's Temple Guards. Torn and beaten, Africanus and Je-Su staggered back to shelter behind the Crags with over Two Hundred Lines of Twenty captured, and most of the remaining wounded.

It was a short battle. And all during the conflict the news was good until Som, other Lor'd Ones of Science, and the somber High Priests of three temples arrived by full dark. A council was hurriedly called and Som said:

"Supreme Lor'd One of the Empire, we scientists have recalculated after the fierce Westsun just three Eastsuns agone. All scientists of the Empire will now agree, the Westsun will collide with the Pleasant Planet after only two more Westsuns.

"The next after the Westsun coming, Lor'd Som?"

"Yes."

"Fifty-three Eastsuns from now?"

"Yes, Lor'd One."

"Thank you for letting us know this, and please let us know if there is any further change."

A-Sar-U turned slowly, his face placid, as if relieved from a long strain. "Lor'd Bes, please let the Drums send the signal that the Empire has agreed upon to instruct all tribes to assemble at their closest temple at this earlier time.

"Send the message as joyous news. The waiting is over

"The blessings of the Supreme God-e is upon our Pleasant Planet and its people.

"Let all people know how soon they may meet their final doom or reach eternal life.

"And, please, say we love them, each one."

51

The Last Breath

The huge Drum had been speaking throughout ten East-suns including the darks. Surely by now every creature on the Pleasant Planet knew that the inevitable was fast approaching, and that this was the last two-thousand breaths. The citizens had come to Po-Si-Don Temple in a joyous, almost frivolous mood. It was not that they did not know that the last Eastsuns were speeding by. Now, in the dew of the second watch of the Light on this very last Eastsun, they danced and gleefully sang:

If we fail, Horus will save us,
If we die, A-Sar-U will raise us.
Life on Ayr Aerth is almost assured
If spiritual travel can be endured.

There were tribal dances, mixed tribe dances, a mixing of tribes such as had never occurred before. In the assemblage of citizens, A-Sar-U detected no bitterness, no fear of death in the awful doom that would come.

A-Sar-U stood at the edge of the porch in the Window of Ra, in plain view of the thousands assembled in the temple precincts below. Bes, Som, Ram—all the God-es— were near, each busied with assigned and practiced tasks leading toward the last drumbeat that would ever be heard on Pleasant Planet.

A-Sar-U's mind raced. He felt as if a thousand thoughts crowded into his head. Now that transmutation of flesh or physical death was assured, he let his mind drift over his life.

He was God-e Supreme. He was the God-e. Yet, there was no joy in his thought. He owned everything upon the planet, in his own right, his own name as God-e, the One Supreme Lor'd. He had no pride of possession.

He stood on the arch of the second balcony of his great Temple. His heart ached with love for those thousands who crowded around him on the ground below. His mind was clear. He had done what he had to do out of love for mankind—and no one had said he was right or wrong.

Even Thoth, his beloved Master Teacher, had never said he was right or that he was wrong, had never complimented him on his ingenuity or on his skill or his lack of it. It was a conspiracy of silence. A silence that let him lead himself and seven million people onward on a pathway to death or to divinity; to burning in fires hotter than ten million imagined fires or to living in the spirit eternally. Now there was no turning back. No other choice.

At the other temples throughout the planet he knew that equal thousands were assembled under the guidance of his priests. How strange and how different. Once he had battled to wrest control from Je-Su, who promised to those who had faith in him, eternal life in the spirit.

Now he stood, along with seven million, and he promised only the hope of escaping physical death by going into the eternal life of the spirit. How slight the difference. Yet how great the difference. Je-Su had promised salvation only on the basis of belief in him, faith in the undefinable, in acceptance of a way of life that meant abject subjection and even degradation now, in the hope that there might be eternal life as a reward hereafter.

A-Sar-U promised nothing except as a reward for the practice of Sacred Exercises requiring extreme disciplines. He asked no one to have faith in him. They needed only faith in their ability to make the Sacred Exercises and disciplines work for them. They, themselves, by the use of will and work, were the source of their own eternal life, if eternal life they were to have.

Was he any better than Je-Su? As a man, no. Je-Su had been convinced that his way was the only way. He had fought for that conviction, even as he, A-Sar-U had fought for his belief that man must be his own eventual savior by using sacred skills and creating his own Spiritual and Radiant Body and giving it eternal life. Who had won? Perhaps no one. If the sun did not collide...

His thoughts were scattered by the soft voice of Horus.

"Father, may I ask a question?"

410

"Yes."

"The citizens say and believe we are Gods. But in your mind you wrestle that question. Are we Gods?"

A-Sar-U gathered his scattered thoughts upon the question that he knew would be asked down through ages to come, if there were to be ages to come.

"Would what the Divine Thoth taught me be enough answer for you on that question?"

"Thoth is your Master. You are mine. It should be enough for all men for all time."

"Thoth taught me this poem. He called it: 'To See God.'

He who does not see a Perfect God
Firmly enfolded in blackest sod
Goes from life to useless death.
Even that which does not seem to be God, then,
Is His true essence and has ever been
Wedded to Him as is the Soul to Breath.

God, Supreme, Holy and Magnificent
Stands in human heart and in firmament,
Small as nothing, large as the Universe.
As water into water pouring
Stays the same, all things to be enduring
Must meet and mingle in this Universe.

The mortal lives not by flowing breath
But by principles higher than even death
Which undergird mortality and sing:
That living fire which in the world turns
Like unto each of the things it burns
Is God, different in each mortal thing.

"Father, I interpret that to mean that God is in all things and in all living beings if we but have the eyes to see and the wisdom to understand. That we are Gods, for we have *become* Gods."

"Yes, in the same way that all who wish to make the effort may become divine. All are potential Gods. We might say to all persons, 'Know you not that you are Gods?' "

Satisfied, Horus turned back to his instruments.

411

A-Sar-U looked out upon the citizens of the Pleasant Planet and in his heart knew they were Gods. They were agreeing with his efforts to solve the problems of the planet. Well, at least the millions around him and his temples throughout the planet knew that the scientists around him agreed that the inexorable onrush of the Westsun would put it on collision course. If not this time, then in the very near future. The explosion was inevitable.

Some believed it would mean little to the planet. Some believed that it would burn a black hole in the entire sky to last to the ends of time.

Some believed, as he had taught, that aided by the excess energy generated by the heat of the approaching Westsun, they could raise their Spiritual inner, Radiant Bodies with full consciousness and powers of mind. Once raised, they could send their Spiritual Bodies, perhaps bearing their transmuted physical bodies, speeding across the sweeps of space, guided by his mind power, and under the protection of his knowledge. Je-Su demanded that everyone believe in him as the Son of God-e. He, A-Sar-U, asked millions to perform a miraculous spiritual feat.

He knew, and the millions knew, it was possible under training conditions. But now, in these last few moments (if the calculations were right) before the collision and explosion...with tensions mounting...with only sixty Westsuns' discipline and training...

He jerked his thoughts back from turning inward. It was short training, but it had to be enough! Holy, God-e, let it be enough for them all!

He must have spoken aloud, for Horus took his eyes from the eyepiece of the visio-scope with which he tracked the Westsun and looked at his father. "Two things, Holy Father. You see to your right the pitiful sight of Je-Su, battered and tattered, but trying still to assert his wisdom and divinity."

"Yes, Horus, I see. Just like we are."

"What is to become of his physical body when..." He left the thought unfinished.

"The Lor'd Thoth said we could take any physical body with us if we learned to loved enough."

"Could you love Je-Su enough to take him with us?"

"What would be hard about that? He has only done to me what he thought he had to do to promote his great love for the Empire. He has always done his best for the Empire."

"I've thought the same thing about Set. He only did to me and my Divine Mother that which he was pressed to do by circumstance, or thought he had to do. He was only trying to overcome the handicaps and limitations he was born with. Father, they have been wrong in only this, they do not accept the Divinity in everyone. Their intentions have been good from their viewpoint."

"That must be right, Horus. You seem to be thinking that we, too, were born with limitations and do many things to overcome them."

"Do you think we could take them with us, even though they dislike us?"

"Thoth said only that we could take any body if we learned to love enough. He did not say they had to love, or even be good, or kind. The majesty of the Divine Law works its magic for those who obey, even, perhaps on those who are not aware of love."

"Shall we take them?"

"We really should try."

"Good." Horus began to turn back to his work, but pulled his head up with a jerk. "Lor'd Father, about Africanus and his people? They have not trained with us, and they seem to dislike us very much. Should we try to take him...them?"

A-Sar-U considered carefully and long before he began his answer.

"No."

He saw the momentary flicker of concern on the face of his son. "No, Horus. It would be a waste of effort for us to try to take Africanus and his people."

As Horus began to turn back to his work, A-Sar-U added, "You see, Divine Son, there are races that have specific characteristics. We have dark-skinned members even in our tribe. But Africanus is a part of a different tribe. His great ego, his showiness, his wild robes and wearing apparel, his flouting of custom...in fact, his whole style of life, comes from that inner racial impulse which he has inherited."

"Then it is not because of his dark skin?"

"No, Horus, it is because of a capacity of his race that, in general, is better than our race. His race has a natural thrust toward the spirit. They live at a higher rate, love more intensely, laugh more easily, hate more fiercely, and are confused by the very things that disturbs their minds even as it is thrusting them toward Divinity."

A-Sar-U was silent as he considered the special, unappreciated abilities of the tribe of Africanus. He wondered if, in ages to come, they would find a culture, a world, in which their special genius would have room to swing.

"They seem different and difficult to us because they do not readily adapt their special abilities to the demands of our society. They do not make good Warriors. Not because they lack strength or courage, but because they do not have the in-driving will to make war, to join combat. In our culture, they do not make good fighters, but they make great friends. And someday, in a place of freedom, or in their own community, they will find a place that will make them great in the eyes of all peoples."

He stopped, surveyed the throngs below, and turned back to his son. "No. We cannot help them in this divine use of inner wisdoms. They have not trained, as we have. But when the need is upon them, they will intuitively know what to do and how to do it. They would not accept—but they do not need—our help. But...let us try to help them, anyway, shall we?"

Horus smiled. "Great idea. Thank you, Father. You know so much!"

"I know so little. It is the Supreme God-e who lends me thoughts."

Horus turned back to his work. Calmly he said: "One thing the Divine God-e should know. The Westsun is crossing the line into field ten. We have one thousand breaths to go."

A-Sar-U heard the calm voice, the confident voice of his beloved son and it gave him courage. "We have..." simple words, yet a statement of unity in belief, of acceptance.

A-Sar-U nodded to the Commander of the Signal Crew. The flags went up. The notes of the trumpets cut sharply into the hush of the crowd. A-Sar-U knew that in each of the fourteen Temple Complexes, in all parts of the planet, some half million persons were standing in expectant, serried, circling ranks as were these beloved ones below him.

The citizens did not stir. There was no murmur of anticipation. Each person was busy with his own stilling of his outer thoughts so that he could reach the inner peace needed to create, free, direct, and send his Radiant Spirit and transmuted self toward the distant goal of Atl Antis or On upon the planet Ayr Aerth.

Far out at the rim of the hill, the shattered but determined ranks of Je-Su's army moved. They were in pitiful battle formation. In no way a threat to the might of his arms, but a hazard of incredible harm to the concentration of the people who sought only release into their Spiritual, Radiant Selves.

Je-Su had sworn he would destroy all possibility of escape from the planet. "If you are to die it is the will of the Supreme, His judgment upon a false generation. I, Je-Su, Only Begotten Son of Supreme God-e, will serve His will. You shall not escape even if you could by your stillborn method."

Sanctimonious to the end, justifying hate and destruction in the name of the Supreme, to the last.

Even Set, Commander of the Warriors of Je-Su, was dedicated to disrupting the effort. His personal hatred was even greater than that of Je-Su, more directed toward A-Sar-U. He had sworn that no one had power to make decisions affecting the people of the planet. No one had the right to decide for themselves what they would believe or practice in religion. He would fight to the death to see that no person escaped his demand for complete obedience...

"Lor'd One, the Westsun is crossing into field four. It is directly west and it is not curving northward. It is as Som and you predicted. Destruction is now assured."

The almost complete monotone of his son impressed A-Sar-U with its calmness.

A-Sar-U nodded to the Signals and they flew amidst sharp blasts of the trumpets. He signalled Bes, who was with the Drum on the fourth level of the Temple of Po-Si-Don. The Drum began the beat that had been practiced so many times by the seven million citizens to be ready for this moment.

415

This time there was a slight murmur and shudder from the people below, but it passed like a sigh of despair. They became calm again, settled into their discipline. They now knew that the Westsun was not curving away, but was continuing on toward the Pleasant Planet.

Collision was immanent.

Yet the people seemed to be more steady and at peace with their destiny. Doubt had been removed. Certainty had replaced it. People thrived more under surety of hardship and danger than under doubt!

A-Sar-U gave the signal for the three spaced blasts on the trumpets to begin the synchronization of all breathing. The effect was instant. Every breath in the thousands around him began to slow, to be made synchronous with his.

With one last swift look he estimated that the advancing remnant of Je-Su's Warriors could not possibly reach many citizens or to him before the collision.

They could fall upon the outer ring of his people and disturb his believers. He felt impotent, he with all his power, to stop the disturbance. He closed his eyes and concentrated upon the task of turning inward.

He had done the best he could, it was up to God-e to make it good.

"Crossing into field three." That same calm voice of his son. He opened his eyes to look once more upon the pleasing face of his beloved son. But they were held by the activity far beyond the last circle of believers.

The floating gossamer gowns of the Virgins of God-e moved toward the advancing Warriors a few paces, and then ranked themselves so that no soldier could possibly pass without touching one of them. This touching would be a heinous act which not even Je-Su had been able to outlaw, for it was a firm conviction in the minds of the citizens. The soldiers stopped with confusion.

"Attack." The bellow from Set came across the distance a short moment after his sword was waved. Not a soldier moved.

"Attack. Attack. Attack." When he saw his commands could not make his soldiers move against the Virgins, he leaped forward, seized one of the slender Virgins and began to lift her away from her place in the ranks of the priestesses.

The astonished, angry murmur of the soldiers could be heard across the temple yards. To touch a Virgin of God-e without her expressed permission was still to invite instant death. It still was the religious duty of the nearest by-stander, on pain of his own death for treason to the planet, to execute the culprit, even in the midst of the act.

Three spears were hand-thrust into the body of the Commander of the Warriors of Je-Su. Set stood in shocked surprise, turned slowly, and fell.

The ranks of the defeated soldiers closed.

The Virgins of God-e moved back into their place and the ranks of priestesses locked out the might of war-like men more effectively than armor could possibly have done.

"Crossing into field two."

The Drum was racing now toward its climax and the final beat. A-Sar-U knew that the time now did not matter so much as the concentration and discipline of his follow-ers. Twenty breaths, if the calculations were right, and they now seemed to be.

The sweet cadence of chanting rose slightly.

"A-Sar-U, God-e, Source of Eternal Life,

"At the last please raise us."

He repeated the words in his own mind as he strug-gled to go to the center of inner peace against all fear and tension. He knew that even a thought of terror could de-feat all his efforts. The murmur of chanting voices rose slightly, but not enough to signal the onset of terror or any crumbling in the resolve of the faithful followers to seek for ultimate release of the Divine Radiant Body...the release of the radiant inner-self freighted with the radiant Trans-muted Body—from the cell body under conscious control and at the exact beat desired.

Release it, then send it at ten times the speed of light through the spheres to the point in space—a small planet called Ayr Aerth. They all were now only a few breaths from the beginning of a new life or ultimate annihilation.

"Crossing into field one. Seven breaths to go!"

The Drum was thundering its last few beats.

Seven! A-Sar-U willed his mind into complete detach-ment. It did not matter now if he and the experiment failed. He was totally detached, not caring, yet fully concentrating on the outcome. He was more relaxed, yet he was even more highly conscious than any other moment in all his life.

Six! God-ette felt the divine energy begin to form in each and every cell of her body. She felt the warm, radiant blow of physical cells giving birth to their radiant duplicate. She felt the strength and charge of each cell lighting up with the duplicate of its self. The energy flowed out of each cell like a warm, golden tidal wave toward each neighboring cell.

Five! Set, stricken Commander of the Warriors of Je-Su, was dimly aware that he had begun the sacred disciplines automatically. Funny! The thing he had learned and said he despised while working as a spy for Je-Su in A-Sar-U's training! Funny. Yet he longed to live, and he knew that the spear thrusts had opened gashes in his being through which his life blood was swiftly seeping away. He tried to form words. He would have said, "Win or lose, explosion or miss, I must leave this physical shell swiftly or I die." He felt no pain. A higher sense was on each nerve. He felt the radiant power of each cell reach out and lock powers, as if joining divine hands. He felt the billions of cells turn from flowing radiance to a single Radiant Body. That body lay inside his body, an exact duplicate of each and every cell. Yet it was free of the flesh and floating upon an energy that bore it up as clouds bear up rain. It was a glorious feeling! It was exactly the feeling A-Sar-U had said he should feel—in his spy days—in the Temple...

"How foolish I have been!" He tried to form the words. Not an apology to A-Sar-U and the Believers, but an apology to Je-Su for failing as a general, an apology to all those he now realized he had wronged, an apology for his wasted life based on beliefs that had no foundation better than that caused by the emotion of doubt and fear. But his mind was throttled to numbness by the force of the Radiant Body rising in his cells and reaching for unity.

Four! Horus leaned comfortably against the visio-scope and let the Radiant Body within him begin to tug at each cell individually. It was a pleasure unendurable, a joyful pain. It was a love too sweet to bear, a love too pure to share. The Radiant Body was a ghost within each cell, and combined with its neighbor to become a soul of energy inside his material body. The sensation was incredible and lulling. The senses spun and sank like a bee with too much honey to bear in flight. It pulled upward toward flight, but was held down by the tugging of the cells.

Three! A-Thena felt her Radiant Body rising inside her cells. It was indeed a pain too sweet to bear! The spirit formed itself into an entity exactly filling the inside of each cell of her body. It tugged upon each cell with a divine insistence, like a happy balloon anchored in each cell but longing to fly upward into total and endless freedom. She felt her Radiant Body, an exact duplicate of her physical body, as if from the manger of each cell a bright spirit was born. No! It was as if from all the cells of her body at one time a radiant God-e arose into glorious life—but could not break free of the skin and thus was body-bound.

Two! Big Warrior felt within his cells the Radiant Body begin to rise. It broke free of each cell with a strangely sweet tingling sound. He could feel—also hear!—the Radiant Body being formed within his body as it freed itself from each cell. He could feel, too, the intense pleasure of his body and his Radiant Spirit Body, It was a joy beyond any pleasure he had known in a life of seeking sensual pleasures.

This was a happiness that rose beyond any belief into a place and beauty unspeakable. His Radiant Soul at last seemed free of all cells but those inside his head at the base of his skull at the back of his brain. He felt a tension there. It seemed as if all the universe pulled upon that area of his brain. It seemed as if a million suns streaked out from that spot; as if all the joys of a million minds, the loves of a million mothers, and the excitement of a million battles almost won, all combined within his skull.

There was a searing golden light that engulfed his brain. There was the dull-sharp crack of a war-club at the back of his head. There was unbearable joy, delightful pain, world-filling golden light!

"Oh, God-e," he thought, "you were always right. The pleasure I sought, you offered me all along."

He felt his physical senses begin to spin, to slide downward toward a friendly blackness that he knew was

419

eternal. He accepted the inevitability of physical death. His Radiant Self leaped upward.

The Drum raced to the climax, and gave its last, strong beat.

One! A-Sar-U felt his Golden Radiant Self, freighted with his transmuted flesh turned to Golden Spirit, burst free of the constraining hold of his physical body and soar into space. He was suddenly aware of his physical body and could see it swaying now as it began to tumble before the energy released by the exploding Westsun. He saw from physical eyes and from spiritual eyes. From each he saw the same thing.

The heavens erupted into flames lashing like uncoiling serpents through the visible universe. The flames traveled toward his tumbling body like the onrush of a wall of death. His physical cells felt the terrible heat for the slightest fraction of time. Then it was no more.

Sight was in his Radiant Body now, and he seemed to see with a million eyes. Infinitely small things were made large. Enormous things were brought down in scale to his immediate view.

He saw the bodies of the Warriors of Je-Su evaporate from the plain, and the plain turn to nought.

He saw the bodies of the Virgins of God-e disappear into a strangely beautiful golden vapor.

He saw, too, the almost invisible Golden Bodies that streamed after his in the universe, bearing upon his, trusting him even in physical death for their eternal salvation and lives everlasting.

He saw God-ette as a radiant angel, rising from the background of a planet being vaporized by heat.

He saw Horus, valiant and calm as ever, coming toward him in a Radiant Body that traveled a hundred million times faster than the swiftest spear.

Behind them, traveling in the spirit bodies they had grown in only eighty-four Westsuns of incredible toil and trust, came the people of the former Pleasant Planet, millions upon millions. Oh, God-e! Oh, Good God-e!

The unmistakable thrill of success ran through his spiritual self, like a physical ecstasy.

He looked upon them all with love and poured out the power of his thought upon each one.

He turned his attention then to the things about him. He knew he was traveling greater far than at the speed of light. He was traveling at the speed of thought.

Galaxies moved by as blurs of light. Suns flamed a billion miles ahead and then a billion miles behind in the same instant. Present, past, and future were there at the speed of thought. Ahead, just there, lay Ayr Aerth.

He felt the attraction of its pull upon his Radiant Being. It was the resonance of his desire echoed back by that strange law of attraction and repulsion. He desired Ayer Aerth very strongly. It desired him and pulled him toward it unerringly through the endless space.

More than all others, he desired to be with Ast-i-ankh, Beloved Chosen Woman. Desire answered desire, attraction multiplied attraction. He oriented his mind upon that spot which pulled him so completely, and joyed in the ways of God-e.

She was there. She was alive! Oh, he knew. He knew!

He laughed with joy.

As his Golden Body came into her presence he knew that Thoth, his Divine Master, As-Tar, and the Divine Ra waited. And, Divine as they were, they could wait. For Ast-i-Ankh, his Divine love, was near.

He had done the best he could. He would leave it to God-e to make it good.

Lion's Wing Press
Our Purpose and Mission

We live in a time of tremendous transition and upheaval as the old paradigms fall away, to be replaced by new models of reality straddling science, religion, social structures, and personal ideals. These accelerating shifts result in skyrocketing stress and increased anxiety for the planet and its inhabitants. The need for clarity, balance and peace is experienced by all.

Fortunately, in great transitions, there are those rare individuals who emerge to articulate their insight and vision, helping others in giving shape and meaning to a future still unformed. Truly they are the treasures of the time, and the way-showers of humanity. They are the "People's People," expressions of reason and intuition, and their very words are the fabric of revelation.

Lion's Wing Press is dedicated to identifying, attracting, and supporting these unique individuals and their mission. Their mission will help define the "New Art and Science of Living" for the twenty-first century, and its quest for a brighter and more peaceful world.

We are pleased and proud to present *Genesis*, a remarkable book by a remarkable man. Dr. Whitworth is a way-shower in the highest sense of the word. We are honored to be working with him in disseminating his unique insight and wisdom.

May *Genesis: The Children of Thoth* be recognized as a meaningful contribution to this dawning "Golden Age of Man."